CROWN JEWEL

Ralph de Boissière was born in Tri
to Australia in 1948, where
salesman, car assembler and
published two other novels in
(1956) and *No Saddles for Kan*

Crown Jewel

a novel by

RALPH DE BOISSIÈRE

PICADOR
published by Pan Books

First published in Australia 1952
First published in Great Britain simultaneously by Allison and Busby Ltd
and in Picador by Pan Books Ltd,
Cavaye Place, London SW10 9PG

ISBN 0 330 26350 1
Printed and bound in Great Britain by
Richard Clay (The Chaucer Press) Ltd, Bungay, Suffolk

Prologue

It was July 1498.

For eight days the three ships had drifted beneath a naked blue sky. Wearily creaked the ships' booms as the vessels submitted to the ocean's listless movement. Such a thirst was upon the sailors that in fear and guilt they mumbled prayers to the Holy Mother. In groups they muttered at their admiral, Cristoforo Colombo, and his crazy dreaming of new lands.

Then on the last day of July Alonzo Nizzardo, the look-out at the flagship's round top, gave a shout of "Land!" and crossed himself and climbed down, shouting: "Land! Land!" not feeling the bruises he inflicted upon himself in his haste. The men on deck wept, embraced one another, praised the admiral they had cursed and, despite their parched throats, sang the "Salve Regina".

When Columbus saw three peaks rising into the blue sky he remembered the vow he had made in his thirstiest moment, and he called the island Trinidad, meaning Trinity.

It was a lovely land, full of sparkling streams, and broad savannahs where the wild deer roamed; and the woods abounded in meat and fruit and were bright with the flight and scream of birds. The Indians called it Cairi, Land of the Humming-Bird. They did not know that their days were come as a fruit that is ripe and soon must fall. Paddling out in their canoes, awed and curious, they watched these strangers from an unknown world. Columbus offered the Arawaks beads, knives and nothings, and asked for gold. They shook their heads and, showing him pearls instead, pointed to Margarita Island for the land of gold.

Years went by, two hundred years, during which the Spaniards sporadically fought the Indians. The island itself was of little moment: they panted after El Dorado, whose image flitted before them as a sound in the night. Upon Trinidad they caught their breath, caulked their ships at the Pitch Lake and scanned the horizon afresh for the land of gold.

But squatting in the doorways of their *ajoupas* the Indians gazed narrow-eyed upon the days that were past. They did not fight, or dance the war dance, or play the ball game called *bato*, and they scarcely tilled the land; for after two hundred years of warfare they were but scattered remnants of a vanquished people.

Spain was as a mother whose drying breasts no longer give milk to her children. When the governor bade the council buy a book to keep the minutes, they wailed that not one sheet of paper was to be had among all the members; and that indeed they were so poor that they had among them but one suit in which they might properly take the Communion.

In 1783 a Frenchman came with word from the king of Spain. To each white settler, be he man or woman, the king offered thirty-two acres, and for each of his slaves half of that again; so that a man with a wife and twenty slaves would have three hundred and eighty acres to call his own.

Frenchmen came in thousands, driven there as cows by thirst to a pond in the savannah. They were revolutionaries and royalists, white men, and free men neither black nor white but somewhere in between. They cultivated cane and cocoa as never before. Fortunes were made and fortunes squandered.

Soon the scent of trade drew England's warships that prowled the oceans. When on an evening in 1797 they entered the gulf the Spanish admiral, from fear and weakness, burnt his vessels at night and retreated overland from Chaguaramas. English soldiers came with the dawn and surrounded the capital, Puerto de Espana. Chacon, the Spanish governor, saw the landowners tremble for their riches; and having looked with sadness at his eighty soldiers he gave up himself and the island to Ralph Abercrombie.

In this way another jewel, tiny, scintillating, with a value as yet unknown, was filched unnoticed for Britain's crown. One soldier's life was all the price that Britain paid.

The free people of colour were thrice as many as the whites, and multiplying fast; and the slaves were yet three times more, fresh importations constantly adding to their number. Fearing lest the free people of colour make common cause with the slaves, the new masters ordered them to carry a lantern after dark and show a pass if challenged. Thus from the beginning did they urge them to rid themselves of the shadow of Africa that darkened their skins.

In every generation of Black men hopes arose which were in no way different from those of Blacks before them. None were realised. Slavery was abandoned, no longer suiting the merchants' need. A new slavery rode in its wake, a new contrivance which repudiated the whip but tied men to the estates on which they laboured. So were men and women from India tied to the Land of the Humming-Bird. India being not Africa its history was not lost, trampled in the dust, denied. And Indians stood proud, conscious of greatness behind them, not warped by schooling as were the sons of Africa who learned of England's greatness, indeed, of the superiority of all pale men. They went out of the school doors into the world with England's greatness like a noose about them. And they saw that there was no profit in Blackness, only sorrow and woe. The pathetic handful who could afford it sent their children to England, taught them to speak with good English accents, even married them to English women; for they would have all men know that they were not what they seemed. . . .

But had Columbus returned to Cairi in 1935 he would have found her still beautiful as on that July day four hundred years before. Though the red monkeys might have retreated, their howling would not have changed; the humming-birds, vanishing spirits of the exterminated Indians, their wings like humming rainbows, would pause in mid-air before the flowers in the woods; and the flight of red ibises across the gulf would resemble the flight of an arrow of flame. A red sun would go down swiftly, and as if in sinking it had burst, gold and violet would splash the sky, and the green hills would lose their lustre, and night would cover them quickly as if a curtain had been drawn. Then the stars, unveiled, would shine like those jewels in the El Dorado of dead men's dreaming.

Chapter one

They gripped the spokes of the two-wheeled timber cart and threw their bodies forward.

"Heave! . . . And again! . . . *And* again!"

The flooring boards projected five feet front and rear. Grasping the boards with his massive hands the helmsman struggled with an angry, desperate look to balance the cart while steering it through the traffic according to the wheelmen's shouted orders. The asphalt, soft in the heat, braked the huge iron-shod wheels.

Now they made a brisk pace, the wheelmen throwing themselves forward and grunting with revenge as they approached the gateway. The trick was to swing across the road without loss of impetus and with one last mighty heave rush the overburdened cart up the incline into the gateway.

"Swing you' swing!" shouted the wheelman on the left.

Jacob, the helmsman, swung left, pressing down on the boards to raise the front end, his teeth clenched, his eyes reddening with the effort.

"Now, all-you!"

They rushed at the incline. The cart clattered over the gutter, faltered at the rise, then rolled into the huge covered timber yard. Jacob let go. The cart up-ended itself with a clatter and stopped. The men flung themselves prone on a pile of timber. Their furrowed black faces ran with sweat. On their great bare arms the veins stood out like cords.

In their skill and their strength was satisfaction, and in the union, also, of their several motions that made of them a team. Without that unity each was helpless. Using his skill creatively man rejoices at the sense of fulfilment he experiences in its exercise. So now they praised themselves and derided other carters. Jacob joked about how one had let the boards slip, scattering them about the street.

"Lordy, Lordy!" he cried. "I nearly piss meself laughin'."

The light died. The heavens split. Thunder rolled and cannoned across the purple sky. A deafening white torrent shrouded hills, buildings, trees and cars and made of the street a swirling stream. A cool wind came in and dried their sweat-drenched bodies.

"Ah! That nice, that good!"

Joe Elias, the Syrian, came up and stood looking at the rain. His broad figure seemed to take up half the gateway. The men, seeing him, rose. He was a good man, Mr Elias, he liked black people. But he was an important man, a clerk; it didn't look good to lie down in his presence. Jacob was first to rise. (He bowed to white people and his eyes never dwelt long on their faces. You had to live.)

"Take a rest," Joe reproved them. "Nobody goin' to see you."

Popito Luna came up to them with his open smile. They didn't think of rising for him. Mr Luna wasn't educated like Mr Elias. But he was a good man too, a good heart.

He was a bit over forty, a Venezuelan, with the South American's broad features and high cheekbones. He came up with his brisk, thoughtless, bowlegged walk and slapped Jacob on the shoulder. "Well, now! What's good, friend?" he said with that kind, guilelessly open manner and smile that made everyone trust and like him.

"Dat's a nice rain, Mr Luna."

"The next load goin' to be easier," Luna assured Jacob. "It goin' to stay cool now for a while and the pitch goin' to be hard down South Quay."

"You know the thing, you know it good," Jacob replied with an appreciative laugh. "But one t'ing you don't know—the weight of dat wood."

"I know it, man! I only have to watch you and I know it."

A bird flew with a wild glad cry to a mango tree across the street. They all looked at it.

"Free as a bird," Popito said with a smile.

"How the young ones get on in the rain?" one of the wheelmen asked.

Jacob said to Popito, as if it were he who had put the question: "When the rain done, Mr Luna, they does shake theyself and cry out loud with happiness. They more happy than we."

"That's right. What he got to trouble him?"

Joe Elias, who had wandered away from them, came back in time to hear Jacob's remarks. He laughed and looked around at everyone to draw attention to himself because to impress others with his cleverness was both necessity and pleasure for him.

"Very poetic, Jacob, very poetic," he laughed indulgently, "but I think there's a more commonplace reason for the little bird's hilarity: it is probably the thought of worms."

"That's it, that's the reason!" Popito said at once and willingly, in deference to Joe's use of words.

The bird dived out of the tree.

"Look, look, look!" Popito cried. "Now, if I was to win a sweepstake, say about fourteen thousand or so, man, I would be free too."

"Fourteen thousand!" one of the wheelmen echoed, and rocked with laughter at so crazy a dream.

"Then you would make others work like Jacob." Joe laughed, and his laugh was a biting mockery of man.

And Jacob laughed knowingly. "Man must live off man, Mr Elias."

Popito looked with animosity at Joe's handsome face with its now bitter, rapacious expression. "It's people like Dollard live off other people!" he declared, speaking from the heart as usual.

He uttered the name in a loud challenging tone, forgetting where he was: the name of the Managing Director, the President of the Chamber of Commerce, the un-elected member of the Legislative Council; the name of the millionaire director of oil and shipping companies; the name of one of the unofficial governors of Trinidad. Not white. No. Look at his mother's picture: she's not black, she's not even brown, but she's not white. No matter: her accent, like Willie's, was that of the cultured English. A likeable man, Willie. They all liked him. But Luna forgot to tremble when he spoke the name, and now even added:

"It's them people we have to get rid of!"

Joe laughed scornfully. "I wish it was as easy as that. Man will always have someone to push him around. *I* tell you so." He slapped his meaty chest. "Don't be led by the nose, Popito."

No one wished the rain to cease but a little black boy who had taken shelter in the gateway. He itched to make use of his sling. He kept stretching it and aiming. Suddenly he raised it and let fly—and gasped in triumph. The bird fell into the swirling waters, fluttered desperately and was swept away.

"Look, he killed it, he killed it!" Popito cried.

The men sat up with exclamations of pity and reproof.

"Hey, you! What you do that for?" Popito advanced on the boy. "What harm the poor bird did you?"

The boy ran away through the rain, frightened, looking behind him, not understanding.

"Death is a terribly sobering thing," Joe said, glancing at the faces around him furtively. "All of us will be brought down like that bird —all—without ever being able to fly."

"Dat true. . . . Look Mr Dollard comin', Mr Luna. Go and get rid of him, man," said Jacob slyly.

The knot of men dissolved in all directions at sight of Dollard's tall, lean figure in the distance. Jacob went to another gate where, screwing up his eyes and shading them with his hand, he pretended to be searching for someone up the street.

The talk had angered Luna as the picador maddens the bull with his lance. What he had wanted to forget rose up in him again: that morning his sister had come with tears asking for five dollars, there was neither money nor food at home. "My God, Aurelia, how you let this happen?" he had reproved her gently. In his pocket he had just enough to keep him till payday. He had had to approach Brassington, the English boss of the hardware department, a man he hated, and ask him to countersign an advance of five dollars on his pay.

"Not gambling, are you?"

"Just living is a gamble." Popito looked straight into the other's eyes.

Brassington had looked at the Venezuelan, hesitated, then signed the chit.

And Aurelia outside in the street waiting, hoping, and Brassington watching, so that Popito had to send someone to her with the money in an envelope. What maddened him was not Aurelia's inability to manage her affairs, or the fact that his pay would be five dollars short (he knew that she, with the best will in the world, would never succeed in repaying him), it was Brassington's indifference, his general demeanour, which indicated an assurance that he was secure for life. Whoever heard of an Englishman getting the sack? From the way he moved about the store, his hands crossed behind his back, you could see he had forgotten there were others beside himself who had to live. "Why life treats people so?" he reflected, sorrowing for Aurelia and feeling animosity towards Brassington rise up like a huge dark cloud behind this sorrow. When Joe said Man would always be pushed around, when he laughed to scorn the notion that workers would free themselves of Dollard, Popito almost choked with hatred of the world around him especially because he felt deep down that Joe was right. He wanted to cry out, to lash out with his fists, to drag down the guilty and humble them.

With careless, desperate strides he returned to the hardware department, pretending not to see Dollard go by him.

Popito's undisciplined style of work, his emotional temperament, his loud voice, his walk—all jarred on Brassington, who in everything was calm and orderly. He knew Dollard had a soft spot for Luna. Once when he had wanted a man for a job Dollard had said: "If you need help take Luna."

"Luna won't obey my orders, perhaps he'll take yours."

"Don't tell me he's dissatisfied," Dollard growled warily.

"I'll tell you what I think—he's a Red."

Dollard smiled. "You think he wants to blow us up, eh? No, man, look here. . . ." He grasped the Englishman's arm familiarly under the armpit as he strode beside him. "We have to try and soft-soap them, my dear fellow. A little joke goes a long way. They're a rather ignorant lot, you know. . . ."

Popito strode into the hardware department now hoping he wouldn't see Brassington. And perhaps he would not have seen him if his every nerve, like radar, had not been attuned to pick the man out from wherever he was. The first person he seemed to see was the Englishman. The long, scrawny red neck, like a chicken's, and the prominent large ears caused Popito to swagger and joke in an unnecessarily loud voice with another clerk because he was conscious of his power to irritate and anger Brassington with the very sound of his voice. He could talk if he liked, couldn't he? And he would talk. To hell with you!

"Must you make such a noise?"

Popito heard the wearied tone of patient boredom. Not what he said but the tone, the accent, grated. He looked, said nothing, turned away. Two minutes later some words jumped out at him.

"You'd better give them to the stupid Venezuelan. . . ."

Brassington was not referring to Popito at all but to a Venezuelan fisherman who had come in earlier that morning. Popito swung about and grabbed Brassington by the shirt front. "Who's a stupid Venezuelan?" he roared and butted him twice, with lightning speed, in the best Creole style.

The speed and unfamiliarity of the mode of attack left the Englishman defenceless. Blood gushed from his nose. Clerks stared open-mouthed, waiting to see what Brassington would do. Some turned away and laughed silently, with joy.

"Go to the cashier and get your pay," said Brassington in a sharp voice somewhat muffled by the handkerchief he held to his bleeding nose. He went to the cashier himself. "Pay Luna off!"

"Yes, pay me, pay me!" Popito cried, pushing his hand impatiently under the grille. "And don't take out more than five dollars, I don't owe you a cent more. Make it up, I'll go and put on me jacket." He moved away. "I had enough from you—you lucky I didn't kill you, you lucky I didn't squash you like a white cockroach!" he shouted at Brassington's retreating figure, his voice getting louder and louder.

On some of the faces he saw looks of apprehension. Yes, they were fearful of him. He felt good. He took his money and went out, talking loudly as he bid the others goodbye. He went through the timber shed. The news had reached the shed already. He laughed with them, he gave the story with embellishments, and again he felt fine. Thank God he was out of here, he would go and look for another job right away. "Goodbye, boys!" And off with his bowlegged stride.

Walking down Marine Square he savoured his freedom and touched with a sense of security the wad of notes in his pocket. He recalled the momentary look in Brassington's eyes when he butted him, the awkward look of timidity that revealed in a flash he was nobody to be afraid of. "I gave him good!" he said to himself.

He went to the hardware store of another big firm and asked for a job.

"Where did you work before?"

"Dollard's."

"Did they fire you?"

"Me and the boss couldn't agree, so I asked for my money."

"You asked for your money. Well, let's see."

The man picked up the telephone and Popito came down to earth. There was no job for him here. He said to himself, "This isn't the only place in Port-of-Spain where I could ask for a job, it got plenty other places."

And he tried. But by closing time he could not hide the reality from himself any longer: there was really no job for him here in Port-of-Spain.

Chapter two

Two days before, Aurelia had been beating her brains to find the rent. There they sat, she and Elena, silent, imprisoned by toil, hungry and apprehensive, yet buoyed up by wild hopes they dared not utter. The whir of the sewing-machine alone broke the silence.

An old friend came in and the dam burst.

"My dear child, I get the work, but who pays, and hummuch?" Aurelia was saying. "So many little girls today calling themselves dressmakers and sewing something for you for seventy-five cents, a dollar, one twenty—anything to get a little food to put in their stomach when day come." A vein in her neck began to swell and throb. "And people who can pay will not pay," she continued, her voice rising without her being aware of it. "Last week I took my *own* money to buy some materials for a dress, made it, killed out meself, strain my eyes till one in the morning, and now yesterday when I send for the money the white wretch take the dress and tell Elena: 'Aoh, tell your muther'—" she twisted lips and neck in her efforts to imitate the accent—" 'she can send to me at the end of the month.' "

She scarcely expected to make up the rent by means of her sewing, although she prayed thrice daily and kept candles lighted on the shelf beside the press for the souls in purgatory. Popito helped her every month; but apart from this she had always "settled my business" by means of the sou-sou. This month, say, Juana would get her "hand", fifty dollars, a purse made up by ten sou-sou members at five dollars a head. Next month it would be Popito's turn, and the next Aurelia's. And so if she had the first hand she would draw fifty dollars after paying only five. Once or twice a year on receiving a sou-sou hand she would repair the damage to respectability caused by time or the bailiff, buying clothes for Elena or some piece of furniture surrendered as ransom. Elena, who would soon be contributing to the upkeep of the household, had ventured to say in surprise the last time:

"Mother, you didn't even pay one month's rent? What about the other machine, it's still in pawn."

Whereupon she had seen the vein in her mother's neck swell. "When you're a woman for you'self you can do what you like with you' money!" Aurelia shouted while weeping, recalling aloud all the unpleasant aspects of her life, past and present, to prove how she had turned misfortune to the best advantage, but somehow conveying the impression that she had miraculously survived despite her own bad piloting.

But now the sou-sou hand was not due for some months. Popito would give, but his gentle reproaches would crush her; and he had burdens of his own. She held off for a day, hoping for a miracle, but in the end she went to him. . . .

They came from Venezuela's poor. Seventeen years before, the Venezuelan rancher, Henriques, had seduced Aurelia, a full-bosomed girl of sixteen, and married her under pressure after Elena was born. Shortly afterwards he returned to Venezuela. She never heard of him again. She lived now near the waterfront in a tiny ancient house of tapia. A three-foot passage separated this house from the one next door and led to the two rooms in the yard. In one lived Rose the prostitute, in the other Cassandra, one of Judge Osborne's maids.

Yesterday Cassandra had come in to say that Mrs Osborne wished to see her. Her two daughters, not long out from England, were in need of dresses more suitable to the West Indian climate. Cassandra had recommended Mrs Henriques.

Now Aurelia put on the good shoes that hurt, and the corsets, stuffed a pad in the hollow of her broad back to improve her figure and pulled her best dress over her head. This summons, she felt, would prove to be God's blessing for all she had suffered these days past.

The Osbornes lived in St Clair. St Clair, with its "Whitehall" (an enormous white stone and marble mansion), its replica of Balmoral Castle, its huge baroque and ornate houses, relics of the good old days of cocoa, is one of the oldest and most fashionable districts of Port-of-Spain. At its feet lies the Savannah—the Grand Savannah—that two hundred acres of parkland where in the long, long ago slaves had planted and reaped sugar but which was a sea now of young green grass that rolled like waves beneath the wind; a haven from the town's clang and pain and evil where you could suck up the peace of earth, of grass and sky and listen to the inner man if he had not already abandoned you. Here Gwenneth, the elder of the Osborne girls, rode horseback, generally accompanied by the handsome English police officer Sub-Inspector Primrose.

Not having the tram fare Aurelia trod the Pitchwalk, which circles the Savannah. At nightfall the poor, strolling on the Pitchwalk, admired the great two-storied houses encrusted in history, the new cars, with eyes that hungered for beauty and held no envy. Who would envy God? In the hot sun Aurelia had no eye for this beauty. She was hungry; the shoes pinched. She concentrated on making a dignified entrance without limping.

Cassandra, the second maid, received her and smilingly conducted her to the big drawing-room. Aurelia, unaccustomed to polished floors, nearly fell, and flushed deeply with embarrassment. Gwenneth invited her to sit down, Cassandra she despatched for fashion books. Gwenneth, proud and strong-willed, could not bear not to be in the limelight. She was rather short and held herself very erect as if to compensate for her small stature. She chatted amiably with the dressmaker, gazing at her with a frank curiosity she would have concealed had someone of her own class been the cause of it. She did not know in what category to place this woman who was broad and shortish with a skin ruddy brown like cedar, large dark sad eyes and close-waved black hair. She did not look Negro yet was so dark.

Cassandra returned with fashion books.

"Thank you. Call my mother and sister, will you, Cassie?"

Esther, the sister, came in, nodded to the dressmaker and joined Gwenneth in picking out the styles that pleased them both.

Aurelia felt gratefully that they were going to be her best customers. She had but the vaguest grounds for coming to this conclusion—their English accents, and they were so pleasant and so wealthy, the furnishings were of such good quality and God was so good that it must be so. No matter what troubles tried to push Aurelia under she always managed to shake them off and bob up to the surface like a cork. And like a cork she was spun about by life's every eddy.

A heavy rapid step was heard. Mrs Osborne came in—large-boned, fleshy, red-bosomed, perspiring. Her head on one side, she was smiling that insincere smile common to society women who entertain a great deal and head various committees. Aurelia was struck by something coarse and insensitive about her man-like tread. She felt that the judge's wife was looking not only at her but through her. Aurelia bristled. At the same time she felt uneasy, so that she smiled awkwardly as she inclined her head in greeting.

Mrs Osborne sat down and rested her elbows on the arms of her chair, letting her red hands, adorned with several rings, hang loosely.

She began to question the dressmaker. How long had she been sewing, whom did she sew for, had she had experience in making evening dresses? Then, gathering from the flushed brown face before her that these questions might be offensive, she added with a smile, her head shaking (it was a nervous affliction she could not control): "I'm very particular about the kind of work I get."

"So am I too. Have no fear of that, Mrs Osborne."

Having chosen styles the girls produced materials. Aurelia took their measurements. At last, amid pleasant smiles and goodbyes, she parcelled up the material and went home with it.

As soon as she got home she unfolded the cloth, felt it between her fingers, held it to the light, estimated its price and began to consider how best to cut it. What nice girls they were! She felt with pleasure that their confidence in her was already established. This stimulated in her a desire to do her best. She was certain she could satisfy them. If anything went wrong God would help her, for the rent would soon be due. Certainly, too, there would be more work in the future. People like the Osbornes were the very hub of society, the world revolved around them. They needed and could pay for expensive dresses for parties and hardly stopped to count the cost. She thought also how the Osbornes would recommend her to their friends, and those friends to others. Who knows, she might soon have a large clientele of rich people and be able to employ a girl to help her, take the other machine out of pawn, pay her debts and live in greater comfort. She determined to put all her skill, which was great, into making these dresses. But suddenly she remembered they had not discussed price. "Yes, I ought to have mentioned it," she thought uneasily. "However, they are ladies, and will pay."

That night her friend Hortense came to see her.

"Eh, Hortense, you just in time for dinner. . . . Nonsense! Come along, do. Elena, make some more cocoa for Miss Richards. So how is Barbara, my dear?" Aurelia smoothed the material out on the table. The scissors made a crunching sound on the wood as she cut the cloth.

Hortense Richards had come on a delicate mission concerning her own security and peace of mind. She had been uncertain whether she would accomplish it tonight, seeing that the only thing predictable about Aurelia was that she would be unpredictable. Aurelia loved to laugh, but grew very angry or wept in a moment with equal ease.

When she laughed others could not help laughing with her. "*She's* a sport, boy!" they said. When she was angry they would grow frightened at her red-faced shouting. Now she was in such a good mood that Miss Richards relaxed and replied in the complaining whine habitual with her :

"Barbara, my dear? A big girl and gettin' well rude, I tell you."

"Chile, don't talk, it's hard, really hard, to bring up your children. I myself would have gone to the United States several times but always it was Elena who kept me back. I knew she would grieve. She has that disposition that keeps a thing inside, eating her away, she is so soft," said Aurelia, her eyes filling with tears that were pleasant to her. "Not like me, I like to let off steam."

"Yes, chile, and we gettin' old. . . . Such a trouble I find myself in now!" Miss Richards said, sighing and clucking in the roof of her mouth. She told Aurelia the rent was a month overdue. She had been given till tomorrow to pay it but was "short of five dollars", and did not know where to turn. She began to shed tears.

Aurelia's eyes, too, filled with tears. "My God! Why didn't you come to me before, my dear? I know very well how you feel. The only thing, my dear, I would ask you," she whispered, "my rent is due on the fifteenth—"

"Yes, yes! Eh! How you want me let you down, child?" Miss Richards whispered gratefully. "God will bless you—"

"But not five. My dear, I didn't have a cent today, I had to borrow from Popi. But four, I could lend you four."

"My sou-sou hand is due in two days, I'll give you back then."

Aurelia went into the bedroom and came out enclosing the money hurriedly in an envelope as if it was something that, exposed, might sully their friendship. She did not wish Elena to know.

"Ah, chile, you do not know what you have done for me tonight!" said Miss Richards, opening the envelope to see if it really contained four dollars and thrusting it quickly into her purse, suddenly ceasing to weep.

"We have to help one another in this world, my dear," said Aurelia, not looking at Hortense. There are things about a friend one tries not to see for fear of losing one's moral support in a hostile world.

She remembered an amusing story and, still holding the scissors, turned aside to relate it, doing so with relish. The story acquired many colourful details in the telling. She could not have said which were factual, which imaginary. Nor did it matter, for they were all without malice. She collapsed in a chair and peals of laughter rang through the house. All felt happy, especially Elena, who was outside in the kitchen : she felt reassured when her mother laughed, life seemed lighter.

"Mu-ther!" Elena called.

"Hoo!" Aurelia replied and, raising her shoulders, ran with a comical girlish skip into the kitchen. ". . . Yes, but you didn't put enough milk," she told Elena, throwing some cocoa into her palm and tasting it. "Put more, put more! And what about frying some little figs? Miss Richards likes them. Don't forget fresh pepper; she can't do without that and I meself like a piece." She was softened by her kindness and her story.

When the meal was ready she ate heartily, forgetting all about her debts, forgetting everything unpleasant. She laughed, her face flushed with eating, and she was happy. Miss Richards flattered her as thoughtfully as others remark on the weather.

"Chile, you have a good mother, pray God to bless her," she said to Elena. "There is no dressmaker in this Trinidad to match you, my dear." And: "God is just, you bound to get your crown, my dear. . . ."

Elena fell silent. What particularly irritated her was her mother's obvious pleasure in the flattering, almost mocking remarks of her cunning old friend. But the deeper cause of her irritation became clear to her only when she returned to the kitchen to wash up. An instinct told her that Miss Richards had left at peace with the world because her mother had given her money.

Elena went to bed oppressed by an ugly foreboding which she did not look in the face: there had never been any sense in doing that. She thought of everything but her foreboding—of school, the exams, of Joe Elias, whom she knew was in love with her, of Erica his sister, and of some vague future happiness which would surely succeed her present unhappiness. But the feeling of oppression did not lessen. The walls of the room, which was extremely narrow, seemed to close in upon her slowly, inexorably, squeezing all life and joy out of her mother and herself. She wanted to get up and run away but there was nowhere to run. There was no ceiling, and in the dim light coming in from the street lamp she gazed at the hated cobwebby rafters, where she always imagined something lived that was vicious, evil, nasty. Suddenly there plopped on to her pillow a long piece of dried-up putty enmeshed in blackened cobweb. It was as if evil spirits were pelting her. Too frightened to scream, she covered her head with the sheet and rolled against the wall. The bed shook with her noiseless sobbing for long before she slept.

Chapter three

When Popito lost his job, Aurelia felt as though something she had long been leaning on had unexpectedly collapsed under her. Weeks after she remarked to an old customer:

"Indeed, I can tell you some people really bring you bad luck. It's as if they put a *dwen* on you. From the moment Hortense borrowed that four dollars off me things started to go bad. Everything, everything! Popito lost his job, a customer I was really depending on disappointed me, I couldn't pay rent—I tell you, it was hell!"

The Osbornes' dresses were to be ready for the twenty-fifth of July. The rent had fallen due on the fifteenth.

One morning months before, the agent, a bulky Negro of fifty, had squeezed through the doorway and filled the room with his malodorous person and rough voice. Like a turkey cock just released among some hens he had pulled his long moustaches and congratulated Mrs Henriques on "looking so nice and fat". She, growing red, rose up like a whirlwind and ordered him out. "All right, all right," said he, blustering to cover his confusion at her anger.

Then it started. More than once Leah, the half-day servant, had gone to him with fourteen dollars on account. "What I want with fo'teen dollars?" he would say. "Woman, go bring my round fifteen dollars for me or you' madam going to miss something when the end-a the month come."

Aurelia now had six dollars put aside—"The last," Popito had warned her, "till I get work again." It was somewhere in a drawer of her dressing-table among bills, receipts, paper patterns, pins and a tin of powder. Five dollars apiece for the Osbornes' dresses and she would have the rent and a dollar over.

On the twenty-third she went to the Osbornes for a fitting. While she was away the agent came in with noise and bluster which grew louder when he learned that Mrs Henriques was not at home. He demanded the rent, threatening shame and misery unless it was paid by the twenty-fifth. Aurelia on her return sent Leah to collect from five customers who still owed money. "Leah, tell them I have to make up the rent, explain the position. . . ." Leah came back with but a dollar fifty. Only one customer had paid, all the others had told her to "come back at the end of the month".

Aurelia gave Leah a shilling to buy lunch for the three of them. At noon Elena came home with the sole of one shoe torn off—her only pair. Elena was sitting for her senior certificate; she had no hope of securing a government job without it. It was imperative that she return to school. Besides, Aurelia hoped to be able to say carelessly to her friends: "Elena has just passed her Higher Certificate, my dear, I don't know how, she didn't study so hard." What shoemaker would distress himself repairing the shoe in half an hour? She sent Leah to buy a cheap pair. Two dollars gone, five twenty-six left; five dollars to go with the ten she would get for the Osbornes' work, twenty-six cents for dinner. . . .

The twenty-fourth dawned. Elena stayed home, she had no examination that morning, and neither was there breakfast.

From early in the morning the sun seemed to draw closer and closer with its fire. The rafters snapped as they shrank. A shimmering haze covered the asphalt. The cicadas sang ceaselessly. In the whole motionless, choking atmosphere was a sense of expectancy, of ripening, of that stifling pressure that precedes a thunderstorm. Rose, the prostitute in the backyard, was singing a hymn to forget and jerking rhythmically over her jooking-board. In the street a limping, barefooted peasant was pushing a two-wheeled horse-cart. One of his trouser legs was stretched tightly over its limb, which was swollen to thrice its size by elephantiasis. Gripping the shafts of the cart he strained forward, the sweat pouring in streams from his black face, while he cried in resonant pleading tones: "Sweet potay-toe? Mammy, look Pappy. Sweet potay-toe?" Then for an instant a strange hush seemed to fall on the town, a hush broken by a sigh as Aurelia shook her dress at her bosom to cool herself.

"Mrs Constantine?" she reflected. "No, she paid. Miss Wharton owes me but I have borrowed so much from her already I feel shame to send to her again. Mrs Moore. . . . Ah! Leah!" she cried. "Go and ask Mrs Moore what about the fifty cents she have for me so long now. Hortense has gone to the country, she hasn't paid me *yet*!"

Presently Leah returned: ". . . and she vex, *oui*? She say not till the end-a nex' week. She say she ehn't 'custom to pick up money easy like you."

"And no credit in the shop any more," Aurelia thought. "I'm owing Chee-Awai fifty dollars—my God, when I going to pay that? And he, 'self, the fool, why he let it mount up so?" Going into her room she unlocked the dressing-table drawer silently for Elena not to hear, took out a much-fingered brown purse, counted the contents for the tenth time, sucked her teeth in vexation and locked it away again. "Damn it to hell, man, she's a dog!" she suddenly began storming. "She can afford to pay and won't pay. . . ." Saliva rushed into her mouth at the tempting odour from Rose's pot.

All this time Elena was silently helping her mother with the sewing. An hour passed, then two. ". . . and Elena blames me, but how can I help it? Never complains. . . . She has a good appetite." Shaking the dress at her bosom she went to the window. She saw a semi-paralysed dumb Indian beggar tottering towards her. His eyes were wild and staring from the effort to express something with the sound issuing from his throat. He paused before her, held out his paralysed hand, whose fingers could not uncurl, and coughed, trying to maintain a precarious balance. Aurelia went hurriedly to the brown purse and took out a penny.

"Mother! No, no, leave it *alone*!"

Aurelia leaned out and put the coin into the pale, dirty palm. "How some people suffer in this world," she remarked to the cutting table, avoiding Elena's eyes.

"Mother, how could you do that?" Elena cried in a loud shaking voice. "What do you think I went hungry all morning for—to feed a beggar whose pockets are jingling with coins? That's what I don't understand with you: you either blowing hot or cold, sometimes you lose all sense of reasoning and fling everything to the winds and then run to God to complain—"

"Not a word more!" Aurelia shouted, advancing threateningly with uplifted palm.

Elena bit her handkerchief and fled to her room.

"And Popito too," Aurelia reflected, wiping away tears of shame with her palm. "He worries, he's drinking heavily, a thing he never used to do. He would give me, yes, heaven knows where he gets the few cents from, Joe or some woman, but he would turn round and want to murder somebody. Joe, yes . . . well, I am forced to do it. Better he than Rose. You have to swallow pride. But Elena mustn't know. I'll write a note. . . ."

But no sooner did she begin to write than such a chill feeling of shame overcame her that she tore the note in pieces.

At last the dresses were finished, the basting threads removed. Aurelia put on the shoes that hurt, the corsets, the pad without which she was sure she looked too fat in one place, and set off on foot for the Osbornes' through the burning sun.

She was in a cold sweat when she arrived. Cassandra came upon her sitting on the front step, very pale. "Something happen?" she whispered, glancing about, concerned lest others observe her state and fearing a reprimand should Mrs Osborne notice the dressmaker reclining on her front step when the proper entrance for her was the side door. "You want some water? Come." She helped her in. As before, Aurelia tried to avoid treading on the thick, magnificent coloured rugs. This time she was careful not to slip on the floor.

Cassie showed her into a bedroom. Gwenneth Osborne came in with her short, quick steps, proudly erect—indeed, there was something in her bearing both compellingly attractive and coldly imperious.

"She smiles as if she loves herself and expects me to do the same," thought Mrs Henriques, irritated by hunger and depressed by a feeling that she had failed in life—a feeling intensified by Gwenneth's energetic self-assurance and pink cheeks, which seemed to say: "It's your own fault, not life's."

"What, are you really ready, Mrs Henriques?" Gwenneth said with unexpected warmth and kindness, seeming to glow with satisfaction as she took the finished dress in her hands and held it at arms' length. "You *are* a treasure. It's lovely! Hold it, will you? I'll take this off." Hurriedly she removed her house dress. She tossed her hair back petulantly when the evening frock stuck over her bosom. "I don't need your help," she said sharply as Aurelia stepped forward. Humming and smiling proudly, she turned this way and that before the mirror. "It's awfully good."

Mrs Osborne came in. She kept smiling around her as if hoping she had missed nothing. "I think it should be slightly longer, don't you?" she suggested. It had suddenly got quite dark. Thunder rolled in the distance. She switched on the light.

Gwenneth replied coldly: "This will do very nicely as it is, thank you, Mother."

Mrs Osborne's head was shaking nervously. She cleared her throat patiently, as if making a sacrifice of something she held dear. "Very well," that sound seemed to say, "your own dress . . . old enough, I suppose. . . ." She examined Esther's, turned it inside out, looked at the seams, and made another sacrifice. "Yes, that seems all right," she remarked, not looking at the dressmaker, while the negative shaking of her head seemed to convey the opposite opinion.

"Is she dismissing me?" Aurelia thought, and the pulse in her brown neck beat faster.

"Hm," said Mrs Osborne, smiling at her handsome daughter who was examining her back in the mirror.

Aurelia suddenly understood from something in that awkward smile that while looking at the dress apprehensions and decisions about price were going through her mind.

"She looks almost regal," Mrs Osborne said to the dress, dropping a tiny laugh like a sixpence.

"Oh, yes, it takes her," Aurelia agreed quickly, not sure what regal meant.

"At this age most styles suit them, I suppose. They really aren't difficult to sew for." Another sacrifice.

"Yes, she has a very good figure," Aurelia agreed. "Excuse." She stepped forward, plucked a thread from Gwenneth's hem, shook out the hem with a nervous gesture and stepped back but did not sit: this time somehow she feared to sit in her employer's presence.

A smiling pause followed.

"Oh, do take it off, you'll get giddy!" Mrs Osborne glanced at the dressmaker and laughed with a louder tinkle, like a penny.

Gwenneth, who could sense atmosphere, felt that the unpleasant business of bargaining was about to begin. With a feeling of embarrassment she hastened to pull the dress over her head.

"Don't tear it, for goodness' sake!" from her mother.

"Thank you, Mrs Henriques," said Gwenneth, flushing, and left the room in her slip.

Frowning and at the same time smiling, as though deriding herself for having to trouble about money, Mrs Osborne began : "Well, let's get down to business. How much are the dresses?"

"Five dollars each."

"Good heavens! Nonsense! Why, I understood your charges were quite reasonable."

"But what would you call this, Mrs Osborne? These are dresses I could get five dollars apiece for anywhere."

Lightning stabbed. To the crack and crash of thunder they paid no attention.

"I never dreamed of paying such a price! Why, I never pay more than three dollars apiece."

"Not for this class of work—"

"Oh, in thread and buttons . . . surely . . . a couple of shillings each at most," Mrs Osborne waved her coarse red fingers with their rings. "And you—"

"Sixteen hours a day I worked on these dresses, Mrs Osborne," said Aurelia, flushing and raising her voice. Rain and wind were lashing at the windows. Thunder rolled majestically into the distance.

Mrs Osborne rose and took up her bag from a table. "Very well. Say no more. I'll give my work to someone else in future. Now—what do you want on account?" Her head shook more rapidly than ever.

"I don't keep accounts, it's cash I always work for," Aurelia replied, panic-stricken.

"Indeed. Well—"

"I have to make up the rent by tomorrow morning for the latest!"

"I can't give you more than three dollars on account, till the end of the month. I'm sorry. We all have to arrange our affairs to suit our pockets. Can't always do what we'd like." Mrs Osborne was moralising to the wall, eyebrows raised. She put three dollars on the table and fussed in her bag.

Aurelia grabbed the money and left the room. This time she did not avoid the splendid woollen rugs but scraped her shoes over them. Cassandra took her to the servants' quarters. There they waited for the rain to pass, looking out on the big garden where the handsome trees were reeling madly. A dog, a thin stray, huddled against the house, ears back, tail between his legs, too spiritless or sick to shelter. The lawns were flooded, the earth churned to mud. After a while it grew lighter. The clouds broke and fled. Now the scent of drenched earth, which had followed the scent of heat, was followed by a cool, sweet, heady odour of wet trees and battered flowers, of grass, of life refreshed. The sunlight coloured the raindrops falling heavily from the trees. Aurelia looked at it all without knowing what she saw. Her own eyes were full of water.

Chapter four

That night Aurelia bought chicken pilau and pastelles. Sumptuously did they feast to make up for their vain fasting and Aurelia's feeling of guilt towards Elena. No wedding feast graced with the finest old rum could have been sweeter than this, consumed so to speak behind the battlements while they awaited the enemy's assault. It gave body and soul new life; it incited laughter, and hope awakened. They mocked their tormentors. Each with her laughter gave strength to the other, and in them arose a defiant satisfaction that they had not been crushed, would not be crushed. They felt close, very close.

They went to bed soon after.

At two in the morning Aurelia awoke with a feeling of oppression and fear. Though she took great gulps of air something kept squeezing and choking her. She put her hand where her heart should be. It wasn't beating!

"God forgive me! God have mercy on me, a sinner!" she prayed rapidly, terrified now, her eyes roving in the darkness as if expecting to see *it*—the end. Remembering the bailiff and all her troubles, past and present, she felt she no longer had strength or desire to fight *it*. She went into Elena's room, saw her peacefully sleeping, hugging her pillow, one brown leg stretched out, the other drawn up. "As the earth is far from the sun, so am I," she thought, "from her life and dreams." Tears ran down her cheeks. "Let death take me. It's time, it's time!"

She peered through the jalousies into the deserted street. Trams had long ceased running. From the waterfront came the laboured puffing of a railway engine shunting a goods train. A drunken voice began to sing a doleful chant, echoing in the street. It broke off and a sound of vomiting followed. She seemed to hear the town breathe in its uneasy sleep, to hear the mutterings and scratchings of those who slept on the sidewalk beneath the Town Hall gallery. "O God, must I die alone, now, this minute?"

". . . bicarbonate of soda," occurred to her.

She drank some. She belched, striking her chest, and felt better. But she wept for her sorrows and the suffering on every hand against which at this moment it seemed useless to struggle. She went back to bed. There she lay sleepless, pondering, until the first light of dawn. Then she woke Elena. They held counsel and agreed to lock out the bailiff to gain time.

Having made sure that all doors and windows were fastened, Aurelia whispered : "I ought to stop using the machine, I don't want him hear me."

So she cut out dresses instead. Elena basted seams.

Leah arrived and, learning that they were beleaguered, went off to cook their lunch at the home of a friend. Noon came before they heard the front door handle rattled and a woman's voice call: "Aurelia? Aurelia?"

"Fortunately it's not someone who owes me money," Aurelia whispered, cowering down behind the table even though the jalousie blinds were shut.

At one o'clock Leah's well-known knock on the door of Elena's room, which led to the yard, announced that lunch was served. Elena took the tray from Leah and whispered: "Push the door in well behind you."

They ate in silence, hungrily, quickly. At every suspicious sound they ceased chewing and stared at each other, listening with strained attention. The kitchen being in the yard they did not wash up after; that would wait on night's fall. The law forbade a bailiff to exercise his rights between six pm and sunrise.

Four o'clock came without a single interruption.

"It look as though we get away today," said Aurelia. "Tomorrow

Sunday, he can't trouble us. Maybe I can arrange something by Monday, God willing."

Just then they heard a heavy step in Elena's room.

"Who that? Who you?" cried the terrified Aurelia.

Elena slipped into the little dining-room and sat there picking at the tablecloth with her needle. She knew how it had happened: Leah had not pushed the door in far enough to allow the bolt to fall into the socket. She heard the heavy-footed agent step in and say triumphantly to the bailiff, his coarse voice rattling with phlegm: "Come, man, pass this way," and then mockingly to her mother: "Like you want to lock me out."

The presence of that sweaty, big-footed agent in the cherished privacy of her room, the tone in which he addressed her mother, filled Elena with disgust. She forgot her fear and returned to the living-room. Her fingers trembled as she continued sewing.

"Take the washstand and the dressing-table," the agent ordered the bailiff. From his angrily vindictive tone Elena realised he expected opposition from her mother and welcomed it. She tensed.

"You can't take the dressing-table, that is what my customers have to try on before," Aurelia said firmly while removing the contents of her washstand with angry haste.

"You take that dressing-table!" said the agent.

Speaking rapidly in a lowered voice she told him: "If you take one thing more than this washstand you going to take me in pieces with it."

There was that in her voice and reddened face which confused the agent. He began to bluster, protesting he might not get enough when he auctioned the washstand. But the bailiff said in a shamefaced undertone that the washstand was enough. He wanted to go out through Elena's room, but the angry agent insisted that they go through the front door.

A cart was waiting. Elena could hear the horse stamping off the flies. Her mother sat down opposite her at the cutting table and, resting her head on her hand, began to turn over the leaves of a fashion book. When the bailiff opened both halves of the door to permit passage of the washstand and the thin, waiting horse and the curious passers-by appeared as close as if they were in the room, Elena rose with assumed dignity and retired to her bedroom.

She felt both anger towards her mother and a longing to protect her. "How can I help her? She must go her own way . . . to perdition!" she thought with horror. "But my life has to be different, *has* to be different."

At last the agent, grunting, and giving directions for all to hear, succeeded with the bailiff's assistance in placing his plunder on the sidewalk. Then Aurelia closed and locked the door and returned to her former position, with her head on her hand.

An invisible lock had shut the door on happiness from the day she married Henriques. Life had thrown her down a well. She had worked like a cockroach that struggles endlessly and with desperation to climb up the smooth sides of the glass into which it has fallen. It is halfway out but it slips and falls back. It tries again, choosing another side, but fails to get a grip. It falls on its back, its legs vainly claw the air. At last it succeeds in righting itself. It pauses to gain strength, laboriously it begins to climb once more. For a long time Aurelia sat turning over the leaves of the fashion book and occasionally blowing her nose. At length, however, she rose and her scissors crunched again on the cutting-table. Elena came out and conferred with her about basting a collar. She broke off to tell her mother in an eager yet timid voice how lovely was some style she had seen a day or two before, describing it with that minuteness of which only young girls in poor circumstances seem capable. She was trying to say that she loved her, was not ashamed, that she thought no less of her for failing to keep out the bailiff. But Aurelia did not understand this, and Elena was too shy to embrace her and warm her heart. It was strange. It seemed as though in the years gone by so many tears had fallen, so many plans had gone awry, so much effort had been expended in protecting Elena in the midst of the battle that there had been no time, no inclination for the hugs and kisses that others lavish on their children.

At half-past six, when it was rapidly growing dark, Aurelia went into the yard to bathe—for at that hour the little boys in the mango trees would not be able to pelt her in the roofless bath. The stars were shining brilliantly when she came out smelling of soap. The appetising aroma of chocolate came from the kitchen, where Elena was preparing dinner. Aurelia drew a box and sat by the kitchen door and Elena joined her.

"What a lot of stars tonight, ehn?" Aurelia remarked, wearying of drying her crinkly coal-black hair and looking up at the sky.

"Erica said they had such lovely moonlight in Grenada for her honeymoon. Child, you know how sentimental Erica is," Elena added to appease her mother, who was not over fond of Joe's sister.

"Yes, I always heard Grenada was a nice place."

"Gosh! I would love to go there for two weeks."

"Two weeks? My dear, what is two weeks? What I need is a good two months' rest. Since I left school I never had a holiday, and never been sick much, thank God. Sometimes I long to see the sea. Only there's always somebody to get vexed if you don't invite them to spend time with you. It's better to leave Trinidad and go to Grenada."

"When we get rich."

"Eh, you don't want to go, in truth." Aurelia lowered her head and began drying her hair again. "As soon as this sou-sou is finished I going to join Miss Wharton's: ten dollars a month, two hundred when you get you' hand . . . I could well manage it," she continued as if to herself. "By the time I settle up two months rent and a few little things I could go to Grenada with a cool hundred and fifty and enjoy myself very well for six weeks."

"Passage is sixteen dollars return, thirty-two dollars for two of us."

"Travel second-class, Elena. It's only a night across."

"We could even go by sloop. I'd love to sail!" Elena tickled her and laughed excitedly.

Aurelia laughed too, ceasing to dry her hair.

Elena took her hand. "No," she said, playing with her mother's fingers and speaking as one who makes believe, "we'll go by steamer and travel first-class. And we not going to live in town, we going to live in the country—listen, nuh, Mother, stop drying your hair! Erica says—fruit! Chile, she never saw such an abundance of pine-apples, oranges. . . ."

A sizzling in the coalpot warned Elena that the chocolate had boiled over. She ran into the kitchen.

Aurelia leaned back against the kitchen wall, swung her legs and looked at the stars. She was already convinced that she had "seen my way" at last and that in five or six months' time, when she had got that hand from Miss Wharton's sou-sou (which it seemed to her now she would certainly be able to join), she would do everything as planned.

Chapter five

Joe was the eldest of six children and the favourite of his mother, who had always spoiled him. He was indeed someone you could not help noticing. When strangers saw that massive chest, that big, well-shaped head with its untidy mass of overgrown black hair, those piercing eyes and the beaked Syrian nose, they turned more than once to look at him and asked his name. Acquaintances, smiling conciliatingly, would pat his meaty sweat-dampened back as if congratulating him: "Hello, Elias." Joe would answer, "Oh, hello, boy," as if saying: "Yes, it can't be helped, I am really a remarkable fellow."

His father was a broad-shouldered man of middle height, jowly and red-faced. In raw youth he had come from Syria with a pack on his back. Now he had two drygoods stores and several properties in Port-of-Spain. He groaned loudly from habit each time he put his hand in his pocket. In his declining years (he was sixty-one) he had become a sensualist. Just recently, some months past, the family had learned with horror that old Elias had long been maintaining several women besides his wife.

While proud of his son Mr Elias, a simple man, feared his opinions. When Joe swore at the government old Elias would say hurriedly in a low voice: "Joe, Joe. Be careful, the police!" His son's courage and boldness had always been a reproach to his own moral cowardice. Joe entertained all his friends in his room, to which he had a separate entrance. Whenever old Elias passed the closed door of that room and heard loud arguments within about "Fascists . . . Communists . . . this rotten government . . .", he would shake his head reproachfully and sigh. Once or twice he went to his wife and complained in a low voice:

"Look, Mamma, Joe goin' to get in trouble with the police. Talkin', talkin' against the government. What he knows about such things? You better speak to him."

"Oh, be quiet!" she screamed at him, waving a hand and moving off with a rolling gait on her fat legs.

One Saturday afternoon after taking stock in the lumber yard Joe went to see Elena. He had long been in love with her but he tried to pretend to himself now that it was Popito he wanted to see. "Maybe he's there. I'd like to know how he's getting on."

It was two days after Popito had lost his job.

As soon as Joe entered the little cottage he saw Popito and sensed an electric atmosphere of sulky hostility.

"Hello, Joe. How?" said Aurelia because something like that had to be said when a guest came in. Without troubling to remove the frown from her face she continued sewing.

"Siddown, man, take a chair," said Popito in his kindly voice in which Joe now heard regret, fear and agitation. He drew hard on his cigarette, trying to calm himself, and blew the smoke out as if the taste were unpleasant.

The room remained full of hostile silence.

"Where's Elena?" Joe enquired.

"She hasn't come back yet," Popito said.

Joe nodded several times, looking at Popito, and his eyes twinkled. "Well, boy, you certainly fixed up Miss Brassington." (The "Miss" expressed their dislike of the man.)

"Yes, he certainly fixed up himself too," Aurelia put in at once, vindictively, evidently unwilling to give up the quarrel that had raged before Joe came in. "Brassington will eat at the Queen's Park Hotel while you filling up on windpies."

Popito winked at Joe with a feeble pretence at shrugging off the misrepresentations of a woman incapable of understanding all the issues at stake.

"Blood in you' veins, what, man!" she flung at Popito. "It's so you want to go through life with everything. Joe, with Popito, it's always a word and a blow. You can't be always refusing to accept what life brings, man."

"What life brings? It's what man does to you!" shouted Popito. "If I had any sense it wouldn't be a word and a blow, it would be a word and two blows."

"Take it easy," Joe said.

"How you expect to get the better of English people?" Aurelia persisted. "You don't see it's to keep out of their way?"

"The most urgent necessity now is the formation of trade unions in all branches of industry," Joe said. "Do you know what I will tell you, do you know?" Leaning his large body forward so that the chair groaned under him he devoured Popito with his bright blue eyes. "Boisson is lying when he says the British Labour Party has advised him against forming trade unions at the present time. He is afraid to lose his power! So long as we have no trade unions the workers look to him and his little clique."

Boisson, a white French creole from a highly esteemed family, was indeed a power among the workers. Captaining a West Indian regiment during the First World War had changed his mind about many things, especially the position of workers in the West Indian society of that time. When the workers asked their captain to lead the party they had formed, he consented. In those days he had taken a stand against his own class. But many years had passed. Today workers were growing disillusioned: power and his old class allegiances, they felt, were making him a drag on the movement. At a time when the unemployed and half-starved were looking for action Boisson was saying it would be dangerous, the law being what it was, to form trade unions.

"Joe, the unemployed, the unemployed in this country!" Popito said suddenly in a tense low voice. "You seein' them everywhere—sittin' in the squares, walkin' the streets. They put on collar and tie and jacket to hide their hunger. We are proud people. They try to pretend nothing wrong, but they mad with the need to strip off and fight. They don't know what is the right way to fight. They 'fraid the boss might outlaw them forever if they form a union."

"Look here, do you know what really is the trouble with us, do you want me to tell you? The lack of means to bring the progressive forces together. The lack of a paper to take up the fight for the working man. Small as our magazine is, a great deal can be done with it. Oh, yes, you may laugh," said Joe, raising his voice angrily although no one was even smiling, "you may laugh but I'm telling you. . . ."

Popito sighed. He was hardly listening. "Magazines to fight. What would you know about workers?" he thought. "You' belly full and you' father rollin' in money like a pig in mud."

Joe was launching a literary-political magazine with the assistance of two of his friends : André de Coudray, who came of an old French creole family high in the social scale, and Manuel Camacho, a Portuguese. Manuel was of as little account socially as the Syrian Joe Elias because they were comparative newcomers whose families had never owned slaves and great estates as the de Coudrays had done, but the three had been drawn together by an urge to break the fetters they felt heavy upon themselves, and in which West Indian society languished.

At this moment Elena entered and Joe fell silent. Her dark skin and eyes were glowing. She kissed her mother and uncle. "Hello, Joe. How?"

"Good, good. What about you? Been swimming? You got sunburnt a bit. How was the water?"

He talked quickly in the attempt to keep her near him, but she answered his questions while moving to her room and disappeared into it with an apologetic, smiling glance over her shoulder. She was the centre of all eyes and she knew it.

Again silence. Popito envied her youth and her careless expenditure of it. The darkness of his own future seemed terrible by comparison. If her future grew dark it would be because he could not help her. A light had gone out for Joe. How futile and senseless seemed all this bother about a magazine when life was passing him by! Who could tell how much time was left? He loved the swiftly changing clouds, the fecund earth and its scents, the falling rain, the sea, the rising sun . . . but feared their passing. He loved life's strong pulse within himself but did not trust it. It was a fleeting thing, a firefly briefly glowing in an endless night. When death's hand took his own, plans and will and talents, love, hate and fear would all evaporate without a trace. Today life ruled him, he writhed in the frustration of his ambitions; tomorrow death stood between him and life's tempting fruits and he looked on everything with sorrow. . . .

As soon as he got home he picked up the evening paper, retired to his room and shouted for Beulah to bring him iced lemonade. Mrs Elias, hearing a note of irritation in the voice of her favourite son, joined in the shouting for "Beulah! Beulah!" From somewhere in the yard came an answering "Mistress E-li-oos!" on a rising note and the slap of slippers on running feet.

Joe was reading an account of a city council meeting, paying particular attention to the account the mayor had given of himself. The mayor was Boisson.

Boisson, in 1935, was now at the height of his political power. He was leader of the Workers' Party and a member of the Legislative Council. He had won the eight-hour day (with lowered wages), workmen's compensation and old-age pensions that were more symbolic than real—they did not suffice to pay even the meagre rent of a pensioner's room. But the workers had not had to struggle for these gains; they were a hand-out from "White Massa" through the intervention of their white leader. To the great majority he was their god.

A small number of workers headed by the Negro, Le Maître, were demanding the formation of trade unions and a united struggle against the bosses as the only road to higher wages and better conditions. Joe was keen to join Le Maître in drawing away the workers from Boisson's influence. But more important to him was his dream of being elected to the city council and challenging Boisson's power in it.

Beulah knocked and came in. She was young, good-looking, and he took pleasure in her smile and her large black eyes which guilelessly reflected joy and pain.

"Put it there, just put it there," he said, not even glancing at her now.

"Bah! Boisson!" he thought. "If only I could get on that council I would show them what the despised Syrian can do. Only that lecherous old man stands between me and fame, leadership, the leadership of the working class! What is twelve hundred dollars to him?"

He jerked himself out of his chair and went to the window. The room suddenly seemed too small. The first stars were shining. A fresh scented breeze cooled his neck and chest. He inhaled lustfully, feeling an irresistible stream of youth within him, urging him towards the unknown. "Yes, impelling me to greatness. Why not? I see so much more than other men. . . ." He gripped the window in both beefy hands. He felt powerful enough to tear it out of its frame. But what was the use of it all when one's wings were clipped? It was better not to understand more than others but to go along without thinking or looking upwards at the stars.

He heard his father enter the study. The study adjoined Joe's room. He heard the old man spin the lock of the safe and the safe door creak on its hinges. Every Saturday night his father counted up the week's takings and the wages, and checked his wife's accounts. Saturday's money was locked in his safe over the weekend.

Although Joe had many a time seen and heard his father counting and groaning on a Saturday night he began to listen intently now to the old man's every movement. There was a period of muttering as he added up his cash book, then a long-drawn sigh and groan as he finished, then the rustle and clink of money being counted. "Ah, my God, my God!" the old man groaned at intervals, as if foreseeing his inevitable ruin. There were other words Joe could not make out.

With resolute steps Joe hurried from his room—again not seeing Beulah, who was returning for the lemonade jug—and entered the study. Old Elias looked up in alarm and ceased counting.

"Look here, Pappa, look here, I want to have a serious talk with you," Joe began in a threatening tone because he was nervous. "Are you finished? Well, all right, then, finish."

"Talk, talk! Say what you want," said old Elias, prepared to reject outright any request for money.

"Look here, this is a serious matter." Joe seized a chair and thrust it between his legs with an adroit, determined movement that convinced the old man it was indeed no laughing matter. "I will tell you frankly: I have a big job to do in life, a job that will benefit everyone in this community—and you too, you too. That job is on the city council. You could quite easily help me to get there. After all, what is twelve hundred dollars to you? It is not as if you cannot afford it. And you could easily transfer—"

"Twelve hundred dollars?" old Elias interrupted in a frightened whisper, drawing back. "Boy, you mad? And to do what, to go and talk foolishness about breakin' down the good houses that keepin' people like me alive? Eh? I must give you twelve hundred dollars to cut my own throat? I tell you, if it was so I was to give away money, where you would be today? You' head too hot—"

"Shut up, you hypocrite!" Joe shouted in a terrible voice, striking the desk with his fist. "If you had given the money to Mamma and the children instead of to your whores, life would have been pleasanter for all of us."

The old man's red face became redder from shame and anger. "That is none of you' business!" he blustered. "I give you everything that is to be given."

Mrs Elias was fat and her old legs were stiff, but a note in her son's raised voice made her hasten in alarm to the study. She was just in time. Joe had grasped his father by the collar and was choking and shaking the terrified old man.

"Money for pianos and houses for your whores but none for your children and their mother?" he shouted, no longer knowing what he was saying. "We'll soon fix that, we'll soon fix that, you skunk—"

"Joe, Joe! Stop that, boy, stop it, I say!" cried Mrs Elias, striking him in the face.

Joe flung his father aside and strode rapidly from the room and the house.

Chapter six

Joe went to Manuel Camacho's but the latter was not at home. He did not go to André de Coudray's—let André come to him. He was too proud to enter that great house in wealthy, snobbish St Clair where people would regard the presence of a Syrian, some merchant or other, with scarcely concealed disapproval. He sneered particularly at those aristocratic de Coudrays with their refinements of thought and feeling, their finicking repugnance of the world's vulgarity, because he was conscious in himself of something coarse, savage and relentless which was eminently necessary if he were to make life take note of him. It was an essential part of his nature, yet in his heart sometimes he felt ashamed of it.

He phoned André.

"André? What are you doing? Come over, nuh? We'll have a talk."

Because it didn't matter what André was doing. He needed an audience, he needed someone in whose presence he could soliloquise. He went home and waited for him. He thought what a fine fellow he was, warm-hearted, acutely sensitive, unable to hurt anyone deliberately. He forgot entirely that he also considered him a snob who in the company of ordinary working folk closed up and sagged as the Petit Marie plant does at a touch. Joe had the faculty of seeing that particular side to an idea or a situation or a personality which most suited his prevailing mood; and surrendering to it he would turn his back on what he had espoused with equal conviction the day before.

It was this very aspect of Joe's character that mystified and irritated André because his own disposition was the exact reverse. He liked everything to be clearly defined and it was his life's lack of definition that was the cause of the profound unhappiness he concealed from everyone, even from himself.

He had been reared in an atmosphere of tea with gossip at four o'clock, discussions safely conducted within the bounds of official thinking, tennis on private courts, bridge, and languid boredom offset by the assiduous cultivation of the acquaintance (friendship being out of the question) of English officials.

He was the descendant of an old French noble who, with thousands of others, had fled to the West Indies from the Great Revolution. André's father had bought the St Clair home during cocoa's best days. Old Mr de Coudray's father had owned sugar cane estates. Mr de Coudray had rich memories of boyhood days passed in the old ancestral home with its retinue of black servants, some of whom had once been slaves. When his sisters were to be married their wedding gowns were ordered from Paris; besides racehorses half a dozen riding animals stamped their hooves in the stables; there were entertainments, balls; there was a particular set of delicate chinaware that was no longer used but preserved in a glass case—some visiting prince, duke or earl had eaten from it long ago. They had lived on the outskirts of Port-of-Spain, in a beautiful valley many miles from the cane estates that gave them everything. But Papa had died young and Mama, putting her trust in a manager, was soon robbed. Her affairs became so involved that she was forced to sell the estates and the ancestral home to salvage something for the children. André's father, Henri de Coudray, and one old unmarried sister were the two members remaining in Trinidad of that once large family that had wielded great influence in the government circles of its day. Today Henri de Coudray was a distinguished and well-to-do King's Counsel whose presence was felt everywhere : he owned a coconut estate in Manzanilla on the east coast, shares in oilfields in the south and a citrus estate in the north. The family mansion and reputation was set firmly in the west.

Like many another old and well-to-do French family this one revolved like a satellite about the English sun. With one difference: that in the distant past the de Coudrays had got themselves a slave ancestor and their revolutions were as a result confined to an outer circle—they revolved in the moonlight rather than the sunlight, so to speak. Mr de Coudray had sent all his children to England to be "finished", to mix with men and women who knew what was "the thing" and when to do this thing, and who spoke with English accents—above all, the correct accent. It was as if a stamp "Made In England" had to be acquired before this class of West Indian could be certain he was not "cha-cha"—a Creole expression meaning "of no account". One had to convince those whose escapades with the slaves were not evident that one's social rectitude was irreproachable, and that if one revolved in the moonlight it was from preference, a personal dislike of the glare of the sun.

Mr de Coudray was a tall, straight man of sixty who walked with precision and dignity. This walk, his upright bearing and his stern expression, made sterner by his pince-nez, suggested to others that he was threading his way through some unpleasant locality and wished to remove himself unsoiled from it. Just looking at him people often felt that he belonged to a remote and important world. Workmen and peasants he passed in the street sometimes took off their hats to him, imagining him to be some very high government official, and in distant country districts they had even suspected he was the governor travelling incognito. There was a barrier about him which few overstepped. If at any time Mr de Coudray thought his dignity in peril, he adjusted his pince-nez, quickly jerked up his eyebrows and looked over his opponent's head—the effect was more disconcerting than words.

André was the only one who had not been "finished". In early youth he had been in delicate health. Doctors had expressed the view that the cold English climate would not improve it. He had dreams, visions, ideals, gifts denied the rest. At the same time he had from his earliest years doubted his abilities because no one approved his visions, no one valued his gifts. He was the darkest of them all. He had never forgotten the day when, still a boy, he had asked his old aunt Clotilde about his grandparents on his father's side. For it was a question never discussed, and the avoidance of it confused him. She had drawn her chair closer to his although no one else was present, and in a low voice said as if revealing a dread secret:

"La Rosette, my dear? She was your great grandmother. Her father was a de la Clemendaire, her mother a slave. La Rosette was very uneducated, a mere peasant, hail-fellow-well-met with all the niggers, talking just like them. She would come to town without stays, riding on some peasant's donkey cart," said Aunt Clotilde, laughing, her frown expressing the family's mortification. "Yes . . . a dreadful person. So many people knew her that as soon as one referred to Mama as '*La petite fille de la Rosette*'—bam! we were done for."

From that time on André had felt guilty when he noticed that esteemed sign of his brother's and sisters' (there were two) "finish" —the English accent. He knew that he was different, that he was gifted, and like all gifted people he knew it was not profitable to be different. He longed for fundamentals that would explain the world and help man win justice in it, but he thought: "Can justice be for us too? For Blacks? How is it possible?"

Joe was spread out in an armchair, reading, when André arrived.

"Siddown, André boy, siddown," he said with lazy amiability, pushing with his foot towards André the chair on which he had cocked his feet. "So, how?"

"So-so. Almost finished the article on music. What we need is a company that will bring the best from Europe to the islands and South America. If we—"

"You right," Joe interrupted, "but listen a minute. I nearly throttled the old man a while ago."

"What!"

"Man, I don't know what got into me. Mamma saved me, it's a fact, man."

"What happened?"

Joe leaned forward dramatically in his chair. "Boy, if I were in that city council the feathers would fly! You know that?" He laughed bitingly.

"But why throttle him? Mamma is on your side, she can get the dough for you."

"That old man? You don't know him, you don't know him, in truth. However, wait, you goin' to see something."

"No dead bodies."

Joe laughed. "He never had such a fright in his life. . . . Listen, I expect a ring from Manuel. I want to see the magazine out next month." And very sure of himself, like a managing director to heads of departments, he indicated who should write what as he laid plans for the first three issues.

André listened and envied him the confidence with which he pursued his present ambitions. "What are mine?" he thought. "Is it only music I should live for?"

Joe shouted: "Beulah! You there?"

And ever-watchful Mamma from another room: "Beulah! Mr Joe."

"Comin', Mr Joe!"

And in a moment she was in the doorway. She had showered, changed into clean clothes, was scented, ready to go off home.

"I know what you want—more lemonade," she said, smiling at them both.

"Bring some of you' sorrel for us. It's good. When I tell you—it's good!" he added to André with an enthusiastic look intended to flatter her.

She went out laughing. Her hips swayed slightly, her whole figure, so young and strong, seemed to dance. She was gay and her movements were so quick they gave a peculiar sparkle to her personality. André did not know what caused it but every time he saw her he knew he was in danger, and now at her wide bright smile his heart beat fast.

The phone was ringing and Mamma was answering it. "Joe!" she shouted. "Manny!"

Joe went out. Half a minute later Beulah came in with jug and glasses. She smiled and her eyes for the first time held André's. That look suddenly and inexplicably established an understanding between them. She poured him a glass of the red sorrel and watched him drink it.

"Nice?"

"It's lovely. Did you make it?"

"Yes." She came closer and her fingers closed softly on his around the glass as she poured some more. His heart leaped and pounded. It was difficult to breathe. What he was drinking had no taste. She was watching him almost shyly now.

"That is for Mr Joe," she said, putting the jug on a table littered with magazines and papers. "No more for you." And with a smile mischievous, coquettish and bashful she took his glass and flashed out of the room.

All his cherished ideas about his article, music, the magazine vanished in the flood of passion that seized him. He was choking, his hands were icy. He didn't want to see Joe or talk about anything, he wanted to run out after her. "Why did she do this to me?" he thought, furious. Had she guessed the role she had so often played in his secret thoughts? He got up, looked at a magazine but did not understand what he read. Some minutes passed. Joe was still talking to Manny, he could hear him through the open door. "I'll go," he thought, suddenly depressed. He moved to the doorway and at the same instant she reappeared in it.

"Mr André, you come in you' car, ain't it?" She spoke softly and rapidly.

"Yes."

"You could give me a lift home? I want to get home early tonight." Her large eyes were timidly joyful in expectation of his response.

"Yes, come."

"I goin' to meet you outside."

She disappeared in a flash. He went out through Joe's private entrance. None must see him. She was not in the car. He heard a low whistle and saw her up the street at the corner of a lane. All at once he was stirred by the poetic charm with which this act of discretion graced their adventure.

She got in. Having asked where she lived, he ran out of words. It was terrible to drive in silence like this; everything that had happened was going to be wasted! Yet he dared not speak because the tremor in his voice would reveal the extent of her power over him. She kept glancing at him. He put out his hand and took her own. "You make wonderful sorrel."

She laughed and came close against him. The warmth of her, her indefinable sexual power, sent a shudder through him. "You're driving," he tried to remind himself.

She lived in George Street, she had said. It was not far. Even if he had never known George Street he knew it tonight by its smell of poverty and his inward shrinking. The street lamps seemed dim and sparse. Low houses, aged, propped up one another. Small cake shops, a shoemaker's, a coal merchant's cubby hole, were interspersed among them.

"Stop here." It was an alley between two houses black with age and weather. "Thank you." She half got out, his hand in hers. He felt rather than saw her radiant smile and shining eyes. "Come, nuh?" she said softly, drawing him by the hand.

Suppose someone who knew him—even by sight—should see him

entering the alleyway. . . . Yet he followed her as if she alone was in the world about them.

She rented a room in the barrack yard. She lit a lamp on her dressing-table, turning it low. He saw the liquid glow of her eyes and the uncertainty in them. She closed them as he kissed her. She felt a great hunger and shyness in him. She opened his shirt and drew his left nipple between her lips. On the bed, which creaked a little, he was consumed by a flame of savage bliss. He felt himself entering into eternal life, but also into eternal, joyful death. Her whispers, her hands, her little moans, her movements—all told him she was not giving him her body only. She was absorbing him into herself. She was renewing herself and giving him life. This black girl was the first he had touched. It was not as it had been with the coloured ones before her. Now he was all-powerful, among the gods, steeped in joy, aware yet not aware of wings, until a blinding ecstasy burst upon him and he floated down, down, down. . . .

And in her eyes now a fleeting timidity and fear lest she be mortified by his satisfaction, his coldness and his shame. How earthy was earth, how bare, how cruel its demands when they beheld their naked bodies devoid of passion. She covered herself quickly.

"How talk to her? What shall I say?" he thought. Just as he had grasped a vision it had dissolved like mist, and she was again Joe's servant. He pulled away the sheet and kissed her breasts. He felt something in her melt. Her hands caressed his face. Both knew a kinship beyond colour, class, beyond St Clair and all his education. Tomorrow could he take the sorrel with an indifferent "Thank you" and averted eyes? For twenty-three years but one reality. Now he was torn up by the roots. She was a forbidden self that frightened him but which he longed to cherish.

She did not respond when he said goodbye, only looked down, her smile, as his, concealing unspoken questions. Going out he realised for the first time how dark was the yard and how offensive the smell of urine that pervaded the alley.

As soon as he got home and entered the tiled side veranda with its handsome balustrade he saw his father reading *The Times,* his old aunt Clotilde silently rocking her favourite rocking-chair, his white-haired mother crocheting and his younger sister toying as usual with the gold chain on her thin chest as she read a novel: at peace, secure, cut off from that other world.

Aunt Clotilde, his father's sister, was an old maid of sixty-eight. She suffered "from nerves", was irritable and lived in the past when she had been somebody. Her faults were offset by her wonderful ability to laugh at herself. She enjoyed amusing others by making fun of her defects, partly because she was lonely and felt the need for affection. Whenever she came, as now, to spend some days with the de Coudrays in their dull, well-ordered mansion André felt that something slightly improper but very amusing was being indulged in. His father lost his sternness and became kind and lovable. His mother laughed in a restrained manner, with blushes, as if against her better judgment—her soul was apt to creak under expansion.

"Well, well!" said Aunt Clotilde when André bent down and kissed her. (If she knew how those lips had just kissed Beulah, he thought. . . .) Nodding her head reproachfully she held on to both his arms. "Is that how you come to see me? Ah, ah, ah!"

"I've had so much on my hands." He patted her flabby arm in its old-fashioned long sleeve.

"Your hands?" She opened eyes and mouth, straining to hear. "Oh, on your hands, yes, busy. . . . But, my dear, surely—half an hour, will that kill you? Eh? Where have you come from at this hour? Eh? Engaged to be married?" she asked with an eager, teasing look, repeating what she thought he had said.

"Went to see some friends." André bent down to her ear. "Elias. Syrians," he added to annoy his mother.

"Syrians!" cried Aunt Clotilde. "Oh, my, cha-cha people. What things he does!"

Mrs de Coudray assumed a familiar cold, martyred look, closing her thin wide mouth in the way André had learned particularly to dislike. It put an insuperable barrier between them.

"He's a very fine fellow," André shouted.

Aunt Clotilde understood after a while. "Very fine fellow," she repeated, then made a face and shrugged. When André said "Syrian" she pictured a man with a pack on his back, a man speaking bad English while the smell of garlic almost knocked you down.

André drew a chair up close to her. "Did you know Boisson in his young days, Auntie?"

"Maurice Boisson? Oh, yes. Yes. He was the most amiable of them all. The Boissons were always inclined to be a stuck-up lot, you know. . . . But what is the purpose of all these meetings of his? They seem to bring nothing but trouble for all of us, my dear. My cook is telling me now something about a minimum wage: very soon, she says, I will have to pay her not less than ten dollars—with food, if you please! Is that what he is telling the people to do in his meetings? Oh, but no! He should be ashamed of himself, my dear. And the police are letting him do this sort of thing?"

André could not help laughing.

Aunt Clotilde continued: "I said: 'When the day comes that I have to pay you that sum and feed you then we will all be mistresses, you see, and there will be no servants. I want to know how you will get on *then.*' Yes, I said: 'You should be glad to find someone who pays you three dollars with feed.'" And Auntie, flushed, glared at Mrs de Coudray then adjusted herself in her rocking-chair with a twitch and rocked back and forth quickly.

Yvette turned a page of her novel and patted a yawn.

"Times are changing," Mr de Coudray remarked. He switched off his reading lamp and, settling more comfortably into his chair, said: "Clotilde, do you remember the old days, how we used to give the trees names? There was one big one by the cow pens. I called it Madame Boisson, you remember?"

"Yes, yes," replied Auntie, frowning and laughing. "And there was one in what we used to call 'grass field', where Daniel, our head groom, used to graze the horses sometimes. For some reason this same Boisson called it Madame Gransaul. Do you remember?"

"What became of old Daniel?"

"Oh, but he died! Don't you remember, just before André was born?"

"The attraction on the Boissons' property was the old sugar mill and the sling," said Mr de Coudray. "What lovely sling we used to get from the old mill! I remember once some of their big dogs chased us. How we ran!" And Mr de Coudray's usual stern, aloof expression was replaced by an open, mischievous smile that made André feel close to him and wish that he could always be close.

"What's that, what is he saying?" asked Auntie, leaning forward and getting ready to amuse them by laughing at herself. "I'm hearing something about 'big dogs in a case', what is it?"

Everyone laughed, but Auntie more merrily than anyone, with that stifled laughter that made her face red. "Yes," she said, wiping tears from her eyes. "Yes . . . he was always up to some trick or other."

"Go on, more," André felt like saying, "don't stop."

"Yes, quite a nice fellow. It is only since he came from the war that he took to the niggers like this." Auntie turned down the corners of her mouth.

A maidservant stood at the door. "Madame, a lady come—Mistress Knox."

"Who is she?" Aunt Clotilde asked with a vexed look, not wishing anyone to deprive her of their company.

"They're English," Yvette informed her. "He's in charge of the railways." She rose hastily and ran upstairs to change.

Mrs de Coudray, touching her beautiful white hair, was already on her way to the drawing-room.

"Coming?" Mr de Coudray asked his deaf sister for form's sake, and without waiting for a reply followed his wife.

Abruptly all the charm in the reminiscences vanished for André.

"What an hour for visitors! Half-past nine. Knox? Never heard of them," Auntie said with an irritated expression. Rising on her feeble legs she peered querulously in the direction of the drawing-room and took André's extended arm. "English, she says. You wish to go too, I suppose. Well, go on, go, I am too old. Just turn on a light. Why have they this mania for turning off lights! They're not poor."

"I'm not going, Auntie," André said, pressing her arm.

"Yes, yes, by all means. Just turn on a light."

"I'm not going in, I say."

"Oh, you're not going in," she smiled, relieved. "Yes. . . . Well, it's time I was in bed. I won't detain you. Good night, my dear. Kiss me."

Her kiss was warm. She patted his cheek. She ascended the stairs slowly on a servant's arm.

George, who seemed to have scented the English from afar, went by smoking his pipe. André held his nose pointedly.

"The best there is, my boy, I always use the best," George remarked. He took himself seriously.

Yvette came hurriedly down the stairs. She was transformed not by what she wore so much as by the smile of suppressed gratification that lit her cold face.

André turned away his eyes. He went to his room.

Chapter seven

He could not forget Beulah. Unknown to himself, he, the poet, had endowed her with a mystic aura of beauty. Let disaster strike, he would visit her again.

"But suppose she's not alone!"

No, it was better to go to Joe's. He would surely see her there. He would ask for . . . well, something, and she would bring it, would again pour it for him, and her fingers would touch his own, and again he would take her to her room.

He went to Joe's. As soon as he smelled the familiar smells and heard the familiar sounds in Joe's home—all of which was pleasant to him now—he imagined he sensed her nearness.

"What happened?" Joe looked at him, puzzled. "Why you went off so suddenly yesterday? We wanted to see you, Manny came over."

"I was restless. He rang me this morning. Still insisting that the magazine should adopt a revolutionary policy and be anti-religious."

Joe curled his lip scornfully. "Some people have a romantic idea about jail. Why this urge to dive underground in a conspiratorial manner when there is so much to be done above ground? It is trade unions. . . ."

André's ears strained for Beulah's voice and the sound of her footsteps. "Yes, of course," he agreed, forcing himself to think of what Joe was saying. "Now, take Jacob. He is one it would be difficult to get into a union. He distrusts everyone and everything, he's afraid; a lot of them even affirm they are constitutionally incapable of sticking together."

"That can be overcome, it has to be—"

"What about some of that excellent sorrel, Joe?"

"Sorrel? What sorrel?" Joe retorted irritably because he had been interrupted in mid flight. He persisted in outlining his ideas, but now André hardly listened. At length he shouted: "Mamma! Beulah there? What about some sorrel?"

And Mamma's instant shout: "No more sorrel, all finished."

"All finished," Joe said to André, throwing up his hands. And shouted again: "What else? What else?"

"Coconut water!"

Mamma herself brought them coconut water.

He thought he would go to Beulah's room that night. But suppose it embarrassed her?

Next night the thought of her gave him no peace. He parked his car where he knew she would pass, and waited. She would come by, he would open the door and, surprised and happy, she would get in. He would drive her home, she sitting close beside him as on Saturday night.

He heard her voice. One moment a fearful apprehension, the next acute disappointment: she was in the company of another girl. He let them go by and drove away.

And the next night the same.

One scheme succeeded another and he cared no longer about embarrassing himself and her.

On Saturday afternoon he went to Joe's. He slipped in furtively through the side gate and looked about him. The Eliases' yard was a big one with coconut and breadfruit trees, servants' quarters and a washhouse. It had not long rained and now it was sunny, the northerly wind was scented with trees and earth, and the shadows of white clouds swept over the earth like the wings of giant birds. He felt with irritation the contrast between the sunny, carefree atmosphere and the turmoil in his soul. Some freshly washed garments, still dripping water, hung on a line slung between a breadfruit and a coconut tree. He heard someone humming and saw her, hips swinging to her lively step, disappear into the washhouse. She was wringing out the washing and looked up as he darkened the doorway. For long afterwards he remembered the joyful surprise that shone straight out of her heart when she saw him.

"Eh! It's you?" she said softly.

"Been looking for you for days."

She looked down as she wrung the garment with a strong movement of her wrists. "So, how?"

At once he sensed she was on her guard. And now he saw a different Beulah, not the dream who had loved him in the half light but the one with little pigtails sticking out from her head, and perspiration running down her face and darkening the armpits of her working dress. He understood he was mad, that her world was closed to him.

"In hell without you," he muttered. "I'll take you home tonight."

And added in apology for the arrogance he heard in his voice: "If you'll let me."

She was wiping her arms in her apron, neither looking at him nor replying, a soft glow of contentment on her face. With a sudden stab of fear he felt himself at her mercy. He pulled her to him. She let him kiss her, but did not respond, then her restraint broke and she nuzzled him with lips and cheek. "You know where you are?" she whispered. She broke away from him. "This not goin' to work out, André." She seized the garment and again began wringing it.

"Why?" he asked foolishly.

"I have a friend, yes?"

"A friend. . . . A man?"

"Mm-hm."

"Between last Saturday and now?" His disappointment would have been comical had he been able to see himself.

She shrugged indifferently. "That is life. He not goin' to like it."

Everything seemed to turn upside down in him. Then some instinct—the uncertainty in her eyes raised to his—told him she was lying, and he seized her again. She pushed him away roughly.

"Stop it, man, stop it!"

He had only to take one step more to her and she could have been his. She wanted nothing but this although she saw only grief before her. But he did not take that step, he even turned away.

"When you gone is only misery facin' me every day. You think I want that?" she said in a passionate low tone. She took his hand. "Try to understand, nuh, man," she pleaded.

In that second he knew that she was pleading with herself also. He was going to embrace her, but Mamma saved them.

"Beulah-h!" she shouted.

Beulah started and moved away from him. "Ah comin'!" she yelled, and snarled, all shaken up: "Why the hell she don't leave me in peace?"

"Go, don't let her see you," she said to André and flung out wildly.

With hardly a thought for who might see him he crossed the yard to the street. He drove to the Gardens to hide his wound, to escape the confining, the unalterable boundaries of life; and there beneath the trees he flung himself on the still damp grass, wanting to strike someone, to weep, to beat his head on the earth, to get drunk, for only now did he realise how sweet was his regret, how singular her fascination, and what painful joys and joyful pains had been born within him. *She* had not been afraid to face reality. What was this half life of his worth? In that sky with the swiftly moving clouds, in the majesty of forest trees, in the moist scents of earth and tree bark there was such an assertion of life's endless growth that he felt enraged by his own purposelessness in it. O Lord, if he could only decide what to do! Something tremendous, something that would require all his strength, which was endless, incalculable. His fingers tore up the grass, they quivered with the realisation of his potential. Where should he begin? Where, now this minute? He got up and began to run with a joy in movement he had seldom known, as he was inclined to physical laziness. Knowledge, knowledge and yet more knowledge! He drove back to town, to the Public Library. A workers' meeting was in progress in Woodford Square outside the library. Briefly he glanced at the crowd over his shoulder before ascending the steps.

He had read Tolstoy's *What Then Must We Do?* It had turned him inside out with its revelations of man's exploitation of man, man's cruelty to man. It was all there, everywhere around him, and he had not seen it. He had even shared in this cruelty and accepted it. And now, hugging preciously, jealously, the hunger gnawing him for greater knowledge, he searched impatiently among the volumes, reading snippets, picking up one book after another, half hoping that in one of them he would find a revelation of life's meaning and purpose.

He carried off another volume by Leo Tolstoy, who painted life with such persuasive artistic force, with an angry authority that seemed beyond question. (In nothing could André bear half measures, especially in the emotions.) And with this promise of light in his hand he went out and would have driven away but for the voice in the square.

The crowd, which had grown, was silent, evidently transfixed by the words and the personality of the man who addressed them. The anger and sincerity in the great voice, the flow of facts, the dogmatic confidence with which they were spoken—it was all so new, so unlike what he had heard before, yet somehow so suggestive of the prophet who had opened his eyes that André went into the square to listen. Some five hundred people were gathered in a semi-circle about the bandstand. The speaker was a tall, heavily-built brown Negro with greenish eyes and pouting, insolent lips. André asked who he was.

"That's Ben Le Maître," a worker said, looking at André suspiciously.

". . . why Boisson wouldn't fight for a lower franchise? Because he 'fraid we elect barefoot people who would protect *our* interests. Ain't he say you and I are the barefooted and unwashed?"

"Go wash you' foot, boy!" a wag called out.

The crowd laughed. But Le Maître had no sense of humour. He was in the grip of ideas that would liberate men. "Look how Boisson supportin' the capitalists," he continued. "Give them money to plant their cocoa. Give them money to make sugar. What we gettin' out of those thousands of dollars? A couple days' work a week at sixty cents a day. The oilfields payin' us seven cents an hour but he fightin' for preference for oil—preference for them in English markets. Can seven cents an hour feed us?"

"No!" came the voices. "You, 'self, too! Makin' joke, man! Eh-eh! Seven cents?!"

"Then they must split up the bankrupt estates!" thundered Le Maître. "Divide them up among the people. But Boisson won't fight for that, he don't want us independent. . . ."

His words were like rain on parched earth. Falling on leaves and grass the drops break up, run off, coalesce into larger drops, into rivulets and streams. Something similar happened in the crowd when the meeting ended. The droplets of Le Maître's ideas drew men into groups which sometimes dissolved, sometimes coalesced into larger groups as the men weighed their experience against his urgings. Some angrily supported Boisson, others with curses decried him and ardently upheld Le Maître. On the benches the sick, the aged, the tattered beggars sat waiting dumbly, beyond despair. Beneath the majestic forest trees half-naked children ran about shouting, playing some game. Cherubs of stone with distended cheeks blew water into the fountain. The square was alive with the fervour of dearly bought ideas, with joy, cynicism, grief, despair and hope, but André found himself turning his back on it all; crushed by his own pitiful insufficiency in the midst of a life so endlessly varied, so brutal, yet so alluring; so intoxicating at one moment, so horrifying the next. Where was the connection between *this* and *himself*?

And with a feeling as if he had fallen from a great height he went home and shut himself up in his room with Tolstoy.

He put the book aside after a while—*A Confession and What I Believe.* This was September 1935. There were no answers in that book for him or for those people in the square.

Chapter eight

Elena Henriques was like thousands of other girls from poor families in the Trinidad of those days. At eighteen she quite lacked sophistication. She came of a stratum too poor to be entrapped by advertisements in glossy magazines. No night clubs existed. One went to the movies, to dances, to weddings and christenings. Once in a while, almost as infrequently as a comet appears and with all the excitement one engenders, some famed instrumentalist glittered for a night in Port-of-Spain, bedazzling the thousands who came to hear him, and hurried off next day to the big money in South America. From early January until Lent one went to the calypso tents—affairs of bamboo and plaited palm leaves, shadows flickering under slit bamboo lamps. Lord Executor was in his decline, the star of the Roaring Lion was rising. The best seat one shilling and no need for a special dress. No radio hourly inspired expensive desires, how for only such and such she could curl or perm her hair, iron or shingle it. (When the last big fight had come off in New York one lucky possessor of a radio set—he lived only a block away—had taken it into his veranda and turned it up loud for the people's benefit and to show off a bit. A crowd had gathered in the street to listen, hushing one another as they strained to hear the commentator between whistlings, wheezings and cracklings.)

Elena lived in the midst of lust, drunkenness and knavery; she understood the operation of the social meat grinder as well-to-do girls could not; but she herself remained strangely natural, idealistic, even pure, dreaming of a life denied her mother. Except to go to school Aurelia never let her treasure out of sight. Life had its terrors for her. Not the big-city terror of being crushed and forgotten in the ant heap. For there was time for lingering with friends and spilling with sighs one's rancour against white folk or whatever seemed the cause of one's misfortunes. One's heart never grew hard for want of tears or laughter. There was time to sorrow at length since no one sorrowed alone, and laughter trod on the heels of sorrow as daybreak follows night. There was time for the poetry of life, not only its pain. There was time for all manner of simple pleasures—there was always time: weren't you a long time dead?

No, she feared lest Elena be plucked like a half-ripe mango, savoured and thrown aside.

André had danced with her at Erica's wedding the year before. He had not been able to keep from staring at this girl whom he remembered as a child, when he was a child himself, coming into his home by the back door to deliver a dress and collect money. Suddenly, without warning, she was transformed into a glowing brown beauty in a dashing gold bodice and brimless hat that crowned her thick black curls. She had just finished dancing and, smiling on all the world, tried to restrain the quick rise and fall of her bosom. Joe seized her arm as she passed him but Elena, evidently fearing to be without a partner of her own age for the next dance, screwed up her nose and eyes in her impatience to escape him. In André's social circle girls showed a measure of poise, some even affected the blasé. Elena entranced him.

A year passed before he visited her one day with Joe. And again she was different: simply dressed, no lipstick, and a calm dignity that marked her maturity. She had accepted, he felt, the responsibilities life flung at her.

Elena had never forgotten that day. She sensed a loneliness and shrinking similar to her own in this André de Coudray. Joe she considered elderly. He, not yet thirty, envying André his attractiveness to women, went to Mrs Henriques and spoke his heart. Elena said that night, "But I am not in love with him," and opened her black eyes as if unaware of the havoc she had caused with her glances, her frolics and her laughter. How and when could she have given Joe cause to reach a conclusion at once distasteful to her and flattering?

Aurelia could not help remarking in a warning tone as if thinking aloud: "I tell you, not every day you get a man like that." Or: "Well, he's a man who could support you, not like one of these young boys who like a spree." She addressed the cloth she was stitching in the machine. Elena felt like something on sale.

Suddenly she forgot André. She stumbled on a job and life became sterner. A former schoolfriend had whispered she was leaving Hoo's to get married. She urged Elena to hurry. Elena went to see the owner of the business, William Hoo himself.

He was a poorly educated Chinese man in middle life, frail but as resilient as bamboo. Twenty-five years before, he had worn flour-bag pants and slept among the goods, the mice and the cockroaches in the back of his shop to save money. Now he owned a hardware business and by astute, merciless and shady deals had acquired cocoa, copra and citrus estates. He had bought a big house in St Clair among people who did not regard this low-class merchant with much favour. He owned racehorses, some of which he had imported from America at great cost.

"What she say she gettin'?" he demanded.

"She didn't say," Elena lied, afraid to mention seven dollars a week; it even seemed presumptuous.

He seemed relieved. "T'ings bad now. One of these others could do her work, it not much."

Silence.

"Mr Hoo, I'll work without pay for a trial, a month. . . ."

She almost shuddered when she saw the cunning, evil grin that broke the stolid calm of his pallid parchment face. But the next minute there was stern reproof in his tone.

"I don' work so! Slavery done. Anybody who work for me I does pay. Not like some white men I know. Worse again, a girl. If she work for you, pay her, man! Too much thiefin' in dis country a'ready. When you don't pay you encourage thiefin'." And having got on to his favourite pedestal he added: "I will give you t'ree dollars a week to start. If you careful, don' make too much-a mistake in you' work and don't—" He was about to say "don't steal", but the young woman's calm dignity baffled him; besides he had only just suggested there were no thefts in his store. "We'll see what happen, nuh," he went on. "Come tomorrow and learn the work, don' wait till Miss Marley gone. What you' name is? Here, write it."

Elena went home with mingled feelings of gratitude and revulsion.

She had not been in the job three weeks when Hoo, realising her ability, made her "secretary" of the board of a new company he had launched to make coconut oil from his copra. Her job was to take detailed notes of all the friction, backslapping and manoeuvring that went on at meetings. These notes provided him with evidence he might later use against his partners, and clues to personal weaknesses which he could exploit. He always feared that others better educated than he might outwit and despoil him.

Obliged to permit Elena to create all his correspondence he would sign no letter that contained words unfamiliar to him.

"What word dat is? You know what you sayin' there? I never see no word so yet. Too much education does get people confuse. 'Of little consequence'—what does it mean? Change it."

He would strike out phrases in a finished letter, inserting others of his own.

"You can't say it that way, Mr Hoo, it's not correct."

"Write it so! Who signin' the letter, me or you?"

All this for an extra fifty cents a week.

His suspicious, twisted mind oppressed her. It isolated her from the world's goodness.

It was during this period that she met André one night in the Public Library. He walked her home. She asked him in. As she did so she remembered there was nothing left in the sitting-room but three chairs. Awkwardness being a response she had long learned to conceal, she now became more poised than ever.

"Please sit down. Do you still play the violin?"

On his previous visit with Joe, André had been unable to understand why there were only three chairs and a box, no pictures, no carpet. Perhaps they were moving the next day and the other things had gone on ahead? In the life he knew, rent got paid of itself; bailiff was a word in a dictionary. Only because of a remark Popito let fall later did he understand what had happened. He was appalled, then furious, then amazed that they still laughed as if it did not matter. Now a feeling of protectiveness came over him.

"Yes, of course."

"I heard you play once at a school concert."

"What did you think?"

"It seemed sort of extraordinary that someone in Trinidad could play so well." She laughed.

"Elena, have you ever been to the Pitch Lake?"

"No."

"Ever been to Blanchisseuse, or the south? Ever seen them plant or reap sugarcane, or drill for oil, or pick cocoa? Nor have I. We belittle what is ours. They tell us all the good things come from England and America, and we believe it. You thought it extraordinary that I, a West Indian, should play so well. You should have been annoyed I played so amateurishly." He shrugged.

"It's true. I never think of . . . us as a people. Will you go to the States?"

"My father seems to think I'm at a silly age which will persist indefinitely. He has no music in him." With a gesture and an impatient look André expressed the frustration of cherished dreams. "I'd like to compose real West Indian music."

"But is there such a thing?"

"Of course. Nothing, nothing is so important as to discover what one can do best, what *must* be done, and do it with one's whole soul no matter *what happens*."

"I understand that, I believe in dedication." Her truthful black eyes were fixed on his almost imploringly. "But suppose you can't? Suppose you're pinned down like a butterfly in a case?"

"Don't talk of it!"

"Do you believe in fate?"

"What, in sitting down and taking it? Of course not."

"Yes, I know, but . . . sometimes fighting is useless."

"There must be hope, Elena. Don't you see? Otherwise it's too horrifying."

He was no longer listening to the whirr of the machine in the bedroom; he was no longer conscious of her calves, her breasts, her plump arms, her curls; he was aware of a spiritual affinity he had not experienced with anyone. He longed to reveal that inner world which no one valued and at the same time he feared to do so.

"Did you hear Mischa Elman when he passed through Trinidad?"

She sighed. "No. I suppose you did?"

"He crushed me. I hated him and loved him. For days I was in despair. I'm telling you what I was too proud to tell anyone." He blushed.

"You needn't be afraid. Crushed. One can be crushed in more than one way. Do you think I'll be able to find what I can do with my whole soul? How many of us can?"

It was not to be denied. None would employ her but the small, the coloured merchants. The banks took white girls only. Even some of the big companies.

When he left she was unable to forget him. He had stirred up something deep down in herself, thoughts she had never dreamed of discussing with Joe or her mother. Suddenly she was not alone.

She recalled a day when she had been sent to Mrs de Coudray to ask for an advance on work yet to be done. Though but a child her pride shuddered when Mrs de Coudray, with an air of yielding to Fate, rummaged in two purses, pursing her lips disapprovingly, before handing her a crumpled dollar. How well Elena remembered that crumpled dirty dollar which she had at once concealed in her fist. "Hm. When will the dresses be ready?"

"But he is different," she thought, already pitying his private torments, wishing she could help him, not yet realising that she was trying to draw him to herself for her own support.

Soon he was coming twice, three times a week. Whenever he came he knew she had dressed for him, had been hoping he would come. He couldn't take her to a movie, not even for a walk; they were not engaged. It was the Latin custom. But Aurelia made one concession : they talked alone. He, however, as an intruder is conscious of a watchdog, was conscious of her presence there behind the partition, of her listening, of her jealous uncertainty born of suspicion of his class and his intentions. Sometimes when Elena was relating something a voice would come from behind the partition and the machine would stop racing.

"No, my dear, it was not so it happened, it was like this. . . ."

If Aurelia was in the sitting-room when André came she would greet him politely and unobtrusively disappear with her sewing. He felt she was thinking: "Very well, I'm giving you another chance to make up your mind. It's time!"

Elena understood this as well as he. After a few weeks she blushed when he came. She went hot and cold with embarrassment. She kept casting about for some way of suggesting he come less often while at the same time indicating that her interest in him had not abated. She was forced to examine her feelings. To love him, she knew, was folly, but to lose his companionship, their talks, seemed unbearable.

It was Saturday afternoon. They were talking—about Turgenev's novels, he remembered later—when they heard her mother go into the yard. They both fell silent as if the same thought had leaped simultaneously into their minds.

"Do you ever go to the Gardens?" he asked, trying to seem casual. But his eyes betrayed anxiety. "I often go there. On Mondays. It's so peaceful, I can think, you know. Even write a little music sometimes."

"Yes. Sometimes. It's sad there."

"Sad?" His heart beat quickly. Soon he would hear the footsteps returning and she would not have given any indication that she understood. "Why sad?"

"Because . . . I don't know . . . it says something so beautiful and unattainable."

"Why unattainable? Everyone has a right to happiness. God, I hate this country!" he burst out with a strange unreasonable passion.

They heard the mother returning.

"I don't think you do, really. It's just that everything. . . ." She broke off, sighing.

"No, look—*listen*!" He began to speak of a short story recently published in the *Guardian*. It had won praise. "But its claim to merit rests on its mockery of working people—Blacks. It's disgraceful! What great idea is there in life to hold on to?" But of what he hated most, his feelings of his own inferiority, his terror of being nobody—of this he was too proud, too sensitive to speak.

Aurelia was praying before the lighted candles on the shelf. She liked André, his heart, his lighter skin, his family connections; but what did he intend, my God?

She heard the front door open and Elena say, "Come in, Joe."

Seeing André and the happy smile on Elena's face Joe knew that what he valued most had been snatched from him.

"Oh! So you are here too?" And he laughed in such a high sneering tone that André knew Joe hated him. "Where's Popito? He told me he would be here."

"He hasn't come yet," Elena replied.

"So, how, boy, how?" Joe asked with a smile both challenging and cruel. "I haven't seen you for some days, man."

André began to speak of the magazine, pretending he had noticed nothing. The first issue had only recently appeared. The newspapers had ignored it, but it had been eulogised by the politically conscious and those inclined to the arts.

They heard Popito coming in through Elena's room. He wrenched open the door and entered with a blundering noisy step.

"Aurelia, where you, girl?" he called out in a determined drunken voice.

"Aurelia, where you, girl?" he called out in a determined, drunken meal every day. Now and then he earned a few dollars tallying on the wharves. As the weeks went by and he failed to get a steady job Popito, like a tree uprooted and transplanted when too old, began to show signs of withering physically and morally. If he could find nothing to do he would at once seek out company, man, woman or child, he could not bear to be alone. Even when reading the newspapers he must have around him someone with whom he could discuss the news and curse the government. When he came among friends, even relations, it seemed to him that while they addressed him kindly, asking if he had found anything, always a look of distaste at his failure lurked behind their sympathy, as if they feared he might ask them for money and they would have to refuse. It was a distaste, he felt, not unmixed with hatred, the kind of thing the strong young ones feel towards decrepit old beggars who approach them for alms.

"You prayin' again?" he asked now, irritated at seeing her thus occupied. "Man, is all dese damn prayers got you so, yes? You prayin' and the bailiff takin'. God not worryin' wid you, what you worryin' wid Him for?"

Aurelia turned red, a dangerous sign, and stood up, vexed and ashamed at this intrusion into her cherished privacy and his mockery of her faith, which was all she had.

"Get out of my bedroom!" She grabbed the scissors from the machine. "Come one foot nearer and I'll jook you with these!" she cried, disregarding the presence of guests. "When you get drunk do I come and stop you? You leave me to my way of settling my affairs."

"Don't talk to me like that, I am your big brother. Give me those scissors. You don't know I have to protect you from danger?" He struggled with her for the scissors. "I must protect you from those who are foolin' you. You goin' to fight me?" he panted, wrenching the scissors from her hand with a twist.

"Uncle Popi, are you mad?" Elena screamed in the doorway.

Popito swept from the shelf the flickering candles and a framed prayer to Christ. " 'The shadow of thy wing,' " he read aloud and crushed it with his foot.

Aurelia sat on the bed and rubbed her twisted hand. Elena embraced her, kissing her rumpled hair and whispering: "Mother, mother!"

"Go back outside," Aurelia whispered, her face contorting in the effort to stifle her weeping. "Go, go!" And she pushed her aside.

Elena was going out without a glance at her uncle, but he took her arm.

"Elena, listen to me," he pleaded.

She brushed off his hand. "How dare you come in here in this condition?" she said in a low, quivering voice, and went out.

"You against me too? What you know about life? Damn nonsense," he grumbled shamefacedly, picking up objects and looking at them without seeing them. "I can't get a job, the bailiff robbin' you, and you prayin'. God does live in St Clair, in the two-storey houses. He forget us long time. We have to look after ourselves before the Devil take us. Ehn, Aurelia? Look at me," he pleaded, lifting her chin, but she pushed his hand away.

He flung himself across the bed, then got up as if stung. "All right, I am drunk. But why do I drink?" he added, trying to justify himself. "I have no activity. God punishin' me, what! It is the merchants in this town doin' this to me—rich men doin' this to poor men. You think if I was a Limey, drunk as I am—" he lowered his voice, smiling cunningly—"they would not—at once!—find a job to give me? They would give me money to go back home. They would hide me, protect me. They feel an Englishman is a special man. Aurelia, sometimes you don't feel to kill and kill and *kill*? Ehn, Aurelia? You never have that feelin'? You and I have the same blood, don't tell me no!"

Aurelia wept, gazing at the wall as if asking what she had done that made it necessary to go on living.

"Popito? Popi?" Joe called.

Popito went to the door. "What's up, pal? Coudray, you here too? How you' boss, you' friend Mr Dollard?"

"Come, siddown, siddown, Popi," Joe urged in a soothing tone.

"On what?"

"Well, get a chair, nuh."

"Get a chair. Just like that. You could see you' father got money."

Popito went out for a box.

"He's havin' a hard time," Joe sighed.

Popito returned with a box, which he put down noisily and defiantly. He sat down and took out a packet of Anchor cigarettes. "So how you' magazine? You stirrin' up the people to fight yet?"

"To fight?" Joe repeated, sniffing, evidently fishing for an answer that would not irritate Popito still more.

"To fight!" Popito repeated. "You 'fraid, I know you."

"What sort of fight, Popi?" André asked.

"What sort of fight. Look, lemme ask you something. What you know about life? You ever had to go without food for one day?"

"Very easy to lecture, André—"

"I'm not lecturing!"

"Very easy to lecture," Joe repeated, "but just step down from St Clair, where you are so carefully protected. Come out of the clouds. Come down in this world, boy, and you'll understand something of the eternal verities."

André smiled sarcastically, flushing. "You long wanted to get that off your chest."

"That's what I mean," Popito said to André. "Your life is not our life, you can't live like us. You understand me? Furthermore Elena is the dearest thing in life to me. When I look at *her*—I see happiness, innocence. Boy, look, I feel envious, man! I not afraid to confess it: envious and sad—I had nothing so. And I don' want anybody make her unhappy! You get me?" He spoke fiercely, restraining his tears, tears of shame that he had lost her respect, tears of resentment towards life. All that resentment seemed concentrated now in his feelings towards André.

Elena's eyes blazed, they seemed to grow larger than ever. "Uncle Popito, André is my guest!"

"You be quiet! Guest? What you know?"

Aurelia rushed out like a tigress. "Get out of here! You hear me? Get out of my house!" she yelled at her brother, looking like a madwoman with her loosened hair standing out about her head. "Joe, take him outside before I do something I'll suffer for all me life. Take him out! Don't try to run my life for me. I'm sick of you, if you want to know the truth. I have me own troubles, God damn you! You dare to put you' foot in here again in that condition and I'll call the police!"

In her boundless rage she would have struck him down without a thought for the consequences. Popito saw this—he knew her well—and sobered at once. "All right, come go, come go," he muttered.

Aurelia retired to her room, but her voice went on and on flailing Popito. She raked up incidents long past and threw them at him to prove he was gullible and weak. She sneered, she taunted. Elena knew not where to turn for shame. She was unable to meet André's eyes. Her hands clasped and unclasped, she ran her palms down her hips to dry them.

André saw that that which supports a man's soul had collapsed in Popito. He took his arm and pressed it.

"I'll come with you, Popi. Look, I'm not offended by what you said, don't worry about it. Let's go."

"You see how it is with me, Coudray? You see? Is it my fault?"

"Come, we'll talk about it outside," Joe said.

"André, you know I didn't mean to insult you . . . my God! Why I have to say things like that? What devil makin' me hurt people I love, man?"

"Don't bother, tomorrow she will have forgotten it all, she will be sorry, too," said André, showing towards Popito the tenderness he felt for Elena but could not show her.

"It's done. What's the good talkin'? You can't undo it. She's right. Whatever bad you do in this world sticks on to you like shit. Eh, Joe? Eh, pal? Let's get out of this damn place."

They went out. André looked back. Elena was standing half turned to him, on her face an unnaturally strained, frozen expression. She was pretending to look through the half-closed jalousies. For an instant her eyes met his. He pulled the door shut behind him.

She sat down, then, in her uncomfortable straight chair, her fingers agitatedly playing with the hem of her dress. Slowly her tears welled up and flowed. Tears sometimes arise from many causes all at once. It was so with her now. A sudden deep tenderness for André was mixed with sorrow, a frantic yearning for a way out of the life that was choking the family, and hope that couldn't die because all life was before her. Her mother's voice went on and on. Just when her torrent of rage seemed to be abating it thundered afresh and she cried out to God accusingly: "What have I done? But what have I done?"

A wedding procession sped by. Some twenty cars followed one

another blowing their horns, announcing with gay clamour the joy of love, the end of loneliness, promise of a great fulfilment, expectation of perpetual bliss. Elena thought of her friends. Tonight they would be going to dances or parties, or for walks with boys round the Savannah, or to the movies. . . . Darkness fell, and still at intervals her mother's voice rang out. Elena's tears had dried but despair chained her to the chair. She sat quite still, gazing into the darkness. Monday would soon come. Again she would feel isolated by Hoo's crudities, Hoo's suspicions, and the stench of spiritual death all round her. "O God," she thought, "help me! Help me! Help me!"

Chapter nine

Joe could neither forget Elena nor forgive her for the happy, almost rapt smile he had seen on her face when he entered. "The little fool! What does she think? And her mother permitting it. He's not going to marry her. He's like all his ancestors—lechers, leeches!" Yet an unwilling respect for André rose in him. "Cunning, cunning!" Joe thought, trying to crush his feeling of admiration. "He wants that simple-minded Popito on his side. Oh, very clever, Mr de Coudray—Count!" he added contemptuously.

In the efforts he made to encourage Popito not to despair he forgot his own gloom, but as soon as he got home it overcame him. He sought out his mother. She was sitting in her favourite cane chair in the side veranda darning socks.

"Mamma, how? The paper come yet?"

She indicated it with a jerk of her head. He began to read it but soon threw it from him.

"What a life this is!" he said. "What a life! Some little man up there turns the page and everything is changed for you. When you see what people suffer you wonder how they put up with it. Boisson is right—they're like sheep."

"He says that?" Mamma asked unbelievingly.

"He's too clever to say that but it's so he regards them. Why make a fuss? Tomorrow—death. Just like that. And everything is finished, you know? All you struggled for, all you thought was so important —love, putting order in the world, happiness—all of that hasn't the slightest significance any more. The insect is crushed."

"Joe, why you don't get married? Death, and look at you—strong as a bull. If you get married you would cool down." Mamma rested her hands in her broad lap and looked at him earnestly, her head on one side.

"Ah, get married, what? Happiness is an illusion, Mamma, that's all it is."

"But it's nice, Joe, it's a nice illusion. You know what is good and what is bad, boy? You don't know yet, you know. You have to take the fruit and eat it before you talk big." The fingers holding the needle moved rhythmically.

He laughed shortly. "If I knew how to ingratiate myself with girls or if I could be a ladies' man like André it would have been all right. But that sort of thing doesn't come naturally to me, Mamma. Why make a fool of myself?"

They were silent.

"Joe, who is the girl?"

"Don't rake that up. . . . Well, it don't matter. Elena Henriques. Who else?"

"She's a nice girl. But why you troublin' you'self? She's not the only one."

"I know that, but it's not a pound of meat I'm buyin' in the market, Mamma. You can't compel someone to love you. Man has a grossly exaggerated idea about his power to change things in this world. I tell you—fate, you can't escape it." He rose. He stretched his arms over his head till his joints cracked. Sighing, he went with indifferent steps in the direction of his room. At that moment he heard his father's voice raised in argument with the chief clerk from his biggest business. Joe stopped. The old man was accusing the clerk of allowing himself to be cheated by a customer. The blood rushed to Joe's head.

"Mamma, come in here a bit," he said peremptorily. "I want to talk to you." He motioned with his head to the drawing-room.

"What? What's the matter now?"

"Come, come, this is important!" His tone brooked no refusal.

"Help me up!"

He helped her to rise from the cane chair in which she had embedded herself. The very way she lumbered hurriedly from side to side as she entered the drawing-room indicated her impatience with him. She sat down. "What's wrong?"

"Listen, you spoke to him yet? You spoke to that shylock, that fornicator, that rotter?" He shook a finger in the direction of his father's study. His voice rose although he had come into this room so as not to be overheard.

She looked at him open-mouthed over her spectacles. "You goin' off you' head again?"

"Listen, Mamma. You listenin'? Put that sock down for a minute, what I'm tellin' you is important. It's not important only to me, you know, it's important for all of us."

She removed her spectacles.

"I cannot go on like this, you understand me? I'm wastin' my life in Dollard and Company. I'm thirty years old, I'll soon be an old man. What will I have done with my talents? Thousands and thousands are out of work, hundreds of thousands are oppressed. It's criminal! We can't live like this. I have to get on that city council!"

"Don't shout, you not in the council yet. So what about Fate, ehn? First you can't change anything. Now you want to change everything."

In the study there was silence as old Elias listened in alarm.

Joe was sweating. He pushed his long black hair impatiently from his forehead and walked about. "You will certainly see a change if I get there! Who are Boisson's followers? Lickspittles, opportunists sitting on their brains. Do *they* care what people suffer in this world? Don't you see that? And what is holding me back? What—is—holding—me—back, Mamma!"

She made a disdainful face and jerked her chin at the door. "He's listening," she remarked in a whisper.

"So what, so what!"

"Leave it to me, I told you," she rebuked him. "A tomato must be in hot water before you can peel it."

"But the deadline is approaching. I have to give my name to the town clerk by a certain date otherwise I cannot contest the elections this November."

"Joe, if not this November, then next November. You will get the money, I promise you that; but leave him alone."

"What, you expect me to waste away in this condition for another year? Do you realise what you're asking of me?"

"What is a year, Joe? What is a year, boy! A wife would cool you down. You spoke to Elena's mother?"

Joe gripped his hair in both hands. "Yes, yes!" He groaned. "In some ways Elena is still a child: she feels I'm too old. . . . Look, forget it. Tell me what you intend to do." He dropped into a chair and sat with lowered head.

She was looking at him sympathetically and nodding. She put on the spectacles, her fingers began to move over the darning egg. "I goin' to make him give you the money as part of you' inheritance," she said in an undertone. She told him of the plans she had made, trying to soothe him.

Joe only half listened. He was groaning, smiling ironically at his hopes that Elena would love him, and muttering: "My God, my God!" exactly like his father.

The very next day Mrs Elias learned that her husband had put a house in the name of one of his women. She went into his study, swaying from side to side on her rheumaticky legs which seemed bowed under her weight. "Moses, I want to talk to you!" She swung the large wicker chair close to his desk and sat down.

He saw that he would not get rid of her easily. He pretended astonishment. "What happen? Something happen?"

"Yes, something happen!" she shouted, incensed by his shamming. She restrained herself with an effort. "Your own child, your eldest son—the boy is not happy, you understand? He wants to go in the city council. He's not a fool, he's a clever boy, you know that very well. Give him the money, Moses. You hear me! Give the boy the money!"

He cocked his head on one side and nodded. It was a trick of his when preparing to say something sarcastic and unpleasant. It always annoyed her. "You think I pick up twelve hundred dollars in the street, ehn?"

"You are throwing it away in the street! You put property in the name of a black nigger woman, but what about your children? Don't think you goin' to give away what belongs to the children, Moses, don't think it! This house is mine, it is in my name, don't forget that." Suddenly aware that the whole household could hear her raised voice she took two hobbling steps to the door and banged it shut. "If you want to live in peace in it do the right thing."

This time his jaw dropped in genuine dismay. Long experience had taught him that she could make his life unbearable if she chose. In this warm old nest he had only to express a wish and a shout from his wife would ensure its execution. Pleasant meals, clean clothes, papers in bed first thing in the morning—all appeared as and when required. That a single word from her might halt this smooth-running machinery was horrible to contemplate: he hated change, he was too old. He raised his hands to his head.

"Suppose he don't win the election, he not gettin' the money back, you know?"

"You ever ask the woman for the money back?"

"My God!" he exclaimed in a horrified whisper. "I never give twelve hundred dollars to anyone in my life, how you could say that?"

"Silence, Moses, don't anger me! And you will have to put one of the houses in Joe's name, otherwise he not qualified to stand. Yes! Don't open you' eyes at me. And bring him in the business. He must have time to attend meetin's. He should manage one of the stores."

"The last time Joe manage one of the stores the clerks do what they like with him. He lend everybody money. It was two years before I get it back."

Joe had been listening outside. He burst in. "They have to live, damn you, they're human beings!" Mamma jumped up. With unexpected strength from a single thrust of her arm she pushed him aside. "Be quiet! To give away what is not yours is very easy. If he had given it like you what he would have to give you today? In this world you have to live for you'self and you' family. You have brains only in you' mouth. Put him in charge of one of the stores, Moses, he have to have money to live while he's on the council."

"The council, the council. He goin' to reduce the taxes?" cried the old man, spreading his hands.

"You could die tomorrow, the doctor say you' blood pressure too high, it goin' to kill you," Mamma said brutally. "I want to see Joe learnin' the business now. You understand me, Moses? I'm sick of the two of you!" she suddenly shouted. "Let me sit, Joe, I'm not feelin' well." Joe vacated the wicker chair he had commandeered when she rose from it. "Go now, leave us," she added with a motion of her hand.

Joe went out, observing with satisfaction the look of fear in his father's eyes at the mention of death. He went to his room. Beulah had tidied it and was making his bed. He sat down in his reclining cane chair that was lined with cushions. He picked up an American magazine and idly turned the pages while giving little coughs and sniffing as he always did when unsettled. He thought neither of his mother's mental and physical state, nor of his father's, nor of anything except his future in the council. He thought how he would destroy Boisson's image with devastating speeches and how they would elect him mayor. He would dominate the council by playing one faction against the other. From the governor down they would all be apprehensive when his name was mentioned because he would give the people what no one had given them before. The working people would be on his side. At this moment he felt for them a mild contempt mixed with pity. What they needed was a man of education, foresight and knowledge of the world's contending forces who could steer them clear of the futile extremes to which Le Maître seemed committed. In West Indian history he would carve a name that time would not erase. But then he thought: "And death?" Just when he was spreading his wings death overtook him and to no one did it matter, not a soul. He made a desperate effort to push the thought of death aside. He thought of Jacob with envy. He envied him his unquestioning acceptance of his lot, envied his secret, if meagre, spring of happiness, envied the pride and chuckling relish with which he told of his sexual exploits, envied even the way he could twist his tongue to suit the occasion and the company and manoeuvre himself about the pitfalls that beset him. What did Jacob care about death? Spit in death's face, the bastard! "When you and the woman have a nip of rum together, man, and you get in bed wid she dat is the time life really start!" That was what he would say. "Why do I fear death?" thought Joe. "Why do I fear it will take me before I can make my mark? The English don't fear it, they have made history with it. Is that why I fear it? Isn't that reason enough for all of us to fear it, to fear being squashed underfoot before we've had time to live?" He kept muttering and running his fingers through his mop of hair.

Beulah, humming softly, occasionally glanced furtively in his direction while making the bed.

"Riot today, Mr Joe," she remarked with a prankish smile to the clean sheet she was unfolding.

"What's that? A riot?" He looked at her and was suddenly aware of the curves of her youth, the flexible ease and grace of her movements, of her natural charm that no soiled dress could diminish nor the slavey's tasks she had long been accustomed to perform for him. "Yes, you right, Beulah. A riot, in truth. You heard everything? You heard?"

"Couldn't help, man."

He was smiling at her, longing for her, for she was life. What would he not have given now for the comfort of her companionship in that bed she was making? Politics, art, friends, money—take them all and let love stay with him a while and let him drink deep of the simple elemental joys before the scythe descended. But he searched her eyes in vain, no response was in them; he was her master only, not a man who might give her joy. She had joy enough already; no seed of death was in her as it was in him.

Had he guessed what was in her mind he would have been more distressed. Haunted by memories of André and not seeing him for several weeks she feared he had forgotten her for someone else. She had wanted to ask what had become of him. She had thought to lead up to this with a reference to "the riot", but now she had not the courage to ask the question, it might mean too much to her. . . .

Some weeks later old Elias suffered a stroke, a mild one.

"O my God, my God!" the old man groaned in his bed. "Who goin' to manage the business? Christmas comin' on, the only time I could make a little money."

"Moses," said Mamma, "Joe will manage everything. But you must give him the twelve hundred dollars and put the big house in his name. Then he will come."

"What's this? A Chicago gangster? You puttin' a gun to my head?"

"What you want to do? Make you'self worse? Get another stroke and die?"

The thought sobered him. He muttered and turned away from her.

Later that morning he called for his cheque book. ". . . have to buy off my own son," he muttered, putting on his spectacles.

Chapter ten

After Aurelia had raged against fate through half the night, questioning whether the Lord gave proper attention to His business, and after, it seemed to Elena, she had sweated afresh over every one of life's deceptions and injustices—and the list was long—she fell asleep and woke on Sunday as if nothing had happened.

To Elena this Sunday seemed especially dull, and the dullness especially oppressive. If only something new would happen! But the church bells rang out just as they had rung every Sunday throughout her life. From some of the houses she passed on the way to church came the usual smells of Sunday cooking. There was the usual sunshine. The warm air in the church was as usual thick with scents: the delicate rooty odour of *vetiver* which full dark bosoms exuded in their breathing; the eau-de-cologne from the handkerchiefs that fanned perspiring faces; the bay rum in the scanty hair of oldish men. "O Lord, how dreary!" she thought. With a sinking heart she kept repeating the prayers, automatically following the mass but not knowing what she was saying.

When she got home she lay face down in bed and immersed herself in Turgenev's *Fathers And Sons.* She scarcely put it down once till darkness fell. She measured her impressions of Turgenev's art against André's impressions. She thought his wise, the result of deep reflection. The novel, as a consequence, was rich with meaning. She wanted very much to meet and talk with him again, but the thought of going to the Gardens did not enter her head. Not yet. Only on Monday, when she shrank into herself in the atmosphere of moral baseness of many Hoos, especially those in the making, did she think of the Gardens and determine to go. She hoped André would be there also. If not, she would just sit there awhile and think of what he had said, and of Bazarov.

At home she found her mother out. She took the key from its hiding place and let herself in. Unexpectedly she was glad of her mother's absence. She hastened to change, wrote hurriedly on a scrap of paper, "Gone to the Gardens, Mum. I won't be late," then took a route she did not often follow, a route her mother would not take, to catch a tram.

She alighted at the turn-off to St Anns. She did not notice the huge silk-cotton tree, or the saman trees, or the passing cars, the faces because now she knew how very much she wanted to find him there. She imagined—her cheeks hot with guilt and fear—the thunder of her mother's wrath, that awful rage in which Aurelia was unconscious that she was shouting because she was terrified lest some man debauch her treasure.

She wandered about the paths, lost herself among the trees, and at every turn her hopes sank lower. Life was unbearable. She began to feel the dammed-up tears spilling over in her.

"Elena!"

She turned. He was running to her. Instantly, with a skill born of long practice, she assumed an expression of calm composure.

"I've been looking all over for you," he said, panting, taking her hand in both of his. "I didn't know what to think."

His hands, not his words only, expressed relief that he had not been deceived in her, triumph at finding himself alone with her at last. He was not the André with whom she discussed novels. She was aware of a sense of release in him and especially of his persuasive, inescapable charm.

"I love these trees!" she said with a passion that surprised herself, and withdrew her hand.

"These are bay trees." He broke a leaf and held it under her nose. He showed her other trees, all unexpectedly and mysteriously beautiful—the nutmeg, the banyan, the Australian eucalypt. "That scent, listen—I mean, just stand still a minute. That's from the eucalypt, that smooth, white bark. And this . . . I wish I knew!"

"Let's read what it says."

"Doesn't mean a thing to me."

"Anyhow, it's gorgeous."

"I ought to know it, I'm sure we have several on our estate in Arima."

He could have bitten off his tongue. The words had been prompted by his self-consciousness at being seen in public on such intimate terms with a girl so coloured. He took her hand, laughed and ran away from himself.

"Don't run, it spoils everything. Besides, that man's coming."

The stranger, an Englishman, was dressed casually and carried a towel; he was evidently on his way to the swimming-pool. He smiled when about to pass them and said: "Good evening." They responded and walked on silently, almost as if they had been caught out in something.

"The governor," André said, his mood changing.

"He looked like the butler." She laughed.

In the sky streaks of drained white cloud lay motionless, as in a painting, against those more distant and of a purplish hue. The sun was blind. From the wooded hillside came the "coo-coo" of a king-of-the-woods to the notes of *A-men.* That single call repeated at intervals filled Elena with a strange joyous sadness. "I would almost have said you hated *him*!"

"Because it made me feel pleased to be addressed by him!" André beat his knees with clenched fists.

"Don't," she begged, clasping his fist.

He sprang up. They walked through the glass houses, noticing the begonias yet not seeing them. Night followed them swiftly.

On the Pitchwalk he said: "When can you come again?" Now, in the open, he dared not take her hand. "Wednesday?"

"All right, Wednesday. Cheerio." She smiled then went straight to the tram stop without looking back.

All the next two days the Gardens were in her thoughts. They would talk of Turgenev, his Rudin, Bazarov, whose thoughts were somehow familiar to her, awakening her to a new world and her place in it.

But when they met they were both constrained, both aware of guilt in those two days of anticipation. Turgenev was handy, though it was not the words that mattered but their inflections, the quick revealing glances. Once her hand brushed his by accident. He took it. How dare he kiss her? Those others stood before him; to put his arm around her as he had done with *them*. . . .

A huge blood-red disc was sinking. Clouds caught fire. Now with unexpected charm the last rosy rays of the sun tinted the moss and scaly bark on the upper branches of the forest trees. Long, broad shadows lay upon the grass. On the topmost twig of a tree a keskidee balanced himself, threw back his head and twice uttered his impetuous, noisy cry. The poetry of the evening lay about them like a perfume.

She glanced at André questioningly. He took her in his arms and kissed her. She made a startled movement to thrust him back, but then she returned his kisses. Never had she kissed a man before. It seemed to her that those kisses bound her to him for life. "Don't . . . don't!" she gasped. "It's getting dark, we must go."

They sauntered out. She let him come only halfway home, fearing her mother's conjectures if she or neighbours should see him. And no holding hands: in the street it would cheapen what had passed between them.

"Friday?"

"No. You come on Saturday."

"Elena! Why not Friday?"

She shook her head and laughed, eyes glowing. "No. Come home. How would it look if you suddenly stopped coming?"

When she got home she prepared the simple meal they had at night. She hardly knew what she was doing. She would be humming, then break off and stand looking at the coalpot with a smile, then come to herself and make an effort to think what had to be done, and run back and forth fetching what she had forgotten. She felt his kisses, felt his trembling, and such pity and love welled up in her that her face shone with an inner blaze. She longed to sacrifice herself for him. "What happiness! Will it be taken from me?" she asked in terror. The cocoa hissed at her as it boiled over. She took the pan off the coalpot. She stood looking at it, passing her fingers slowly over her left hand where his kiss still tingled.

"Elena, something wrong?"

"No, Mother."

"Well, hurry up, nuh, man, I'm hungry."

Suddenly she felt such an overwhelming pity for her mother that she ran into the bedroom and put her arms around her and kissed her.

"What's the matter now?" Aurelia asked crossly, too preoccupied to look up from the sewing machine and the cloth running away under her fingers.

"Nothing, I'll be ready in a minute."

After dinner she got into bed and lay there in the dark. First, meeting him at Erica's wedding, then Joe bringing him home, and then meeting him in the library. If it was fate, what did it hold for her? The machine in the next room whirred, and she felt with solemn joy how different her own life was going to be from now on. "I want to understand him in every way, every possible way, so I can help him."

Stillness. Darkness. She had not heard her mother retire. She had no desire to sleep. The blaze would not die down. Why had she told him to come home? No, it was best so. . . . She talked to him, advised him, discussed all sorts of things with him. She astonished him with the variety and significance of her views. "Now I understand everything, at last I am at peace, thanks to you," he said. And suddenly her child appeared. She began to weep with shame and a vague terror because it was not the one she wanted. He was arguing with her mother in the next room, she could hear his raised voice. She rushed to him crying: "Take me away from here, take me away!"

"What a silly dream!" How good it was to wake and recall instantly the inflections in his voice, the clean smell of him.

Next day so calm was she at work and so withdrawn that with jealous suspicion Hoo looked at her several times. He had no use for people who took themselves off to another world in working hours.

That night a simple thought struck her like lightning: "Will he love me always?" And her heart shrivelled.

She was sitting in the half-dark waiting for him. What were Rudin and Bazarov beside the beating of her blood? She opened the jalousie window and, leaning on the sill, her face in her hands, looked at the people passing by on the sidewalk. She scarcely saw them. Rapture had died. He had not said he loved her. She must have his declaration. She did not know how to play at love. . . . But no, he had trembled, yes, he had trembled. . . . "Oh, come, come, come!"

Joy stabbed her as with some sixth sense she felt his approach. She reached down from the window and mussed his hair. He opened the door. An empty room! There she was behind it. They both laughed, she with ringing abandon.

Hearing the machine in the bedroom, from which the only light filtered, he called a greeting to Aurelia.

"Hello, André. How, boy?"

"Very well, thanks. How are you?"

"Battlin', man, still battlin'."

"Isn't it time to knock off yet?"

"I can't hear the whistle."

He tooted a long blast. "How about that?"

"Overtime now begin. What to do?" A rhetorical question.

He moved his chair close to Elena's.

"I've nearly finished *Asya*," she said hurriedly, and as if not noticing.

"You have? Yes, it's not very long."

"Something is missing in it."

She tossed her handkerchief up and caught it.

He seized her hands and kissed them. She cupped his face with them and for an instant leaned towards him, then drew back.

"Do you like *Asya*?" she asked in an indifferent voice.

"It's very poetic."

"Yes, it is."

As soon as the sewing-machine stopped they were conscious of a third person with them.

"But really, what does it say?" He sighed.

"Something . . . I'm not sure."

"It's just about dreams and, well, flirtation. Isn't it?"

"No, there's some sort of tragedy. He hints at it only. I wanted to know everything. I mean, why she didn't love him or couldn't love him, or whatever it was. It teased you."

"It was just a poetic picture. I think he was only interested in the poetic atmosphere."

"I don't like that. What about life? Their characters? Nothing is worked out."

"Read *Smoke*. That's much better."

She rolled her handkerchief into a ball. "What's that about?"

Again the machine paused. He said, addressing it: "It's much more substantial than *Asya*. *Asya* is really quite inconsequential. Quite. . . ." It whirred again.

"What are you reading?" Her face, her voice, everything about her had turned, it seemed to him, cold and dull.

"Gorky."

"Still? Why do you think he's so good?"

"Read him. You'll see. Such power! *Twenty-Six Men And A Girl*. That's wonderful and terrible. It's life naked."

Her eyes were resting on his with a strangely distant, enigmatic expression. He felt that something was devouring her. He leaned forward and kissed her lips. She did not respond, neither did she draw back.

"I read one of his once. In a collection somewhere."

And again he kissed her lips. She closed her eyes so he would not see all that was in them. "No, you mustn't!" she whispered, pushing him away.

"I didn't care for that one I read. No, that's not right. It was cruel! Awful. He made it seem there was no way out. I hate that. There must be a way."

Aurelia was singing. Now she broke off. They heard her go into the yard.

"Elena!" He pulled her on to his thighs. He was kissing her breast through the dress. There was thunder in her ears. Her fingers fluttered in his hair and about his face. "I love you, Elena! I love you."

"No, you mustn't. . . ." And her lips sought his. Abruptly she slipped from his thighs on to her chair. Her mother's steps were returning.

Had she come into the room at that moment Aurelia would have been alarmed by the proud, submissive joy on her child's face, but she went on sewing; and even when she heard Elena's spontaneous, happy laughter, so unusual at home, she felt glad for her and hoped that God would be merciful, but did not understand what was happening.

He left at ten. It must never be later. Nor did he forget to call good night to Aurelia when the machine stopped working.

"What have I done?" he thought when he got home. "What have I done?" In her company half an hour before he had been so sure; now in this cold, proud family mansion to which he was bound by twenty-year-old habits of thinking, patterns of behaviour, prejudices and ambitions, those thoughts of marriage seemed well-nigh frivolous.

In the Gardens one Saturday afternoon they met his father strolling with a well-known white planter. Their theme song was the hazards to which the planter today exposed himself for the public benefit. The planter, smiling wryly and waving one hand, was saying something about ". . . the price of a bag of cocoa today is so ridiculously low."

"Hello," Mr de Coudray said, raising his hat in deference to Elena. His greeting and the planter's gliding glance seemed to indicate that they both had witnessed an indiscretion but were too polite to dwell upon it.

Later he asked: "Who was the girl?"

It was almost always at dinner only that André met with his

family. He had learned to listen to their conversations in silence. Tonight his entry had been followed by silence on their part, which Mr de Coudray broke to ask the question.

"Elena Henriques," André replied. "She was once a little skinny kid who used to come here with dresses."

In a tone of reproach tempered with resignation to her fate Mrs de Coudray said: "Not my dressmaker's daughter, André?" and, raising her eyebrows, cast down her eyes.

"The same. Why?"

She rang the bell. A starched white cap and apron appeared and removed the soup plates. No one spoke till the black girl had gone.

"You tell us why," said George.

"Why? How could you understand?"

"She's very attractive," Mr de Coudray conceded. "Very beautiful eyes."

André's heart went out to him. Again all were silent as cap and apron returned with a dish of fish in gravy.

"I intend to marry her," André said when she had gone, fearing the conclusions they might be drawing.

Mrs de Coudray served the fish.

"Not much for me, thanks," said Yvette.

"She makes a very good gravy," Mr de Coudray remarked.

"I had to show her." Mrs de Coudray sounded very prim.

"Cheers to you, Mum," said solid George.

Corn coocoo was brought in, and a salad.

"Mm. Delicious," George murmured, chewing lustily. "She's done justice to your tuition. What's her name?"

"Philomena."

"She must be the fattest one we've had," Yvette remarked.

"Pass the salt, George," Mrs de Coudray said, but her tone said, "What does salt matter, can that change anything?"

Mr de Coudray: "Well . . . I hope you know what you're doing."

Mrs de Coudray, as if André was not among them: "To get married he must be in a position to support a wife. It would be very unfair to build up any illusions in her mind about his prospects." Pink spots appeared in her cheeks. She rang the bell. "The wine," she said to the apron.

* * * *

On Monday she was not at home. Aurelia came out to him.

"Elena had to go out with a couple dresses for me, André. Up in Belmont. She'll be back about nine or so, if you care to wait."

He said he would return another evening.

"Sit down a moment, André, I'd like to talk to you."

She was smiling, but now he was terrified by the moral force of this woman. Ill-educated she might be, ignorant of much that would make her acceptable in St Clair, but to the moral truths dear to her she would cling as to life. He dare not infringe them. He never guessed that she had sent Elena on this errand purposely so as to talk alone with him.

"I have a good idea how Elena feels about you," she began, sitting on the edge of her chair because she was nervous. "She don't talk much but I am not blind either. You must know how you feel. You are more mature, and you been coming here now for some weeks very well. And well, people talk, my dear André. And Elena have no father, as you know, I am responsible for everything. So I feel I must ask you," she added, softening her tone apologetically. Her eyes had grown moist because she was afraid for Elena yet did not want to stand in the way of a good match.

"I love Elena. I want to marry her," he said with firmness.

Aurelia crossed herself. "God is merciful. I really didn't believe you had dishonourable intentions, but you know, André, in this world you really don't know who to trust. That husband of mine. . . !" She blew her nose. "But what about you' parents? I don't think they will agree."

"They don't agree. It doesn't matter."

"And when you think you will be able to marry?"

"I don't know." He felt she required an explanation, a promise, something irrevocable and binding, and they were making some sort of a deal. It was distressing. "I can't right now. . . ."

At that moment it seemed to him quite strange that a few kisses in the Gardens had led to this.

"Don't mind that, boy. In a couple years things going to change. You not black and you not a fool. You bound to get on. You will get a better job."

André did not wait for Elena's return. He went home proudly conscious of the solemn and difficult responsibility he had assumed, and at the same time was awed by his temerity in assuming a burden that could demand more in spiritual resource than he could offer.

Elena's first words when she came home were: "Didn't André come?"

"Yes. He said he would come back Wednesday."

"Oh."

Aurelia saw her disappointment. "I had a talk with him, Elena. He told me he wants to marry you."

Elena shot a reproachful and angry look at her mother and turned aside, scarcely hearing the rest. She understood now why he had not waited. She felt that the precious, delicate love developing between them had been trampled on (she and her "talks"). She could have wept. But she sat quietly on the bed and appeared to listen. To say anything was to call forth lightning, that expression of uncertainty how to deal with life. She had a foreboding now that all his hopes and hers could come to nothing.

Chapter eleven

Popito had gone to see Jacob the porter, who had come down with malaria. Though Jacob was sly and shifty Popito was fond of him: who was he to censure Jacob if life had fashioned him with a harsh and hasty hand? Indeed, having no job, Popito envied the porter. "How the hell he manages to feed a family of eight on five dollars a week?" he thought, and felt drawn to Jacob by curiosity, a sneaking envy and a desire to talk and so minimise his own misfortune.

Through a narrow passage between two walls he entered the barrack yard in Nelson Street where Jacob lived. Shed-like structures divided into dens bordered three sides of the yard. All the doors were open. Sometimes the bleakness within was plain despite the door curtain that tried concealment. Occasionally one caught the gleam of something snatched from life, and treasured: a polished sideboard, an oil lamp of shining brass, chairs from a better day—from the master's home, perhaps. Two women were washing clothes outside their doorsteps. A third was heating sad-irons in a coalpot. Movie songs competed with hymns and both were silenced by bursts of gossip as the women pursued their dreary tasks. In the yard, trodden hard, stony, was not a blade of grass. Some boulders, pale from endless use, were heaped about its middle. Here was the bleach, on which a pair of khaki pants, discoloured by toil and daily sweat, spread its legs obscenely yet unnoticed. Four men, squatting, were playing cards in that part of the yard which the nine o'clock sun was not yet roasting. The smell of darkness and poverty rose powerfully in the heat and, at this moment, oppressed Popito, who suddenly wished he had not come in: he, too, could be flung down here one day. Involuntarily he looked up at the breadfruit tree towering majestically into the sky above the gamblers. Covered with huge green leaves, burdened with fruit larger than cannonballs, it was a symbol of normal, clean and vigorous life, and in its season gave them daily sustenance. Jacob himself had said once:

"Roas' breadfruit, Mr Luna, and a bit-a roas' saltfish wid sweetoil? Man, sometimes that could be sweet, yes?"

Jacob was not married, but he and his woman had lived as man and wife for thirteen years. It was the custom—almost; one's hands remained untied. When he was thirty, youth's vigour still within him, there had been other women, other children, but always it was to this one he had come back. Now, after thirteen years, as often happened, he felt no call to wander. Why marry her? He had no will to make, nor property to bequeath his several children. There they were, pitching marbles in the sun, the younger ones in singlets only, clamorous and wild. They would live as he. Why not? Why worry? To dead before you' time? You, 'self!

As Popito approached the doorway the woman came out of it. She was not quite forty, large, strong and vigorous as Jacob liked them. She called him. Coming out, he greeted Popito cheerfully, but as usual without looking him in the face.

"Much better, yes," said he in answer to Popito's question. "Weak, nuh, but not too bad. I goin' out again tomorrow. So, what about you, Mr Luna? No job yet? A-ah! T'ings bad in trut', man. So much-a people not workin' dese days, I 'fraid to stay home five minutes. But Mr Dollard is a good man, you know? A nex' boss would take out me pay, but not he, man. But I sorry to hear you ain't get nutten yet, Mr Luna. Eh—eh!"

"Well, boy, what to do? So, how the wife and kids?"

"Everybody well, man, everybody well, only the colds have them."

"You should be livin' in a house, man. Nobody wid so many children should have to live in a place like dis."

"House?" Jacob laughed heartily but with gentle irony. "House! Ah, Mr Luna, you good."

But Popito wasn't laughing. "How you could support Boisson? You don' know he owns a place like this?"

"Me? I don't support Mr Boisson, man," replied Jacob, laughing slyly and looking away. "I support me own self, man."

"Why you don't support Le Maître? He's a worker like us, and black besides."

"Dat's true. He and dis trade union business. . . . I don' know if it could succeed in Trinidad, *non*? Man, we Creoles fightin' too bad against each other, man."

"Tchps! Ah, Christ, life is a hell of a thing for some of us, Jacob. Some say is God's will, and then they say you got to suffer in hell again when you dead. I tell you, if hell worse than this it bad in trut', *oui*?"

"It ehn have nutten so, man. When you dead, you dead. Eh—eh! More sufferin' again?" And Jacob laughed his slyly sensuous laugh that seemed to say he had some secret project that could make life palatable even in the face of so unlikely a change in his fortunes.

Popito laughed too. But then he sighed.

"Well, Jacob, I gone. I'll come and see you again, hear? Hold on to you' job, boy, don' get like me."

"Right-o, right-o, Mr Luna!" Jacob laughed. "Keep courage, you goin' to get somet'ing."

Popito went out of the yard.

In Charlotte Street something unusual was happening unknown to him. A crowd of workless people who had come out of the slums was marching down Charlotte Street towards the waterfront, calling on others to join them in their march to the Governor. Many were the placards.

Some read :

WORKERS, YOU NEED BREAD—JOIN US
FIGHT THE CAPITALISTS WITH UNITY
DEMAND THE RIGHT TO WORK
WE ARE GOING TO THE GOVERNOR

"Eh, chile! Like Dry River come down!" said a young Indian woman to another beside her. She had a ring in her nose and a stinking tray of fish on her head. She stood still in surprise, uncertain whether to be afraid of the crowd or to admire the spirit that animated it—a spirit of sulky resentment and determination.

The Dry River is so called because during the dry season no water runs through it. But when, in the rainy season, clouds burst upon the hills that ring the town, swirling, thick brown water rises to the top of the river bank. Then everything that has grown accustomed to the river's long inactivity is swept away by it. Trees, boxes, bridges, fowls, goats, spin helplessly in its grip.

In like fashion now this swelling river of workless people flowed down the street. At every step more were sucked in—grinning youths on bicycles, women with loose alpargats which slapped their heels as they ran, and half-naked children. Their noise, the curiosity and excitement on their faces, their shouts of encouragement stimulated the marchers. Looks of confidence began to replace the expressions of self-derision, of nervous suspicion and resentment on the marchers' worn, perspiring faces. Some ceased to look stonily straight before them and began to encourage men on the sidewalk to join the march. Above the shouts, the comments, the ringing of bicycle bells and the blare of horns one heard the ominous shuffling out of step of their four hundred feet.

Popito had been standing outside a rumshop in a side street. Thirsting for a drink, unable to trust himself to have one only, he drifted about restlessly, listening to the scraps of noisy argument flung out from the bar. He pulled his hat down over his forehead partly to keep off the glare of the sun, partly to hide his face from friends who might see him.

He saw a crippled black beggar crossing the street. His shrivelled legs were quite useless, his back and arms abnormally developed. He wriggled and shuffled himself across the street on his hands and his rear. Traffic slowed for him. Popito looked at him but thought only of the drink he wanted.

Suddenly he saw the crowd as it went past the side street, and at the head of it—Le Maître! Alarm and gladness seized Popito. He ran into Charlotte Street and walked on the sidewalk beside those four hundred shuffling feet. He read the placards with a kind of joyful surprise and pushed people aside without realising what he was doing. His one desire was to keep abreast of Le Maître. The latter attracted all eyes with his big voice, masterful bearing and determined, firm steps.

WE DEMAND WORK FOR OUR PEOPLE,
BREAD FOR OUR CHILDREN

So said the placard he carried. Now and then, stepping to one side and walking backward, he would look down the column and shout in a ringing bass that he obviously enjoyed using:

"Come, comrades, crowd up!" Or: "No straggling, comrades. In step! Left, right, left!"

"How well he marches," Popito thought, longing to walk beside Le Maître at the head of that militant-looking crowd.

"No stragglin'!" onlookers repeated admiringly, hardly able to believe it was one of themselves who was so impressive.

The crowd, like Popito, felt in Le Maître the unabashed resolution of a man incapable of more than one point of view and willing to overturn society to impose it. More, the placards said that that point of view was their own.

Some were debating who the tall man in front was.

"Le Maître, that's Le Maître! Damn good man!" cried Popito, ready in his excitement to vouch to everyone for Le Maître, and pushing his way forward in order not to lose sight of him.

A tram approached, its gong sounding impatiently as the crowd in the street forced it to halt. Automobiles, too, halted or edged forward, horns blowing. Leaving the customers in the shop, or the rice untended on the fire, men and women ran out to see the marchers. Three washerwomen who had come out of a yard were running on the sidewalk. One, stopping to get her foot back into the alpargat that had slipped off, deliberately upset some caps and belts a merchant was displaying outside his store. The others made as if to steal them. They ran away, looking behind with reckless laughter when his frightened clerk abused them. Other women were shouting at the grumbling and frightened Syrian, Lebanese, or Negro merchants who stood in their doors:

"It's more dan work we want—it's money! Why all-you don't pay the people?"

Voices said gleefully: "Beat them up—bitches! All-you frighten now. It's trouble for all-you."

"Come on, you hungry people, join us!" Le Maître cried to some shop clerks on the sidewalk. "You had you' lime-bud tea like me this mornin'. You can't feed you'self and you' mother on two dollars a week, you know that."

The coloured clerks sighed, or smiled shamefacedly, and turned away, glancing covertly at the boss.

A very fat black woman with a sour smell was sitting in a narrow, filthy passageway with her back to one wall. Before her was a tray of mangoes on a box. In one corner of the tray were a few copper coins. She was correcting another woman in her drawling voice: "Governor, what!" she said, referring to one of the placards. "What he goin' do? He white. He kean't see what in we pot, chile. We has a right to what is ours, give us what is ours," she declared as, leaning forward with arms on knees, she peeled herself a bit of sugar cane and sucked it noisily.

When Le Maître said, "Join us!" Popito itched to do so but hung back, remembering he was a clerk, and looking among the marchers for others like himself.

But now a laughing, big-breasted cook with a basket knocked against Le Maître as he stepped sideways to look down the column. The placard fell from his hand. Popito jumped into the street, upset a cyclist and, snatching the placard from a worker who had stopped to retrieve it, ran forward with it as with a banner.

"I have it, man—come on!" cried he triumphantly to Le Maître. "I will hold it."

He looked about him angrily as if defying others to take it from him or deride him. He no longer doubted that he was acting in the only way possible.

"What's your name, comrade?" asked Le Maître, sizing up Popito.

"Luna."

"Out of work? How long?"

"Goin' on four months very well."

"Where you worked?"

"Dollard's Hardware."

"I worked at Dollard's too."

"Man, it was a hell of a thing they did me," Popito began. But at that moment galloping hooves rang upon the road and out of Queen Street appeared two mounted policemen and an officer.

"They giving us an escort, Clem," said Le Maître to a small, pale, thin brown Negro who had been quarrelling with someone in a hoarse voice. "Clem!"

"We not turnin' back!" Clem suddenly began shouting violently.

The officer rode up to the head of the column and, resting his left hand on his knee with the wrist turned outwards, looked at Le Maître and Popito from the height of his spirited broad-backed stallion, which snorted impatiently and tossed its head.

"Who's the leader?" he asked severely.

"I am!" replied Le Maître.

"Where do you think you're going?"

"To the governor. Any law against it?"

It seemed to Popito that the officer changed his mind about something he intended to say. Adjusting himself in his saddle he asked:

"What route are you following?"

"Down Charlotte Street, Marine Square, Abercromby Street and around the Savannah to Government House."

The men were watching the officer, scanning his face for some sign that would tell them how to act. They all knew the spruce Sub-Inspector Primrose with his flaxen hair and moustache and strong pink neck. To their surprise they saw a pleasant expression come over his face.

"Eh-eh! He smiling, man," they said to one another.

A bold one called out: "We not all, nuh? More coming. Prepare for us."

Something in Le Maître's resolute manner had caused Inspector Primrose to assume a disarming expression. "No nonsense now," he said.

"We are unarmed," replied Le Maître. "Not like you."

Touching up his spirited horse, which danced sideways, thrusting his glossy hindquarters almost into Le Maître's face, the inspector trotted off, lifting his rear rhythmically up in the saddle.

The mounted policemen remained with the crowd to keep order.

"So you were at Dollard's," Le Maître continued.

For the hundredth time Popito related how he had butted Brassington. By now he had added sundry embellishments, all to his greater glory, without being aware of it.

"I worked in the soap factory," said Le Maître. "In the Legislative Council Dollard got Government to support the manufacture of local soap. Raised the duty on imported soap. But the big soap people in England played hell because it was cutting their sales. They pulled strings at the Colonial Office and made us refund all the excess duty to the English soap makers. Now English soap comes in cheaper than ours. Dollard has almost closed down the soap factory. Don't you know that? He fired about twenty of us. He's only makin' low-grade soap now, and he has to put the name of the English soap makers on it."

"Boy, you see what money can do?"

"The first lesson you have to learn—you know what is the first lesson you have to learn?" asked Le Maître, sternly grasping Popito's arm because to impose his will on others was natural and necessary to him and now others were looking at Popito and himself. "Keep together, comrades!" he called out, turning round as they entered Marine Square. "You must realise," he continued, "that this country is the Englishman's country and you have to buy what he has to sell you."

"Yes, boy, I always hated those English bitches, you know," said Popito avidly.

"Why don't you join the Negro Welfare?" asked Le Maître, looking at him closely. "Is it that you think yourself too white for us?" he seemed to ask.

"I am ready to join now."

Blowing through his nose and wrinkling his brown forehead the unhealthily pale Clem, like a fly in a bottle, launched an attack upon police, merchants, landowners, city councillors, Boisson and all and sundry. His pallor made his brown skin look yellow. His comrades, laughing, teased him, and Clem Payne (as Popito heard him addressed) attacked them for their levity. "This is no *joke*, this is no time for sky*larkin'*. Members of the Negro Welfare? We have no time to make Boissonites members of the Negro Welfare. Bring traitors into our ranks? We do' want no *weaklings*, no *traitors*. One day we may have to face death!"

Popito looked at the mounted policeman, but the latter was holding his head straight as though deaf. Over the horse's glossy hindquarters Popito recognised some friends on the sidewalk, but he pretended not to see them. All his friends who had jobs, it seemed to him, were now his enemies. They were on one side of the fence, he on the other. In his eagerness Popito mentally prepared words with which to address His Excellency when they reached Government House. He would tell him about that soap business. Let him come, the son-of-a-bitch!

The growing crowd turned into Abercromby Street. They were singing a hymn, a hymn with militant words. All along the route now people stopped their cars, stood on the sidewalk or leaned out of windows and looked at the marching workers critically or with amused disdain. But as if the marchers had cast a seed behind them, long after they had passed people were criticising the government for not taking measures to assist the unemployed. "We black, but we human too."

At length the crowd approached the foot of Government House drive. By the guard house Primrose sat waiting on his horse. The policemen who had accompanied the marchers galloped up to him. The three mounted men blocked the entrance with rearing steeds.

"Cool off on the Pitch Walk, boys. We can't all go to the Governor," Le Maître's voice was heard.

The crowd, some glumly silent, others arguing, others shouting threats, retreated to the Pitch Walk. Presently Popito saw a policeman marching up the drive between Le Maître and Payne. The policeman was buttoning his collar hastily.

It was eleven o'clock. Heat rose off the Savannah in waves. Men and women reclined on the roadside grass, on Pitch Walk benches. The horses stamped off the flies, snorted and champed their bits. At the top of Government House the Union Jack hung limp as a dead coconut branch. Government House stood massive, silent, aloof, as it had stood for a hundred years.

Half an hour passed.

"All-you better hurry, yes?" a flat-chested woman complained. "I leave rice on the fire."

"Must be fry rice by now," a man told her.

"Perhaps he got a little jail of his own in there and he put Le Maître in it," another joked.

Popito was watching a short Indian peasant mowing grass in the

Savannah. The Indian wiped the shining scythe blade and mowed with swinging, tireless motions of his body; stopped and, with a sweeping, practised motion of his leg, gathered the grass into a pile. The sweet, warm, earthy smell of mown grass floated over the field to Popito. The donkey in the shafts of the Indian's grass-laden cart moved from place to place, tearing up juicy blades of grass. Tick birds and blackbirds flew down upon the mown spaces and upon the donkey, and hopped out of the path of the scythe blade, balancing themselves with their tails.

The calmness of that scene, the indifference of the Indian to their demands, irritated the impatient crowd.

"But look that man cuttin' grass, nuh," said Popito.

"What he care?" said another. "Dem so would live on grass like the donkey if you give dem a chance."

At last Le Maître and Payne were seen coming down the drive. The crowd rose and thronged about them as if they had brought food.

". . . has given us an assurance that he will look personally into unemployment," Popito heard, trying without success to get closer to Le Maître.

"What! He still wants proof?" cried Popito.

"It's a move we had to make," Le Maître was saying. "Had we left it to him, he would have found it out from the bosses, and they would have made us out to be vagabonds. . . ."

Already a new move was afoot amongst the crowd.

"Pass the word . . . pass the word," men were saying in low tones. "We goin' to Woodford Square. Boisson got a meetin' there at one o'clock."

Some of the marchers, disappointed at the result of the interview, went home arguing among themselves. On the faces of others, especially Clem Payne, there were sour looks which showed a readiness to vent their frustration on the first luckless victim.

"Come, let me see who are the good hecklers here," said Clem Payne hoarsely, as if there was a clenched fist in his throat.

Chapter twelve

The people had long been inarticulate, blind in revolt, without a leader, without a party—a body without a head. But they had marched into the first world war with rolling drums and streaming flags, and when they returned in their thousands they no longer regarded submission as their fate. They had seen white men sweating and slaving, they had seen them combining against the white boss and winning: black men could do the same. But life, it seemed, had little use for them though they had fought off death in the trenches and, on their return, had been counted heroes. Jobs were scarce, bellies empty. And out of their own experiences and those of English workers now was born their Workers' Party.

Boisson had been their captain in Egypt, a friend of the soldiers, their chosen advocate before the military courts. So, not yet feeling their strength, and overawed still by white man's power, they called on white Boisson to lead their party—Boisson the rebel among the politicians, the mutineer among the masters. "Give us strength and we will make you strong!" they said.

The red-headed Boisson bore a grudge against his class. He abhorred their discrimination against Negroes, who had fought and died no less loyally for Britain's empire than the whites had done. When on his return he saw the fruits of victory handed to those who had earned them least; when he found that his white civilian friends had built nests in his absence, and the very job he viewed with favour was given to some plump fellow who had never heard a gun go off—then he took it into his head publicly to denounce his own class and join with the workers against the bosses.

For many a year when Boisson stood in the squares shaking his fist at the capitalists, the remains of his red hair flying, the workers threw hats in the air and would have trampled underfoot without hesitation the first man who dared to touch him. Like the sailors of Columbus they seemed to see the land at last.

Le Maître's followers, still but a handful, sneered that Boisson was at the end of his tether, the white people had given all they would give: old-age pensions three dollars a month; and the eight-hour day won at the cost of lower wages. As to a minimum wage, the bosses had declared it "an impossibility in this country". All the same, they had given their blessing to a government enquiry. Few entertained illusions about what the results would be. For Boisson to rise in the legislature, abuse the capitalists, threaten them with demonstrations and demand that they make more concessions—whom was that hurting?

But his followers said: "Good! Give them hell. There's a real man, the workers' friend, the workers' advocate. Vote for him, the only man who could help us."

"What all that speech-making give us?" others asked. "For all that talk what more you get in you' pocket? Anything more?"

At the May Day meeting this year someone had made a rousing speech about the stranglehold of the oilfield bosses on their workers: whereupon Boisson had spoken with fervour, even with emotion, on the duty of all the people to be loyal to King George V and especially at this time of his approaching silver jubilee.

"Whatever people feel about crown colony rule, my friends, if we were under dictatorship that same king would by his own devotion remedy all the wrongs from which we are suffering. . . . Every man who thinks right, who has not got a warped soul, should rear his head and bend his knee to the King of Kings to guard and to keep and to bless that Royal Family. . . ."

There was little applause, and in that no warmth. The people needed and hoped to hear that he would compel the government to find work for the unemployed, feed the starving, raise the wages of those who toiled. But of this no word. Only talk of the Royal Family. White people, damn you! Covered in jewels besides. Don't even have to put on their own shoes. Whenever they feel like a bite to eat they just ring a bell, and look it—ham, turkey, whatever take their fancy. What the hell they know or care about us?

André, reading the speech in the press, was seized by a feeling of impotent rage, but Joe roared with fiendish laughter. . . .

Boisson was to address his supporters, his detractors, the curious and the idle, and those who might be persuaded to vote for him at the next municipal elections, in Woodford Square, in the heart of the city. On one side was the Town Hall, where he reigned as mayor; on the other stood the Red House, seat of government, the temple from which, despite all his thunder and lightning, he could not drive the moneychangers. A large crowd was expected: it was Saturday and all business closed early.

When André arrived with Joe and Manny Camacho the meeting had already begun. Camacho was a young Portuguese of twenty who had recently entered the government service as a junior clerk. He had long black hair, rounded shoulders and soft, plump, pale long fingers that seemed made to leaf through books and papers with dexterity. Short-sighted, he had a trick of peering through his thick spectacles with neck outstretched. His sole interest in life was politics, not the personal political response of men to events so much (at his age the fate of individuals seemed unimportant) as the large events themselves and their overall effect upon the political maturing of the mass. He would discuss the future of the world proletariat with the enthusiastic self-assurance which youths easily acquire by reading widely on a subject that attracts them. He was at a stage too when the development of his mental powers over-stimulated his self-confidence. Someone had only to express doubts about our workers' capacity for leadership and Camacho, hands on his broad hips, was shifting from foot to foot, as if his wings were beating, taunting: "Coward! What do you know about them? Petit bourgeois ideas have not got you anywhere, can't you see that? What has Boisson done? Seized the reins and the whip!" Camacho was that same enthusiast who had annoyed Joe by suggesting that the magazine adopt an anti-religious policy.

He had whispered—he had got it from one of Le Maître's lieutenants—that the hunger marchers would invade the square and challenge Boisson in debate. He foretold there would be "a hell of a clash". He, Joe and André looked forward with interest to the result, especially André: in him a vague hope was rising that in Le Maître the working people would find a leader who would make no compromise with white domination, a leader at once militant, incorruptible, upright. Could they, would they, downtrodden and unlettered, schooled for two hundred years to fear White Massa, hating their fear and their impotence to purge themselves of it, submitting outwardly but enraged and warped within (André was apt to apply to all, indiscriminately, his own frustrations)—could they spawn such a leader as he hoped Le Maître would be? A wild hope, doubtless. Crazy idealism. Looking for a Messiah as so many still were doing. "My God, it's not a *Messiah* we want but a man of strength, understanding of the realities, pride!" He was looking, he knew, for someone who could do what he could not, nor any member of his class, separately or together . . . "someone who will give us West Indian pride".

A large crowd, constantly reinforced by workers, by the bare-footed and the ill-fed who had stopped to listen as they crossed the square, had formed in a semi-circle around the bandstand, where the police band played for ordinary folk on certain evenings. Something spoke to André as it had done before of the contrast between this beautiful square with its enormous rustling forest trees that filtered the sunlight, the green grass cool to the bare foot's touch, the fountain, around which black children skipped, playing over cherubs with blown-out cheeks—the contrast between this and the sick who sat on the benches, the aged, the barren, the thieves and vagabonds, the strong, the workers and those who had given up hope of work. No words rose in him to express this contrast. A vague despair, which from habit he tried to ignore, laid a clammy hand upon him. "Beautiful," something in him said as he felt the trees move lazily in the breeze, "but what's the good of it? And all enclosed by massive spiked iron railings."

Boisson now stood speaking in the bandstand. The crowd was listening so intently that when newcomers arrived André could hear the rustle of footfalls on the grass. Boisson's voice was small and high in the open—almost comical, it seemed to André. He climbed on to the ledge outside the bandstand railing. When he saw the black sea of stern, intent or puzzled faces before him he forgot that Boisson seemed comical.

"At next Friday's meeting of the Legislative Council," Boisson was saying, "I am going to move a motion on the minimum wage question. I have no doubt that that resolution will be defeated like so many others in the past, but no matter what our friends do—"

"Not our friends!" cried Camacho in a strained, melodramatic voice. "Your friends!"

"Oh, shut up!" said a voice near to André in the bandstand.

André looked round and saw a well-dressed brown man on whose face was an arrogant, rapacious expression. Putting a cigar between his wide thin lips he drew them back over his teeth in an unconscious snarl. He and those about him were Workers' Party officials who had gathered, thick as fleas on a dog's back, to support Boisson. At one moment André heard them discuss a resolution to boycott the Electric Company, then a card game at someone's house, how much money so-and-so was making, then a humorous remark followed by large-bellied complacent laughter.

"You who have so many lights in your house, what do you intend doing?" asked a flashily-dressed plump black fellow who gave off an odour of perfume as he pressed a freshly laundered handkerchief gently to his forehead and cheeks.

"What I was just saying is this," said the brown man, who was clearly confident of his own importance, "we will cease to support one capitalist organisation in favour of another—the oil companies."

The scented dandy, who was adjusting his tie in its starched white collar, laughed with willing appreciation and patted the brown man's back. "Clever, that's clever," he said. And in a lower tone: "Look, what are you doing afterwards? Let's go to the Hotel de Paris and have a drink. Little matter I want to discuss . . . getting a bit involved, man. . . ."

Some lesser person with a frayed dirty collar about his thin dirty neck stepped hurriedly to the brown man and timidly pointed to something written in an exercise book. The brown man put his cigar between his bared teeth and took the book. The man with the dirty collar and scrawny neck respectfully came closer with head craned to see what was required of him. "No, you cannot word it that way," the brown man said. "Give me the pen." He scratched out something so violently that he tore the paper. He wrote afresh and read his correction in an abrupt tone of finality. "You cannot say that to ignorant people. We must say we desire . . ." André heard him saying.

"I hear Le Maître was on a hunger march this morning," the scented dandy remarked.

The brown man pulled up his pants with a decisive movement. "He's going to find himself in jail soon."

"A dangerous man," the other agreed.

The dandy's healthy face with the skin stretched smoothly over it, and his full red, moist lips began to arouse a feeling of angry irritation in André. He was astonished at the indifference, even arrogance, these party officials displayed to the workers, who were hanging on Boisson's words and occasionally applauding them. The officials spoke of their women, responded indifferently to a policeman's respectful salute and smile, and pretended not to notice people in the crowd pointing them out to others. He jumped down from the bandstand ledge and squeezed through the crowd to Joe. His big arms folded on his chest, Joe was looking upwards straight at Boisson and sniffing as he often did when controlling his irritation.

"Just a lot of petty scoundrels," André said with youthful exaggeration, jerking his chin at the men in the bandstand. "I've been listening to them. They're not interested in the workers—"

"Oh, you've only now discovered that?" Joe said with an ironic laugh. "Half of them are employed by the city council, they got their jobs through Boisson. I'm surprised you don't realise that." Joe was expending on André the frustration bottled up in him. "Not scoundrels. They're an effete mob. One honest man of principle in that city council would make them tremble in their shoes. *I* tell you so!"

André seized Joe's hand and raised it like a boxing referee signalling the winner of a bout. Joe pulled away in embarrassment.

Suddenly a murmur ran through the crowd like wind in the trees. Boisson no longer had their attention.

"Stop them!" shouted the brown man, waving his cigar. "This is our meeting."

"Le Maître . . . The Workers' Welfare . . ." voices said. "Look trouble now . . . Le Maître is a fighter. . . ."

"What Le Maître could do for you? He ehn't white, he have no influence, he ehn't workin' nowhere. Mr Boisson is a kind man. He don' refuse nobody help," a man in a tattered shirt was hectoring another. "Many times I see him put his hand in his pocket to help people. He would always recommend a man for a job. When a boss see the mayor's signature, what that mean? It mean you got a job! Le Maître want to form trade union. Next t'ing he want you go on strike and starve. Who want to starve?"

André again pulled himself on to the bandstand ledge. He saw a column of men sprinkled with women entering the square through the Knox Street gate and Popito at the head of them beside Le Maître.

"Le Maître himself. . . . He means to make trouble. Call the police . . ." the party officials were saying, jostling one another to get a glimpse of Le Maître.

Irresolution seized Boisson. Some of the workers were shouting: "Go on with the meetin'!" Others, laughing, said: "Look trouble now!" and gleefully jumped on the bandstand ledge for a better view.

The brown man, his cigar clenched in his teeth, pushed his way down the steps. "*I'll* clear them out of here!"

"You cannot do that!" Boisson shouted at his retreating figure. "The square is a public place."

But the brown man shook off the hands of those who would restrain him and rushed to the mounted policeman outside the gate.

So many people were now clambering into the bandstand that André lost his hold and jumped down. He tried to push his way through the shifting crowd to Camacho, but the latter was unable to hear his shouts. With pale parted lips, adjusting his glasses that threatened to fall off, Camacho was trying to extricate himself whole from a fight that had broken out around him. Le Maître's men had joined the crowd. Some of Boisson's supporters had abused and attacked them.

The mounted policeman trotted into the square and backed his horse into this struggling portion of the crowd. It broke and men scattered, surprise and indignation on their faces, some abusing the policeman, others their political opponents.

"Comrades! Friends and comrades! My friends!" Boisson cried, holding up his hands. "Do not pay any attention to this interruption. There are certain people who stand at street corners at night and *mauvaise langue* myself and other leaders of the Workers' Party. What I want to ask them is this: what have they done for the people of this island? Is there one single action of theirs that they can point to and say, 'Through this the people have been made happier.'?"

"No! No!" voices cried.

"And what you do? Tell me that!" Popito Luna's voice was heard above mocking laughter from some around him.

The crowd, agitated, undecided, was pulling first one way then another. An ugly temper flared up now here, now there, now smouldering, now bursting out.

"Where you comin' pushin'? Everybody was peaceful till you come."

"Shut you' big mouth! If you didn't talk so much I could hear what the captain sayin'."

". . . their one cry is for unions, unions," Boisson was saying. "Well, let them go ahead and form their unions, the law is there, we are not stopping them. But what I want to know, my friends, is, what is the good of having a union if you have not got the right to strike or the right to picket peacefully?"

"How many workers have you got in the Party, Boisson?" cried a ringing bass voice that it was impossible to ignore. All heads turned to Le Maître as he came forward. Men made way for him. André again fought for a place on the ledge, dislodging someone in the process.

"The Workers' Party can boast of one hundred and twenty thousand members in its ranks today," Boisson answered proudly. "You do not—"

"Then I say this, Boisson and comrades!" roared Le Maître. "I say that if one hundred and twenty thousand cannot force proper trade-union laws out of Government then the Workers' Party is of no real use to the workers. Half that number on strike could paralyse industry and transport. . . ."

"Man, call the police, man!"

"What the hell he know?"

"He right! What they going to do—jail a hundred t'ousand people?"

"No! We don't want no unions. . . ."

The faces of the disputants showed anger, bewilderment, hatred, amusement, disgust. The police charger shook its head and brushed the flies off with its tail.

"Give me a chance to address the meeting!" Le Maître challenged Boisson.

"This is not your meeting—"

"Keep out! Don't you attempt to come up here."

The Workers' Party officials were shouting and shaking fingers at Le Maître.

"What about free speech now, Boisson?" André heard Joe's rather small voice. He stood close to the bandstand. "So you are afraid of free speech?"

Le Maître saw that his enemy had lost control of the meeting. Knowing that Boisson could not compete with him in vocal power he faced the crowd and roared:

"Comrades! Let us form unions now. I am a worker like you. If we have to strike we will strike like men and defy them to jail us all."

Some in the crowd wanted to remove Le Maître forcibly, but others gathered round to protect him. André felt that many of Boisson's men were drawn to Le Maître by the strength they saw in him and would have liked to hear what he had to say. Le Maître's followers were cheering his every utterance. Boisson, red-faced, was vainly attempting to shout him down. Again André was pushed off the ledge by excited workers.

"Talk about unity, you know what is unity?" a man nearby was saying with an angry conviction that drew others about him. He was a narrow-headed Portuguese with a long, blue-veined neck and white knee-caps showing through his trousers. "You want to know what is the Unity of Man, the Brotherhood of Man?" cried he, snatching a coin from his pocket and holding it aloft. "Look at it! Right, brothers? That's the Unity of Man. If you haven't got Caesar's face to show—no unity."

Those who had gathered around him when he began to speak, hoping he would bring them light, now turned away, muttering: "Oh, shut up! Preachin', preachin'. . . ."

Another section of the crowd, with that primitive feeling which makes healthy fowls pick a sick fowl to death, was jeering at Boisson.

"Down with him, down with the traitor!" André shouted, reddening angrily as he remembered Boisson's May Day speech.

Camacho, straining his voice till it quavered on a false note, cried: "You're selling jobs on the Council!"

Another cried: "You're making two hundred and eighty dollars a month as mayor, that's what you're fighting for."

Additional police horses came trotting into the square and pranced in sideways among the people. André saw Duke, the well-known detective and bully, thrusting his enormous shoulders through the crowd and striking left and right with his club. A feeling of revulsion seized André. Suddenly he hated the brown man, hated the lesser official with the exercise book for the way he kept his lips parted in bewilderment and adjusted his thin neck in its dirty collar.

"Scoundrels!" he shouted. "Cowards!"

The whole crowd broke, men ran in all directions before the thudding of horses' hooves. But a furious pride made André refuse to run. He walked away with his clenched fists buried in his pockets.

The leaves of the great trees rustled in an almost stately fashion.

Chapter thirteen

Le Maître, too, had been a soldier. In 1915, when he was twenty, he had joined one of the first Trinidad contingents to be formed. After seeing service in Mesopotamia he was shipped to India. There he was locked up in barracks with other coloured troops during the massacre of Amritsar.

Three years of contact with Australians, New Zealanders and English Tommies, with blood, death and brutality, destroyed whatever respect for Empire and the ruling class he had retained from his schooldays. When he was finally demobilised Trinidad seemed too small for him. He found his countrymen uncomprehending; their acceptance of their lot revolted him; he was sick with the sourness of his own aimless discontent. Once when drunk he beat a policeman and served two months for the assault. He went to sea. He signed on as an ordinary seaman, had a look at Rio de Janeiro, and skipped the boat in New York: under the glitter of the great city there seemed to be the life for which he thirsted. For eight years he remained there, working, reading, sharing the struggles of the working class and gaining some knowledge of how to conduct them.

The winds of fortune blew him back to his native Trinidad during the depression of '29. He learned that his father and mother, to whom he had never written, were dead. His brother, now a druggist, was struggling to achieve respectability on fifty dollars a month, while his sister was bawling her lungs out at fifty schoolchildren for little more than servants' wages—forty cents a day. They got him a job on the oilfields as a pipe fitter in Point Fortin. The pipe fitters' grievances became his own; he was soon their voice. In his army days, feeling in himself the capacity for leadership, he had acquired a reputation for stirring up trouble. Now his confident manner, the manner of an intelligent man who had no doubts about what he wanted, served him well for a time; but when he was heard telling the men they were fools to permit a wage-cut from eleven cents an hour for a twelve-hour day to nine cents an hour for eight hours, the bosses ran him off the oilfields.

He drifted to the outskirts of Port-of-Spain. He was by now a family man, having married and begot twin sons within two years of his return from America, and in '31 he could not feed them. He searched desperately for work. He was evicted for not paying rent, what little furniture he had was seized, and his wife found shelter for herself and the twins in the home of a friend. Le Maître himself bunked with an old schoolmate. But this was only the high wind that stripped the trees. The full force of the storm broke a fortnight later. His wife and the twins went down with typhoid fever. Months of slow starvation had not helped them; in a week they were dead. But Le Maître knew nothing for he lay in hospital too weak to lift his hands, holding on to life because he thought his twin sons needed him.

When he recovered he joined the Workers' Party. Soon he was criticising Boisson and his methods. Then Boisson, fearing this challenging worker who could think for himself and lead others, made haste to expel Le Maître and his followers as "dangerous subversive elements".

Le Maître wasted no time. It was not hard to gather men who felt that the Party owed them something, but whom Boisson had been obliged to overlook when dispensing the limited number of jobs for city council or government workers. They began to hold street corner meetings. With a gasoline lamp and a table they would collect where the workers lived and sing "Glory Hallelujah", a union song and some merry-sounding hymn; and at the sound of Le Maître's voice rolling through the night, and the thumping upon the table, the people would gather, the telling begin.

"Comrades," Le Maître would say, lapsing into Creole, which bound the workers to him at once. "I ehn come to talk to all-you 'bout Gawd, nuh? It's food I come to talk about, how you and me eatin'." The people, smiling, would nod, his words were sweet to them.

An old baker named Winchester took him at nights into the bakehouses, where men worked sixteen hours a day. Naked to the waist they bent over the wooden troughs, mixing with their great arms the flour into dough and pouring into it their sweat; they stood at the wooden table tearing the dough up into loaves and kneading it with easy circular motions of their hands; and while they worked they sang slowly in a rich chorus or as part songs gloomy hymns or songs they had heard at the movies. The singing eased their labour, a softness would come upon their faces and silence follow the songs. To them in the deep night came Le Maître with his talk of wages and better conditions.

He would go into the public squares and talk to the jobless who crowded the benches and lolled on the grass in the hot sunshine. The sun gave warmth and life, but of what use was life? The flowers were beautiful, as was the quivering of grass and leaves; but without food, the pulse-beat of life, there was no beauty.

It was with such men as these that Le Maître marched to the Governor demanding work.

When the police broke up the meeting Le Maître, Popito and three other men left Woodford Square in a group talking and arguing with such heat that they did not realise they were following Le Maître home till already far out of their way. They left him then, after arranging to meet on the morrow. Le Maître called Popito back.

"Let us go and have some food. I want to talk to you. Tell me more about yourself. Are you married?"

Popito told Le Maître about his sister and niece, and how much more difficult life had become for them now he was jobless. Le Maître enquired about men he knew at Dollard's. Popito gave hurried, indifferent replies because he had already surrendered to Le Maître's positive and overpowering personality. He kept glancing with a smile of admiration at the shirt arm that had been torn from Le Maître's shoulder during the *mêlée* in the square. He found it an additional cause for admiration that Le Maître had forgotten about it. But what completely won Popito's loyalty was the humanity expressed in Le Maître's interest in the life of a near-wreck like Luna.

Le Maître took his wrist in a conspiratorial way he had, put his head close to Popito's and said, as if revealing the secret of life: "Never despair! To despair is to commit suicide. So long as you breathe you must fight. It's only so you can be free."

He began to question Popito. "What about this paper you told us about? What sort of fellow is Elias?" He put these and other questions with a distracted air, as if he were thinking of several things at once, and at the same time turned to look at the rear of a woman who was passing.

"Eh-eh! Cassie? That's you, girl?" said Popito, smiling at her.

Cassandra, the Osbornes' maid, was wearing high-heeled shoes with silk stockings and a blue skirt with a white bodice tucked into it. Her face was fresh with youth, health, judicious make-up and the anticipation of some kind of pleasure awaiting her just round the corner. Very different was she indeed from the Cassie he had come upon from time to time in his sister's yard who always gave him a respectful greeting.

"Good afternoon, Mr Luna. How are you? Long time I didn't see you."

"But the girl is damn good-looking!" thought Popito as he replied, noticing her smooth dark skin and her beautiful soft black eyes. She looked at him with such unconscious sly coquetry that he asked where she was going and felt a mad desire to go with her.

"I goin' up San Juan to see a friend. Mr Luna, you workin' now?" And her husky voice, it seemed to Popito, was sympathetic and yielding like everything else about her.

"Not yet, man."

"Oh, gosh, I so sorry to hear! Don't mind, you goin' to succeed soon. I goin' to pray for you." Her eyes teased him.

"You still in the same job?" He was unwilling to let her go.

"I still goin' ahead. Goodbye, Mr Luna. I goin' to catch the bus."

"All right, Cassie, I'll see you. When you comin' back?"

"Tonight 'self," she answered over her shoulder.

On Le Maître's face was a mingled look of envy and curiosity. "She is a servant," said he. "How you come to know her?"

"She livin' in the yard just behind my sister."

"Marriage, honeymoon and all that—it is a very overrated thing," Le Maître remarked unexpectedly, pushing out his underlip scornfully. "The worker who is just married loses all his militancy. I was married for a short while, and all I could think about was how not to offend the boss and how many times a night I could have my wife."

"Marriage is for people with money," Popito flung off, eager to put himself right with this man he admired.

But Le Maître looked back at Cassie, who was disappearing down the street. "She is a very good-looking girl," he remarked. "Clem Payne is one of the few married men among us. I have known him all my life. You know what it is to starve with a wife and three children? I was lucky: mine died before they could suffer. But his are suffering before they die."

"Your family died?"

"All of them—all! In a week. The capitalists are to blame for that. Do you ever hear of them dying of typhoid in St Clair, St Anns, Maraval, where the rich live? No. But we are left to the mercies of typhoid, malaria, tuberculosis, hookworm. These things make a man think. What has happened to you is a good thing, it is making you think. But you are doing a bad thing to send the thoughts from your mind with drink. You must study how to make the workers unite against the bosses. That is the most important thing in the world. When you work to that end you work for all mankind, not just yourself."

"Yes! I believe that," said Popito. "This Payne. He seems a reckless sort of a man, he don't give a damn about anybody."

"He is the bravest of men," Le Maître replied defensively. "During the war I saw him laugh at death. You would see other men get pale and frightened in a bombardment, but he had nerves of steel. He is a very sick man. His hatred of the bosses burns inside him like the eternal lamp in church. His will is like iron. He will die on his feet, he will never lie down in bed for death to take him."

They went through a passage and entered the barrack yard where Le Maître had a room. At the far end, in a mess of rubbish and rotting boards, where black cobwebs draped the rafters, three youths were setting type and working a printing machine. Someone had forgotten to turn off the tap near the bleach and water was making puddles in the yard. A barefooted old woman fanned a coalpot on her doorstep. A young girl came and turned off the pipe and sprinkled some clothes on the bleach. Her dress and bare feet were filthy but her youth and figure seemed to declare: "In spite of everything, still I'm blooming."

"Eh, *b'en!*" said Le Maître to the old woman. "What about Tony?"

"He ain' come."

"Bring an extra plate for a comrade."

"Well, boy, so this is where you livin', ehn?" said Popito in a tone that suggested he was preparing to condole with Le Maître.

"Many of us who have a roof now will have only the Town Hall gallery later. How would you like to sleep under there?"

The Town Hall dated from Spanish times. Its first floor gallery used to hang over and shelter the sidewalk. There, especially on rainy nights, slept homeless beggars upon bits of bag and cardboard with which they shielded their meagre bodies from the unfriendly cold of the sidewalk slabs. Once Popito, drifting homeward, full of the brief contentment won with rum, had stumbled over one of them. Stooping, he had stroked the man's head in apology and gone his way with loud singing.

"I wouldn't mind if I had comrades with me," he replied.

"I would sleep alone, Luna!" said Le Maître, again pushing out his underlip. "If a man lacks the conviction to carry him through, no amount of comrades can help him."

The room was divided in half by a cheap red cloth hanging from a string. The old woman came in, wiped her bare feet upon the burlap bag mat and her hands in her dress. She took two plates from a shelf, went out and returned with them full of pilau. Le Maître, holding his plate in one hand, dug in with a spoon, taking big mouthfuls as if he had too much to do and say to savour what he ate.

Presently he looked up and saw a small thin man in khaki enter the yard. He put the plate in a chair and went out at once, his big head thrust forward in a bull-like manner. The little man, seeing a stranger in the room, halted and turned his back. Through the open doorway Popito saw how Le Maître ceased chewing abruptly as the little man spoke, then swallowed and frowned angrily. The little man spread his hands and began to protest, but Le Maître, turning his head away, insisted in a tone of rising anger:

"Don't tell me anything! You had a right to play on him the same trick he played on you. But you were *afraid*," he added, disdainfully throwing back his head and pouting his lips. "Don't undertake a job if you kean't carry it out. Those were my words to you. But, by Christ, if you put your hand to the wheel let them crush you to pulp and move you in pieces rather than you give in. If you had come and said you were afraid I would have gone myself."

The young girl, singing an "I love you" song, glanced at them and continued to sprinkle the clothes that were on the bleach.

Feeling ashamed the little man cried: " 'Fraid what, 'fraid what! They suspect me. What you want me do? You awright, man."

He went off, talking angrily and waving his arms.

Le Maître came in and finished the meal in silence.

"That fella was givin' you some trouble," Popito suggested.

"He's a good comrade. But his job requires a man with a good *cabez'*. He was afraid of handing out leaflets in the oilfields." Le Maître laughed scornfully, without humour. "What about the Negro Welfare, will you join?"

"Yes. Where all-you have meetin's?"

Le Maître gave him the address in Piccadilly Street.

"You must come and see me again. Don't mind I live like a rat in a hole. One day we will all come out our holes and live in houses."

"I like those words too bad!" said Popito, laughing joyfully and shaking Le Maître's hand. "Nothing in this world could t'row you down. Well, till tomorrow night, ehn?"

"Goodbye, Luna!"

Chapter fourteen

Long ago Percy French had joined the Shouters. To him it had been more than a religion: it was a form of dramatic art in the practice of which he briefly won self-realisation and a release from the rage, confusion and doubt that clouded his thinking. Nowadays he called it "all superstition"; he was reading books and pamphlets, he was hot on the trail of those forces that held the workers down, and thinking how to upset and defeat them. When some of the publications of the Left Book Club proved beyond him, his education being limited, he turned to Le Maître and Payne for help. Long out of work, he lived on breadfruit, saltfish and mangoes. In appearance he was an insignificant little man; yet when he spoke to the workers and instinctively exercised his very West Indian talent for self-dramatisation he loomed as a prophetic giant before his audience. Highly excitable, with black eyes that at times seemed ready to leap from his head, he would rise up and down on his knees as if preparing to spring, hitch up his pants, pace the platform like a caged lion, then suddenly drop his voice to a whisper like an actor in a play. His role gripped him. Often one can see amidst the rubbish and filth of *La Basse* a plant that has taken root, flowered and is about to put out fruit. Such was Percy French.

Manny Camacho knew him well. They both lived in Belmont, French in a winding street so narrow that pedestrians hugged the fences when a car went by and little boys in tattered clothes leaped on the running boards and grinned at the drivers tauntingly. Manny knew a different side to French, he knew him as a practical kindly fellow whose wild look would vanish suddenly in big-mouthed laughter. He laughed with his whole soul, as if he had not a care in the world, but silently, exposing the gum above his front teeth. He felt obliged to help the old folk—cooking for his old mother, putting in a board in the house of the old man over the fence, cutting the limb of a mango tree to prevent the fruit falling on someone's roof. He could not stand idly while the old ones struggled.

One day when he and Camacho sat talking a woman of fifty went by in the street. Her head was tied with a white cloth, Shouter fashion, and she was talking loudly as though possessed by a spirit.

"You know who that woman is?" French said as he returned her greeting.

"Who?"

"My sister. You see what poverty can do? Ehn? And hard work that makes men and bullocks equal and deadens you' mind like chloroform? Worry, venereal disease—look at her!"

She began to sing hymns at the top of her voice. Little boys ran behind, teasing her.

"What you think that makes me feel inside here, Manny?" French struck his chest. He picked up some stones and pelted the half-naked urchins teasing his sister.

When the police chargers pranced into the crowd and Duke lashed out with his club as if squashing flies, Camacho fled with the workers, but a voice stopped him.

"Manny! Manny! Stand you' ground like a man!"

He looked round and saw French standing with an angry expression, mouth open and fists clenched.

"What kind of man are you, runnin'?"

On Manny's face was a smile of fright and shame. At this moment one of the big Canadian horses danced sideways and back and would have tumbled French over had he not skipped out of its way and sprung up on the bandstand ledge.

Manny hailed André, who was walking away. With French and Clem Payne they went into a nearby rum shop. André, lacking any common experience with workers, felt he should behave in some special way, a way unnatural to him, but resisted both this and the temptation to make some excuse and run away. At the bar several men and a woman were laughing and arguing, some tipsily. André followed his companions into a room at the side. There half-a-dozen workmen were sitting round a table listening to one of their number, a middle-aged man, who was saying something about Boisson. French greeted the speaker. The others looked with unconcealed curiosity at André and Camacho. Under their scrutiny André felt conscious both of his unworthiness and his superiority to them; but Camacho, accustomed to mixing with them in his father's shop, was not in the least self-conscious.

"What will you fellows have? Rum? Four rums!" Camacho shouted to the long-faced old Portuguese bartender who put his head inside the door. He slapped André's shoulder. "Well, have you had your baptism of fire, my boy?" he asked with a mocking, boisterous laugh. He thoroughly enjoyed his self-appointed role of political mentor to this "misguided young bourgeois", as he had spoken of him to French.

"I suppose you have had your skull cracked by the police many a time," André retorted with a smile.

French shook with laughter and patted André's arm in so appreciative a manner that the latter at once felt at ease.

Camacho blushed. "We smashed them!" he cried triumphantly. "Eh, Percy? We must attend Boisson's meetings and make him answer our questions."

Payne had a trick of wrinkling his nose and blowing through it contemptuously when some remark annoyed him. He did so now.

"Smashed them? *Smashed* them? Use the right word, boy, we *broke up* the meetin'."

"We must do so again."

"Milk not yet dry on you' lips. . . . We must draw the workers to us by conviction!"

The middle-aged man at the next table ceased talking and looked with hostility at Camacho. "It's hooligans like you tryin' to set worker against worker. What right you have in dis? 'Make Boisson answer questions.' Who you are to question him?"

One of his companions pushed back his chair noisily and approached Camacho with unsteady gait. Slapping his hands on the table he leaned on them and peered into Camacho's face. "You know what the Captain do for the workers? Who are you to talk? And he!" He poked a finger at André.

"He did a lot for the workers. I know. He's a good friend of the workers," André said soothingly because drunks embarrassed him and he feared the freedom liquor lent the tongue.

The man's companions took him away.

"Don't start it all over again inside-a here," one reproached him and, turning to Camacho, added: "You better watch you' tongue!"

The long-faced bartender brought in the rums. "Cheers!" said Camacho, raising his own glass in the effort to hide his embarrassment that no one at this table had supported him.

"Cheers," said French. He took a mouthful, savoured it, nodded approvingly and drank off the rest. The whites of his eyes grew redder.

Payne drank his as if he needed a stimulant. He threw it down his throat, gasped, shook his head and clutched the table.

"You' tongue always runnin' away with you, Manny," French said. "Revolution is not made with the tongue, you know, it is made with the head."

Camacho waved a hand in dismissal.

André asked French: "After trade union, then what?"

Payne laughed mockingly.

"What you want after that, André?" French asked with an indulgent smile.

"The British out of here."

"Independence! You are one of us," French said, again patting his arm. He was no longer smiling. André felt French had taken him to his heart as he was ready to take any man who wanted freedom. "Why you don't come to our meetings, man? Come and hear Ben Le Maître, come and hear what the workers are thinkin' and sayin'. You will learn."

"I'll come, I do want to come. How are we going to win independence? The British aren't going to give it to us."

"We goin' to take it!" Payne burst out. Camacho laughed. "Don't laugh," Payne went on. "Watch the way the world movin'."

"How can we take it?" André persisted with some impatience. "A few shells from a cruiser and it's all over, even if nine tenths of the people wanted independence."

"Defeatist talk!"

"Look, they don't even have to shell us, they could starve us."

"It's true," French agreed. And Payne, who knew quite well it was true but hated this truth, swung his thin crossed leg and blew through his nose contemptuously.

"Independence of mind—that's what we need!" André continued. "Independence of spirit. The courage to think like West Indians, to be proud of being West Indians—"

"Who tell you we haven't the courage to *think* like West Indians, to *feel* like West Indians?" Payne burst out again.

"That's what we are like, whether you like it or not!" André felt an aggressive spirit coming over him as the drink, to which he was unaccustomed, went to his head. "Spiritually and mentally we are creatures of the English—"

"*Spiritually?* What you talkin' about—church? I don't believe in no church."

"Be quiet and listen. Our attitudes, our loves, our bowing and scraping, our fear of ourselves—where does all that come from? British education! Independence of the mind is what we need above everything. Why do we distrust ourselves and fear one another? Because of our subservience to White Massa. You tell me how you're going to fight that. Come on!" André glared at Payne, lips trembling, in his mind the memory of what he had felt quite suddenly the night before : panic at the knowledge that he had bound himself to Elena. It was too soon; he wasn't sure of himself or that he had the strength to face a life of poverty with her. What had he done! He felt an awful, shameful terror of the future with her, cut off, condemned.

Payne laughed his mocking laugh. "He got some fire, man!" he said to French, who was listening with a sad and tender smile.

"Answer the question, Clem," French said.

"Answer it you'self. Who could answer it? To fight, to fight, to fight!" Payne shouted, hitting the table with his fist. He was breathing rapidly, as if he had been wrestling, because his weak body could not contend with the hates accumulated in him.

"You don't know," André said with angry disappointment. "Nobody knows."

"We have to fight, comrade André," French told him. "Clem is right. Form trade unions and make our demands for a better life. When a man is a fighter he don't think as you say."

"Where is he? Show him to me. Have another rum." André noticed French fondling his glass.

"Yes, I'll have another. Clem?"

Clem shook his head.

"I could tell you stories about Ben Le Maître," French said in a tender, kindly tone occasioned partly by the thought of another drink. "That man is not afraid of a single thing. People feel that as soon as they see him. He speaks to bosses as man to man, not impolite, but as if he is the boss. He don't shrink from anything. But he is not a man who could enjoy a joke—you ever notice that, Clem? He could laugh with scorn, laugh in triumph when Boisson make a bad out, but to laugh just for fun—he ain't able. Cheers!" French added and drank of the rum the bartender had just set down before him.

"He speaks to the boss as man to man," André reflected, hating himself because he could not do likewise. "He doesn't value what I have been taught to value."

"You must hear Ben," French was saying. "Attend our meetin's, talk to him."

To hell with him, thought André, and was suddenly revolted by the smell of rum on French's breath, by his smile and by everything in the horrid little room.

When they went out his head was swimming. Payne laughed at him mockingly and went up the street. To be mocked enraged André; but to be mocked publicly by this black worker was almost more than he could bear. He flushed and turned his back. But a moment later he realised that that mocking laugh could express both approbation and contempt. It had become so habitual that it replaced all the others Payne had been capable of long ago—kindly laughs and laughs of love and joy. And behind the dislike he felt for Payne at that moment there lurked an unwilling feeling of admiration for him, and respect.

Chapter fifteen

At last Joe had managed to shake off Dollard and Company. His father had appointed him manager of one of the shops. Joe felt he had won freedom—so it seemed to him—and he was bursting with plans for the future.

The value of his management lay principally in the fact that his presence discouraged his father's clerks from helping themselves secretly to those articles or the cash they needed. They liked Joe. His heart was not yet cased in iron and the pleas for assistance they made to him in lowered shame-filled voices rarely went unheeded. Much of his day was passed in talking with customers or holding discussions in a back room with the workers, clerks or intellectuals who read his magazine, admired his brilliance and felt stimulated by his company. Sometimes their discussions were on literature and the arts; more often their nature was political. They were always fiery. Without Joe's forceful personality and the challenge of his unorthodoxy they would have lost heat and died. His admirers expected much of him. They needed someone through whom to voice their accumulated indignation and their aspirations. Joe was their man. He knew the use of words; he feared nobody; he was better educated than most of them; and they, thirsting for education, were drawn to those who were crowned with it. Some saw him as that coming political figure behind whom they, rallying to his banner, would attack the system under which they groaned. Joe for king. They were ready to begin campaigning for his candidature in the 1936 elections.

At last old Elias had put a house, the "big house", in his son's name. It was too soon to begin campaigning, but Joe felt the time had come to make himself known to his electorate. He joined both Boisson's party and Le Maître's, and attended their meetings.

Formerly he had paid scant attention to "that crank, Le Maître". He acknowledged Le Maître's intelligence, but those he had gathered round him were in Joe's opinion a group of ignorant men inflamed by a sense of injustice that fitted them only to lead sheep-like workers in some foolhardy adventure. Now that he was disposed to regard them as possible allies in his struggle to win a seat on the city council, his opinion of them underwent modification. "In their own way," thought he, "they are heroes. They can never succeed. And they are not aware of it."

So varied were the points of view from which Joe apprehended life that he lacked stability and gave the appearance of lacking will. He would veer now to the left, now to the right, and now go into reverse, bewildering equally friends and enemies yet resolutely pursuing each new conviction as if it were ultimate truth, and displaying a prodigious disdain for the abuse he called down on his head for abandoning former concepts. It could never be said that he lacked courage.

Le Maître was following that course which to him was a spiritual, intellectual and moral necessity. He liked power but his love of it was directed outwards to the service of a class, a great body of people among whom he lived every moment of the day and whose collective voice he heeded. Joe sought power because only with power could he impose the ideas he valued and put an end to his insignificance. He wanted to give life a shake and compel it to obey his will, even for a brief moment.

"Le Maître," he reflected, "is wasting his time and his talents among too many ignorant people. It is in the city council that he and I will do most good. His party could put him there. It should not be difficult to persuade him: he loves power."

One night he walked with Camacho from Belmont to the schoolroom in Piccadilly Street where the Negro Welfare held its meetings. It was a distance of perhaps two miles and Joe perspired, became hungry and arrived at the schoolhouse in a fidgety, petulant mood that was almost feminine. He saw a small, partly bald man shouting and gesticulating from a platform to some thirty other Negroes, and his feeling of irritation increased. "The futility of that Percival French," he thought, laughing cynically.

The men listening to French were mostly journeymen bakers. French was urging upon them the need to form a trade union in their industry.

"Ask yourselves," he was saying, "what Boisson can do for you. He has never won a wage increase for you. Do you think the master-bakers will give it because they have kind hearts? Do you think they will reduce their profits," he bent his knees and straightened up as if preparing to spring when he uttered the words "reduce" and "profits", "in order that you might eat better? No-o! They must be forced to give you more. How is Boisson goin' to force them? Tell me that, comrades. I am waitin' for you to tell me. Is *he*, an owner of property, a capitalist, goin' to fight other capitalists for *you*?" French laughed. Joe saw he was completely carried away. "You have to forge a weapon for you'selves and belabour the master-bakers with it! You have to form a trade union. . . ."

Afterwards Le Maître came up to Joe. "What did you think of

the meeting—the speakers?" he asked with a proud smile. "French was specially forceful tonight."

Joe shook his head, lowering the corners of his mouth. "Tell me something : do you really think this is the correct approach? At a time like this, when the police are attacking meetings and driving you from the streets, do you think we need a firebrand to encourage the police to strangle the people's voice?"

Le Maître uttered a loud scornful laugh. Camacho remembered that French had said he could never laugh "just for fun".

"Percy!" Le Maître shouted. "He says you are going to encourage the police to silence us."

French, grinning amiably, came up with Popito and Payne.

"So what is your idea?" Le Maître continued, his green eyes resting on Joe with amused yet watchful tolerance.

That look offended Joe's vanity. "Oh, so you want to know what I think?" he remarked with surprise, as though expressing his satisfaction that the conceited Le Maître was at last prepared to listen to other opinions besides his own. "Well, let me tell you this. Do you want me to tell you something? The most urgent necessity now is the destruction of Boisson. Do you realise that? Have you realised that before you can form trade unions, before you can take one step forward, you must show him up and discredit him? It is his hold on the masses that stands in your way!"

Only a few months before it had seemed to Joe that the "most urgent necessity" was the formation of trade unions.

Payne blew through his nose angrily. "Uh goin' to catch up with you," he said in a loud rude voice that ignored Joe Elias, and he left the room.

"Yes, yes, Clem!" said Le Maître. "And how you propose to do this? I know already—you will try to get on the city council and show him up." Le Maître smiled and spread one hand. "Isn't it so?"

"And what is wrong with that?" Joe demanded aggressively, embarrassed that Le Maître had seen through him so readily. "Don't you understand the importance of taking the council out of the hands of businessmen and putting it in the control of the workers' genuine representatives? You should be there! That's where you should be. There with me! If the workers' representatives really controlled that council Government would be very much embarrassed—"

"Look here, Elias, while you are flattening Boisson in the council the workers are starving, they are looking for a place to sleep, indignities are being heaped on them in their own country by foreigners. What sort of service to the workers is that?"

"You don't understand the position. . . . Look here, I am absolutely ravenous," Joe remarked to Camacho. "You think it's possible to get a *rhoti* around here?"

"*Rhoti* at a time like this?" Camacho laughed in astonishment.

"Listen, now," Joe continued, turning his back on Popito, who had begun to say something, and whom he considered of no account. "What we want is a socialist party. You call this party the Negro Welfare. The name is a bad one, it's racist. You want not only Negroes, but Indians, Chinese, everyone—"

"You are right. We chose the name because it would draw the Workers' Party members in Port-of-Spain, where most of them are Negroes."

"Well, all right. Such a party could back candidates for the city council, it could put you there."

"And you?"

Joe laughed, pleased with his own cunning. "I have other plans. I will get Boisson and his party to put me there, and once there I will do everything for his destruction." He shook a finger. "Wait and see!"

"I didn't realise you were so cynical."

The man's bluntness confused Joe. He assumed a look of surprise. "Cynicism? But you are compelled to beat the enemy with his own weapons!"

"We live like lilies in the field, Elias. Our roots are in the earth. I intend to organise the workers wherever possible—the bread industry, in the city council, in the oilfields, anywhere. They must learn to fight for themselves. Don't you see what slavery has done to us? The people still feel that if a good white massa came along he would solve all their problems. Their spirit was crushed in the first place by being rooted out of Africa and deprived of their years of history. Their descendants became a people without memories. They knew only the whip and white massa." Le Maître was shouting, shaking his hands before Joe's face. "And you tell me about getting on the council. To hell with the council! The people need to stretch their muscles and realise their strength. They need to make themselves into a people they will respect. It is time they stopped laughing at themselves."

All those who had remained in the hall after the meeting had gathered round and were listening. "Hear, hear!" voices said with earnest, almost solemn approval. And Joe himself thrilled to the man's power to move others.

"If there is arrogance in him there is also deep humanity," he thought. He, artist-philosopher, embittered by the terrible social conditions of his time, controlled by his moods and swaying from idea to idea as the weeds of the ocean do to the ebb and flow of the tide—he, too, longed to help his fellow man but was conscious of his own weakness as much as his strength. In the face of Le Maître's overpowering authority and conviction he stood silent. "How is it possible to be so impervious to doubt?" he thought with envy. He understood that the truth which Le Maître had grasped was rooted in history. It sprang from a broad perspective uniting past and future. But Joe was indifferent to history, he valued more the struggles of individual man to break the spiritual bonds with which life fettered him. "Each of us has a contribution to make," he thought. "Each must go his own way. But I will achieve more than he ever will, I am convinced of it." And he chuckled sardonically, glancing at the faces about him, partly from the need to reassure himself and partly to display his own independence of mind before all these people who submitted so unthinkingly to Le Maître's convictions.

Chapter sixteen

After that day spent marching in the streets and attacking Boisson in the square, Popito became so friendly with Le Maître and submitted so completely to his influence that it was difficult to be content for long without his company. Le Maître provided the moral sustenance that was so necessary to him at this time. If Popito were missing for a day or two Le Maître would give him a welcoming smile when he turned up and say: "Popi! Where you been? What happen? I didn't see you yesterday or day before." He understood all that Popito was suffering, he had been through it himself.

When, therefore, Popito ceased to attend meetings because the police were keeping an open, intimidatory watch on the hall Le Maître did not rebuke him. Popito said from a sense of guilt:

"I am tired of doing nothing, man—tired! I would like to sweep all these damn parasites from the face of the earth. I myself would like to kill some."

Le Maître, sitting in his old bentwood rocking-chair from which half the seat was torn away, remained silent. Popito felt worse. He turned his back on Le Maître, flung away a matchstick he had been chewing, then got up and said he must be going.

"I have been thinking about you," Le Maître said. "It is no use to hope for favours as a brown-skinned clerk. You realise that?"

"All that is over. I'm not a fool," said Popito, though he still hoped.

"You are over forty years. You look like forty-five. Employers will say you are finished. Your only hope is to stick with us."

Popito aimlessly broke a bit of stick and tried to fling the pieces into a patch of sunlight near the door. He said: "Once they catch me I am done, you know. No hope of a job again. This country is small."

Le Maître leaned forward. "What is the alternative? Give way to despair, let death creep into you like the woodlice that have rotted these walls? You goin' to hold you' hat out before you as creatures broken by life are doing out there in the street now?"

"I still have me freedom."

A child began to wail and beg for mercy. Popito looked up. In the yard a tall, long-breasted mother was beating a thin little girl with a stick.

"Where the hell you been so long?" cried the mother in a tone of exasperation. "So—so long I send you in the shop and dat—dat—dat—" she was emphasising her words with blows—"is what you let the Chinee man give you for six cents? You lose a cent! Don' tell me no, you well lose the cent, you well—well—well lose the cent."

"Gawd damn it!" exclaimed Popito, enraged and hurt as if the blows were falling on him. He stepped out but Le Maître called him back.

"You must take a more detached view of these things. As you see her there, she is exhausted with work. That is freedom. Look at it well. You want that?"

"But how you live, man!"

"Food and shelter are not everything, Popi. Look at Payne: he is a very sick man, he has a wife and three children, he can't do hard physical work, but he lives! He lives intensely as you have not lived yet."

"How all-you manage to eat, to pay rent?"

"The workers help us. Like you we get an odd job now and then. Camacho helps us. Has he ever told you? No? That's how we live. Would you prefer us to submit to police intimidation? To submit is to die like some Baboolal or other in the square."

Popito lit a cigarette with fumbling hands.

Le Maître relaxed in his rocking-chair. "You cannot live without danger. Look at the ants in the road. They cross. If hundreds are killed others take the chance and they get over. They survive and build nests."

Popito drew hard on his cigarette. He looked at the indifferent sunshine, the barefooted young woman who was singing, the old women washing clothes at the pipe nearby, and from it all he felt cut off as from life itself.

"Come and go with me to Fyzabad," Le Maître said, getting up suddenly. "It's no good for you to sit here like this. We will meet some of the oilfield workers, I want to have a talk with them."

Popito said to himself determinedly: "You can't bring back the past, you have to make something of the future." But as he went out of the yard with Le Maître he could not shake off the feeling that he was heading into a storm he might not survive.

They took the bus "Sweet Violet"—it wasn't hard to find, its name was painted, entwined with flowers, on the rear—and got to Fyzabad at five that afternoon. It was a village of shacks set in an area from which oil was sucked day and night. A vampire desists when sated, but these pumps were never sated, they seemed to work without cease. Yet this and the workers' shacks, some crumbling, some painted, others old and weathered, Popito took for granted, it was such an ordinary sight.

The Negro Welfare used to hold its meetings in a hall above a grocery shop at the Junction, as the crossroads was called. This was the principal part of the village. Here were houses whose solidity indicated the owners' faith in life. "Cartage contractors and garage owners live there," Le Maître told Popito. A few little shops were stuffed with the haberdashery and hardware that oilfield workers could afford to buy. A roadside market lay open to the sky.

Fifteen oilworkers attended the meeting. Le Maître was no stranger to them, some were old workmates of his. Popito saw that just as in Port-of-Spain his views, his confidence, his voice all gave them strength. He heard it in their weighing of weakness and strength in the oilfields, in the clash of personalities that drew fire and wild recriminations and in their full-bellied sensuous laughter that suddenly swept the storm aside as the wind drives the rain clouds from the face of the sun. The sun came out and they went downstairs to drink in the rumshop.

The rhythmic thunder of approaching drums beat on their ears. A semi-trailer carrying lengths of oilfield pipe had been trying to get by a line of trucks and buses parked on the roadside but had been forced to a halt by three buses approaching from the opposite direction. Two of these were occupied by Indians celebrating a wedding. They were singing Indian songs and beating cymbals and drums with such an exciting, gay, infectious rhythm that everyone stopped to look and little boys in the street danced and shook their bodies. A big glossy car claimed their attention as it stole up behind the semi-trailer. At the wheel sat a liveried chauffeur in a cap with a glossy peak. In the rear seat, reading a document of some kind, sat a broad-shouldered sunburned Englishman with broad, sharply-defined features.

Le Maître pointed him out to Popito. "Major Bottomley, my old boss. He is the big shot on these oilfields."

Some black youths stood gazing in a state of sycophantic rapture at the lines of the great boss's car. "That is car!" they said. "Eight cylinders, *oui*?" One knew a girl who was the chauffeur's niece. This raised him to a particular plane of importance among the others. As the car moved forward silently behind the truck a little boy ran swiftly forward and touched the rear fender that was gleaming in the last rays of the setting sun. His playmates uttered shrieks of admiration at his daring.

Le Maître took Popito to the shop beneath the hall and introduced him to Yankee, who owned the building. He was a brisk round-faced, jolly Chinese man of indefinite age—thirty or forty—in white shorts reaching below the knee, slippers and a cotton singlet. A flour-bag apron covered his front. When he laughed his eyes narrowed to slits that glittered so merrily that the friendly Popito liked him at once. He had got his nickname because he spoke with an American accent acquired during many years in New York city.

Yankee greeted Le Maître heartily. Some four years before, when he had just set up his grocery business, he had got into the clutches of a rich Chinese merchant. By following Le Maître's advice he had managed to extricate himself from his dilemma. From that time he had felt obliged to Le Maître to the point of feeding him without charge on the rare occasions when Le Maître came to see him. Le Maître did not outstay his welcome.

"Your fliend?" Yankee asked. Like many Chinese he experienced difficulty with his r's.

"One of my best friends."

"Name?"

"Popi."

"How?" Popito held out his hand.

Yankee's thick hand did not return the pressure and this made an unpleasant impression on Popito.

Le Maître ordered bread and a tin of salmon. "He's out of a job," he said, opening the bottle of stout Yankee put before him.

"A-ah! Long time?"

"Five months, goin' on for six," replied Popito.

"A-ah!" Yankee looked at him long. "Where you work? Dollard, eh? Customs work?"

"No, but I have done that, you know," Popito replied at once.

Yankee had taken them into the back room, which was piled high with stock and was stifling with its mingled smells of saltfish, sugar, onions, flour and pickled pork.

"You must be rotten with money now," Le Maître said with a half-envious, half contemptuous look, glancing about him as he ate.

"Money? I don't know the last day I see money, man," said Yankee, grinning, his restless plump hands caressing the top of the pine table at which they were sitting.

"But you have laundry as well now."

"No money, man, no money."

"Why you don't give the Negro Welfare the hall rent free? When we succeed in winning higher wages for the workers it is here they will spend their money."

"Good guy, smart fella," Yankee said to Popito, patting Le Maître's arm, and spoke of something else.

Popito visited Yankee again the following week, this time with a list headed by several people who had contributed money to the party's funds. Yankee looked at the list a long time when Popito pointed out to him that a Chinese doctor of their acquaintance had given ten dollars. Then he laughed as if to say, "It can't be helped, I'm caught," and gave Popito five.

"Still out of work?"

"Still, man."

"You have wife? No wife? That's the best idea. Woman give a man hell when he ain't got dough. Hard times for you now, eh?"

"Give me a job, man!" Popito burst out, slapping the counter. Then uttered a shamefaced laugh that he had let his suffering be seen.

Yankee caressed the counter. "When you come next time. You come next week? We see then."

Fyzabad was sixty miles from Port-of-Spain but Popito was there on Monday. Yankee took him into the room in which he slept. It was right behind the glass cases with their laundered and labelled suits. Again one wall, a bamboo cot. For pillow, a folded blanket. A dirty hammock hung from a ring. A sooty oil stove stood on a stained and scorched little table. Two tin trunks, one under the table, completed the furnishing of this room. Yankee drew a folding camp stool from beneath the cot and handed it to Popito.

"Want do customs work?"

"Anything, once it have money in it. How much you goin' to pay?"

The answer staggered him: "Twenty dollars eve'y case you clear."

"How many cases?"

"Four—fi'—six. Sometimes more."

"Every month?"

"Sometimes twi' in one mont'."

"Two hundred and forty dollars a month! What you have so in those cases?"

"Wine, good wine. One case have special mark. Don't let customs open that case or no job for you again."

Popito grunted and looked down.

"Good money for you," Yankee urged.

"What you have in that case? Opium?"

"No, no, man! Nothing dange'ous."

"When you want me to start?"

"Tomollow. Shut you' trap. Don't say anything to Ben. Understand?"

"Suppose I land in jail?"

"No jail, man, not even fine for you. Police watch me. You know Duke?"

"The detective?"

"Yeh. A no-good fella. Velly c'uel man. I see he st'ike a young girl, cut up her face. He suspec' me but he flaid of me. He know I can ploove he take glaft from people."

Popito had seen Duke using his baton that day in Woodford Square. An uneasy feeling spread through him from his belly but not from the fear of Duke's baton; it arose from fear of what Le Maître would say if he found out.

"You look flighten', man. I get a nex' man wid guts for the job."

"Who say I'm frightened? When you goin' to pay, it's that I'm considerin'."

"Soon as you bring the cases to me here."

"What about an advance?"

"No advance."

"I got to have an advance. I goin' to have expenses."

"Okay." Yankee gave him two dollars. He brought out the papers from one of his trunks and revealed the mark Popito should look for.

"I can always give it up after a couple of shipments," Popito thought as he hid the papers in his inner jacket pocket and rose. In this shipment there were eight cases of dried fruit and wine. By tomorrow night he would have a hundred and sixty dollars in his hand. He would give some to Aurelia, he would hold his head up, the load that was breaking him would lift.

Next day Popito sought out the customs officer in charge of the shed where the goods were lying, and to his joy found it was a self-important mulatto with whom he had previously had dealings and whose weaknesses he knew. Popito chatted with him in the friendliest yet most respectful fashion for some minutes, calling him "Mister" several times. Having found the cases and had them wheeled up before the officer, he adroitly opened three and put two bottles of wine and a box of dried figs on the officer's desk.

"Beautiful wine," Popito said in a confidential murmur. "As you know—you're an expert."

The officer smiled his thanks, stepped down from his platform and asked, pointing: "What's in this?"

"Same thing. You want me open it?" Popito held the hatchet aloft. His heart beat fast. How ready he was at that moment to love or hate this customs officer! It was the marked case.

"All right. Never mind. Nail them up."

Popito dropped the hatchet with a clatter. The officer returned to his desk on the platform and signed the papers.

Popito hired a truck, helped load the cases on it and went off with them to Fyzabad. For a long while he, usually so friendly and talkative, said not a word to the driver. He was thinking: "One more shipment and he will pay me forty dollars a case—the son of a bitch, the bastard!" He flung his half-smoked cigarette out of the window.

Chapter seventeen

Often in the last few weeks Popito's thoughts had turned to Cassie. Once or twice he had met her in the yard and this prevented him forgetting her as he wished to do. He thought of her with a sad, hopeless longing because she was young and so attractive, and he was penniless and full of years. If there was warmth in her eyes when she spoke it was from gratitude, nothing more: she couldn't forget the day when she was down, right down, and he had given her all he possessed.

"Neighbour! Neighbour!" a girlish voice had called tearfully that day.

"Yes, who you?" Aurelia cried irritably.

Popito followed his sister to the back door. There stood Cassandra, the Osbornes' maid, so agitated she had forgotten she had on but a thin dress through which the sunlight outlined her body.

"They takin' away me things and I haven't a cent. You could lend me four dollars till the end of the month, Miss Aurelia?" The timidity in her husky voice indicated that this was a last desperate effort to raise the four dollars, that she was uncertain whether to give way to fear, grief or rage. "I have a friend who does pay it for me every month. He's a po-leece, but he broken bad dis month. If again I used to pay irregular for me furnitures I would say they have cause to take them; but I does pay every month, as soon as he put the money in me hand, and the first, first month Uh miss you goin' treat me so?" Her trembling voice kept rising. "And he takin' everything, everything, even me bed and mattress!"

"But what wretches!" Aurelia cried, her face going red. "Are they men? A set of *soucouyants*!" she shouted, shaking her fist at the men she could not see behind the fence. "It would be good to kill some of you! O Lord . . . chile, I'm sorry. And I, 'self, not a cent in the house."

"Pies, hot pies!" came the nasal wail of a pie woman going by in the street.

Cassie returned to the yard where men were calmly carrying away all of her possessions; and sitting upon the wooden steps of her room she appealed to invisible persons, whom she clearly imagined to be judges in some high court of justice, to see what was being done to her, "O Gawd, O Gawd!" And she reiterated as if for their benefit what she had last said to the policeman, how he had promised to bring her the money, how she had told his repossessor he was expecting a five dollar sou-sou, "but the man don't want to hear me, my Gawd!"

A butterfly had settled on a weed a few feet from her, an enormous and magnificent blue butterfly with tails, a rare sight in the city. Slowly it fanned itself with its wings; it felt secure; no one saw it; no one had time to pay attention if he did.

When Popito, who had followed Cassie, saw the men carrying her belongings out of the room and setting them on the earth, when he saw what was so personal and so richly associated with memories of pain and pleasure exposed to everyone's indifferent eyes, he sullenly kicked the stones beneath his feet and sighed.

"Lift it up, man, don't drag it!" the black repossessor was saying in a bullying tone, trying to sound important and authoritative to conceal his shame. "If you break the foot of that dressing-table you going to pay for it."

"All right, chief, don't quarrel, we goin' to lif' it good," replied the barefooted Indian cart driver with a whip over his shoulder.

On an impulse, muttering a curse, Popito took all his money out of his pocket—three shillings—and offered it to her. She thanked him but refused it.

"Girl, take it!" cried a woman's harsh voice. "You think is every day you does get somebody to give for nothing?"

Popito glanced up at Rose, the prostitute, who was standing in the doorway of her own room.

"Yes, take it," he begged in a low tone. "What will I do with it? Get drunk? Take it, man." He put the coins in Cassie's reluctant palm.

He went out of the yard saying to the repossessor: "All of you are bastards! You hear me? Bastards!"

"Oh, shut up, man," the repossessor replied. But the words had wounded him for after a while he muttered: "Every man have to earn his bread some way. . . ."

That night the old dresses and lengths of cloth Aurelia kept between the coir mattresses and the bed spring to make sleep sweeter came in very useful. She gathered them into Cassie's empty room and, laughing and joking she laid sugar bags on the floor and spread the old dresses on top of them.

"God bless you, Miss Aurelia," Cassie said. "Like you know how hard Flora bones could be."

The circumstances of her earlier life had not been such as to coarsen Cassie into the usual servant pattern. She had known both father and mother; she had had a home; both parents had been employed even in the hardest of times. Six years before, when she was thirteen, her father had died of a fall from an oilfield rig. There was no workmen's compensation then. The burden of carrying the family grew too heavy for Cassie's mother. Broken by work and poor food, worn out before her time, she was reduced to pushing a little box cart from door to door, buying or begging empty bottles and selling them to drug stores till death claimed her. Cassie had to live. Who could do so on eight dollars a month? Along came a policeman who had been a playmate of hers. Soon he was keeping her, providing her with furniture on the instalment plan. But he had begun to tire of Cassie; not she alone had charms. And one night when he could not have his way he beat her. She seized the pot of urine and threw it over him. So it ended.

If Mrs Osborne spoke harshly to her, tears of fright and embarrassment would fill her eyes. When something pleased her she would hum a tune, clap her hands to its rhythm and do a few dance steps. More than once she had come running into the yard late of a morning because she had been out dancing the night before. Hastily pinning on her cap and tying her apron strings behind her she would run into the house and, still breathing heavily, lay the table for breakfast. If Eldica, the other maidservant, came in then to clear away the litter left by last night's guests Cassie would eagerly, in a low voice, give account of the night's adventures, but without making a single mistake, without forgetting a knife or a spoon or mixing up the table napkins.

And now tears.

"You too foolish," said Eldica. "When a man beat you is because he love you."

"That's you, not me," Cassie replied haughtily.

Eldica was an older girl who had already had three keepers. Her tears had long dried up, she had learned to kick life in the face.

They lay talking in the servants' rooms, which were detached from the house. Just then they heard Justice Osborne's car crunching the stones of the drive. Cassie jumped up in haste, slipped on her shoes and ran to the pantry away from Eldica's mocking laughter. The judge's cold, clipped voice, his English accent, his unsmiling countenance as he said: "Clean that up," or, "Martinis for three," without glancing at her, made Cassie feel he was not subject to ordinary human failings. She wanted only to please him and escape unscathed from his presence as soon as possible. She measured the drinks into the shaker and while shaking them up with ice—perhaps it was the ice rattling like a shak-shak that caused it—she realised she would seek help from the *Orisha*.

It was a cult the slaves had brought from Africa. It had come to be known as Shango, a misspelling of Chango, son of Ob, who was but one of many great gods. Cassie's mother had belonged to the Shangoes. Once, she had told Cassie this story :

Late one night when she was alone at home a middle-aged man, a friend, had come to see her. Her husband was at work; Cassie, barely five, was sleeping soundly. The visitor, full of drink, tried to bully her into lying with him, and, when she ordered him out, pursued her through house and yard, round and round, determined to lay hands on her. In a certain part of the yard she had buried a cutlass (symbol of the god Ogoun), as instructed by the *hounbonor*. It was required that thrice daily, at sunrise, noon and sunset, she should sprinkle water on the spot, and that if she took a drink of rum she should cast some on that spot too before the glass touched her lips. She did it all faithfully, never forgetting. Now, her legs trembling with fear and with running, she was cornered in the yard by her unwelcome visitor, seized and flung to the ground. She thrust a foot against his chest and with all her remaining strength hurled him backwards, scrambled to her feet, ran inside, picked up the sleeping Cassie and fled to the home of a neighbour.

"Nex' day Uh find the cutlass there in the yard. Nobody dig it up. Ogoun 'self draw it out-a the earth to strike the man down if me strength did fail me. If it wasn't for Ogoun—I tell you!"

As a child Cassie had attended Shango meetings and had seen her mother become possessed by the spirit, fall shuddering and writhing on the earthen floor and dance with controlled abandon, unaware of the world around her, to the merciless beat of the drums. And she herself had become possessed and danced when she grew older. Cassie believed in Christ also and prayed to him; but Christ was unapproachable and far, while Shango, Damballa and Ogoun were potent and close, she had seen the evidence of their presence beside her. Feeling now the need to win a measure of mastery over those forces in life that were rolling her back and forth as the waves roll pebbles on the beach, she attended a Shango meeting in John-John village and shared in the sacrifice. She didn't catch the spirit this time, only sang with the rest and prayed for help. The vision of help that rose before her was what it could only be—a man.

Night had long fallen when Popito returned from Fyzabad. He went straight to his sister's, intending to give her some money, but almost on the steps he met Cassie. As soon as she saw him she gave him a smile so spontaneous, open and bewitching that he was shaken from head to foot. He felt a wonderful new strength surge through him. With a hundred and sixty dollars in his pocket and more to come age would be forgotten, fear demolished; happiness was his to take and give. The mad thought came to him to throw a few bills in the air just for the hell of it, to prove he was master now.

He seized her arm. "Cassie! How, girl?"

"Good, yes?"

"You still workin' at Judge Osborne house?"

"Still holdin' on. What about you, Mr Luna? No job yet?"

"I workin' now, man. It was high time. A good job too."

"What you sayin'! I glad to hear, Mr Luna. Miss Aurelia must be well glad too, she always worryin' 'bout you. So where you workin' now?"

"All about, man, doin' customs work. Only now you come home from work, Cassie? But lemme see you good—eh-eh!" He took her hand but at the same time stepped back a pace and looked her up and down. "In spite of all the hard work you lookin' nice, you know."

Cassie liked Mr Luna because he was kind, and because of his sister, her friend and benefactress, who had lent her money to buy a bed and made dresses for her for nothing. She laughed and looked aside, thinking he had had a drink or two. Popito felt with irritation that she was laughing at him.

When the morning sun warms the mimosa weed—Petite Marie—its tiny leaves unfold and its branches raise and open themselves to the sunlight. Popito's admiration warmed Cassie like the sun, her heart opened, she was ready to flower.

"Come and go to pictures with me tomorrow night," he said impulsively.

She laughed loudly, mocking herself and him, and pulled away from him. "Look, lemme go and sleep, do. I don't go to pictures." Mr Luna of all people!

The street lights had been turned off, the moon being three quarters full, and now the moonlight's mystery transformed everything it touched. Cassie's eyes were irresistible—large, liquid, soft as the night itself. "How you mean 'don't go to pictures'? Let us go, man, Cassie! You will have a good time."

"Eh-eh! But Mr Luna, you could ole-talk good, yes?"

"Look!" He fluttered the wad of notes before her.

"Well, now you have money you could get a lot-a nice women to go with you," she remarked indifferently. "What you want with me? I not your colour."

"To hell with colour! What a strange girl you are! Eh-eh! The truth is you have a boy friend."

"I have no boy friend, Mr Luna. But what you think Miss Aurelia goin' to say? She's the one friend I have, yes? Go and sleep, man, I don't want trouble." She moved to pass him.

He took her arm again. "What I have to do with me sister? She not supportin' me, it's I helpin' to support her now. . . . All right, then," he broke off suddenly, waving an arm and turning away.

And he was not Mr Luna, just a disappointed middle-aged man over whom she had power. What the hell, it was only to the pictures, she wasn't going to let it go any further than that.

"I wouldn't have a free night tomorrow," she said, looking down and rubbing her arm.

"When you will have one?"

"Saturday. Saturday I comin' home early, four o'clock. You want to go Saturday night?" And her smile now was one of coquetry.

"Good, ehn?" he said triumphantly. "Where you will meet me? At the corner. You . . . because of me sister—"

"You see? You would be shame if she knew."

"Oh, shame, what! She will give me hell because she want to protect you. It's a date. Saturday night eight o'clock. Okay?"

"Yes, good." She laughed mockingly and ran from him. "I gone! Goodnight!" she called without looking back.

They went to the Empire Theatre. He wore his good suit, she a flowered frock his sister had made for her. Even more attractive did she seem to him than on that day he had met her going to San Juan. She had thought they would sit in the pit with the workers but to her joy and pride they went through the front entrance among the well-dressed white and coloured folks and sat in the soft seats of the stalls. He put several bars of chocolate in her lap. She was amused.

"Like you buy a week's supply one time." She counted. "One tonight, one Sunday, one Monday, one Tuesday, one Wednesday—what about Thursday, Friday and Saturday?"

"Eat them, eat them," he urged, confused by her banter.

"What time you tell the chauffeur come back for us?"

"He waitin' outside."

"You buy chocolates for him too?"

The lights went out. He took her hand.

"You's a young boy again?" she whispered. He heard the smile in her voice. She put a bit of chocolate between his lips to ease the sting.

"Again? I ain't stop yet."

"What! Since all that time?"

"I look so old?"

"About a hundred, Daddy. Times change, yes? Nowadays hundred-year-old men playin' handsy-handsy."

"That is only to start."

She cocked her head at him in tart surprise. "It's so? Never start what you can't finish." She withdrew her hand and leaned away from him.

After the show they strolled to Lord Harris's square and sat awhile. He kissed her. "Eh! But you affectionate too!" she said, withdrawing.

"God, why am I chasing behind her?" he thought, feeling driven to prove himself still young. The very sound of her voice, husky, round, brimming with youth and the power to confer happiness upon whomsoever she favoured, maddened him into kissing her again and, when coldness persisted, caressing her breast.

"None of that, please, Mr Luna," she said in a dull voice, and rose.

He saw she felt ashamed for him. He tried to laugh it off. "You so touchy?" And thought in vexation, "Mr Luna!"

As they strolled homewards he, well-behaved now, asked about her work and life and what kind of people the Osbornes were and how they lived. For the first time that night she did not mock or rebuff him.

"Why you don't join the Negro Welfare, Cassie?"

"And what is that, now?"

"A party to protect the rights of the workers."

"They have rights, nuh! I didn't know," she remarked with such cynicism that he replied :

"If you don't fight for them you wouldn't have any. Come to a meetin'. What about Wednesday?"

"I don't know. What they could do? They got any strength?"

"It's by stickin' together we goin' to get strength."

"Oh. I see. Which part of Trinidad that happenin'? I never hear it yet. I seein' white people stickin' together, not black people."

"The times changin'. Ain't you say so you'self?"

"Yes, Daddy," she teased.

They were near the corner now. He kissed her good night on the cheek. She did not draw away this time: after all, wasn't it his due?

And some days later he took her to a meeting of the Negro Welfare.

Cassie was surprised to see that the workers felt themselves on an equal footing with Mr Luna. They called him Luna, sometimes Popito. And really he was one with them, no different, because when Mr Le Maître gave him some instructions (in a tone that showed he was confident they would be carried out) Mr Luna accepted the job quite readily.

Le Maître spoke of holding street-corner meetings more frequently despite police persecution, of all comrades taking part in speaking at these meetings and trying to get their workmates to join the Negro Welfare. "Comrades Payne, French and myself are going to Fyzabad. The rest of you must take more responsibility. I propose to you now that we change the name of our party. What we are aiming at is all workers united in trade unions, no matter the race."

Someone proposed the name Socialist Union Party.

French disagreed. He proposed the name Workers' Welfare: the word "Welfare" would appeal to all workers.

After discussion the meeting accepted French's proposal.

Popito rose. He spoke of the need to bring workers' wives into the organisation. "They have a big influence on the men, you know. We must show them we are strugglin' for shorter hours and decent pay. We have to bring servants into the party. Their highest wage is ten dollars a month, and some gettin' five and less."

French supported Popito. Cassie was one of three women present. When French expressed the hope that they would join the party the men looked round at them with encouraging smiles and comments. Cassie sighed. The other women giggled.

From that night Cassie's distrust of Popito dissipated. He was of her class. She could not believe in this unity yet, she must wait and see; but she believed in French and Le Maître quite simply, without any inner disputation, as if she had heard the gospel. The need for unity was a need she had inherited from her parents, from generations of workers. It was a dream no less powerful because she looked with cynicism at the possibility of its realisation.

"I hear the workers have big strikes in America," she said when they were going home. "They ever win?"

"Win, yes!" Popito assured her. "Sometimes the government brings out soldiers to shoot them, you know? Some die. You think that frightens them? Man, other workers strike in sympathy! Without trade unions what would happen? Look at us."

"So much-a trouble in this world to live in peace. It's not right, man. How it could be right? What we do wrong?"

Suddenly he was furious. "Do wrong, what? Do wrong, what!" he shouted. "We have any strength to do wrong? It's them who have the money doin' wrong. They killed you' father. What they give you' mother? Look at Aurelia—so kind, my God, so kind, and look what life doin' to her. They pushin' under the earth all the good human beings, Cassie."

"It's true, it's true," she said, and took his hand. "You have to take it cool, don't get upset. Life stronger than you."

They went to the movies again, and then he asked her to go swimming. "You want to take a sea bath at Carenage on Saturday?"

She smiled teasingly. "But how you could guess so good? That's the dead thing for the po' tired servant girl. No, man, I haven't a bathin' suit."

"Leave it to me."

"No, thank you. I will get one meself one day."

"Cassie, I have the money, man!"

"So what?" She wanted very much to go swimming; not since childhood had she splashed about in the sea; but to accept a gift from him meant opening a door.

He, feeling rather than hearing the lack of firmness in her refusal, said: "I'll get a nice two-piece one. I saw one only yesterday."

She made a "tchps", sucking air with a discontented sound through lips and teeth.

The day they went it was sunny and hot, the calm water flashed in the light like molten lead and dozens of black, mahogany and yellow bodies glistened in it, churning it to foam amidst shouts and laughter. Cassie put on the bathing costume he had bought her. She hardly understood the emotions that turned heart and head upside down. Now she wanted to be seen and admired by everyone and now she was ashamed of being seen so bare in public; now she felt with a thrill of pleasure that her figure would attract all eyes, and now she feared what the world might think; now he was too old for her and they would laugh, and now they would envy her because his skin was lighter than her own; now they all were enemies and now they all were friends; now she was a fool and would have done better to stay at home. . . . But at this point she walked out of the dressing shed into the light. She felt a light breeze search her thighs, arms and bare belly. She folded her arms against it, against the curious, admiring, lascivious glances that seared her as the sun seared her back. She raced for the concealment of the water, flinging herself into it.

"How I look? All right?" she asked with a laugh as he ran in after her.

"Champion!" he assured her. "Not one here good as you."

"It warm and nice!" she shouted joyfully, looking at Popito with elation. She flailed the water, blew laboriously through pursed lips, held on to him laughing and tried to throw him over. He dived, got his shoulders between her legs and tossed her over his back. She rose choking, a little frightened but laughing still, dashed water into his face and hid behind him. She put a headlock on him as the policeman had shown her. *He* had never taken her anywhere, only kept her to lie with him. Playfully, proudly too, she slapped Popito's strong and gleaming brown back and arms.

They ate under the trees. He had packed a basket with mangoes, bread, ham, cakes and two bottles of mauby. "So, like you think of everything, Mr Luna," she remarked with a laugh.

"Yes, Miss Walcott."

"For a hundred years old you not bad, nuh? Still takin' the girls for sea baths."

"Here, fill up you' face, you talk too much."

She felt ensconced by his maturity. He talked of what was always in his mind: why for so many there was no work; how Dollard's workers were divided; how many clerks, who looked so superior and well-to-do, were forced to borrow on next month's pay to live. Her comments, acute and apt, delighted him, showing she had long acquired an instinctive understanding of what weighed upon them. There came over him an unexpected tenderness for her, so that his former feelings towards her seemed coarse and evil.

While talking with him about life she was estimating him, the man, with her instinct, which listened to his voice, the quality of his laugh, and the layers of other meanings beneath the meaning of his words.

He was a good man. He would not hurt anyone. In all things was he generous. But there was something unreliable. . . . A gesture with his arm and the way he turned his head as he drew a hasty conclusion, which she instantly refuted—such signs as these confirmed for her a weakness in him. And nothing else drew her so close to him as this instinctive understanding that he needed a moral force behind him.

They frolicked in the water again, then sprawled on the shingle and finished what was left in the basket.

"Look, while we talkin' sun goin' down, yes?" she said. Laughing happily at the tenderness she saw in his face for her she ran into the sea for the last time.

The sky in the west was burning gold, overhead the clouds were red, and the still water reflected both the red and the gold.

"Look at the sun how pretty!" she exclaimed. "What is that, the sun? No, the clouds," she added, answering her own question. Lovingly she cupped the water in her hands but even as she did so the colours escaped her. "Look, like a carnival costume. Ehn? Pretty, man!"

The beach was deserted. The sea caressed the shingle. The old caretaker appeared and, leaning against one of the sheds, looked at Popito and Cassie and yawned as if appealing to them to give over and release him, but being a man of experience he sat down on a stone and lit his pipe. The gold in the west turned to blood. Imperceptibly a purple mantle rose and covered the hills. The sky paled as in death. A pelican skimmed the water, silent as a shadow, without a motion of his outspread wings, and disappeared into the stealthy night.

Popito put his arm round Cassie, flesh against flesh. For an instant he was sure she was his, but the light went out of her face and she eluded him. "You don't see the man lookin'!" she said, but he knew it was not the caretaker's presence that had turned her from him. She began singing while thinking: "He too old to marry someone and leave me. The younger ones, I know them—big stupid talk, ignorance, showin' off. . . ."

"Time to go out," she said, throwing water at him, and ran away.

When they were dressed they walked hand in hand up the undulating road beside the shore in the darkness fragrant with earth and ocean. A bus going to Port-of-Spain went by but they did not think to stop it. Such a day had never been.

She put her arm through his. "They say every star is a world."

"They no good to us. What they say is on them?"

"You askin' me? What I say is what I read in the papers—every star is a world."

"If the scientists say that they should be able to say what is on them too. They only guessin'. One thing I feel sure of: they have no bailiffs up there to persecute people."

She laughed. "Stop. Le' we look. You know any of the stars? Some of them supposed to represent bears. Another set, a man with a belt—Orion. Show me Orion."

"Orion is a sensible man, he gone to bed. No Orion there tonight."

"Well, if nothing else in you' head you have a quick tongue, that sure."

"Man don't know what is on earth and he investigatin' what up there. He can't settle his business down here and he talkin' about life up there."

"Yes. All the same, when you have time to look at it as we lookin' at it now, it's beautiful, really beautiful."

"Yes . . . beautiful," he said reluctantly and with such sadness that she pressed his arm. He put it around her and she did not resist. They came to a track leading down to the beach. He descended it cautiously, drawing her behind him.

"You not goin' home tonight?"

"Listen to the water, smell it. Smell the night. You not smellin' the sea at home."

"When a man start talkin' poetry to a girl—hm."

The shingle crunched beneath their feet. A fishing boat lay on its side. Long ago a young coconut tree had fallen in a wind and grown upward in a curve.

He drew her to him and kissed her hungrily.

"Tomorrow you spread your wings and gone, gone like the pelican," she murmured. She gripped his ears in both hands. "I will pull them off, yes? Gone like the pelican. . . ."

"Don't say that! My God, how you can say that?"

Never again, he knew, would he find someone so young and lovely to want him and to sweeten the sourness of his swiftly passing life.

"Help me to live, Cassie. Life hard. With you I can begin again, I have something to live for."

"Not you alone want help, Popi, I want it too," she whispered, her breath coming quickly.

Nervously at first she let him take her, then her doubts fell away and her spirit melted into his.

Little wavelets kept flinging themselves on the beach and sighing.

Chapter eighteen

On the following night Popito, entering the yard like a thief for fear his sister or niece might see him, went with Cassie to her room.

Sitting on her tin trunk he noted the little pine table covered with new oilcloth, the single chair pushed under it, the nails on which she hung her garments as she removed them one by one. "She got those nails from a soap box," he reflected. "She beat them with a stone to straighten them and with that same stone she drove them in the wall." Aloud he cursed the bailiff.

"I forget the set-a them long time," said Cassie, smiling over her shoulder as with quick, expert movements she made the bed she had risen from so early that morning. "If I was to keep thinkin' of people so and what they does to others I would be old a'ready."

Down to brassière and pants, she sat on the bed, on her face a barely discernible smile of self-mockery and submission. She rubbed one arm and looked down, avoiding his eyes. Her huge shadow leaped in the candlelight as though reflecting a struggle within her. Suddenly he sensed her desperate efforts not to sink like Rose next door.

He took her in his arms. "How old you are, Cassie?"

"Nineteen last month."

He held her off. "Only nineteen? So young? I have forty-one years. But I can still love, Cassie."

"I see so," she smiled, embracing him.

They were lying side by side. "You must move out of here," he said. "I will get a better room than the one I have. You will come with me?"

She made no answer.

"Popi," she said at last, ruffling with a finger the thick black hair on his chest, "you know the sayin', 'New broom sweep' clean.' Everything is nice to start but afterwards come blows, and all is yours and nothing mine and you could t'row me in La Basse when you please. I don't want that. I will come and live with you but the day you raise you' hand to strike me don't look for me again. I ehn't make for war, I make for peace." She sighed. "If you kind to me and treat me good, as now, you needn't be frighten' I would leave you for anybody else."

She was telling him not to leave her for another either. Suddenly he felt the weight of his responsibility for her happiness, for her moral and spiritual health. He had spoken from his heart without thinking, as was his way; she had revealed to him the full meaning of his words. Could he carry this burden—the deliveries for Yankee and now her? He said:

"Cassie, God strike me dead if I ever raise a hand to you! Whatever I buy is for cash and in your name. If we cannot agree take the things and go, take them and go, man! What is the sense havin' a woman who don't love you? Take it all and go!"

She said nothing: she was listening to his other voice. Again she had an indefinable sense of frailty in him intertwined with goodness. She felt she was saying goodbye to the dreams of girlhood, goodbye to the hope that she would love a young man who would marry her. "So be it," she thought. "He's not a bad man, I feel sure. Only God knows how long he will stay with me."

"Marry her," he was thinking. "No, she likes fun and dancing. She will love some young chap, then what? Besides. . . . But who are you to think your skin too light for hers, Popito? Who are you to think you'self too good for a black girl, a servant? All that life pass' now, everything change up for you, man! She herself don't expect it. . . . Anyway we'll see how things go. . . ."

Holding him by the ears she said merrily: "You see? This is what I will do you if you beat me." But suddenly impelled by an urge to protect him she pulled his head on to her breast and with a mother's hand caressed him.

Three weeks later Cassie moved into a room in Belmont with Popito. His thoughtfulness amazed her. He rose before she did, at five in the morning, lit the coalpot and boiled coffee so she should not go to work hungry. When he saw how tired she was sometimes when she came home after nine at night he angrily told her to leave the job.

"What you wearin' out you'self for for a miserable eight dollars a month?"

"Jesus Christ, help me and let it remain so always!" she prayed, feeling frightened.

Cassie's devotion to him grew day by day. When his desire for her could not be satisfied he made no complaint but hastened to ask if she had pains and give her pills to allay them. She recalled how in a similar situation the policeman had abused and cuffed her. Nor was he constantly dissatisfied like some young barnyard cock. And so when she gave herself to him it was not her body alone she gave him.

Occasionally—and self-consciously because of his age—he took her to a dance. She had always more partners than she could please. With a happy self-assured smile she would say to those who offered themselves: "You too late, boy, I have the next one with Fred. Come sooner next time." Like bees around a big bag of raw sugar the young men hung about the girl with the husky vibrant voice and the eyes that shone with gaiety or flashed in sharp anger. She forgot all about Popito. But one night when he danced four times with an unknown woman who looked part Spanish and whose skin was light Cassie called him and said: "Take me home. I'm tired."

"It's only twelve o'clock," he said, wondering what had upset her.

"Nevertheless it's time to go."

"All right, come, I'm ready. Who trouble you?"

"Nobody trouble me, nuh? Left to you you would dance whole night wid dat woman."

It was a happy task, and a rewarding one, persuading her that he wasn't straying: it rejoiced him to know that she was still all his.

One day he went out promising to return by nightfall. She came in late as usual, undressed and dropped asleep at once. Around midnight a consciousness that all was not well jolted her awake. She felt in the bed beside her; he had not returned. She looked at the alarm clock on the shelf—twelve-twenty. Silence and darkness covered everything like a blanket, stifling her, crowding her mind with fears. She lay awake for hours. Her ears seized on every occasional footstep. She wept. "The Spanish woman! And I so foolish thinkin' he really goin' to stay with me for good. No, it can't be true, I never saw anything, he's just the same. . . . Killed! O God, no!" She saw him in the road, bloody, crumpled up, disfigured. Terror seized her. She got up, lit the oil lamp.

She tried to read a magazine her mistress had thrown out. Behind the words were other words: "What part of the country? What does he do? What keeps him so long? Perhaps he gambles, perhaps he's drunk. He needs me, I should be there with him. What you sayin'? He not a child! Maybe so, but you have to watch him."

Hearing movements about the yard she opened the window and the dawn burst in. Before it some of her fears dissolved but other fears grew sharper. No, it was not a woman. An accident. She refused to look at death, the morning was too bright for death. "Ogoun, Damballa, help me!" she cried to the sun.

Let madam make her own tea. She sat at the table mending one of Popi's shirts, the need for food forgotten.

At ten o'clock he entered. "Cassie."

"Popi!" she cried, starting up. "Where you been?" She took a step to him angrily, ready to give vent to her rage or weep with relief. "What happen?"

"Nothing happen. What could happen?" he replied with a fond smile that seemed to her to be hiding something from her and begging forgiveness at the same time.

Tears filled her eyes—tears of relief at seeing him well, tears of rage that he had been happy while she suffered and of jealousy of that Spanish woman. She was suddenly sure it was the Spanish woman and saw her in his arms and smiling at him as she had done that night.

"What could happen to you—yes! Ask me that. Whole night I didn't sleep because of you," she cried. "If nothing happen to you then where you went? Only one thing to keep a man out whole night and that is a woman. What you take me for, a coonoomoonoo?"

"Hush, man, hush!" he interrupted in a low severe tone, quickly shutting the door. "I don't want everybody to know my business."

"You haven't even the shame to deny it, 'self!" she shouted, longing to punish him because she was tied to him by economic and spiritual bonds and was horrified at the thought of breaking them.

"Be quiet, man! I haven't been with any woman. The truck broke down last night, we had to sleep in it. This morning we had to get a tow into town."

She fell silent, ashamed. She sat on the bed. "O Lord, I was so anxious! I hope I never pass a night like that again." She wiped away the tears with the heel of her palm.

He sat beside her and soothed her but knew he was soothing himself too, for now he appreciated much more fully how slender was the thread between them and disaster. Suppose he was discovered with the drug—the opium—whatever it was? He was finished. And she?

Cassie listened to his words but as often happened some inner ear was listening to his voice. With abandon she threw her arms round him and pulled him down upon her on the bed. Her mind was full of "whys". She kissed his unshaven cheeks, his lips, and pulling up his shirt caressed his muscular back. "Why you have to go so far?" she murmured. "Why you never talk to me about it?"

The spell she had cast disarmed him. From his heart overflowed the fears he had long wanted to reveal but had long suppressed. "If you know how dangerous is what I am doin' you wouldn't even ask that."

"Well, tell me." She kissed him, pressed him to her, her heart sinking.

"If the police catch me they will jail me, beat me up. You mustn't tell a living soul, Cassie. I believe is opium I take from customs. It's in the goods I clear for this man in Fyzabad. That's how I make money. I help Payne with it, though, and I help the Welfare to print pamphlets. But they don't know how I get the money. My life is in your hands now. If I wrong you is only one word you have to say to the police."

Somehow his body had become very heavy, she felt she was stifling. "Don't talk stupidness. Sit up, you heavy."

"Why?" he asked playfully. "Why?"

"No, not now. Sit up, sit up!"

She rose but he grabbed her hand. "What's the matter? You disappointed in me? You vexed? Speak the truth!"

"How I could be vexed?" she asked with an innocent expression, opening her eyes wide. "Everybody have to find a way to live, that is life. Let me go, Popi, I have to cook, I haven't eaten since last night." She pulled away from him and went out.

And that huge weight which had seemed to press upon her now pressed upon him. He lay on the bed motionless.

When after some time she came in with what she had cooked for them both she was singing. His heart, deceived, grew lighter. He praised her cooking and spoke about the truck, how the engine petered out, what the driver thought and how he, Popito, disagreed with him and said it was the coil, and how he had got a lift to the nearest telephone at seven in the morning. Now and again she made noises appropriate to the sympathy, surprise, amusement or admiration he wished to evoke. She went out to wash up and he to shower. When she came back in he was fresh and clean. He had made the bed and was lying on it. He called her with a smile, but knowing what it meant she said, "Comin'," and went out again. She returned with a bucket half full of water, a scrubbing brush and soap: it was some time since she had scrubbed the floor and now the task seemed urgent.

"It's now you goin' to scrub?" he reproached her. "All night you didn't sleep. Take a rest."

"And finish this when?"

"Leave the damn job, man! How much money you makin' so? Leave it and you would have time for this."

"Leave it and you get in trouble and then where I will be?"

He sat up. "Cassie, why you holdin' this thing against me? You don't see nothing leave for me? All the months I been out of a job you think I didn't learn that well? There is nothing for me to do now except fight, Cassie."

She paused in her sweeping of the floor and looked round at him. "Dishonest fightin'? Ben Le Maître know what you doin'? I don't think so."

"For Christ's sake keep you' mouth shut and don't tell Ben anything, he suspect me already."

She continued sweeping energetically. Suddenly he realised they were far apart. Fear of and hatred for her rose in him.

"I'm not a boy, I'm not young, you don't understand that? No chance for me now except what I could take."

"Just lift you' feet, please," she said without looking at him and with a patient air that expressed her disillusion.

He jammed on his hat and went out without a word. He had thought he knew where he was going but after walking two hundred yards down the street he turned back. He returned to the room. Cassie, on her knees, her dress tucked high over her legs, was scrubbing the floor. "Damn it, she's in my way and I am in hers!" he thought, flinging his hat down. She spread a sugar bag for him to step on, bade him remove his shoes. He lay on the bed and read the paper, scarcely making sense of it. Above the rasp of the scrubbing brush he heard her singing an old lullaby in French *patois*.

"Little darlin', sleep
Befo' you see one-eye *diable.*
If he come papa kill him,
Tie 'im in cocoa bag,
T'row 'im in ravine deep.
Shut eye, darlin', sleep,
darlin', sleep."

She sang it gently as if it were a sweet reminiscence of an event that could nevermore recur.

"Cassie?"

She glanced at him with that same coldly reproachful expression.

"A hundred dollars, a hundred and eighty-five dollars—that's not something you throw to one side like fig skin. This morning I come back with over a hundred dollars. Look." He pulled the bundle out of his trousers pocket to show her.

She turned away indifferently. "You not gettin' it by honest labour. If it is opium this man not smokin' it himself. It's you helpin' him to ruin the lives of Chinese workers. How you could say you fightin' for workers and yet you doin' this thing to them?" She faced him. "Get a nex' job, Popi, I beg you. I want to love you, yes? Let me feel you are honest, true—no matter what happen."

The strap of her slip fell down on her arm. He remembered it falling down just that way on the beach that night in Carenage and how she had not troubled to push it back, and how it had magnified his sense of intimacy with her and excited his desire. Now the balance between them had shifted. He felt helpless before her, stripped of the power she had conferred upon him as a result of his maturity, his money, his masculinity.

"*Carramba,* man, we have to live!" he cried. "You goin' to love me if I come home day after day without a cent in me pocket? Answer me that! And how you think I will feel to live on you? You think I want to live on *ma ca fou'chette* from Judge Osborne table? My God, Cassie, try to understand, try to understand!"

She continued scrubbing.

Terror came over him and with it an annihilating sense of his complete uselessness to himself, to her, to anyone, to any idea. It was so strong it almost robbed him of breath. He lay motionless with his face to the wall. He kept thinking of death, the thought would not leave him.

All day he lay like this. His unrelenting gloom distressed her, she had not expected to see all she had uncovered in him. Night came. She took him in her arms. Life came back to him. Her need of him gave him strength; her voice and her love fought off his despair.

Chapter nineteen

Next morning she vomited after drinking coffee. She thought she had had too much curry the night before, but the recurrence of the vomiting over several days convinced her she was pregnant. The last of her girlhood fled with its jokes and gay flirtatious glances. Uneasily she sat at home, her mind full of strange new thoughts to which she tried to grow accustomed. As soon as she began to show Mrs Osborne would fire her. How could she be hard on Popito now? When in self-defence he said only rich Chinese could afford opium, not the poor, she only sighed. In truth, no one wanted him. He could find no other work. Formerly he had saved little, he had given so much away; now he was saving for their child. She saw the jobless in a quite new light—men with families they couldn't feed. Her interest in Workers' Welfare grew apace and she read the booklets Popito gave her. Often those simple tracts on economics were too abstract for them both. Then they sought help from Ben Le Maître, from French, from Payne, whoever was handy, and argued, refuted, weighing experience against books, seeking the path out of the forest.

One evening there was talk of raising money to print a booklet when up jumped Popito.

"Leave it to me, I will get it."

Le Maître looked sharply at him then took him aside. Journeymen bakers were gathering for a meeting before taking up the night's toil and Le Maître did not wish them hearing him.

"Where you get this money from?" he demanded.

"I am working, you know that. How you mean, where I get it from?"

"Listen to me, Luna. You are working for Yankee, you are taking goods from customs—"

"So what? He has a shop, he's a wholesaler, so what, so what?"

"How much is he paying you?"

"That is my business!"

"It is my business too because we are comrades and what you do affects us all." Le Maître spoke deliberately. "You have a woman in your care now. She's going to have a child. Even a customs clerk without such responsibilities cannot stand the cost of publishing a booklet, far less you. I have heard rumours about Yankee and the opium trade. You are helping him. Answer me—is it so or not?"

"What you mean by 'helping' him? He pays me to take goods out of customs, he never tell me what else is in the cases." Popito looked at Le Maître defiantly.

"Naturally. But you are not a fool. You know very well he pays you plenty to keep your mouth shut. You have lowered yourself to his level."

French had come up and stood listening, looking down. His presence embarrassed and agitated Popito still more, but it stimulated Le Maître, who was accustomed to having an audience and needed one.

"We have the task," he continued in a louder voice, "of raising all workers to a higher level, of inspiring them to sacrifice their jobs in the struggle against their oppressors, even their lives. But you are making a good thing of driving them still further into the jaws of the vilest capitalists, men who will stoop to anything to make a cent. Popi, come to your senses, man!" he added in a loud angry whisper, grasping Popito's arm. "If you had faith in us—conviction—it would not be so."

Popito wrenched his arm free. "What you know about me, what is goin' on inside of *me*!" he said with trembling lips, striking his chest. "Who the hell you think you are to tell people how to run their lives? A lot of big words and books—"

"If you did not have that girl in the family way I would put the police on you myself!" Le Maître interrupted, speaking slowly and angrily.

"That's not the way to speak to a man," French rebuked Le Maître calmly.

"How else you want me speak to him? He is—"

"That is no way to speak to a man, comrade Le Maître." French's tone warned Le Maître he had gone too far. For an instant their eyes met and flashed.

"All right, you speak to him," Le Maître said, and left them, his lips compressed.

Popito too was moving away but French took his arm and led him to the back of the hall apart from everyone.

"Ben don't know how to speak to people sometimes," French said. On his face was a kind, persuasive smile but there was steel in his voice, Popito felt. "He is right, though. I know you agree. Ain't it so?"

Popito was doubled over as though something was tearing at his entrails. "Right, what, Percy? What he knows about me?" he insisted. "What you know about me? Month after month a man goin' like a homeless dog from one boss to the next and all you gettin' is kicks. I am a man, not a dog, I have a right to live!"

"That's true, Popi. That's true. But if you persist in doin' this thing we kean't keep you in Workers' Welfare."

"Right. I will leave now!" Popito jumped up excitedly.

French took his arm again. "Wait, wait," he said, smiling gently. "Hear me. You know what Cassie will do then? You know? She will leave you."

"You mean all-you will try and make her leave me!"

"By no means. But I'm tellin' you I can see the strength in that girl. She believe in us. She wants a better life."

"And I mean to give her a better life. I want to educate the child, I want to rent a house, I want to marry her, I want to live an honourable life. Look, keep away from my life. Leave the girl alone or it's blows between you and me!"

"Keep cool. Nobody want to encourage the girl to leave you."

"The day you do that do me the favour to kill me one time and done."

French nodded thoughtfully. "Man, look at me—glad to be alive though I don't know where the next meal comin' from. It's not to say I am not frighten' sometimes, but I take it cool, I don't bother wid it. You goin' to wait till you have money to say, 'Now I am goin' to live'? Man, life passin' all the time, you have to use it as it come' to you. Look at our West Indian people. How many have a decent life? But they live, man, they laugh, man, they make themselves happy. Since slavery times it was so: we had to find a way to enjoy life—or dead!"

Behind French's smile something flashed in his eyes like the glint of the sun on a blade; at the same time Popito smelled his warm breath malodorous from rotting teeth, and he envied the man's indomitable courage and fanaticism that made him ignore personal suffering.

"Raise up you'self, man," French added. "What you say? We need you, Popi."

"Comrade French!"

Le Maître was calling him to the meeting, which was about to begin. Popito reluctantly followed French and joined the others.

They began discussing how to organise the journeymen bakers. Le Maître, French and Payne had by now confined their activities almost exclusively to the oilfields; a man was needed who would visit the bakeries at night and persuade the men to join the union that had been formed. "They are ripe for unionism," Le Maître asserted confidently.

Silence fell. One sighed. Another shook his head.

"I will undertake that job," said Popito.

"We need someone with experience of the trade," Le Maître replied, lowering his eyes.

Popito sprang up. "What experience? What you talkin' about? You need experience to convince a man to come to a meetin'?" he challenged, looking as if only his distance from the platform prevented him from attacking Le Maître physically.

French too stood up. "What sort of reasonin' is that, comrade chair? Where is Luna to get experience—"

"Right there," voices interrupted. "That's right, he must do the work. He could work with Winchester. . . ."

"Comrade Luna, are you prepared to carry out this task?" Le Maître rasped.

"That's why I offered to do the job. What you think, I want to hear the sound of me voice?"

Laughter.

"Very well. If you have any difficulties, call on one of us. Are you all in agreement?"

Heads nodded. One man said humorously: "Give them a good shake up, comrade Luna. We need a stick to beat the others with, man."

Winchester, with whom Popito was to work, was one of the leaders of the journeymen bakers. He was a very thin and tall man close to sixty, with a long face dried-up and lined, and long, thin grey moustaches stained yellow from smoking. He read a great deal and was possessed of an uncommon facility in the use of words. They flowed from his lips with the noisy frothing of a shallow stream; he was continually on stage; a single question from an unwary interlocutor was enough to call forth a half-hour lecture on the intentions of Hitler or the role of Stalin. He disliked Popito because Le Maître had sent him and because Popito "treated him slight". "Luna?" he would say with his unpleasant sneering cackle. "Luna-tic. You have either dropped the 'tic' or they forgot to put it on, one of the two."

"Oh, you damn ole fool," Popito said, turning away.

With a few words peppered with a laugh Winchester tried to prejudice the men against Popito. When Popito went into the bakeries they returned his greeting with smiling condescension that puzzled him. "You was ever a baker?" some said. "You ever work in a bakery? No? Eh-eh! And you tellin' us. You good, man!" Or: "What union you in? No union? How you know it does work then? You come and you get money out-a we and we ain't seein' nutten for it. What it is, at all?" But all the same they listened because he was transparently sincere and didn't "talk big" like Winchester. They felt he was one of them.

Meetings were held on alternate Saturdays, very small meetings, no more than a dozen men. Popito had misgivings about old Winchester from the start. Bull-headed, enjoying the sound of his weak voice, the old man talked to the workers at length, scarcely giving them a chance to express their views.

"Boisson wants our vote. Is he raising our wages? No. Can he raise our wages? Of course not. Can he tell the master bakers, 'Raise these men's wages'? They would laugh him to scorn. It is we, united in a union, to force them to put their hand in their pocket. Look at the transport workers in England, man, look at the general strike some years back, they didn't beg nobody, man, they tie up the whole of England!"

"Yes, but black people not united man, that's the trouble," some were saying to others.

"Union kean't succeed in Trinidad. Some fellas in the rumshop now—"

"Some feel Le Maître not white, so what he could do?" a squat bright-eyed man broke in.

Winchester became impatient, waved his hands disdainfully and abused these men, calling them fools. One shouted back, some laughed with angry scorn. Popito felt the men's morale disintegrating. With his swift bow-legged stride he went to the platform.

"Wait a minute. You talkin', talkin' as if you swallow a gramophone needle," said he, ignoring Winchester's protests. "Comrades! I goin' to tell you something I was readin' only yesterday. When the English workers was formin' trade unions they didn't have it sweet, you know? The police pick up two of the organisers and sent them to Australia as convicts. Suppose the workers had said, 'Man, trade unions can't succeed in England,' where the English workers would be today? Nearly two hundred years pass since that time. Unions all over the world now. The chief obstacle to formin' a union here is ourselves. Don't mind what the boss say, he can't live without us."

"All right," said one. "We strike and he take on unemployed workers. Who going to feed us? You?"

Very slowly did the meetings grow. But the feeling among the journeymen changed sharply some weeks later when the master bakers began to talk of laying off men and cutting wages. It was at this time that Joe began to attend meetings.

Winchester, introduced to him by Le Maître, said in his bombastic little voice, laughing incredulously: "Want to join us?"

"Elias is supporting the Welfare in his magazine and giving it publicity," Le Maître told him. "He is standing for this area, the most impoverished in the whole of Port-of-Spain, in the November elections. He wants to learn first-hand about the people's conditions. He will be useful to you. Let him join the union—why not?"

"You have already formed a union?" Joe asked.

"We are not registered, Mr Elias." (Since he was sure to become a councillor and his father had money it was as well to give him the Mister, Winchester thought.) "We are trying to bring in a majority of the journeymen bakers. But come and talk to them. Why not?" He laughed unpleasantly.

One Saturday more than eighty filled the schoolroom in which they met. It was in the upper half of an old George Street building, the lower being a dwelling house.

Among those in the hall was a short man called Ellis. He was a master baker who was too poverty-stricken to side with the big men. He had an oven beneath an old shed among the cesspits of Clifton Hill, employed two men to help him with the baking and delivered bread by bicycle to a few shops in the district. He went regularly to church and had come to rely upon his Bible for guidance in all his affairs, both his affairs at home which he termed "matters of state", and his business affairs, in which he always did his best to be scrupulously just. Sometimes when his men were working he would read aloud from his Bible, seeing with difficulty through an old pair of metal-rimmed spectacles hooked to one ear with string. He read aloud not for anyone's benefit but because the words meant more and were more beautiful when he did so. Reading in a grave voice, absorbed in what seemed to him the truth, he never noticed when others smiled.

He had gone about that week encouraging the journeymen bakers to attend the meeting. His interest in doing so lay in the fact that the big bakers were driving him out of business by dumping bread on the shops. Whatever remained unsold was no loss to the grocer, the baker purchased it from him and gave him a commission into the bargain. Ellis could not afford this. The conditions under which he worked made it impossible even to deliver bread on time: frequently the weather delayed the rising of the dough, or the wood for the oven was wet. It was cheaper to side with the journeymen in their demands for higher wages and call for the abolition of commissions to grocers and sellers.

On this Saturday Shorty Ellis stood near the doorway reproaching newcomers for being late, admonishing them as if they were children and he an earnest but overworked school teacher, and urging all to "go up, go up and take your seat, comrade". He wore a long jacket, clearly not his own, a buttoned-up but collarless shirt and a pair of unlaced old shoes that made a clopping sound as he walked about.

Joe, accompanied by Camacho, came up the stairs. (Before, when the meetings were small, Joe had thought it not worth his while to attend them, he could make no thunder.) He shook Shorty Ellis's hand and greeted him in a tone of contemptuous banter, winking at Camacho.

Ellis was no fool but he pretended to notice nothing. "Glad to see you," he said gravely. He was about to say something more but broke off, grasped Joe's arm and in his usual loud, fearless voice cried out: "Brother Winchester! Brother Winchester I am talking to you. You see we have spies in our midst today?"

Men turned to look. They saw two detectives in plain clothes who had just come in. One of them was the notorious and hated Duke. This flashily-dressed man, so well-known for his cunning, savagery and persecution of his victims, was sitting sideways at a school desk that was too small for him, his enormous shoulders hunched and his crossed legs thrown carelessly in the aisle while he leisurely picked his big white teeth. Some women had come in, Cassie among them. They asked him to move his legs. He did so indolently, provocatively appraising their figures as they went by him. He and his companion paid particular attention to Cassie.

Cassie, too, had seen Duke but she kept her head straight, knowing well his reputation.

Making a clopping noise with his loose shoes Shorty Ellis came up to the table on the platform. The crowd was animated, consciously or unconsciously expecting some good result to come out of the meeting because of the numbers present and their evident militancy. Winchester rapped loudly for silence.

"Brothers and comrades," said Shorty. "Now, that is not the way. Time to start business. Pay attention. Consider, brothers, the jep-jeps. Touch the nest and what happens? They fly at you like bullets. They sting you and drive you away. Yet you are thousands of times stronger than them. One jep-jep you would stand and fight—all of them if they come singly. But why are they stronger than you?"

"Unity," said someone.

"That's the thing!" cried Ellis gladly, looking about, clapping and nodding. "Unity, brothers and comrades. Unity will put this whole island in our hands. Remember what Saint Paul say to the Corinthians. All-you don't read you' Bible, but you could always find somet'ing in that book to suit you when you want it. Don't laugh, you in the front row there, Saint Paul say a wise thing." Ellis raised a finger and shook it as he quoted: " 'The body consists not of one organ but of many; if the foot should say, I am not the hand and therefore I do not belong to the body, does it belong to the body any the less for that? If the ear should say, I am not the eye, and therefore I do not belong to the body, does it belong to the body any the less for that? The eye cannot say to the hand, I have no need of thee, or the head to the feet, I have no need for you.' " And he gestured emphatically with a downward motion. " 'It is those parts of the body which seem *most contemptible* that are necessary to it.' And again: 'If one part is suffering, all the rest suffer with it; if one part is treated with honour all the rest find pleasure in it.' Like Saint Paul see us gathered here today and he say those words for us. What you say? Right or wrong? You who was laughin', what you say?"

"I ain't laughin' now, pal. Saint Paul know his business."

"Like he was a baker," said another facetiously but without irony because the crowd was with Ellis, waiting on, anticipating, his conclusion.

"Some of you talkin' of strikin'," Ellis continued, "but strikin' without unity—I tell you, you might as well go to Duke there and lash him and let him take you down. . . ."

They laughed, they shouted their approval when he sat down.

Winchester, inflamed by the numbers in the hall and their mood of hopeful expectation, felt impelled to show the tyrants what sort of a man he was; he would show the workers too there were other leaders besides Le Maître; Le Maître was not the only one! And carried away by the scent of power he began in spite of himself to speak fiercely and without discretion in his weak, bombastic voice, his long moustaches jumping up and down.

"Why have they sent their spies? They realise the anger of the workers. They want to use the police against us if we strike. But they will not succeed, *I* tell you so! If every bakery in the city go on strike they will fear for their profits and give in to us." He outlined the case for the journeymen, comparing their wages with the cost of living. "I say, comrades, let us demand a meeting with the master bakers and demand a fifty per cent increase—otherwise we strike!"

Some cheered, some laughed, some mocked the cheerers. Joe, clearing his throat and sniffing as if he had a cold, looked fixedly and with irritation at Winchester. The old man had tried to patronise him, harping on his youth and inexperience; he tried to show Joe he was unwelcome by continually lecturing him about "my people", "we Negroes", and did not openly scorn the Indians only because there were some among the journeymen.

Joe started up from the bench and in his small voice commented sarcastically on "this haste to strike". A strike was a last resort to be used when every means of negotiation had broken down. "To strike is all very well, but where is your strike fund? And I tell you frankly, to make a demand for fifty per cent increase is absurd. They will never meet it. And even if it were possible for you to force them to meet it they would raise the price of bread and everyone would suffer, you most of all."

Manny Camacho could contain himself no longer. Joe had not yet sat down and he was up. Joe perceived with irritation from the way Manny shifted from foot to foot, hands on hips, head thrust forward, that his friend was stimulated by the crowd and anxious to display his political muscles. In a determined voice that rang nervously he said:

"We must teach the workers the meaning of militant trade unionism. Why is the comrade afraid of facing the issue? Why this red herring about increased bread prices? The struggle calls not for friendly-society speeches . . . reading of minutes . . . filing of correspondence," he threw out his pale soft hands scornfully, "it calls for militant action, the struggle of class against class, not class collaboration—"

Approving shouts interrupted him and drove him on.

"Sooner or later we will have to man the barricades!" he cried, adjusting his glasses. "It will come to that. Some of us will die but we will not run when the police bring their rifles—"

Popito, on the bench behind, grabbed his arm. "Shut up, man! Look police takin' down what you sayin'."

A foolish embarrassed smile came over Manny's face and he sat down.

Ellis was saying: "Brother Camacho, that is not the way. You come here with you' head full-a book-readin' and you want to plunge the workers in sorrow and misery." Joe laughed uproariously at this, nodding approval. "Let me ask you this, is you goin' to support the fatherless children if police shoot a few workers and put the rest in jail?"

"Shootin', what, man, shootin', what! The man is foolish," Winchester snorted. "Nobody wants war, we want money."

At last one of the journeymen, a peelman, got up. He was a young mulatto with a grim, hard expression and long blue-veined arms from which the shirt sleeves had been rolled back almost to the armpits.

"Mr Camacho not a baker, he have no right to talk for us. What we want wid war? We want food. He got all the food he could eat, his father got a shop. I say, gentlemen, let us form a deputation now to meet with the chief bakers and talk dis t'ing over. They kean't live without us, bread sellers kean't live widout us. We is the key men. I agree fifty per cent too high. We call for twenty-five per cent."

There were more speeches. A skinny little Boissonite with a tremendous voice kept trying to break up the meeting.

"Listen to the dotish ole men," said he, referring to Winchester and Ellis. "It's they going to lead you out of Egypt."

In the room below the hall a woman hammered the ceiling in protest against the noise of stamping boots, but no one heard her. After Ellis had lectured the Boissonite sternly and made everyone, even the skinny Boissonite, laugh, a delegation was elected to meet the master bakers. The meeting came to a close. Everyone tramped downstairs talking, arguing and laughing.

Chapter twenty

They all gathered in knots upon the sidewalk, arguing as they had feared to argue upstairs; feeling deceived, despairing of improvements in their lot; growing angry with one another and swearing; seeking relief from the image of their weakness in bellowing laughter.

Duke pushed them aside. "Break it up, break it up!"

A spark seemed to jump from man to man.

Cassie, adopting a sneering tone which she evidently wished Duke to overhear, said: "And what about when they raid the whey-whey gamblers? When they kean't get evidence they does put whey-whey marks in you' pocket and say they find them there."

A short, long-chinned woman replied: "Yes, chile, yes. And I hear they hold Boysie. It's true?"

"Yes, in the rum raid Saturday night up John-John. About twenty police and detectives surround the place, but Albert get away," said Cassie, lowering her husky voice delightedly.

Duke seized her. "What you know about the rum raid?"

"But what's wrong with the man?" cried Cassie, looking about her with frightened eyes. "Let me go, man, let me go-o!" She tried to pull away.

The knots broke up. All came together with a collective roar about Duke and his victim. Some pushed forward, others back. Duke smiled when he saw their strength, knowing they didn't know how to use it. His eyes searched the faces for the one he wanted. His grip made Cassie wince.

Joe saw the short, long-chinned woman looking up angrily and fearlessly at the tall Duke, whom she abused, crying: "It's a shame, it's advantage—takin' advantage! You's a dog!"

"Take her down," Duke said.

The other detective grabbed the short woman and dragged her protesting down the street like a bleating, resisting goat being taken to the slaughter.

The roar grew louder. People came running to the crowd from all directions.

"He lookin' for promotion," said a man of about forty with a shiny and bumpy bald head. "It's a stripe he want from the white people."

"But I heard what she said," Joe protested to those about him. "A perfectly harmless remark. I heard—"

"Go to the station, Elias, go, boy! That man is a criminal, he will kill her!" said Ellis.

The crowd began to follow Duke, who was alternately pulling Cassie and pushing her before him. He said something to her with a smile and she suddenly ceased to resist him or cry out. Around them voices were advising Duke what to do to himself and making encouraging remarks to Cassie; bicycles accompanied them with ringing bells; cars forced through with horns blaring.

Popito and the young peelman with wiry, blue-veined arms had stayed upstairs, discussing how to approach the master bakers. The shouts of the crowd brought them down to the sidewalk in a hurry. When Popito saw Cassie being carried off he was about to run to her but Joe held him.

". . . no doubt of that," the man with the bumpy bald head was saying. "I see one time he suspec' an Indian jeweller of stealin' silvers and meltin' them down, but he couldn't prove it. That time not everybody know he's a detective. So he start visitin' the jeweller's wife and makin' himself nice wid she. And you know he make the woman leave the man? It was six months before he could get she to lay down wid him, but when at last he have her like a tame fowl she tell him how the husband stealin' silvers and meltin' them down, and where he have the furnace. Duke arrest both-a dem. The man and the wife. The man get three years and the wife six months. And the judge congratulate him on a fine piece-a work. . . ."

"Mr Elias goin' to the station," Shorty Ellis was saying. "Who again hear what the girl say? Step forward, all who hear. We have to see justice done, man!"

"I hear but I 'fraid to put foot in the station, me dear," said a woman. "Let Mr Elias go, he big and strong."

Duke hailed a passing taxi. The two detectives pushed the women into the taxi and got in with them. It sped off. Bicycles raced after it recklessly and merrily; women followed, running.

"Of course I'm going, don't be absurd," Joe was saying to Popito, who was obviously agitated. "Are you frightened? You're so pale, what's the matter? But my God, to what depths of degradation human beings sink!" he added half to himself with horror and disgust. "One might as well live in the jungle . . . sons of bitches!" He kept wiping his forearms nervously.

Popito whistled a taxi. He pushed Joe in. "Besson Street station," he said.

A group of women was standing outside the station when they reached it. Some said they had heard that the girl Duke arrested had stabbed a man. A woman breathing rapidly from running came up to them, a hat in her hand.

"I get she hat," she announced with pleasure. "Quite in Prince Street it blow off."

Joe and Popito, having stated their business to a young constable in the entry, were taken into the charge room. The sergeant was sitting at his desk, his belt and collar unbuttoned. The short, long-chinned woman, who never ceased shouting, had woken him from a nap. Before him stood Duke and Cassie.

Popito gazed at her horrified. From her swollen, battered lip blood oozed; her entire personality was altered by the expression of hate, cunning and desperate resolve in her eyes. The blood sang in his head; but a look from her made him pull in the reins, a look not of fear—there was none in her now—but of warning.

Duke smiled. "You know this man?"

"Yes."

"What is his name?"

"Ask him you'self."

"Don't look at me like that," he said, and struck her with his heavy hand across her mouth, jerking her head back.

The blow made the hate burn deeper in her dry, glittering eyes. She spat out blood at his feet. Popito clamped jaws and fists.

"Look here, sergeant," said Joe, trying to control his indignation, "I can clear all this up. It is a pure misunderstanding. I saw everything that happened."

"Where you were?" the sergeant grumbled irritably.

Joe noted his dissolute, twisted mouth and felt from his tone that he wished to be rid of him and the embarrassment of Duke's brutishness as quickly as possible.

"I was right there when she was arrested. I heard what she said."

"Why you didn't come before?" the sergeant demanded of his blotting pad with a sulky look. Then realising the folly of his question he said harshly to the young constable: "Constable Ward, take a statement from this man."

Joe, glancing at Cassie, followed the iron-shod heels clanking before him. From the constable and the rooms there emanated a harsh, pungent odour of disinfectant which was ever afterwards associated in Joe's mind with the fetishes of police discipline and man's hatred of man. In a subdued tone the young constable asked Joe his name and address. He made two attempts before writing the name correctly, his attention was distracted by what was going on in the charge room. Joe felt that all these words he was putting down were absolutely no use to Cassie. He, too, kept listening.

The sergeant had asked Popito for his name and address.

"You know this woman?"

"Yes, she's my wife."

"Your wife? You are Luna and she is Walcott?"

"Isn't he keepin' you?" Duke said to Cassie.

"Yes."

"What you know about the raid in John-John?" the sergeant asked Popito.

"Nothing."

"Do you know that one constable was killed in the raid and another severely wounded?"

"I know nothing about that and my wife knows nothing about it."

"Walcott, where were you on the night of the raid?"

"Nowhere!"

"So you were nowhere. You mean you were some sort of a jumbie?"

"Yes."

"Be careful how you answer in here, woman."

"Where was Luna that night?" Duke asked.

"At home."

"Don't lie. Luna came home late. Isn't that the case?"

"No!"

Popito saw Duke's enormous black, smooth, perspiring nape bulging over his collar. He felt he was going to hit Cassie again and he shouted: "I was at home!"

And at that moment Duke punched her in the belly, forcing her breath out in a grunt.

"She's expectin' a baby and you lettin' this animal beat her up in here?" Popito shouted, quivering.

"If you don't keep quiet I'll put you in the cells. Don't make no noise in here," the sergeant warned.

"He came home very late, isn't it so?" Duke's fist was poised. "I don't want to hear about no babies, I want the truth. He came home very late. Speak the truth." Again he punched her, again she grunted.

"Watch you'self, Corporal Duke!" said the sergeant.

Cassie was looking fixedly at Duke, like a snake. That look exasperated him. He had begun to realise that with every blow he struck her he was forging a piece of steel, a keen-edged sword. "He came home late from Fyzabad, isn't it so?" Duke looked at Popito. He began to twist Cassie's wrist. Her eyes never left his face. Her nostrils flared. Suddenly she lowered her head and bit him. He struck her savagely across the mouth. She staggered, licked the blood from her lips and spat in his face. Just in time the sergeant saw the cold bright spark in Duke's eyes.

"Watch you'self, Corporal Duke!" he shouted, banging the desk.

Duke's fist remained poised. He opened it and pointed to Popito. "You were in Fyzabad that night."

"I was not! And besides, you have no right to question me, I came in here of my own free will, I'm not under arrest."

"You had better speak," said Duke, "because she is under arrest."

"I was not in Fyzabad, I tell you!"

"What was the last date you were in Fyzabad?"

"Explain you'self," the sergeant said with irritation. "What his being in Fyzabad got to do with the rum raid?"

Duke went to the desk and whispered to the sergeant.

Joe came in wiping his forearms. The sweat was pouring out of him now.

The sergeant read his statement. "All right. You can go."

"I can go?" Joe repeated with angry surprise. "You are holding a trial behind locked doors and I can go?"

"You keep quiet, Elias," the sergeant threatened, rising and buckling his belt, evidently with some sort of guilty awareness that he should at least mitigate the irregularities of his subordinate's behaviour by observing the regulations in regard to his own dress. "You keep quiet or I will arrest you on a charge of obstruction. Constable Ward, put this man outside." He buttoned his collar.

"If you think you can get rid of me so easily you're mistaken. I'm going for a lawyer and I'll be back in here with one in half an hour!" Joe flung off the constable's hand and stamped out.

The threat urged restraint on the sergeant. After attempting to frighten Cassie with a severe warning he released her from custody. She said not a word, only looked at him with those same unblinking eyes in which hate burned.

Outside two taxis were prowling. Popito signalled one and took her home. She lay down in that same silence, numb, quivering, aware that everything was changed in her, nothing would ever be the same, and she needed time to understand the change.

"Oh, God, Cassie, it's my fault, it's my fault!" he whispered.

She pulled him to her breast and stroked his head.

The pains began, then she began bleeding.

That evening she lost the child. The doctor he had rushed to call ordered her to hospital.

"Popi, don't get discouraged," Cassie begged him weakly. "We could always make another baby." But she remembered how only that morning he had put his hand on her belly beneath her nightdress, hoping to feel his son's movements, and how she had laughed and said he wasn't big enough yet, it was much too soon; and she wept for Popito now though she had not shed a tear for herself before.

Chapter twenty-one

André was dressing for the Lorrimers' ball. In an agitated frame of mind he looked in the mirror at his face. It displeased him, but there was nothing to be done about it so he looked away. His dress suit seemed to him ill-fitting, or perhaps not fashionable or something. "It's time I had another, I've had it four years."

His social indiscretions, he reflected, would scarcely be unknown to the Lorrimers, and he was not a familiar in their circle. The invitation, reaching him only a week before the ball, suggested a reluctant recognition that he was in some degree a social obligation. In childhood he had romped with the children; it was Phyllis's twenty-first birthday party; he worked with her at Dollard and Company. To fail to invite at least one member of the de Coudray family, who were very well-to-do, might have given unnecessary offence. (Why, it was wryly conceded in certain quarters that had he chosen to live in France Mr de Coudray might have been no ordinary "*Monsieur*" but a "*Monsieur le comte*"—some people held that it was his right.) And then the two families did pay each other social calls. No oftener than once a year. Your turn this year, mine the next.

Despite all this, however, despite the offensive fact that the invitation had arrived only six days gone, he was flattered and eager to attend. He would find himself in the very cream of Trinidad society. Most likely he would be the only coloured person present. He wanted to forget for a while the onerous pledge he had given Elena, it frightened him. At the same time he felt uncertain of his reception by this crowd of Trinidad and English whites. The bowtie would not stay right and for the fifth time he unravelled the knot with angry fingers that would not obey him.

The invitation said "from 9 p.m.". He arrived at a quarter to ten, long after the dancing had begun: he must not seem too eager. He had given thought to the mode of conveyance. The Lorrimers' home was little more than half a mile distant; but to walk to a ball was impossible, a tram unglamorous, his old car absurd. He called a cab. When it stormed up over the loose white pebbles of the drive like some hot-blooded steed and skidded to a halt at the veranda steps at least half a dozen women, and Sir Richard himself, came out to greet the new arrival. He had achieved the desired effect.

He detected, however, a certain disappointment in their greeting. "Oh, it's you, André. Do come in." Evidently some very important guests had not yet arrived.

He bowed languidly over Lady Lorrimer's hand. He offered congratulations to Phyllis, who had rushed out, and kissed her hand with an air intended to amuse and charm the elderly ladies and Phyllis herself. He succeeded. And all the time while going through his performance he was conscious that he was a coloured man and everyone knew it, but nevertheless he was triumphing. Phyllis took him inside and introductions followed.

Some eighty guests had already arrived and more were expected. Two huge rooms on the ground floor of this old mansion in the Spanish style had been turned into one. Everywhere were bright lights, baskets of yellow and red flowers and potted palms. Through inner doors one glimpsed a platoon of spotless servants. The polished floor shone. Faces were bright with expectation, even the faces of the servants. The girls moved about like gaily coloured birds, chattering, squealing, expecting wonders. They looked continually at the new arrivals, afraid of being outshone and hoping to see *him* among them, that him who tonight took one form and tomorrow another.

Loneliness came to André and stood between them all and himself. He looked idly at Betty de la Mare, who seemed dazzled by her own splendour. Her gown invited him to look on her plump arms, the top of her bosom and the whole of her beautiful back. She was waiting nervously for someone to look at and approve her. She saw André, to whom she was always distant, and now waved and smiled. Then she blushed and absently touched the strap of her gown. She smiled and glanced at a stranger, who did not notice her, then as if not wanting her smile to waste she glanced around for someone who might welcome it. But at that moment there was no one and she wilted. The black musicians struck up a tune. André went to her rescue. At once the sparkle returned to her eyes.

Suddenly she twisted in his arms. "Ah! Brian *Foster*!" she breathed ecstatically. "Bryan!" she cried, waving with her free hand.

André released her. "You're free to go."

"Oh, no. . . ." She was embarrassed.

When the music ceased André joined two girls he knew. Others fluttered up like moths to light. They bathed him in the poetry of their sex. He wanted to bury his nose in their hair and their bosoms. On his left was Marie-Louise. His eyes never left her face but he saw all of her through her gown. He understood that his attentions, his eyes, his voice were arousing desired responses in her.

They danced. The feel of her body against his, firm yet yielding, set his heart pounding. In the back of his mind appeared Elena with her beautiful black eyes that were luminous with trust and incapable of deception. He remembered her kisses. But he drove her from him because she had no place here. He was ready to fall in love now, this minute, with Marie-Louise.

The music stopped. He went into the unlit side veranda and with his hand he struck one of its cold, fluted iron supports. "What is love?" he thought. "How is it possible to feel *this* for her and at the same time *that* for Elena?" He did not hear the low voices of the couples sitting in the scented semi-darkness.

A car rolled up the drive. Lady Lorrimer was standing at the head of the steps. "Here you are at last," André heard her saying in her most amiable tones. "We thought you were never coming."

And now Phyllis by her side cooing, "Hello, Gwen!" with happy, grateful, even respectful intonation.

The new arrivals were the Osborne girls, Gwenneth and Esther. Evidently these were the important guests for whom, André thought, he had been mistaken. Esther was colourless, he did not give her another glance. Gwenneth's personality drew all eyes to her. She was below medium height but in her erect carriage, her short, precise prim step and her blue eyes with their fearless direct gaze he perceived a haughtiness that repelled him. He took an instant dislike to this girl with the upper-class English accent he considered affected. When they emerged from the room in which stoles were removed—it was February and the nights were cool—and wear and tear made good before a mirror Phyllis introduced them to those who seemed most worthy.

A black maidservant in stiffly starched white cap peered round a doorpost and tried to catch Phyllis's eye. When she thought she had done so she gesticulated hurriedly, exposing the whites of her eyes and stretching her mouth unnaturally to shape words, evidently wishing to convey that some misfortune had occurred. No one had time for her now.

The music began again. Some of the old folks in the veranda looked in with paternal smiles—"Never mind me, I'm just enjoying the sight of young people"—to see if their sons were dancing with the Osbornes.

As soon as the dancing stopped Phyllis rushed with her heavy gait to Gwenneth's side. Now Gwenneth laughingly asked the plump, plain Phyllis before some admiring young men to confirm that something was quite, quite true, wasn't it? And it seemed to André that this English girl was pleasantly aware that though she was simply dressed the contrast between herself and Phyllis was entirely in her own favour. He felt too that the simplicity of her dress was in some way an indication of her indifference to the company, and this also irritated him. Someone called her name. She turned with a frown to see who was interrupting her. It was Jack, Phyllis's brother, a cumbersome, perspiring person famed for his skill at soccer. A bored expression of mild distaste came over her face. Having dropped him a few words she clasped Phyllis's arm and went off with her, stepping primly in her very high-heeled shoes—she did not like being short.

In between dances Arnold Walker appeared, almost the last to arrive. He was a thin blond of thirty who spoke rapidly in a soft voice and with a merrily conspiratorial, seductive smile, either holding the hand of his interlocutor or putting an arm around him. About Arnold there was something slippery and pliable that André did not like. Especially was this the case when Arnold met "nice people". Then his eyes would grow moist as he bowed and he would suck his breath in through his teeth as if hungering for them. He pounced on Phyllis, who was not dancing. Bending over her hand, which he pressed fondly in both of his, he was laughing at his own pleasantries as he always did.

"Hello, diplomat!" André called to him.

"Ah, hello, André. Having a good time?" said Arnold, coming up and shaking André's hand while looking around for more important people.

Suddenly he could not nod and grow moist-eyed fast enough. He moved towards Gwenneth Osborne with his arms outstretched. He began to dance with her.

The black maidservant peered round the doorpost and tried to catch her young mistress's eye. When she was sure she had done so she again gesticulated, exposed the whites of her eyes and laboriously formed words with her mouth. She was too intimidated by the company to step on to the dance floor and convey the disastrous tidings that salt had got into the ice-cream they were churning by hand.

Phyllis pretended not to see her.

That careless buoyant feeling with which André had come to the house, that youthful assurance that the world was his and they could not help but like him if he chose—this feeling was now quite dissipated. When he danced with Marie-Louise he was conscious of her sensual joy in the touching of their thighs and hips. But not only Marie-Louise tormented him; Gwenneth Osborne, she above all, with her strutting about, her toleration—so did he imagine it—of the obsequious Lorrimers and her pleasure in the court others paid her—it was she who infuriated him.

Swelling out his fat brown cheeks the saxophone player behind the potted palms blew into his instrument and the music began once more. Someone had called for a Paul Jones. Girls formed circles within circles of men. The girls skipped around in one direction, the men in the other. All sang:

"There's a brown girl in the ring,
Tra-la, la-la, la . . .
And she looks like a sugar and a
Plum, plum, plum."

Then a change of music and a scramble for partners.

André found himself facing an elaborate coiffure from what he termed "the Osborne retinue". For an instant its wearer seemed uncertain whether to submit to the fate before her. Smiling, not looking at him, she put a hand on his shoulder. Again the change of music, again the scramble to form concentric circles and again a boisterous rush for partners. Gwenneth, looking about her with laughing eyes, was about to drop out when she spied André standing alone. She saw from his ironic smile that he would have been glad to be released from this childish game which grown-ups were playing. That he was different from the rest attracted her. She ran to him.

"Come on—quickly!"

They danced.

"You're André de Coudray, aren't you?"

"Yes."

"Do you play the violin?"

"I do."

"I thought so. I often hear you practising in the mornings when I go for a ride. Yesterday you were playing the first movement of the Tchaikovsky concerto."

She was probably, he thought, the only one here who could recognise the music. "You know it! Like it?"

"Oh, I do! You played it awfully well."

"Thank you. Do you play?"

"Long ago I fiddled a bit. But no more."

"Whom did you hear in England?"

As most of his musical knowledge had come from recordings he listened with avid attention to the details she gave him about Kreisler's use of the bow, Heifetz's technical mastery, and how, when a string had broken during a performance of a Bach chaconne, he had simply ignored it and made do with the rest. Now they sat and talked music. To all music lovers it seems that they alone understand the hidden significance of their favourite compositions. She kept trying to explain the significance he had missed, and even Heifetz missed, in the Tchaikovsky concerto.

A pair of immaculately creased pants came up to claim her for the next dance, which had begun.

"Oh, is it your turn?" she remarked indifferently and, with a smile at André, she floated away.

He noticed her look at him from time to time as the night wore on. Her glance seemed to say: "Why don't you come and talk to me or ask me to dance? No one treats me this way, and besides it's unpleasant." At last with a quickening pulse he obeyed that glance. They danced for a second time. Then a third. After that he avoided her.

To his surprise Arnold Walker came up and, while fondling his hand, asked him how he was getting on at Dollard's, he had not seen him for such a long time, and had he met Miss So-and-So who plays the piano? "Come, I'll introduce you," Arnold said.

It was after two o'clock in the morning, supper had been served, and the men in the study, which had been turned into a bar, were telling dirty stories. Some of the guests were leaving but André had no thought of leaving now. He had danced with Miss So-and-So who played the piano, and she was not bad either. Several times, inadvertently, his eyes met Gwenneth's.

It was going on for three when the Osbornes said goodbye.

Gwenneth turned to André: "Come and see us, won't you? I'll be at home on Saturday. We'll have a musical feast."

She spoke like a thoroughly self-assured English society girl to whom it never occurs that anything she says or does can be out of place, and everyone around heard her.

André bowed with smiling insouciance.

Not long afterwards he walked home well content with the evening, his conquests, and with Gwenneth herself.

Chapter twenty-two

Not until next day, when the night's glamour had dissolved, did reality assert itself. He would go to the Osbornes', listen to some music with Gwenneth, and then what? How could one live on two levels? It necessitated insincerity, downright dishonesty, from which he shrank. How could one, on the one hand, espouse the cause of black workers and, on the other, ingratiate oneself into the company of one's British rulers and command their respect? Pride stood before him. He did not go to the Osbornes'.

Some days passed and Gwenneth phoned him. Wouldn't he come on Saturday afternoon? She had just received a new recording of the Brahms concerto. Had he heard it? Oh, he must!

And, pride appeased, he went to the Osbornes'. After all, he said to himself in extenuation, why seem ungracious?

There are some people whose walk clearly expresses some trait of character, and Gwenneth was one of those. When he entered and she came rapidly towards him on her high heels with her firm short step, holding herself very erect, André felt uncomfortably that she would have her way in spite of anything anyone might say or do. Yet the next moment her radiant smile and her funny little half-bow as she shook his hand seemed to say that with him she felt obliged to submit to his will and was glad to do so.

"I'm so glad you've come. I'm all alone this afternoon. There won't be a soul to disturb our concert."

"So she planned it this way," he thought, "and her parents don't know she invited me."

They looked through her records. She put on the Brahms. She began to do what he detested, to hum bits of it, smiling with closed eyes in imagined rapture. She spoke of Schnabel, the pianist, whom she had heard, but smiling in such a way that he felt her enthusiasm was less for Schnabel than a form of flattery towards himself. She put on a jazz record. "Shall we dance?" He pretended horror. He begged for Tchaikovsky's second piano concerto.

The sound of a car in the drive broke the spell they were weaving. Doors banged and the judge and a strongly-built Englishman of twenty-eight or so came up the steps. Gwenneth introduced her father and David Primrose.

The police inspector, thought André as he shook hands.

In the judge's large blue eyes there was a bored expression. He had an unpleasant trick of blinking. Though thick with the flesh of middle years he held himself erect, like Gwenneth. He was the product of a long line of landowners and merchants. In the eighteenth century a famous ancestor, overburdened with riches derived from West Indian sugar, had built himself a great showpiece in Surrey, Morden House. Later he had been knighted. After this it became the tradition for all young male Osbornes to attend Eton College. Selwyn Osborne had long been nourished by the traditions of his forebears and—though he did not clearly realise it—the traditions of his country that had once ruled the waves unchallenged. They formed a kind of impenetrable shell in which he moved secure. At forty-five he was high in the service. He felt he could look up with confidence at the plums within his reach.

"How do you do?" he said. "Are you the musician? Yes. I've heard about you. My daughter seems to think you're rather good. I know your father. Very able, very able. . . . You will have a martini, I s'pose. Do you like them dry?" he added, in his tone a suggestion of careless condescension that was due to André's youth.

Cassie, all fire suppressed, stood just within the room, a dull-faced black girl neatly clothed in cap and apron.

"Four," the judge said.

"Yes, sir," Cassie said and disappeared noiselessly as she had come, avoiding André's eyes as he did hers.

Sub-Inspector Primrose said: "Cigarette?" to the judge. Then, eyebrows mildly raised, silently held out his case to André. The latter noticed with animosity the breadth and pinkness of that powerful golden-haired hand accustomed to holding in horses and controlling Blacks.

The sub-inspector remarked: "I had a rotten time trying to telephone from the club this afternoon. They need a telephone booth there very badly."

"Mm. Yes. I've not had very fortunate experiences with booths," the judge replied in a bored tone, removing a shred of tobacco from his lip. "But at least in a booth you don't have to take it lying down."

He drew down the corners of his mouth and blinked rapidly as he always did when he said something he considered witty. Gwenneth and the guests laughed politely but the judge, unsmiling, went on to say he had had a slice at the fourth hole, it was damned awkward. Sub-Inspector Primrose said he had got into the bunker at the fifth and had had to pick up. The judge said the seventh green was in an atrocious condition, didn't anyone bother to speak to the greens-keeper?

"The mole crickets are very bad this year," remarked the sub-inspector.

"André, do you play golf?" asked Gwenneth.

"No. Tennis only." André would have liked to give some rein to his personal charm, but in the presence of this Englishman who was large with the authority derived from a foreign land, a man whose background he could not even guess at, whose experience of life was so much broader than his own, he suffered a strange paralysis.

A black hand put down before the judge an embossed silver tray heavy with martinis, and withdrew.

The sub-inspector waited politely for André to finish what he was saying, then remarked to the judge that the headlines in the evening paper were not encouraging, the Indians were at it again.

"All of this trouble with Gandhi would not have arisen if England had not educated the Indians beyond their intelligence." The judge, who had spent many years in India, addressed this remark to his martini. He interrupted himself to sip it (the others taking the opportunity to do likewise) and continued: "Culture is something the Indians are incapable of assimilating. You will come across cultivated Indians but you can rarely call them cultured."

"But they've had a very ancient civilisation," André protested, his ears reddening.

"Barbaric. Barbaric," the judge commented, sipping. "They're a very intelligent people, there's no question about it, but still too immature to make proper use of the knowledge England's given them. Plagued by superstitions and holy cows."

The sub-inspector chuckled appreciatively at the "holy cows".

"Not a Hindu, are you, Mr de Coudray?" The judge blinked bored eyes rapidly.

"Yes."

An instant of shocked silence. The judge's mask fell. Then he laughed. "Splendid!"

The sub-inspector smiled at his martini, caressing his blond moustache.

Just the moment for an exit, André thought, and smiling also, rose.

"Must you go, Mr de Coudray?"

"Yes. Pleasant meeting you, Mr Osborne."

Gwenneth went out with him. "Till next Saturday?" she said, drawing a quick breath as she grasped his proffered hand.

He saw that this proud girl felt embarrassed at the very idea that she might find herself in the position of having to accept a refusal from him.

"Till next Saturday."

"Why did I say that?" he kept thinking on the way to Elena's, feeling uneasy. "I'll call it off."

It was good to be with Elena. On one side of her lived an Indian jeweller who worked in a cubby-hole downtown, fashioning wonderful filigree bracelets out of silver. From his house came Indian songs on a gramophone with a metal horn, and the scent of the coconut oil they used for cooking. A schoolteacher lived on the other side. Every night he rode off on his bicycle to give private lessons to backward students. An appetising odour of black pudding being fried came from his rented wooden house which sun and rain had blackened. This, André felt, was truth, earthy and bitter, hateful yet dear.

Elena was alone, preparing dinner.

"Hello!" she said joyously. "I knew you were coming."

"How did you guess?"

"I felt it."

He held her hands and kissed her. She blushed with happiness.

"Guess where I went?"

"Where?"

"Valencia. We have a friend up there who manages a big cocoa estate. It was wonderful wandering under the cocoa trees. So shady and cool. And slippery too after the rain. Year after year the leaves fall and decay, and that scent mixing up with nutmeg mace, it was so poetic I wanted to cry, and so *good*—I mean, it wasn't only beauty, goodness too, you understand?"

"Yes. Beauty and goodness. . . ." How like him she was inside! All the same Turgenev was mixed up in it.

"And the river—simply roaring, you had to shout! Suddenly a huge yellow bird flying out from the forest. Honestly, I felt so soothed and excited and . . . frightened and happy, wanting it to go on and *on*."

In her glowing black eyes was love for himself. He, the spirit of him, had been in that forest. He wished he hadn't gone to Gwenneth's. She began moving about, putting butter in a saucepan, breaking eggs in it and whipping them.

"Have you had dinner?"

"No. I was hoping you'd invite me."

"Of course." And a smile over her shoulder.

Almost three weeks gone she had said: "Mother told me she spoke to you. I'm sorry she did it." Her face had been cold, almost severe. "I don't want us to become engaged yet. I don't think either of us is . . . sure." He only looked at her and she saw what she had hoped not to see. "And we mustn't see each other too often," she added desperately. His eyes dropped. She had decided rightly and he knew this.

She had begun going out more, had even been to a couple of dances with old schoolfriends; but she had only felt more hurt and lonely than ever. Now just to look at him was happiness.

"Did you do anything special this afternoon?" she asked while they were eating. All along she had talked to keep from asking this.

"I was at the Osbornes'. Gwenneth phoned me. She wanted me to hear the Brahms."

"Was it good?"

"Yes, very good."

Just a tiny pause before she asked: "What is she like?"

He shrugged. "Not bad. Rather arrogant, I think."

"Does she play an instrument?"

"No. You know something? It's most unpleasant when someone invites you to listen to that kind of music and starts to hum it at the same time."

"Did she?"

"I can't stand that."

"I suppose she knows a lot about music, though."

"She's listened to a lot. She has a certain feeling for it."

"Have some more bread."

"No, thanks, I've finished."

She got up and cleared away. They went into the sitting room. She didn't turn on the light.

"André, you do feel quite free, don't you? I want you to." Again her face was cold.

"Elena . . ." he began and broke off, blushing. He took her hands.

She crushed his fingers in hers but turned her head aside. "No, don't." She pushed him away gently.

Suddenly he exploded. "That arrogant old fool! 'Britain educated the Indians beyond their intelligence.' I felt both insulted and helpless."

Elena looked at him silently, in her eyes reproach. Why couldn't he forget those people? Gwenneth and her father were like a crown of thorns on his head.

He left early. For long Elena sat there in the half-dark like a wilted flower.

Next Saturday he went again to Gwenneth's. . . . There is fascination in looking down from a great height and feeling compelled to grasp the safety rail, which suddenly seems quite insecure.

They played more records. This time her mother was at home. He heard her voice calling something to one of the servants from upstairs. "Does she know I'm here?" he thought. "She must. She doesn't come in. But if I were Inspector Primrose?"

He began to comment on the music, the execution of a phrase, the orchestration, the weakness and strength of the composition; he picked out and named chords, named instruments, as if he were the conductor at a rehearsal. He was reassuring himself, asserting his strength. He saw that to her he was brilliant, almost a magician. He wanted her to feel that beside him she was quite ordinary. Her interest was still at its height when he assumed a look of boredom and rose to go.

"Oh! Are you going?"

"Yes. I have an appointment I must keep."

She nodded slowly, almost a regal consent to his departure. "It's been wonderfully interesting," she said, going to the front steps with him. "I wish I knew half what you do about music."

He began to say goodbye but she, ignoring this, asked, suddenly making a decision: "André, do you ride?" She blushed but looked straight at him.

He made a motion of dismissal. "I've never ridden in my life."

"Will you come riding with me?"

"Impossible. I'd fall off." He laughed and took two steps down.

She followed him, arms folded as if holding in eagerness. "You won't, I'll see to that. Don't you trust me?"

"Should I do so?"

She tossed her head. With that gesture she seemed to say she would not be fooled with. Nevertheless, she crossed the lawn with him. She glanced at him from the corner of her eye. He saw not only admiration for himself but determination to have her way and vexation that he had reduced her almost to the point of pleading.

"I'm a very good horsewoman."

He laughed. "I'm not questioning *your* ability, Gwenneth."

"I didn't think you'd be afraid," she remarked, disdain in her smile.

"I'm *not* afraid!"

"You will come, then?"

"At least I'm afraid for my hands." He looked in her eyes and resistance left him. They said: "It would be so pleasant to be with you out there in the Savannah, by ourselves." He said: "Ring me. Will you?"

"All right. Cheerio." And in her smile now was triumph.

He was just going out when the judge's car swung into the drive. They nodded to each other.

And at the dinner table the judge: "Where did you meet this young fellow?"

In Gwenneth's eyes, raised to her father's, came a distant blank. Esther said: "At the Lorrimers' ball."

Mrs Osborne's head was shaking on its thick red neck. Silence but for the clink of forks on plates. Cassie, standing at the judge's elbow with a dish of pigeon peas, glanced from the extreme corner of her eye at Gwenneth.

"Lower. Don't lift it into the air," the judge scolded.

As usual Cassie was unnerved at sight of his pale, black-haired hand as he helped himself.

Mrs Osborne cleared her throat.

"Clearing the decks," occurred to Gwenneth.

"He's a musician, I'm told," Mrs Osborne said in a tone that implied: "It takes all sorts to make a world."

"A very good one too. I think he's brilliant."

"Nice to be friendly, I'm sure," the judge continued, "but you don't want to get mixed up with the wrong people."

"He's the first real gentleman I've met."

Her mother cleared the decks again. "We hope you'll meet others."

A sound of munching and crunching. The potato chips were very crisp. Eyebrows lifted, Mrs Osborne glanced at Cassie. "Beer for the master."

The judge, over his upraised fork: "Popular in the district?"

All looked at Gwenneth. She tossed her head. "An intellectual? I shouldn't think so."

Cassandra stole the plates away. She brought the beer and tried not to look at "Justice's" hand as she poured it for him.

"He seems to know the Lorrimers very well," said Mrs Osborne in a tone that disclaimed responsibility for the Lorrimers' actions.

Cassie's discreet exit, and her discreet re-entry with the sweet: stewed guavas.

"Poison fruit," said Esther. It was the accustomed family joke about this dessert.

Mrs Osborne, head shaking in denial, said: "You do them very nicely, Cassie."

Cassie always stewed for the cook, who could not do them well. A sudden shy smile lit her face and made it beautiful. "Yes, ma'am," she whispered.

"Coffee for me only," said the judge. "I'm much too fat."

Gwenneth felt firm ground once more beneath her feet.

"You should come riding with me."

"Largo is what I need at my time of life, my dear, not one of your bouncing prestos. I'll stick to golf, I think."

The atmosphere at the de Coudrays' dinner table was quite different. André had not turned up for dinner and the family was speculating on how he had "managed to get in there". A stranger could have been forgiven for making the assumption that they were discussing a difficult son who had unexpectedly passed his finals with honours and was about to be launched on an enviable career.

Chapter twenty-three

They went riding in the Savannah. It was his first lesson. The mare was quiet and he had not disgraced himself. They dismounted and lolled on the grass beneath a tree while their horses grazed.

"Were your parents born in France, André?"

"No, in Trinidad."

"But your grandparents came from France."

"No, you'd have to go much further back." He sensed what she was after. In an indifferent tone he gave her the old family legends about his white ancestors.

"Are they old-fashioned, your parents? Mine are real fuddy-duddies."

She loved parties, late nights, picnics, galloping about the Savannah on a frisky mare. Her parents did not always approve. They liked her association with David Primrose.

"What's he like?"

"Frankly, rather dull."

There was a subtle flattery in these confidences. Her eyes seemed to say that if he wished to he might kiss her and she would not fuss too much. But he pretended to notice nothing.

In a society whose intellectual level does not rise above bad movies, or gossip in the veranda after four in the afternoon, picnics and parties are essential to pass the time. It was inevitable now that the Lorrimers should plan a picnic down the islands and that André should be among the first to be invited. It was a long weekend. Nearly all the guests had gone to St Mary's bay on Gasparee island on Saturday afternoon. Gwenneth had not found it possible to sacrifice the party at the Colonial Secretary's home. She had persuaded André to go down with her on Sunday morning.

From Stauble's bay on the mainland they crossed by hired launch to Gasparee island. The beat of the motor echoed lazily across the glassy ocean that was blinding in the early light. With a flap of his great wing a pelican rose from the water, circled, dived, sat with a kind of lazy contentment and, throwing his head back, swallowed the catch. An old fisherman rowed by, the bow of his boat cleaving the thick water that curled lazily before it like molten glass. He hailed the launchman. They spoke in *patois,* the old man never ceasing his long, easy strokes with the oars. Gradually his voice died away in the distance.

In the inlet they were approaching the shadows were still deep and the water seemed especially cool and tempting. Figures were running down to the covered jetty to meet the launch. Bare legs and arms and excited voices surrounded Gwenneth. The usual crowd, André saw: Marie-Louise, who gave him a look tinged with reproach, Betty de la Mare, Bryan Foster. . . .

They ascended a steep path between enormous rocks to reach the old wooden house. André lingered in the side veranda, his eye caught by a garfish motionless in the blue-green water. He remembered—the veins of sunlight in the water brought it back—that time of adolescent purity when, with the shock of revelation, he had realised the beauty of early sunlight on dew-drenched grass, the magic of the bush, and earthy odours had awoken desires that frightened and delighted him. In the mornings, beneath the trees, far from the sounds of "ordinary" human life, he would watch the awakening light, feeling truth in him and all around him, in the ant, the flower, the rustle of leaves, a cow's plaintive lowing. He wept for this reason and no reason, despising his tears. To return to the dreadful everyday sameness, ugliness and loneliness of home was torture. The adolescent awakenings he bore within him were a torture. No other had such secrets, he thought, and none was teased as he by glimmerings of understanding, by the bewildering consciousness that with his senses he could grasp the inexpressible while his mind knew nothing. It was exasperating that he knew nothing while conscious of his potential for creating something immense and vaguely grand. How simple, pure and even happy now seemed those distant days compared with these. What had become of truth that had seemed so clear and simple?

Gwenneth pulled him away from his reflections. "Aren't you coming? We're going to swim."

An hour later a March easterly had sprung up and the sea was capped with white.

He took Gwenneth for a walk: he could not bear the antics of the muscular fool, Jack Lorrimer, and Phyllis's moist, expectant glances. They walked in single file, following a red earth path between the massive rocks and trees. The trunks were black, the branches entangled in a lusty thrusting growth. Cut off from the wind the leaves barely fluttered.

"What millions of mosquitoes!" Gwenneth fussed. "Where are you taking me?"

"You can go back," he said coldly.

Her eyes flashed. She almost said: "How dare you!" But she knew she couldn't say this to him. "What's the matter with you?" she demanded in irritable reproof.

They came to a glade. She sat in the shade of a mango tree and looked about her.

"Has something offended you?"

"I'm just the moody type," he said. With a stick he had idly broken some wild marigold plants about him and now, diffusing their pungent odour in the sunlight, the fallen flowers submitted to the bees and wasps that probed them. A moist heat from the undergrowth enveloped everything. Dragonflies darted, hovered, shimmered, mosquitoes and bees buzzed. Suddenly came a rustling as a lizard pursued its mate among dry leaves. Only then, when it was broken, were they aware of the stillness and behind it, as an accompaniment, the distant pounding of the sea on the rocks below.

"Smell it?"

She nodded, smiling.

"Don't be silly," he thought. "You're not pure, boy, you can never recapture that again."

"Some of these rocks are twice as tall as you."

"Yes. And do you see the holes where thousands of years ago crabs and shellfish sheltered in them? There's not one of these rocks that hasn't been under the ocean."

She took his stick from him and broke a piece and with it traced patterns idly in the earth among the fallen leaves. Although he looked at the patterns and the stick André saw only the movements of her hand and plump white arm and felt the stillness like a presence around them.

The sunlight faded. Masses of black clouds that tore themselves out of the horizon darkened the sky. A wind chill with rain burst into the glade.

"It's going to rain."

But she rested her cheek on her knees and continued silently tracing patterns.

"I'll get soaked, won't I," she said at length, not changing her position. "Have we time to go back?"

"Why go back?"

She turned her other cheek on her knee and smiled at him.

Heavy wind-driven drops burst through the foliage. Everything roared. He took her hand and ran with her to the lee of an overhanging rock. There was barely room for two. From her upturned, wet and laughing face he knew she expected him to put his arm about her, but he ran into the rain. "Wonderful, wonderful!" he cried. "Harder, harder!" He flung his arms out and opened his mouth to catch the soaking drops.

". . . are you ma-ad!" came her voice torn away by the wind.

And as suddenly it was over. The trees creaked in the wind, which, like a great hand, wiped the eastern sky clean and drove the clouds to Venezuela. The wind went with them. Everything was still. Earth and rocks steamed. Water dripped heavily from the leaves. He felt the reverberations of the tormented sea below the cliffs and himself was rent by inexpressible longings.

"I look absolutely awful!" she wailed. "Look at my hair!"

"Damn your hair," he thought, moving away.

"Wait for me—André!"

He waited, smiling. How ill did her proud step suit her now, he thought in triumph. They walked in single file along the narrow track.

They changed into dry clothes, then he rowed her to Bombshell Bay. He went in and out of the inlets, hugging the rocks and caves because the thunder of the sea within them was music to him. He used the oars with skill, swinging the boat to ride the bigger waves and steer clear of the rocks submerged. The bow rose up on a wave that carried it to the cave and he lay back on the oars. With a prolonged hiss and a roar the half submerged cave spewed foam, the swirling water became a tender green that carried them forward and he felt the joy of danger, of pitting his strength against the sea with Gwenneth near him. She was laughing, not for her the calmer waters. Once he wasn't quick enough and a big roller heaved the boat among the barnacled rocks. Gwenneth's knuckles paled as she gripped the gunwales. He pushed mightily with an oar, the boat slid off the barnacles with a rending sound and they both laughed joyously.

After lunch she deserted him. The others were making much of her and nothing gave her greater pleasure. He lay on the nearby rocks and threw pellets of bread to the brightly striped parrot fish. Some pellets they took, others they rejected, just, he thought, as he was drawn to her one moment or repelled the next by her ringing laughter that said she loved Gwenneth.

The moon rose after eight that night well past its full. One arm of the bay kept out the light for which they all were waiting. The tide was high. In the hammock on the jetty Betty and her Bryan were scuffling. They squabbled in low voices with sudden, inexplicable bursts of laughter. From the rocks somewhere in the darkness came the voice of Marie-Louise. Phyllis, overhearing, sang out:

"Do you know him, Marie-Louise?"

"I met him at the last Country Club dance."

Jack Lorrimer from somewhere else: "That nut!"

Betty: "Who are you talking about?"

Indistinguishable replies and laughter light as foam. A voice floating up: "When's the moon going to rise?"

Someone singing, talk rising like flying fish that spear foaming water. Empty and idle, André thought, in the effort to resist the insidious poetry into which he felt everything sinking.

Gwenneth put her arm through his and took his hand. It burned him. They were sitting with bare feet on the wooden steps of the jetty. Imperceptibly the water rose and fondled their feet. A crab scurried by with a scratching sound.

"The steps are moving! Can you feel it?"

"It's the water lifting them," he said.

The moon flooded the jetty and the rocks with light. Its glow spread over one's thoughts, one's heart. Someone began singing. It was a quite ordinary girl's voice but because the night had given it birth it became exceptional, unique. "How sad. How sad and joyful," he thought, not knowing why it was so. "Why must it pass?" The voice fell silent. Now other voices were heard and other songs were sung, rising and falling like an aroma over water, trees and rocks. The water rose and fell back from the rocks, trickling and gurgling.

The moon was high. Somebody yawned. They moved up to the house in twos and threes. Now everything was still. A cutlass fish, plagued by the moon, leaped out of the water and broke the silence.

"The hammock's empty," he said, rising, and pulled her into it.

"André!" she protested because her giving scared her.

To him she was not only Gwenneth, she was an English girl, a stranger whom he had yet to know; she was that entire class, hard and cold, that did not understand it was crushing hearts and warping minds. And with his lips and touch he sought the softness in her, her tenderness and kindness and, maybe, warmth.

She laughed, and the flame was snuffed out in him. How could she laugh? He did not know it was a mask, he had no use for masks. He listened to the water chuckling among the rocks. "How mysterious, how pure, how cruel is all that beauty!" occurred to him as he looked at the gleaming water and longed to merge himself with what was true and only true. "How unapproachable and sad it is!"

While she, offended by his sudden coldness, passionately kissed him and felt with excitement his instant rising response. The spear of desire impaled her as his lips found her breast. She gasped, tried both to push him away and embrace him as his teeth seized the nipple.

"Don't!"

She sat up. He lay silent, motionless.

An unbearably long time seemed to pass. Why didn't he say something? "Don't you think we ought to go up?"

"Go if you want to."

"I don't want to, don't be silly. I was only wondering what they'd say about us."

"About us or about yourself?"

"André!"

He pulled her down. "Stay with me, don't leave me now," he whispered.

She gave in to that whispered plea. Gently he encroached upon her deeper self. She felt the almost unbearable delight of being discovered and, when her initial shyness was blown away, of discovering him; the joy in her power over him; the pain of resisting, of hurting him with her resistance, and the longing to yield and discover still more. They wearied each other, yet continued to pass from one degree of torment to another without understanding that this was happiness. Words were followed by laughter and laughter by frustration, resentment, fear, bewilderment and wild assertions of love.

The moon was low in the sky, heavy with all it had witnessed everywhere.

"What's the noise? It's like a river."

"*La remou*, the turning of the tide. Come and see it."

The tide was low now and eddies swirled viciously among the rocks as the powerful riptide raced past Gasparee.

"I'd love to swim in it," she said.

"You can't challenge everything. That's a force greater than us. I don't want to be flotsam."

Chapter twenty-four

Gwenneth was bored. She was conscious that her life, her talents, her beauty were running to waste, and this agitated and saddened her. In England she had been accustomed to people of quality, as those in her strata understood quality; she had mixed with men and women whose mental calibre was not generally beneath her own. Trinidad was a different world. The whites had little to offer, and in the coloured "respectables" she met she often felt an instinctive prickling resentment whose cause she could not detect. Thinking it something personal she assumed towards them a proud and indifferent air which not infrequently evoked dislike. For a while she had enjoyed the general adulatory atmosphere that surrounded her in the island's best society. But she had tired of these sycophants, they bored her, they isolated her. Here were no London or Paris nightclubs where one could commit follies and frolic without attracting the world's attention. Here a cold was cause for comment in the social columns; an indiscretion committed tonight could reverberate throughout the island tomorrow. One had only to attend the carnival tents and listen to the calypso singers wittily recount the latest scandal to roars of laughter to discover in what scant respect the people held their rulers. One danced and drank, played tennis, rode horseback, swam or lounged about all day attended by two or three black servants. That was all. There was no white man she had met, English or otherwise, who was not dull, who was not tiresome.

André alone was different and a challenge to her. And her pursuit of him was socially dangerous: he was coloured. It vexed her that he did not succumb to her personality and status as others did. But after that night spent in the moonlight with him he had acquired a power over her and there was no resisting it. She phoned him at work. They had already arranged he would come to the house, but it was not enough, she couldn't wait, she must talk to him *now.* She had to know how he felt towards her: didn't he perhaps despise her? But he didn't, she could tell by his voice, and she flushed with pleasure and excitement.

Her mother was in the drawing-room when he walked in.

"We're going for a spin, Mother, we won't be long," she said.

And off they went.

"She spoke as if she'd known him for six months," Mrs Osborne reflected. She had a strong feeling that something she would not like to know was going on behind her back. "She's as headstrong as her father. She'll have her own way at any price if I try to stop her," she thought.

And they, not wishing to arouse her suspicions, returned quite early. Next day she met him secretly. André was restrained. He did not know whether he was happy or unhappy. He could no longer face Elena and could not stop seeing Gwenneth.

One afternoon they went riding. When they had dismounted beneath their tree she, conscious of the reluctant lover in him, asked: "There's someone else, isn't there?" And flushed, the thought being so offensive.

He frowned. "Let's say there was."

"Are you still in love with her?"

"No questions, no answers."

"I'm in love with you, André." She kissed him. And everything stopped.

Coming back into the world they heard the horses grazing and the wind in the trees. She hoped he would speak about marriage, because no one had yet proposed to her; and no one before had had those liberties. But he was silent.

"Come on," she said tartly. They remounted and set off.

For a week after this she could not see him. A cocktail party here, visits that had to be returned, a dance at some English official's home, invitations that could not be refused; it was a week of social flittings about from which she could not escape. She was furious but no one would have thought it. She experienced no difficulty in putting on a mask and concentrating the attentions of others on herself. She thrived on subterfuges, anxious waitings and concealments. Inactivity was as unnatural to her as to a mountain stream.

She had promised to go riding with David Primrose on Saturday afternoon. She did not put him off. She longed to see André but even more did she hope to hurt him and so compensate for the tormenting thought that though she had given him so much he still nurtured precious memories of some unknown girl, some Marie-Louise, some . . . O God!

But after her ride, and just before dinner, she phoned and invited him over to hear some music. "Do come, André, I've got some new records. I'll be alone," she added lightly. "Mum and Dad are going to a bridge party."

Two hours past he had seen her riding with Primrose. He had been frightened by the jealousy that raged in him, frightened by his entanglement. "Okay," he said in an indifferent tone.

They had just left when he arrived. Only the servants were still about. She put on a record and they listened, but now what they heard did not matter to them.

By nine o'clock they were alone. She turned off the lights to discourage visitors. In the half-dark she fetched a box of chocolates from somewhere.

"Hard or soft?" he asked.

"Mixed. No, no, you must just pick one."

"I can't see in the dark."

"You're not supposed to." She was laughing.

"Which is the one with the strychnine?"

"I'm keeping that for David. Come on, you've got one second." She drew the box away. "There, that's enough."

"Bring it back, I haven't picked one."

"Too late now."

She escaped him, laughing, and he pursued her among the chairs and through the dining-room. She raced up the lighted stairs hearing him close behind her. She was in the grip of an intense excitement, a terrible anticipation that infected him also. Had one of the servants appeared at that moment he would have knocked her down without a thought. Near the top he stumbled. She ran to the door facing her. "If she shuts the door before I get there I'm through with her!" he thought wildly. He flung himself at it like a footballer, just managing in time to thrust his foot between it and the jamb. The laughing face that looked at him around the door seemed indescribably alluring. There was fear in it and something he could not read but which drew him on. He threw his weight against the door and burst in.

"Cut it out, we aren't a couple of kids. This could affect our whole lives."

He did not know what prompted him to say this, the words astonished him. He did not know whether she heard them or whether they made sense to her if she did because she stood with head down, looking at him from the corner of one eye with a nervous, hesitant expression. His arms were round her. He kicked shut the door. Then they were on her bed, he trembling as he undressed her, both in a hurry to take possession of each other for fear that loving might escape them.

And she, afterwards, frightened, almost in tears: "André, what's going to happen to me?"

He emerged from a sort of mist. She was an English girl, foreign to him, no Beulah whose breasts he would kiss submissively. "Happen?" he said, suddenly turning angry and cruel. "I don't know. It could be a very dark baby, much darker than me. Could you survive?"

"I don't want a baby!" Tears in her eyes now. She embraced him. "André, I love you. We could go home. We could marry and settle there. Will you?"

"What if there's no baby?"

"Oh, please! Don't be angry. We couldn't live here. Could we? Please!" She sobbed.

He wiped her eyes.

Chapter twenty-five

Ever since the bailiff had seized the washstand Aurelia Henriques had wished to move, and now she was more than ever determined to do so. Her difficulties had convinced her that a curse had been laid upon the house. This curse was the root of all her bad health, her misfortunes and André's suddenly ceasing to visit Elena and taking up with the Osbornes. It seemed to her that if only she could get into another place she would feel well again and good fortune and happiness would visit them. But to find a suitable house was no easy matter. Once she had rented a suburban house and in three months had lost all her customers; it was too far. It was all very well for Popito to get angry at times and tell her to rent a room in the city, but how many customers and what sort would patronise a dressmaker in a room? They preferred to entrust their appearance to someone successful, my dear. Who would believe that dressmaking in a room would invite success? How could she charge her customers one-fifty or two dollars when they would come just because she lived in a room and so ought to charge but three shillings? And then what about suitors for Elena? What would they think?

"Life is just one fight after another," she complained one day to a good friend and customer while trying a bodice on her. "Sometimes I feel as if I'm goin' mad and it's time to put an end to all this. Such strange thoughts come into my head," she added, her eyes filling with tears.

It was two in the afternoon, she had not eaten since the night before. She had given Elena everything that was left from the evening meal.

The friend, a fat brown woman of fifty, clucked sympathetically in the roof of her mouth. "You have to see for you'self these days, I tell you. . . . Just raise this a little higher."

"I will have to put in a dart," said Aurelia, sighing.

"My child, I say sometimes Gawd don't have time to hear all the prayers. Eh, my dear, when you consider how many millions of people in this world, and all prayin', and sometimes two and three times a day, not to speak of before bed, even if he is Gawd, my dear, it must be difficult."

Aurelia began to laugh despite her tears.

"No, no, I am serious," the customer continued. "I don't know if you believe in these things but I know somebody who could fix you up very well indeed."

Aurelia looked at her in the mirror as she tucked the bodice with a pin. "Some of these people don't know how to do the right things and they rob you."

"Not this person," the customer replied with an air of knowing much more than she was allowed to tell. "No, my dear, not this person." And in a low voice, in a tone of awe, she related how "this person" had saved a man from a court conviction; how for several nights stones had fallen on the roof of a house in which a thirteen-year-old girl was living, how the police had surrounded it but found no one and how "this person" had attended to the girl and the pelting had ceased; and how she had cured a friend of a ten-year-old breast ailment, the doctors had wanted to cut off her breast because cutting makes a lot of money, my dear, but "this person" had treated her and in six weeks—six weeks!—she was well.

So Aurelia, full of renewed hope, asked for the address of "this person".

She turned out to be a small Negro woman with suspicious black eyes. Her first question was: "Who send you?" After they had spoken of the weather and "the 'flu going about" the little woman took her into the bedroom where, ready waiting, was a small table with a lighted candle, holy images and water. Sitting at the table she muttered prayers and appeared after a while to go into a trance. The seance began. A voice which it was hard for Aurelia to believe was not the woman's now asked her to speak. Aurelia told her troubles. The spirit said, sighing:

"It is hard in your world, it is hard. . . . And after a pause, again sighing, it told her what to do to "seal the lips of your enemies."

First she must catch clear rain water in a basin and set it on the floor of her house. Then she and Elena must run three times round the basin while saying one Our Father. They must jump over it three times, taking care never to spill the water nor touch it with their bodies. This done, they must urinate in the water and throw it away in the drain behind the house. Thus would they still the tongues of their enemies and keep evil from the household.

Then somewhat as when Elena had been ill in babyhood and at last after three days Aurelia had raised the money to pay the doctor, and he had come and named the illness, prescribed some powders and said the fever would abate in the morning—as at that time Aurelia now experienced a feeling of glad relief and a confidence that all would shortly be well again, and she wondered why she had not thought before of obtaining help from the spirits. She hastened home to tell Elena.

Elena pined for André but not for the world would she have let anyone see it. She went about her daily tasks as usual, laughed, ate well and seeemd even plumper than when she had met him. She lived two lives. The first was in the office, where she skilfully wrestled with the responsibilities heaped upon her and forgot André; the second was at home in the dream world that sheltered her and made life tolerable. Her love pervaded her being like a dream. She read all the books he valued and that had influenced him. When she saw Erica smile at her husband it seemed to her there was a prodigious meaning in it, a haunting mystery that it was painful to behold; yet endlessly sweet was that pain. She never thought: "I must have André," or: "My life is finished if I don't forget him," or: "I will die without him." In reading, in thinking of him, in loving him her spiritual and mental being struggled to assert itself, to grow, to rise above the horrible world of Hoo, of debt, of shame that had been stifling her so long. She held long conversations with him—not about love because that opened the wound. They were dream-discussions about the books she read, the questions they posed and her reflections about life. Only not all reflections either; not reflections, for instance, about her mother or her conduct of affairs because she felt he would judge her harshly. It was distressing that she couldn't talk over *everything* with him in her dreams. But if she did not protect her mother whom should she protect? Among all the multitudes in this world her mother was alone, quite alone. It was painful when she put herself in a position to be mocked. Without her mother who protected her in her own way, just by being there, what was in the world for her? Only the dream. And at this point the dream became terribly painful. Because it might never be realised.

It was half-past ten at night when Aurelia got home. Elena was reading *The Life of the Bee.* The author's blending of scientific observations with poetic, brilliant flights of imagination seemed to illuminate all the corners of her mind and soul. She sat bunched in a chair, her feet on its rail, her cheek on her hand, rapt, a faint smile making her face glow. At her mother's entry she started violently. The smile vanished. A cold stern look replaced it, as when the bailiff had besmirched the privacy of her bedroom. In the precise and business-like manner she had acquired in her service to Hoo—a defence against that world that was bare of beauty or promise—she gave her mother a message from a customer who had come in an hour before.

"Yes, yes," said Aurelia, brushing her aside, and at once, with gesticulations and in a loud excited whisper, began to relate what the spirit had bidden her do.

Elena listened with an expressionless countenance. Long experience had convinced her that argument was not only futile but dangerous. So as not to appear to be sceptical that salvation was at last to hand she asked her mother some questions—when the ceremony was to be performed, how many candles were required, and so on.

Early next morning before dawn it rained. Aurelia was sound asleep and ordinarily would not have awakened, but it was as if someone had shaken her and said: "The rain water, Aurelia. Now's your chance, don't let it slip." She jumped up from her warm bed, threw over her shoulders the first thing she came across and caught the necessary water as it spouted from the broken roof guttering. At five she woke Elena. Dawn was just breaking. They went into the sitting-room. Aurelia set the basin down in the middle of the floor. Having made sure that everything was tightly shut and no one could see she wondered in a whisper whether she should run north, east, south or north, west, south. She wanted no loopholes for the devil to step in and frustrate their efforts. With a sleepy martyred look Elena said it didn't matter. "Didn't she say run around?"

Crossing herself Aurelia began to run north, west, south around the basin while mumbling the Our Father. The sight of her fat mother mumbling and running in her nightdress made Elena giggle helplessly. Aurelia laughed too but said as if afraid of laughing:

"Come, nuh, man, do the thing. How you want it to work if you laugh at it?"

Elena wiped her eyes.

"Say a prayer," said Aurelia, wishing to evoke the right atmosphere.

"No, let us do it one time and done," said Elena. Her features grew set and cold.

Again Aurelia began to run, mumbling, trying to make the last word of the prayer coincide with her completion of the third round; it seemed the proper way. She took a step back, pulling up her nightdress and jumped. She was about to do it a second time when Elena sobbed.

"What's wrong?"

Elena had suddenly become conscious, unbearably conscious, of the contrast between the joyous rain-scented wind that was trying to get in through the back door, and her mother faithfully jumping over a basin of water in the hope of saving herself from the bailiff; of the contrast between her love and André's indifference; the contrast between her and the cunning of Hoo, who did not care whom he ground into the dust in passing.

"I can't, Mother! It seems such a . . . mockery." She ran into her bedroom to hide.

Aurelia flushed as if coming to herself. "But you're a fool," she said sharply. "People give you something to help you'self and you goin' to turn you' back on it?" She opened the window and dashed the water through it. She started to comb her hair, tugging angrily at the knots without noticing the pain. "You think anything in life comes to you on a silver dish? You have to fight for it and each of us must fight his own way. For twenty years I have fought alone. Show me someone who could have managed as well as I in the circumstances—show me!" she shouted, weeping with shame, wounded pride and despair and advancing into her daughter's room. "You know what it is to love God? What trials you have passed through? What trials?"

Outside cocks were crowing. A beautiful new day was dawning.

Several days later, Elena's friend Maria told them of a house that would soon be vacant. Next morning Aurelia went off to see it. She was delighted with the yard, which was bigger (though what advantage it was to her she did not stop to think) and the rooms, too, were larger. But the chief thing was that the house was in lower Edward Street, almost in the heart of the city. She lost no time in interviewing the agent. When he demanded a month's rent in advance she cried out in dismay. It was short-lived. She conjured fifteen dollars from a couple of friends on the strength of a sou-sou hand due to her in "a few days". She paid the agent. The occupants were quitting on the twenty-third. She proposed to move in the following day.

A difficulty faced her. The agent for the house she now occupied was entitled to a month's rent in lieu of notice as well as the month's rent that would soon be due. Elena privately considered this an impossible situation. She said nothing, it was fatal to say anything at such times. She saw that it was imperative for her mother to quit this scene of their several defeats and humiliations.

Aurelia was not long short of a solution. "One day when God smile on me I will pay him. We have to live, after all, not he alone."

Leah, the half-day servant, was the only outsider admitted to the conspiracy. Leah knew of a reliable carter who would move all their belongings at night. He turned out to be her nephew. This cheerful and muscular young man agreed to do the job but only after some hesitation during which Aurelia smiled amiably upon him and Leah mocked him for his cowardice.

While Aurelia, bubbling with new plans for the future, chattered about the furniture and curtains she would buy Elena unobtrusively took charge of the packing. She arranged with the carter how many trips he should make and instructed him to bring a tarpaulin in case it rained.

On the night of the twenty-fourth Aurelia, despite her former excitement, talked in anxious whispers, conscious for the first time of the embarrassing situation into which she had thrown Elena and herself. She said the mosquito nets ought to go in a box. Elena called out from where she knelt on the floor surrounded by neatly folded piles of household linen:

"No, Mother, they will go on the cart. I have arranged all that."

"Don't talk so loud," Aurelia whispered, running in on tiptoe from the dining-room, where she was packing crockery. "Suppose it rains?"

"Wilfred is bringing a tarpaulin. Why isn't Leah back yet?" Elena flung the hair back impatiently from her damp forehead.

In the warm, still night air the candle flame stretched itself and quivered. Their lights had been cut off, for three months they had not paid the electricity bills.

A jazz band struck up near by. Elena peeped through the jalousies. A dance had begun at the Chinese club over the Chinese grocery at the corner. Well-dressed Chinese girls alighted on the sidewalk from the automobiles that drove up one after the other. She shut the jalousies abruptly. Kneeling in her former position she tried to decide whether only sheets, tablecloths and towels should go into the suitcase; but she could not now understand anything about these matters, to reach a decision seemed both difficult and futile: she kept seeing in her mind's eyes the light-hearted gaiety of the Chinese girls in their dance frocks.

"One big crowd! How we going to pass without being seen?" Aurelia muttered, peeping outside.

A crowd had gathered to listen to the music and look over the dresses of the latest arrivals.

There was a knock at the front door. Its handle was turned irritably and vainly. A familiar voice cried: "Elena!" It was Maria.

"Coming!" Elena piled everything anyhow into the suitcase and pushed it under the bed.

Powdered, scented, and with lips heavily carmined in true Venezuelan style the square-faced Maria was dressed for the dance. She had come to have Mrs Henriques oversee the final details of her costume. A cloud of cigarette smoke behind her betrayed the presence of her admirer.

"Come in," smiled Elena, holding the candle higher and looking only at the dress. "That's the one Mother just made? It fits well."

Maria turned this way and that. Elena offered the escort a chair and said to Maria that a cowl might have suited her. Aurelia darted in and, forgetting to greet anyone, forgetting the fancied necessity of speaking in a whisper, assured Maria that a cowl, though fashionable, would not have suited her at all. She noticed at once where a tuck was necessary, and suddenly the three women, all talking at once and gaily, went in a body into the bedroom. Maria was once more turned about, tucked and adjusted.

Elena saw them off at the front door. When their footfalls had retreated an oppressive, stale and guilty silence filled the house.

Hours passed. Rain fell and ceased. Everything was packed. Elena lay on the mattress with her hands beneath her head and looked up at the rafters and beyond them. Aurelia fell asleep. When she awoke and heard everything quiet as in the early hours of the morning (the music had temporarily ceased) and only the *pick-pack, pick-pack* of water dripping into a basin from the leaking roof, she rose agitatedly and asked :

"Wilfred hasn't come yet?"

"The rain must have kept him back," replied Elena, moving her lips only, her wide-open black eyes still gazing beyond the rafters.

Aurelia suddenly thought: "I hate that André de Coudray."

At half-past one they heard the unmistakable rumble of an approaching two-wheeled cart. It was Wilfred indeed. Aurelia admitted him. She sewed pieces of cloth at the machine in the effort not to hear the noise he made dismantling the beds. Leah was given a suitcase and sent on ahead. As soon as she stepped out she saw a policeman and stumbled back in. The four of them waited silently behind the door. The policeman's slow and measured tread came nearer and nearer. He saw the cart but gave no thought to it. He stood a while looking up at the dancers and listening to the music. At last he went around the corner.

Now the dismantled beds were placed upon the cart. One of the heavy springs slipped from Wilfred's hand and fell with a clang on the other. Elena went hot all over as if the neighbours were looking. The dressing-table mirror was sandwiched between the mattresses, the meat safe and the dressing-table placed on top of them, boxes were wedged in where possible and over everything Wilfred spread his tarpaulin. He seized the shafts and, straining, threw his weight forward. Aurelia made the sign of the cross. The loaded cart, its lantern swaying, rumbled down the street on its two enormous wheels.

Nothing now remained to be done and they must patiently await the cart's return. Aurelia, sighing, opened a window. Elena's shadow heaved on the wall and the candle went out. She groped for matches and relit it.

"Always shut up like some damn criminal," Aurelia muttered, closing the window.

Not until three fifteen was the third and last trip made.

"We should have broken down your basin shelf," Aurelia said vindictively. She tried to smash it with her hands but it resisted her. "Take the old scrubbing brush, take it, don't leave one thing!"

They went out. She locked the door and flung the key in through the jalousies. The dance was breaking up. The music sounded sleepy and dull. Some lone tipsy voices were heard. A car roared past with its hood down. In the rear seat three Chinese girls were singing. One threw out an empty cigarette package. Its inner tinfoil wrapping flew up in an eddy of air and brushed Elena's face.

In the new house all was confusion, yet at the very sight of their belongings thrown anyhow in these new rooms their spirits rose.

At five in the morning, after feasting on bread and cheese, they flung themselves just as they were on the unmade beds.

"Oh, gosh, Elena! I was so agitated I forgot all about this," Aurelia called out. She got up and took from her handbag a little packet wrapped in tissue paper. "I got Mr Lutchman to make these for you," she said a little shamefacedly, holding out a pair of gold bangles.

"For me? Mother!"

Their surfaces had been cut into tiny diamonds that glittered in the light, adding to their fascination. Elena wanted to say accusingly: "There was no need for us to run away with the rent and feel ashamed, there was no need for you to go without food." But she said nothing like this. Not the body alone had to be nourished, it was just as important to nourish and protect one's soul. One had to surround it with beauty, with love, with dreams or in the struggle for spiritual existence one would not survive. Then what would be left?

"I don't know what sort of mother you have," Aurelia said awkwardly because Elena seemed in her heart to condemn her. "I suppose one day I'll take it and pawn it to pay rent."

"I'll never pawn this, Mother. Never."

For a long time they examined the bangles, marvelling at the skill of their fashioning and their glitter in the candlelight. They put them on and took them off and, again putting them on, looked at themselves in the mirror. A warm, rich, adventurous and hopeful feeling soaked into them. They were ready for the fray.

Chapter twenty-six

The heavy storeroom door of the giant U.S. firm Ganz Products Incorporated creaked laboriously on its hinges. Hal Barker squeezed out. Forty-eight, well-dressed, plump, with a pink round face he was the American manager of the Trinidad Branch; yet he squeezed out of the storeroom circumspectly, like a child who has stolen sugar, and ran flat-footed into the office.

Behind the storeroom door a storm was brewing that might affect his future adversely.

"Wahker! Say, Wahker!" he cried anxiously, clearing his throat nervously as he always did. "We gotta git Chin Toon here. *An*dré! You better take my car and fetch Chin Toon. Tell 'm he's *got*ta come. God damn it! These bakers can't reach agreement without him, they'll be arguin' till seven o'clock tonight, they'll—Say, *An*dré! You be darn careful how you tahk to Chin Toon, now. We don't want any of his workers git'n' to know. . . . You want somep'n'?" he broke off as a customer approached the counter. "Wahker, hey, Wahker! Customer out there. You through with your reports, André? Okay, okay, you gotta fetch Chin Toon, don't worry—Say! Get some cigars for me, will yuh?" he shouted as André took off.

Arnold Walker nowadays regarded André with heightened favour since the latter had received the imprimatur of Gwenneth's interest and was received at her home. Indeed, his regard had been inflated to such a degree that he had offered André a job at Ganz Products. André accepted. The salary was higher and the job more interesting than at William Dollard's. All day long he was out among the bakers in towns and country districts throughout the island, selling and delivering bakers' supplies. He met Shorty Ellis and old Winchester, both of whom often kept him in talk, airing their views about the sickness in the industry. He dealt only with the masters but all the same was fully aware of the unrest among the journeymen.

As he drove away he heard Barker telephoning the grocery for beer. "Barker. No, Barker. Bark, bow-wow. Yeh, you got it, Mr Bryce!" he laughed with placating eagerness.

André, understanding all that was agitating Barker, was overcome by such contempt that it exploded into a physical dislike of the man. Because Barker had the knack of exploiting other people's talents, having few himself, and neither realised it when he placed his staff in invidious positions nor cared if he did so. He had learned how to maintain himself in his position by fostering the most friendly sort of *bon vivant* relations between his superiors and himself. A case of very old rum, some special frogs from Dominica, a sheet of stamps with a slight imperfection in the printing—with such friendly gestures did he keep in the good graces of the men who mattered: the District Manager stationed in Jamaica, the head of the foreign division in New York. It was not talent that would make him District Manager one day; "It isn't what you know, it's who you know," he always said with a slyly knowing grin.

From the storeroom now came a buzzing of indistinguishable but angry voices.

"Pay peelmen seven dollars a week?" one master baker was saying. "That is ruination to me. I am a small man."

A paunchy, wily Chinese man of middle age, sitting sideways to the table and cleaning his teeth with a disinterested air, suddenly laughed at this man. "How many peelmen you have? Two, I have six. Peelmen want ten, we offer seven—"

Shorty Ellis, in hat and coat, but without shoes today, began to speak in his loud, firm and fearless voice. He rose the better to be seen. "Bread sellers should be cut out. Then you can pay peelmen. The sellers takin' commission from all of us and the shopkeeper don't care how much he buys because it is all taken back without loss to himself."

He was so angry that he forgot to sit down after speaking and remained standing open-mouthed listening to the next speaker.

A fat, pale-faced Portuguese began to speak rapidly with a Madeira accent, smiling about him. An Indian, shouting angrily, tried to drown him. The first man declared: "It payin' a big man like Chin Toon to have sellers. Why he don't want to come here and talk?"

"Yes, he should come," said the Chinese man, laughing, so that it seemed to Shorty Ellis as if he said: "What do Chin Toon and I care about all of you and your resolutions?"

Barker slipped into the storeroom. "I sent for Chin Toon," he said to the Chinese man because he was the biggest baker among those present. "Yeah, he'll be along." Then, to amuse the others, he turned with a bantering smile to the angry Ellis and teased him.

Chin Toon came half an hour later. He was a small, quiet Chinese of about thirty-five who at once stood out above everyone by the condent, careless movements with which he sat down and leaned sideways on the table, his casual nod to Barker, and the cunning smile with which his glance swept the company.

"What's the matter?" he said to the only important baker present, the paunchy Chinese, speaking rapidly as he always did. "Can't reach agreement without me?"

Many Chinese were well acquainted with Chin Toon, the gambler, for they had lost large sums to him at baccarat and poker. They had the utmost respect for his knife-sharp, astute and daring mind. The bakers around the table feared him. All save Ellis. Ellis rose and repeated the argument he had already offered—that a saving could be effected by acceding to the demand for higher wages and cutting out the purchase of stale bread from the grocers. Chin Toon listened attentively, his eyes fixed on the table. He looked pleasantly at the paunchy Chinese when Ellis finished. He spoke as if it was not Ellis who had addressed him, but this Chinese.

"All advantage on the side of the small man," he said rapidly. "A big man employing sixty men can't pay as high a wage as a small man employing five men. The big man's loss to the shopkeeper bound to be less than the increase in wages to his sixty men."

"It depends on the wage," said Ellis.

"I hear you askin' for fifty per cent," said Chin Toon, turning to Ellis at last with a mildly contemptuous smile. "You a baker or a journeyman? I hear you go to journeymen's meetings. You advise them what to do. Now you come and want to advise us too."

Barker gave Ellis a frightened look.

Ellis, rising, held forth on the moral aspect of the course he proposed, upbraiding and warning the master bakers to beware of their contempt for workers, while they waved him aside impatiently.

Chin Toon spurned any agreement and consequently the big bakers, who had to compete with him, would not consider an agreement either.

After a while the small bakers rose and left the meeting. The others, laughing, drank the cold beer that had arrived.

André went in search of Popito. He found Cassie alone in his room. It was her day off.

"Come in and take a seat. Popi only gone down the road for a minute."

Her smile was assured, friendly, but above all, kind; she was a woman of charm, not the Osbornes' Cassie at all. And suddenly, only at this moment, because he was still naive and lived in a world of his own, did he realise she was living with Popito. She continued the mending he had interrupted. He thought of all Popito must have told her about Elena and himself, his rejection of her love.

"So how?" Cassie asked.

"Oh . . . nothing to talk about. I've come for some proofs for the magazine. Wanted to see him too about the bakers. . . ."

"Plenty to think about if nothing to talk about," she smiled.

He shrugged aloofly.

"Where is the sense in that?" he asked, raising his eyebrows superciliously, so that he looked just like his father. "What does all the thinking do? Does it alter anything?"

She sewed silently for a while, then, while cutting the thread with her teeth, glanced up at him. "So Gwenneth in love with you now," she remarked carelessly, re-threading the needle.

He waited, looking at her, hostility rising. Who was *she* to talk to him so carelessly of Gwenneth? All of him seemed to concentrate on the way she curled one end of the thread over her forefinger and knotted it with an ease born of long practice.

"You knock out the Inspector," she added almost to herself.

Still he said nothing.

"You have to watch now somebody don't knock you out."

She smiled at him almost tenderly. He blushed. He felt with alarm that she was taking happiness from him. Yet something in him that he felt was true compelled him to listen, though with a heavily beating heart.

"In these things you have to study you' head good," she sighed.

"What does all the thinking do? Does it alter anything?" he said and was annoyed with himself for repeating exactly his words of a moment before.

"Yes, I know how it is," she replied sadly after a moment's silence. "The heart sayin' one thing and the head something else."

He longed to ask her what she knew about Gwenneth, but he was afraid to know, and it was an offence to his love to ask any such thing of anyone; besides, it was humiliating to have to learn anything bad about Gwenneth from her servant.

After a while he left, confused and unhappy, and unwilling to face Popito.

Chapter twenty-seven

Winchester approached the master bakers and asked them to meet a delegation of journeymen. The master bakers agreed: their workers were restive and the press had publicised their demands; also, they were becoming organised and no one could tell what might happen; it was well to try their strength. So a time and place were arranged.

But when Winchester set out the new scale of wages the men demanded—a twenty-five per cent increase—their masters laughed and some even took up their hats and went home.

"Let us hear your offer," said Winchester.

"What offer?" the fat Chinese baker hedged blandly. "What I can afford the small man can't afford. Start with the smallest man, ask him."

This was not the workers' point of view. After lengthy and fruitless argument the meeting broke up.

And further meetings were held but never did all the master bakers attend, and the absence of some was seized upon by the rest as an excuse to avoid reaching any decision.

The anger of the journeymen was rising.

One day Chin Toon dismissed a peelman who had cheeked him before all the men. He was that same peelman with the wiry blue-veined arms, George, who had sneered at Manny Camacho's wild talk about "barricades". That night instead of forty men only six turned out to work. Chin Toon sent word to George offering to let bygones be bygones, but George sent back the messenger with a demand for twenty-five per cent more. Chin Toon, the baccarat and poker player, smiled and said, speaking rapidly as usual:

"Close the bakery. Plenty bakers out of work, man. When their bellies get empty they will come to me—cheap, cheap."

Winchester called a meeting. Journeymen from all over the city packed into the schoolroom, and with them Cassie and Popito and Joe Elias.

The skinny little Boissonite with the big voice was one of the first to speak. There was little that was new in what he said, but he spoke with such force, such conviction, and without fishing for words that many who had come resolved to strike were shaken, sighed, and cursed themselves and him. "And suppose you win?" he concluded. "So many people out of work now he goin' to say to himself: 'Monkey say "cool breeze".' And as soon as things quiet down he will fire the lot-a you and take on a next set."

"Then we will strike!" a voice cried.

"Strike?" said Phillip, the little Boissonite, scornfully, turning his back on the chairman to face the speaker. "Think, boy. All-a we who makin' less money must go on strike for a few men to make more than we? We so coonoomoonoo?"

"Phillip talkin' sense," said voices.

"So what you say we must do?" George demanded truculently, rising and pushing his rolled shirt-sleeves yet higher on his wiry arms.

"Apologise to Mr Chin Toon and go back to work," said Phillip with rising confidence. "You not married, you have no responsibilities, no children. We are workin' peaceful and you alone want to strike. Well, strike by you'self."

Angry growls and laughter greeted this. That laughter, the doubt of themselves that it expressed, its submission, its eternal hated submission that she hated in herself, suddenly incensed Cassie now. Turning round in her seat she attacked Phillip in a spiteful tone.

"What sense it have in workin' peaceful? All-you work peaceful all you' life, that prevent them robbin' you? Instead of lettin' the people fight for more money you want them lie down and let the boss trample them in dirt. I was very peaceful! And what Duke do me? What? You all know what."

Phillip raised his voice. "Who you is? Since when they have lady bakers? You, Mr Elias and all sort-a people does come here and try to incite the workers to strike while you keep out the fire—"

"Anybody could join the union and I join it!" cried Cassie, facing him now with her hands on her hips. "I have a right to speak. You and Boisson want the men to starve? Steal and let police beat them? Drag on their bottoms in the street? Strike, yes! Strike now!"

"That's the spirit," Winchester cackled.

Many applauded Cassie's advice, laughing and nodding. Not so Joe Elias. He was on his feet, waiting for her to finish.

"There is a great deal of sense in what Phillip has said," he began with dogmatic assurance that seemed to brush aside what everyone else had said; even Phillip, though Phillip had indeed said some sensible things which he, Elias, would now enlarge on. "I have argued from the start that any exaggerated claim on the master bakers is unrealistic. We are not a recognised body, we are not even sure that we are a body at all. What happens now could well break us into fragments."

Grumbling and restless movements and sighs were heard.

"Hummuch to strike for, man, that's what we has to decide," cried an angry voice.

And George: "Who is Mr Elias to tell us when to strike? He got a store. What he know about what we sufferin'?"

Joe moved a motion that negotiations continue with the masters. It was defeated. Then seeing the necessity to manoeuvre he moved that the masters be advised that if a settlement were not arrived at within a week the men would strike.

Popito jumped up. "No, man! What you sayin'? Forewarned is forearmed. You know what they could prepare for us in a week. If it's to strike, it's to strike sudden."

Winchester put the motion for a strike. An overwhelming majority of the journeymen raised their hands. The undecided, glancing about, raised theirs too. Very few remained in opposition.

All of the bakeries in Port-of-Spain and its environs were shut down next day. Some of the men hung about the streets, others picketed Chin Toon's bakery, driving off with threats of violence the handful who came to work, and yet others drank to celebrate what already seemed a victory.

Le Maître came in from San Fernando, forty miles away, urging on Winchester the need for daily talks lest idleness and inexperience break the men's morale. He gathered them together and discussed tactics in the struggle, and afterwards the men yawned, slept on the benches in the hall, smoked or played cards till hunger called them home.

On the fourth day the master bakers offered a compromise, an increase of ten per cent and, in a few cases, of twenty per cent on existing wages. When Winchester brought the news to the journeymen most were disappointed. The more militant made lurid suggestions concerning the use to which the bosses could put their offer.

Grim-faced, George shouted: "What they think we strike for—charity? Make them understand it's food we want!"

"Let the strike continue!" cried another. "We have them paralysed now, you don't see?"

Joe spoke against continuation of the strike, urging a compromise. This would in itself be a victory; they would have compelled the bosses to recognise their powers; they would give a lead to other workers. To lose now with hundreds in other industries looking on and waiting would be fatal.

Some supported him. George was angry that this shop owner who could go to work when he pleased was gaining influence over the men.

"I'm tellin' you," he assured them, "this whole town feel the master bakers are to blame. Even the papers not against us. They against the strike but not against what we fightin' for. Let us continue the strike, ask for fifteen per cent all round."

Endless speech-making followed. Joe said: "How can you fight without funds? Chin Toon can starve you into submission in a week."

A majority had set their minds on a wage that would permit them to live as men. Every age, every society, every people has its own measure of life that is worthy of men. And every section of society measures differently, some with buckets and casks, and others hardly daring to think beyond the teaspoon. The journeymen wanted but three meals a day for themselves and their families, something to smoke, a drink or two. To hold firm within this narrow orbit took all their courage. Who would dare dream then of homes and holidays, or clothes, or schooling? And now they hardly dared to dare continue striking. The majority behind George was not a big one, and everyone was restless and apprehensive even though the militants assured them that the strike was bound to come to a victorious and speedy conclusion.

Chapter twenty-eight

When he entered the office one huge depressing fact weighed on Barker like a sin he had committed and for which he would never earn forgiveness: for four days the bakeries in the city had bought no yeast.

Only last week New York had written to say that they were glad to see his sales were "looking up", had congratulated him, and he had felt fine, felt secure. And now this damn Chin Toon was spoiling everything, wouldn't come to the party with a small increase that would have headed off a strike. He was the cause of it all, greedy son of a bitch! You never knew what New York would say. If this strike lasted a couple weeks it could make such a hole in sales.

To Arnold Walker he said: "I wish we could do something to get New Bakeries business. That would give us an extra hundred pounds of yeast a day."

The obsequious factotum replied: "Quite right, Mr Barker, that would be very fine indeed, sir. However, with Dollard importing that cheap yeast. . . ."

"How much of an interest do you think he's got in New Bakeries?"

"The bakery is an outlet for his flour, sir."

"Is it? That cheap yeast is driving all these bakers crazy." Barker put on his jacket and went out, saying: "I'll see Duff, the bakery manager. He's over at the club."

It was almost closing time when he came running back in.

"Wahker? Come in here. Shut the door. Siddown, siddown. We've got this thing sewn up. . . ." And he told him what to do. "And we've just got to do that, Wahker, that's all about it," he added defensively, pouting. "We'll never git that guy's business any other way, you know that."

Raising his eyebrows gravely Walker drew on his cigarette. "I don't know what the journeymen will think, sir. It could rebound. It's bound to leak out—"

"God damn it, Wahker, you've just got to handle it right so it won't leak."

Chapter twenty-nine

The news had come to Cassie that a Shango priest in Diego Martin was preparing to make a sacrifice "for better days". She went to see him (she had known him since childhood days when she had lived in Diego Martin) and asked his help. He invited Cassie to share in the sacrifice that he was making. Cassie offered up two fowls and rice and peas. Others provided a goat and candles. All was ready.

But not till the day before did she summon the courage to tell Popito of the intended sacrifice. She did not reveal to him its purpose but in his heart he guessed it: to win protection for him from the police. He did not ridicule her or stand in her way; she revealed but little and was too firm in what little she said. Besides, though he did not believe, his mind was open to belief and he did hope, deep in him, for protection not from the police alone but from the disasters that faced all men of his years and station. Nor was he different from hundreds of thousands throughout the land.

That very day André had discovered one of the bakeries in Diego Martin supplying bread to Port-of-Spain. He passed the information to Popito.

"I'll go tomorrow," Popito said at once. "Those devils!"

"Not before tomorrow night," André warned. "The owner is an Indian—Singh. He's never home between five and seven. You should be able to talk to the men then."

It was the night of the sacrifice. Darkness was falling when Popito went to the bakery. In a shed close by the bakery cows were lowing. There was a smell of cows and fresh dung. In the bakery seven men were working by the light of a single oil lamp hung from a rafter draped with cobwebs black with years. The peelman, an old man, was humming something in a subdued bass.

Popito greeted the men and asked without preliminaries how it was they were working when everyone else was on strike.

No one answered. A muscular man who was mixing dough in a trough straightened up and wiped the sweat from his glistening black body. The peelman stopped humming.

Popito spoke again, saying a compromise offer had been received from the master bakers. The face of the man who had been mixing the dough grew thoughtful. He said that Singh had promised them twenty cents a day extra. Popito pointed out that it was a promise only; besides, what would they do if their comrades won thirty cents instead of twenty?

By now all the men were listening. Even the old peelman who, with lazy expert motions, drew the loaves in their plantain leaves from far inside the oven and tumbled them into the wicker basket at his feet.

Popito tried to show them that by breaking the strike they were cutting the throats of their working brothers as well as their own.

He urged them to force Singh to join the other master bakers in making an agreement with the journeymen; otherwise they would be unable to make Singh honour his promise.

At seven o'clock Popito left them. He felt that some agreed with him and that he had stirred them all up.

It was now pitch dark. Popito looked up between the branches of the trees but could see no stars, so cloudy was the night. Occasionally he passed a hut. A candle or oil lamp burned within and this feeble but friendly flicker cheered him. The streets in those days were unlighted.

After a while he began to hear the sound of drums. Next he came upon three women. Going in the same direction as he was they were laughing and talking loudly to give themselves courage in the darkness.

"You goin' to the Shango meetin'?" he asked.

And at once the laughter and talking ceased. Only their footsteps were heard. One woman peered at him in the darkness. Another grunted suspiciously.

"I am goin', you know. I have a friend who goin' to dance tonight. I only ask because I don't know the way."

"Oh," said one. And after a further silence another said: "Yes, we goin' too."

"Black night tonight," Popito said encouragingly.

"Black, black like the devil himself," the third, who had not yet spoken, said in a frivolous tone.

"He ain't always black," said the first.

"Mister, you goin' to catch the spirit tonight?" the third asked teasingly.

"Don't laugh at dat, chile," said the first, who was older. "You don't know what the Power could do, I tell you!"

In single file they began to ascend a track that wound up a hill. The sound of the drums was loud, demanding, frightening to those who knew them, and yet irresistible. Their peculiar broken, compelling rhythm agitated the women. One stopped and, cupping her mouth, called:

"May-zie! Miss Mayzie, ohi!"

Evidently they were expected, for the red light of a *flambeau* was seen coming down the hillside. The light threw into bold relief the dark shapes of cashew trees, and the red earth track between them.

In that shifting light the cashew trees seemed to twist and dance grotesquely to the rhythm of the drums.

A thatched bamboo shed had been erected behind the priest's shack on the hill. Dozens of people sat or stood close-packed around its sides. Under a mango tree near by stood Aurelia Henriques's statue of the Virgin Mary. Several candles burned before it, and before the candles a woman knelt, touching the earth with her forehead. The sound of the drums was deafening now. Popito, insinuating himself among the close-packed bodies in the bamboo tent, felt suffocated by the hot smell of the people. Looking everywhere for Cassie he hardly noticed a tall well-developed Negro in singlet and shorts who was dancing with a lighted candle balanced on his head.

Cassie saw Popito but neither took notice of him nor ceased to sing till the drums stopped beating. Then she whispered to a woman who sat with an arm about a child. Without returning Popito's smile, seeing yet not seeing, as a priest who faces his parishioners before the altar, Cassie drew him further into the tent and bade him sit beside the woman, who took the child upon her lap. In doing so they brushed by the man with the candle, and for the first time Popito took note of him. With wide-open unblinking eyes that seemed to look through and beyond everyone, and with jaw thrust forward, the *hounbonnor* or priest was walking back and forth with the bold majesty of a god accustomed to fearful obedience, his breath coming and going hungrily through his thick parted lips. He said something to Cassie.

"Yes, Dada," Cassie replied in a timid, eager-to-please tone.

(Dada Mazookoo was the name of the god who had now taken possession of him.)

She handed him a calabash with water. He sprinkled some before her bare feet and some behind her. Then he sprinkled the four corners of the tent and went forth from it. Those at the entrance made way for him with respectful assiduity.

"Jim, come, boy, I tired," said the beater of the biggest drum, the mamma. And he wiped the sweat from his grey head.

Another took his place. In a hoarse voice an old man with a bumpy, shaven head chanted something in an African dialect. Some women replied. The drums began to beat. All joined in the chorus.

Without interrupting her singing Cassie stepped forward and gave Popito a *shak-shak,* motioning him to shake it and not fold his arms

—by folding his arms, the belief was, he would "tie the spirit" and prevent it entering him. The woman beside him, closing her eyes, sang with fervour. The child in her lap was fast asleep.

The drums beat rapidly, fiercely. The whole world seemed filled with drum beats that struck at Popito's navel like whips. They hurt inside his head, and he shuddered; a strange feeling of breathlessness came over him. Just when it seemed to him that he must run outside from those whips and that pain the drums and the singing ceased. The old man with the shaven head shouted a new song. The drums began to beat again. Popito, feeling foolish, shook the *shak-shak* to the rhythm of the drums as others were doing. He was conscious that all were . . . waiting. The mother beside him complained: "The Power not strong tonight." With sleepy looks some of the women adjusted their shawls.

But now the former drummer returned, and, wiping some drops of rum from his lips with the back of his hand, took the mamma firmly between his knees. The shaven-headed man with the hoarse voice chanted with long-drawn, quavering notes, in that strange tongue that was yet familiar, and with his eyes fixed before him, so to speak, upon the song.

"Sing, all-you, sing!" cried he, angered not by the response so much as by the fact that his voice cracked and failed him.

He chanted again, this time in a major key, and all the tent took up the new three-noted chorus:

"*Ah, coo, la, la-a,*
La hoo, la Yea-a!"

With a passionate angry look the middle drummer leaned his grey head over his instrument and beat:

Bam, m'bam. Bam! Bam-bam-bam. Bam. Bam-bam. *M'bam*!

His sweating grey head was cocked to the drum as if listening to some reply none else could hear. His beady black eyes glanced quickly among the singers and fell on Cassie.

Cassie was not singing now. She sat with eyes fixed on the earthen floor. Popito saw that no longer did she hear anything except that mamma's invocation. She began to shudder from the back of her neck downwards. Others, not ceasing to sing, cleared a space about her. Suddenly she gave a great leap into the air and fell flat, with a tremendous thud, upon her face. Popito rose with horror, but others pushed him back. The drums beat faster. Cassandra rolled convulsively from one end of the tent to the other.

"Abobo! Abo-bo-bo-bo!" all cried, becoming excited and rapidly slapping their open mouths with their palms.

Still singing, women grappled with Cassie and lifted her to her feet. She swayed like one drunk. Popito dimly noted that her face was not even bruised; but what impressed him painfully was the fact that she was no longer Cassandra Walcott. Some Unknown looked through her unblinking eyes. Hastily the women searched her head for hairpins, removed pins from her dress and banded her waist firmly with red cloth. She took two great plunging steps forward with legs wide apart, staggered, grunted, put her hands with a defiant gesture on her hips, then, raising them to her temples, rushed forward and flung herself upon the drums.

The drums and the singing ceased abruptly. Only Cassie's heavy breaths were heard. The mamma drummer was afraid to touch the possessed woman, who lay half upon his knees. He looked appealing at another woman, who came quickly and raised her up. On the earth before each drum was a lighted candle. Cassie had upset one and the woman, first touching the earth with her palm, relit the candle and replaced it.

The drums beat fiercely again.

Ah, coo, la, la-a,
La hoo, la yea-a!

was repeated wildly again by every throat on the three notes

C, C, E, E,
E, D, D, C.

The little girl beside Popito was still asleep. She had slipped forward on her mother's lap. Her curving lips were slightly parted, and her little hat had fallen forward on her long-lashed lids.

The singing was like a triumphant welcome to the god that had come among them through Cassandra. Now she began to dance not as the priest had done but aggressively, with abandon, grunting, prancing with body inclined forward, as one driven or ridden. With untutored grace she moved her bare, dust-covered feet swiftly in an intricate pattern upon the earthen floor.

But now the drummer's fierce look was turned upon the other end of the tent where people were drawing apart with awe and respect. It was the *hounbonnor* himself with those terrible eyes fixed unblinkingly on nothing yet on everything who came forth dancing with the lighted candle on his head.

A young man fell down from the bench and beat the dust like a beheaded cockerel. Others wrestled with him to get off his shoes. The singing grew yet more frenzied. The onlookers stood upon boxes, raised themselves upon each other's shoulders and, open-mouthed, gazed at the dancers or commented briskly upon them. The dim light and the shadows cast by the bamboo lamps intensified their looks of excitement, fear and awe.

The drums ceased only when the mamma drummer was worn out. Cassie staggered from the tent. When after a long while she did not return and the drums began again, Popito went out of the tent to seek her. He found her prostrate before the shrine, whose candles had now shrunk to the earth. He looked about first to assure himself that none observed him, then went up to Cassie and shook her.

"Cassie?" said he doubtfully.

The effect was like the severing of an umbilical cord. The Cassie he had known so many months came back from the close, yet distant unseen world, looked up at him and rose as if from sleep.

"What happen?" he asked. "You all right?"

She crossed herself. Then straightened her dress and evidently feeling embarrassed replied: "Wait, I'm comin' now." She ran away into the house to tidy herself while he stood by in the dark and waited for her.

Three days before this Popito had taken six cases out of customs for Yankee—"the very last time I'm workin' for him," he assured himself. It was a safe shipment this time, there was nothing there but what was written on the invoice. What prompted him he did not know, but instead of taking the cases to Fyzabad himself he hired a truck driver to do the job. Duke was in the shop waiting to arrest Popito. His search of the cases was ruthless and thorough, but the bird had flown—or maybe, he thought, had escaped his too eager eye, and he searched again, crushed, destroyed, but was again compelled to retire frustrated. He was angry with himself: he had shown his hand and scared away the quarry.

The idea grew that Popito had concealed the drug upon his person or in some cache until the moment for delivery was more opportune. He had Popito's room watched. Informed that Popito and Cassie had gone to Diego Martin—Cassie had unwisely told a neighbour—Duke scented an accomplice. He decided to join the detective assigned to patrol Diego Martin village: Carr, a young man, big, agile and strong.

Both were riding bicycles. The enormous Duke, feeling too big for the machine, rode with his heels on the pedals, his toes and knees stuck out. The bicycle chain creaked beneath his weight.

At Singh's they stopped to see if all was well. Years before, Duke had secured a conviction against Singh for watering his milk. Judicious bribes had bought Singh immunity from further scrutiny. It was after eight o'clock when Duke entered the yard. He was surprised to see the bakery door open, dough uncovered in the wooden trough and no one about. The only sounds were Singh's high, thin voice raised in anger against someone, and the gentle moaning of a cow.

Duke entered the house without knocking. Singh and his girl wife were moving about their tasks and stopping every now and then to say hurtful things to each other. They spoke in Hindi but the anger in their voices could not be mistaken. Singh, a short plump man of forty, was so angry he ignored Duke—of whom he was secretly contemptuous—till the latter seized him with bear-like fondness and said to the wife:

"Kalaishi, what he doin' you? You want me take him down?"

"You come too late, man," Singh said in English, shaking his arm free.

He had come home, he said, to find all his men enticed from the bakeshop. Kalaishi had observed "a Spanish man" talking to them. Soon after he left a quarrel had broken out among the men. Three, refusing to work longer, went out saying they would get others to come and beat up the rest. The remaining four, finding it impossible to continue alone, had walked out also.

"What the Spanish man wearin'?"

But Kalaishi was unhelpful, she had paid little attention to him, her first-born being sick.

"Okay," said Duke. "Singh, what you have good for dry throat? Come, man, let's take a friendly drink before we go down the village."

At her husband's bidding Kalaishi fetched a bottle and glasses. Having had two drinks and washed them down with water Duke rid the unhappy Singh of his presence.

"He didn't pass us going back to town, he must have gone to the other bakery."

Carr disagreed. "The other bakery not workin'."

"I feel positive he didn't pass us."

"He could have taken another road. She said he came walkin', but he could be way ahead of us if he is on this road." Carr laughed. "Singh was real mad. He was hopin' to get all the trade around here now the others idle."

"Man must eat man to live, yes?"

"What to do? That's how life is in this Trinidad."

"Anywhere you like to name," Duke said cheerfully.

They were silent a while. The bicycle chain groaned.

"Hear the drums?"

Besides the distant sound of the drums they heard only the high, long-drawn, restful notes of grasshoppers, the croaking of *crapauds* in the grass-grown earthen drains and the groaning of the protesting bicycle chain. It was pitch dark.

It was after ten when Cassie and Popito descended the hillside track, Popito feeling his way in the darkness with a heavy stick he had picked up for protection against stray dogs. On his way up one had snapped at his heels and scared the women. When they had run the last few yards to the road Popito said: "You must be well tired after all that dancin', girl." He told her of his fear and horror when she had leaped in the air and fallen on her face, and his surprise that she rose unhurt.

"I not tired. It's seldom when the spirit take me I feel tired. I feel fresh as ever, as if I just wake up from sleep."

"So you really believe in this thing."

"Look—" and now she spoke with confidence—"Duke better not try his monkey business now, I tell you! It's he and Ogoun who will fight it out."

"Who is Ogoun?"

"The spirit who was ridin' me tonight."

"Cassie, you mustn't talk to anyone about this, you know. Le Maître don't believe in this sort-a thing at all."

"And you?"

"Girl, I don't know what to think, it have me beaten. Before we left they brought live coals in the tent. I watched the *hounbonnor* put his bare foot in them as if they was cool water. How he could do that without burning the skin off his foot?"

"Dada Mazookoo was protectin' him."

For a while they were silent. The sound of the drums grew more and more distant. The sound, the darkness and their talk of strange gods gave Popito an eerie feeling.

Duke had wanted to run his eyes over the spectators but had decided against it—he was too well known; and in Carr the people would have scented a detective at once—he was too well dressed. He decided to wait at a bend in the road. Maybe Popito would come by.

And not long after he heard voices. He let the figures come closer. Then he recognised the woman's voice and threw the light of his torch on their faces.

"Hold it! Stop where you are, Walcott. Luna, it's you I want a word with."

The shock of hearing Duke's voice in that dark and lonely road momentarily unnerved Cassie. She at once, with terror, recalled the beating. "What you want?" she cried, standing her ground.

But Popito did not know her well, and though she stepped forward the sound of fear in her voice triggered action in him. With one vicious swipe with his stick he struck the torch from Duke's hand and made him cry out in pain. Then they were off like the deer, Cassie leading the way because she knew the district. She jumped the earth drain and ran into the little savannah beside the road. Here and there clumps of bamboos or bushes loomed up before them but Cassie with cats' eyes avoided them all. Popito, following, hearing the clang of falling bicycles and the running of heavily booted feet, felt they were lost and it was all his fault.

Why am I running? Why did I strike him? Why? Because he knew it had come to a final trial of strength. He could not run like Cassie, he was panting, his legs were quivering, but no matter what happened he would not let them take her down and beat her up again.

"Run, Cassie! Don't stop!" he urged her, and ran back to his pursuers.

"What you want with me?"

"You take the girl, Carr!" Duke cried.

Popito flung the stick at Carr. By a piece of good fortune it caught between his legs and tripped him. Popito rushed at the approaching

Duke like a goaded bull, aiming a kick at his groin, but it caught him in the belly and partly winded him. Cassie, crouching in the bushes behind a clump of bamboos, heard Duke call Carr in the tones of one apprehensive of being mastered. She wanted to run on while there was yet time to do so unhindered but the sound of blows transfixed her.

"O God, have mercy! Ogoun! Dada Mazookoo!"

"You son . . . bitch! Got a knife? Look out, Carr, he like a mad dog!"

She heard a terrible thud. And again. And then a third, less resonant, so that she knew it for a body blow.

"Don't hit him again," said the unfamiliar voice.

She saw the dim light of a torch and heard the unfamiliar voice say: "You hit him too hard, man," and heavy breathing.

"Take him to the standpipe," Duke said.

There was a sound of something heavy being dragged through the grass.

Cassie began to crawl away behind the bushes. Never afterwards did she forget their pungent smell.

"He had a knife, you know, he had a knife. . . ."

"Must be in the grass. . . ."

The light of the torch fingered the ground in her direction. She stopped. She heard the Shango drums beating wildly like her heart and the distant song of praises to Ogoun; and it seemed to her that all was well, that he was knocked out, would be arrested but would come back to her before the dawn. Feeling the strength of Ogoun in her, her whole being chanting the wild song they were singing up the hill, she ignored the torch and crawled away, scarcely noticing that she put her hand in the fresh dung of a cow that had been tethered there that evening.

Chapter thirty

That day Walker had said: "This strike worries me, André. When I think of all the thousands of little children and old people who have no bread . . . this handful of men taking other people's lives in their hands. . . ."

"Aren't you expressing it too colourfully?"

Walker's cheekbones grew pink. This coloured intellectual with his superiority irritated him. "I'm just expressing my sympathy, you know what I mean?" he said, his eyes gliding over André's face before turning away.

"Keep it for yourself, Arnold. The workers will get along all right on johnny cake and breadfruit."

Walker's ears reddened. "You are a card, André," he said, laughing with an air of appreciation and slapping his junior's knee. "Listen, my boy, that's all right, but Barker has a job for both of us tomorrow night." And he outlined it.

"I'm not going to be a party to strike-breaking."

"I told Barker it would be inconvenient for you because you have to deal with the bakers, but he insists."

"Does he? I wonder if he knows there are certain things a man can't do?"

Walker's eyes grew moist and greasy, he took André's hand persuasively. He was genuinely fond of him despite his airs. "Boy, you have the queerest ideas. These are irresponsible people. Could they give you a job? How could it benefit you to support them?"

"It won't. But if I actively worked against them, I would despise myself."

"So you are leaving me to do the dirty work for you, is that it?" Walker flushed but laughed and turned away to hide his resentment. "What am I to tell Barker?"

André shrugged. "No one is compelling you to do it."

The rebuff hurt Walker. He had always been ready to give his heart to André but had rarely been able to get through to him. "I like my bread and butter, André," he replied coldly. "I hear you're getting married."

"Who told you that?" André asked sharply, flushing.

With his nervous hand Walker squeezed André's knee, laughing in a manner that seemed to say he knew how to keep secrets even in regard to such absurd ambitions as André entertained.

"Whoever told you that was a fool and those who believe him are still more foolish." André got up. "Don't count me in on this exercise," he said, and left Walker's office.

Oppressive was the foreboding that haunted André. To possess her and be possessed by her, yet be unable to reach her deepest self; to suspect vaguely in the inmost recesses of his mind, where he refused to look, that her self was alien to his own spirit or that a void was there—this was bitter. Into his love crept a taint of hate. To cause her physical pain was sometimes pleasant—"because she hurts me and will always hurt me," he told himself. But then he despised himself for this and would have liked to strike her because she had made him despise himself. He had not realised it yet, but it was not the falling of the early blooms that troubled him; it was the failure to find a spiritual haven, that need to be secure in someone else because he shrank from himself, of whom he expected much but feared to test and doubted. His thought sometimes turned to Beulah. To compare Gwenneth with a black girl was unfair, yet he could not hide from himself that in that brief episode with Beulah had been a giving and receiving, a oneness, he had not achieved with Gwenneth. She had no need of oneness. To conquer or be conquered was her joy. Should he give up the battle her interest would wane, the excitement pall. Her need of combat and his need of someone to stabilise the best within him held him in relentless, exhausting pursuit.

The following day, not wishing to come into too open conflict with Barker, he phoned the office that he was unwell and would not be in. But he went to Popito's.

Cassie had got home after midnight. She waited, waited, counting the hours, listening to the peaceful, echoing silence while fighting the dread visions rising in her. Then she flung aside the hope that he would come. "He's in the lock-up. I must bail him out, I have the twenty dollars he gave me two days gone. No, I must see a lawyer first. You have to know what is the right thing to do with the police, otherwise it's no good. I will wait till half-past seven. Take patience, Ogoun goin' to protect him."

The sun was just rising. She washed, put on clean clothes and combed her hair. She thought she would eat something but nothing would go down. She drank some coffee. Near seven there came a knocking. She flung the door open. André stood before her.

Her appearance disturbed him. Her face was drawn. Her eyes were sunken and burned with a desperate fever.

"Good morning, Cassie. Is Popito in?"

"No, but he might come any minute," she said rapidly. "Come inside." He went in. "You want coffee?"

"No, thanks, I've just had breakfast."

"Take a seat."

She sat before him on a bentwood chair, smiling with her lips only, waiting, listening for Popito's footsteps.

"Is something wrong?"

"No, nothing wrong."

"Where did he go this morning?" he asked after a pause. "I only ask because I have something very important to tell him about the strike."

"The strike?"

"You know, the bakers' strike."

"Yes, I remember."

He looked at her uneasily. "He must try and get as many men together as possible—fifty, sixty men—to picket New Bakeries. The boss is going to get men from the country tonight and drive them in. Popito must get to work at once or they will succeed in breaking the strike."

"Yes, I understand, they will break it." She saw his smooth, happy, good-looking face that life had not yet scarred; but the word "break" called up again the terrible blows she had heard and the body being dragged through the grass. And suddenly, like a knife, reality severed her from Ogoun. She seized her head. "O God!" she wailed. "O God!" And tears poured out unheeded.

"What's the matter? What's happened?"

He took her hands, and hers clutched his and crushed them. "André! André!" She held them to her face, she twisted in her agony, pressed her head against him for solace, then flung him aside violently and beat her forehead on the table. He had never seen such abandonment to grief and was alarmed, tried to stop her hurting herself, but she rushed away with a cry behind the curtain and fell on the bed. He followed her. She was rolling from side to side.

"Cassie, what is it? Tell me, you must tell me!" He lifted her, held her against him, and again her hands crushed his and her head swung back and forth on his chest.

"André! André!"

Her grief stripped bare something in him, he knew not what, but he too wept. What he had tried to hide from himself was all at once clear—Gwenneth's love would not last because she was the product of a hostile world, and he could not altogether tear himself from Cassie or Elena.

"Come, tell me, tell me," he urged, pressing her to himself while rocking her a little, consoling both himself and her.

In between her sobs she told him, and he froze.

"I must go to the hospital and see if he's there. If he's not there perhaps he's in the cells. . . ."

"No, you can't—you mustn't. Listen, *I* will check on the hospital for you. Don't go there and above all don't go to the police. They want you now."

"I must get a lawyer, I can't leave him like that!" she pleaded piteously.

"You can't help him now—I mean, you must stay with people you can trust. Come with me to Fyzabad. We'll go to Ben Le Maître. Stay away from here for a bit."

The coffee was lukewarm but he coaxed her to drink more of it and drank some himself, then coaxed her into his car. He rang casualty. No one of that name had been brought in, they told him. He went in search of Winchester and, having warned him of what was afoot, drove through back streets to the Southern main road.

All that sixty miles she wept. The main thing she had hidden: the mortification, the awful consciousness of being abandoned by Ogoun and God; the feeling of utter helplessness before the world. She cared not where André was taking her, she felt only that she must stay with him because he was someone in the world and she was nothing.

He knew where Ben lived, having visited him before when in the south on business, but now Ben was not at home. They went to the Fyzabad sport ground and waited in the shade of some trees. At the appointed hour they returned. Ben was surprised to see them and almost from Cassie's first words guessed that the police had taken Popito.

Cassie told him everything.

"You danced?" Le Maître asked.

"I belong to them, man!" she answered with angry irritation. But the tears flowed again when she spoke of the clubbing, and she could not go on.

He waited. "Who told you about the opium?" he asked at length.

"I didn't need anybody to tell me that."

"And you haven't told a soul?"

"What you take me for?" she asked in surprise. She related how Duke had beaten her to make her tell what she knew and she had kept silent.

"You are a girl a man could go through hell for," he remarked, evidently thinking what a fool Popito had been not to realise this sufficiently to protect her. "André is right. It's better not to go back right away. Wait and see what's happening. I'll get you a place to stay. Have you eaten? No, no, you must eat," he insisted when she said she wanted nothing. "Let's go to Yankee's."

They made a meal of bread and fruit and black pudding. Le Maître and André talked of the strike, but Cassie remained silent because she kept holding on to some last shreds of hope and could think of nothing else. Outside the shadows lengthened.

"Wait here for me," said Le Maître. "I'll see a comrade about a place for you."

"I have an aunt, I could stay with her," she said indifferently.

He looked at her curiously. "All right, I'll buy a paper."

He went out. After about five minutes he returned looking grim. He silently put the *Evening News* before her. The headline MAN FOUND CLUBBED TO DEATH IN DIEGO MARTIN was like a blow. She cried out.

"Wait! What was he wearing?"

She described his clothing. Le Maître released her arm.

They listened awkwardly to her sobbing.

"Take me back, André. I goin' to the police."

"Don't do that, Cassie," André pleaded. He had read the cold, impersonal, even gory tale and felt sick with bitterness and hate and horror.

"Take me back, André, take me back!"

"André is right, you know," Le Maître counselled.

She jumped up like a tigress. "So what I must do? Duke killed him! I goin' to Colonel Cambridge himself!"

"Hear me, hear me. Duke has a witness. You have none. You think

Cambridge will take your word? You think any jury will take your word? Who are you? If you cannot produce proof stay silent. You want to open yourself to more police persecution?"

"O God, it must have justice in this world somewhere for us. It got to have justice somewhere for poor people!"

"You want revenge against Duke. I, too, want it. Popito was not only a comrade, he was dear to me." Le Maître struck the table a blow. "But revenge will make matters worse for us. We need unity, unity. It is only so we can help ourselves." He seized her arm and shook it as if hoping thus to rouse her from her despair. "The whites despise us but they are afraid of us. So long as Boisson leads us they feel safe. But when one of us begins to lead our own workers they get into a frenzy of rage, become terribly cruel and use all means to crush us. Don't do anything rash now. Our time will come. Go, bury him. But don't stay in Port-of-Spain. Come back here with us, we will keep your courage high. I will get you a job. You understand me?" He turned to André. "Can you give her some money to bury him?"

Cassie shook her head. "I have. . . . It was too good to last, I knew it."

"Don't let me hear you say that again!" cried Le Maître. "Nothing in this world is too good for our people. Don't give way to despair. If we stand together we are like rock, Cassie."

André was looking at him, surprised both by the statements and the intense conviction with which they were uttered. He felt like laughing, yet at the same time longed to feel that what Ben said was true.

Le Maître in a low voice, and holding the fingers of his left hand one by one as he made his points, told her what not to say to the police if questioned.

"You have done a lot for us, André. We're very grateful to you."

"I didn't do it for you, I did it for myself," André replied sharply because Le Maître's words seemed to indicate he had no right among them; and he felt still more annoyed because he flushed and made an issue of it.

"For yourself?"

"Yes, for myself. Every man has to live with himself."

"Thank you, comrade. So you will take her back now? Good."

It was long after dark when they got back to Port-of-Spain. She went first to the hospital to identify the body. Looking through the policemen as if she did not see them she answered their questions briefly in a low, monotonous voice. She said she had left the Shango meeting with Popito, that he had excused himself to speak to two men, telling her to go on, he would be late. No, she did not know the men, nor could she describe them.

Then André drove her to Mrs Henriques's. Popito had given her the new address. André was ashamed to go in, ashamed to face Elena, but there was no help for it. Cassie told them the same tale she had told the police, and in the same monotonous low voice, as if her tears had dried at their source. From the moment she had seen Popito's face in death something hard and ineradicable had begun to cover her wound.

Aurelia shrieked and held her head. "O God! This and all—even this?"

Elena tried to console her. Cassie looked at them dry-eyed. André thought he saw in those eyes the accusing question: "Have you more right to weep for him than I?"

"I will bury him," she said, and waited jealously, for his sister had more right than she who was but a servant and not his wife.

"Not even that I can do for him, not even that," Aurelia said, weeping.

Cassie rose. "Mr André goin' to drive me home, Miss Aurelia," she said, slipping back instinctively into the role of servant now Popito was gone and she was in the presence of his sister and niece.

They drove home in silence, Popito's dead face between them. When he pulled up outside her place André said:

"I'm afraid for you, Cassie. Be careful."

"Don' be afraid for me, better be 'fraid for you'self."

She opened the door and was getting out but turned and took his hand in both of hers and pressed it. "Thank you, André. Good night."

At that very time Walker was earning his bread and butter. Three taxis filled with men recklessly charged the picket line that had been strengthened before New Bakeries' gates. The pickets scattered, cursing. The gates opened at once and the cabs rolled through.

It was not long before Barker arrived to see how business was progressing. Some pickets were still about and Barker, seeing himself recognised, addressed them jovially.

"Hi, there, Arthur. How's the strike goin'? What're you fellers goin' to do about that offer? Not takin' it. That's the stuff. You give 'em hell, Arthur. Mr Duff just called me up. I'm goin' to see what he wants."

He almost ran into the bakery. "Hi, Duff! How many did Wahker git yuh?" His eyes glistened. He lowered his voice but only as he finished the sentence. He glanced around him and cleared his throat nervously.

"A dozen. That will do for a beginning."

"You didn't have to use the police as you thought, uhn! By Jeez, Duff, you think Dollard will be pleased? When's your first batch comin' out?"

"Four o'clock. I used double yeast."

"You did, uh, Duff? That's damn good. Tell Dollard yet? Pleased, is he?" Barker chortled. "O Jesus! That's damn good noos."

"I'll make a special loaf for you, Bow-Wow."

"You gimme that yeast business. That's what I want. Now you got a damn good chance before the other bakers catch up, see, Duff? You c'n get all that business. . . ."

After the funeral Cassie packed her old suitcase and Popito's, left in Aurelia's care what she could not carry and went down to South Quay to catch the bus "Sweet Violet" to Fyzabad. Walking down George Street behind the barefooted old Indian man in the *kapra* who was carrying both suitcases on his head for twelve cents Cassie saw Duke on the opposite sidewalk. Duke saw her at the same instant and gave her a searching, sly sidelong look. But there was no fear in her now. The terrible glow in her eyes showed him she was a very different girl from the one he had beaten up in the station. He turned his head aside and continued on his way.

Chapter thirty-one

Once, only once, André took Gwenneth to his home. It was no pleasant time for him. He tried to shut his eyes to his mother's claims to good society with her prim social airs, but he was glad, too, that she was not capable of the Osbornes' cool impertinence. Gwenneth's personality sparkled, it set the tone of the conversation and their laughter. They were captivated by her and, he felt, by the unapproachable world in which she moved with indifferent ease. *And she expects homage in our world, she enjoys it,* flashed into his mind. The longer the visit lasted the more painful it became for him. *Is this love? These torments, this uncertainty—are they happiness? I want truth, and yet I turn from it.*

Before it was decently time he rose to go. His parents forgave him with their smiles, which said they knew he wished to be alone with Gwenneth and found it a pleasing wish.

Some days later Mr de Coudray had a talk with his son. He offered to set André up in London. "If you intend to marry her you'll have to get away from all this." His mother urged acceptance. "You're only ruining yourself here, my dear," she commented with eyebrows raised, lids lowered. Her sigh made it clear to him how much she had suffered on his account in the past and what high hopes rested on him now.

At first he saw happiness before him, but then what he had not foreseen became suddenly evident: in what circles in that distant England would he live and survive with Gwenneth?

He thought she would be delighted when he told her of his father's offer. They had been driving through Maraval and had stopped in the bush beside a stream. For some reason she had been withdrawn. He hoped to bring her joy. It was one of those perfect afternoons. There was a light cool breeze. Low white clouds moved swiftly across the sky. From the grass, the swaying trees, the water came subtle fragrances that made him long to embrace this world in which his roots were buried.

"Did he?" she said when he told her of the offer. Her whole face brightened. She looked down and said nothing for a while, rubbing the back of his hand lightly and hurriedly with her fingers. "André, did you write an article for a magazine?"

"Yes. Why?"

"Why didn't you tell me? Didn't you want me to know?"

"I didn't think it would have interested you."

"Father saw it."

"I won't listen," he thought. "I don't want to hear. It's not important. Only this earth, these trees, this sky—only this that is me is important."

"I think David showed him."

"The police? Interesting."

In their magazine *Forward,* which Joe was editing, André had written an article on the city council. It expounded the view that certain government circles resented the existence of the council as a vestige of self-rule and felt its authority an affront to them; that British residents resented control of their water, sewerage and streets by sundry black members of Boisson's party; and that this attitude was the principal inspiration for the everlasting tirades in the press against the council as well as the niggardliness of the government grant to municipal funds.

"What did your father say?"

"He wasn't pleased."

"I didn't write it for him."

He saw in her eyes an imperious flash of displeasure that he had placed her in an awkward position. "He said you were associating with people who needed to be watched and that you were anti-British. Why did you do it? It was . . . a sort of lark, was it?"

"A lark! Good God, it was something I had to do."

"Something you had to do?"

"To live at peace with myself. Can you understand?"

She was looking at him in silence. "I suddenly wondered if I really knew you. You aren't anti-British? That's absurd."

"Is it?"

"But why?"

He got out of the car, slamming the door, and flung himself on the grass beside the stream.

She followed him. "I might understand if you told me."

Crickets answered her, and a frog that had stopped croaking when he slammed the door began again.

He seized her arm, squeezing it painfully. "You, your English friends, all of you despise us. *You* haven't stopped to realise it, that's all." He threw her arm aside because he wanted to embrace her, to crush her, to be cruel.

"What's *wrong* with you?"

He heard uneasy apprehension in her voice. He had never associated fear with her, and the sound of it gladdened him.

"What do you think of your servants, Gwenneth? But why ask that, it's unnecessary. What do you think of black lawyers and doctors, say?"

"What are you getting at? I haven't met any."

"But would you go out with one? They're your class, they're educated, they've got money."

"I don't despise them, if that's what you're trying to say."

"Well, me, then. You've never been even to a movie with me."

"But we go riding together."

"In that huge Savannah hardly anyone sees us. It's a safe place."

"Are you saying I feel guilty about you? You know perfectly well it's because of what my parents would say."

"And your friends."

"I love you and you know it—why, how could you dare to doubt it, André!" She was flushed. "How can you hate us? Why?"

"I don't hate *you*, I love you and I wish I didn't! Every day you lord it over us, here, Africa, India. You hold us in contempt, you bomb us, you bayonet us, you suck us dry. You keep the top jobs. You educate us to despise and fear ourselves, to fall down before you, to speak with your accent. We go abroad to study and come back squeaking with the accents of governors and heads of departments. Those who do that are neither Englishmen nor West Indians, they're less than men—apes, puppets!" He was quivering, choking.

"How extraordinary!" she said, because she did not know what to make of it all.

"There's love and love. If I go away with you I'm in a foreign land among foreign people. Not English and not quite West Indian. I'd be a spiritual nonentity, a man without identity. I hate this island. I hate it and I love it! And you can't stay here with me, you can't live our life, my life—"

"I could!" Her lips sought his avidly.

"No," he whispered, succumbing joyfully.

"Yes," she whispered, not knowing what she was saying because she wanted to exorcise his demon and soothe his hurt that was beyond her understanding.

There was a power, a magic, in him she could not resist; and in them both was the fear of being deprived of their happiness, and an urgency to enjoy it while it lasted.

Neither of them suspected that Mr Osborne knew more than he had revealed. David Primrose had informed him that André had taken Cassie to Fyzabad to see Le Maître. The judge had been more puzzled than shocked. He could not in the least understand what a sensitive and not uncultured person like young de Coudray could find to interest him in the company of a common servant and a rabble-rouser with whom the law was much too lenient. He said nothing to Gwenneth: he could not reveal that the police had their spies in Workers' Welfare. Fearing, too, the streak of obstinate perversity in her he was cautious in expressing disapproval of André. He wanted happiness for his daughter. Obviously, being the woman she was she would never find it in a marriage outside her set. He pressed his wife to take her away on a holiday somewhere.

After her father's remarks about the article Gwenneth discovered that André's strangeness, which had so intrigued her, was too strange. What was he seeking, what would he achieve, she asked him.

"West Indian self-respect. A decent life for everyone. Even independence, mad as that sounds!"

"Suppose," she pursued, "we *had* done all you say we did in Africa and all that . . . it was for the good of those people, they'd have murdered one another without us."

He reddened. "Our good? Look in the streets, look all around you. Is this the good you want for us?"

She was silent, his passionate sincerity compelling her to realise for the first time that there might be quite valid points of view besides those she had grown up with and come to regard as irrefutable. Yet why this passion about a matter so remote from them? What had the people in the streets or in Africa to do with him and her?

"You don't know us," she chided gently. "You don't know the English, you really don't. English people are . . . oh, goodness, civilised! We have poor people too, André, lots of them. I wish you'd come home more often. They don't know you, the real you, André, and I want them to get to know you. I don't want to be meeting in secret all the time. And you don't either. Will you?"

" 'Once more unto the breach, dear friends,' " he said with a mocking laugh. "Must I come and *prove* my worth to your parents?"

"Oh, nonsense. But at least give them the opportunity to recognise your worth. I don't like hiding, it's degrading. Please, André. For my sake? Just once. . . ."

And so one evening he paid them one of his now rare visits. He heard strange English voices. The old feeling of insecurity seized him, but this made him so angry that he took the steps in two bounds. He entered the drawing-room with a stern cold look just like his father's.

"André! Come in," said Gwenneth, rising and to her own annoyance blushing. She blushed because she sensed surprise and displeasure in her mother's expression as she fell suddenly silent. Her father's smile turned sour. And her blush convinced her she had made a mistake by inviting André.

Everyone stopped talking to look at him. He immediately interpreted those looks to mean that they would have been happier if he had not turned up among them, he had destroyed the intimacy of their gathering. Mrs Osborne smiled at Gwenneth with a questioning look, her head shaking nervously. Gwenneth introduced André to Arthur Symmonds, the colonial secretary's son, who went riding with her and had recently been paying her much attention. A dashing lad, physically strong and very good at sport. Then to a pale English bank manager, Jim Bord, who was interested in Esther. He was, it struck André, despite his loose mouth and projecting teeth, inflexibly self-assured, conscious of his place in this intricate scheme of things. This was evident from his handshake, which seemed vigorously to assert his reliability on even the most ticklish of occasions, though he contrived to convey this without looking at the visitor's face but somewhere in the region of his right ear. David Primrose wore a thinly innocent smile. André tried to avoid looking at his golden-haired hands, which he hated. The judge nodded, grimaced, adjusted his neck in its collar.

There was a movement of chairs.

"As I was saying," the judge continued, turning to the sub-inspector, "my personal impression was that he was completely guilty. . . ."

"We were just talking of the tennis finals, André," Gwenneth was saying. "Have you been watching them?"

Ridiculous, thought André: she knew he had. He said: "Yes, I saw Richards win his set."

"Oh, Richards is jolly good!" Jim Bord announced, solemnly enthusiastic.

"I say, wasn't his opponent weak, though," from Arthur Symmonds. "He barely made it interesting. I could have done better myself."

"Could you?" André raised his eyebrows innocently, sensing with a lover's instinct something between Symmonds and Gwenneth.

"Do you play tennis?" Mrs Osborne came in quickly with a smile, her head shaking in negation.

André inclined his head. "I try."

But Symmonds, seeming not to have understood André, was saying something to Gwenneth about badminton. Esther in her languorous way was asking the bank manager if he would enter the next badminton tournament. There was a taunt in her laughter.

"André, were you at the Bolton concert on Saturday?" from Gwenneth, unsmiling, tossing her hair back—defiantly, André thought. Was she brushing off Symmonds?

"Yes, it went well. She has a good voice." Suddenly the temptation was irresistible, his tongue ran away with him. "She sings with taste too. So many of them who come here are tasteless mediocrities. And her accompanist was good—in fact, quite good. A really good accompanist is a rare . . ." he waved his hand, ". . . quite a phenomenon. They're either not satisfied with a supporting role—want to make a noise of their own—or they tend to superimpose their own conception of the music on the singer. It's like those pianists who have little respect for Tchaikovsky's music. His second piano concerto, for instance. They chop it up because they're jealous of the prominence given to the solo violin. . . ."

They were silent, all of them, listening to him. They were surprised he should be heated. "And why does he talk so much?" their silence suggested to him, so that he blushed.

And Esther remarked with a sly smile, lazily: "How strange. I met someone yesterday who thought the concert was awful."

Mr Bord laughed. "Oh, I say, jolly good. That's always the way, isn't it?"

Mrs Osborne asked him if he knew anything that would stop the ants eating her roses. He communed with himself gravely for several seconds before assuring her that he was "ter'ib'y sowwy," he could think of nothing.

The judge and sub-inspector were on murder trials.

"What are the qualifications for jury service?" André broke in, smiling straight into the judge's eyes.

The judge's eyes fell, the faintest look of distaste appeared and vanished around his lips.

"Sixty dollars a month, isn't it?" said Primrose, looking at his host.

"Yes, I think so," the judge said.

"Much too high, you know," André commented, sighing.

The judge seemed not to hear. "If he had come before me he would have got a stiff sentence," he said.

An Alsatian dog trotted in.

"Mick! Lie down," said the judge.

"Splendid dog," Mr Bord announced.

"Six months. Pure Alsatian, you know. I paid forty dollars for him."

André said with a smile: "Almost as much as a juryman."

Mr Bord chuckled, thinking this rather witty, while looking like everyone else at the forty-dollar dog. They were smiling at it and leaning forward in their chairs with an interest that suggested they appreciated both the judge's good fortune in being able to acquire such an animal and the dog's good fortune in coming by such a master.

With the entry of the dog André noticed what he had only perceived unconsciously on previous visits. The Osbornes' drawing-room was functional but tasteless. In his parents' home much time had been spent over the years in artistic embellishment. Drapes, rugs, pictures, vases, flowers all contributed to the enjoyment of one's safe anchorage. At the Osbornes' there was comfort too, but it occurred to him now it was more the comfort of a temporary camp till they moved on elsewhere.

David Primrose pulled Mick's ears. Esther patted his rump. Mrs Osborne went out to get him a biscuit.

The judge offered cigarettes in a polished Indian box rich with inlay.

"Awfully good Camels," David Primrose remarked. "Where d'you get yours?"

André lit the judge's cigarette. The latter put up a smoke screen, half closing his eyes, and nodded thanks. "I had a surprisingly good game yesterday," he said to Primrose. "Bogey for every hole except the third."

"Really!"

"What happened at the third?" André enquired.

The judge removed a shred of tobacco from his lip. "Sliced."

"Pity. I know a chap who has done that hole in one on at least two occasions."

"I don't seem to have heard of him." A warbling, gurgling after-dinner sound issued from the judge's belly but everyone found it inaudible.

Drinks were brought in, and dog biscuits and sweet biscuits. André was wildly tempted to offer the judge a dog biscuit. He drank two brandies and sodas one after the other, and almost at once, because he drank but rarely, he was seized by a spirit of belligerence. Eyes glittering, he told Mrs Osborne that he was going to London, where his father had connections.

"There's nothing here. You can live and die in this place without ever knowing you're alive."

"It's the same in London, you know," she replied, impressed by the word "connections".

"I shall probably spend several weeks in Paris too," he added.

"Do you speak French?"

"I used to once. It won't take me long to pick it up again. I have relatives there in business. They do handsomely."

"Oh, you'd certainly have more of a future there than here."

"Oh, much, much, much more," he said, suddenly unable to control his tongue, and waving his arms and speaking loudly. "Why, what are you faced with in this country? Sycophancy and the worship of sycophancy; the enthronement of insipidity; deliberate discouragement of talent; the crushing of the intellectual; hatred, fear, a prison atmosphere! That's what confronts us." He paused, thinking, *By God, I'm good!* It seemed to him that his words were like brilliant flames and claps of thunder. He looked at the faces.

Esther giggled : "I never thought it was that bad." The others were either shocked or bewildered, numbed, and Gwenneth was embarrassed. Should he tell them about Cassie? he thought. Should he tell them how the coppers killed Popito? But at that moment Mick, who was weary of being rubbed, jumped up barking and wagging his tail in response to André's arm waving and trotted up to him.

Everyone laughed, especially Gwenneth.

"Oh, you are an impolite doggie," said Mrs Osborne, and an animated discussion followed on various breeds of dogs, their virtues and the climates most suited to them.

It was not yet ten o'clock when André rose.

"Must you go, Mr de Coudray?" the judge remarked.

"So nice to have seen you," Mrs Osborne added with the smile reserved for moving votes of thanks at the Young Women's Christian Association.

Gwenneth went out with him, smiling as far as the door. On the lawn she whispered angrily, "André! How could—" But he cut the words off with kisses.

"Tomorrow night in the alley?" she whispered.

"No. In the light, where everyone can see us. It's that or nothing. Goodbye, Gwenneth."

Chapter thirty-two

After the guests had departed the judge told Gwenneth: "I'm not prepared to have that young pup come visiting here any longer."

Humiliated by André's behaviour, her sympathy going out to him for the hurt she sensed but improperly understood, Gwenneth shook back her hair with a defiant toss and blushed. She was about to go upstairs but the judge stopped her.

"You ought to know this. He was seen driving with one of our servants some days ago."

"André? With one of our servants!"

"The young one who went off without notice."

"Cassie? Who saw him?" she demanded.

"Who saw him doesn't matter, the authority is reliable."

"Where was he driving?"

"On the Southern Main Road. Why wasn't he at work? You might find it profitable to enquire."

Gwenneth ran up the stairs and locked herself in her room. For long her eyes searched the gloom, her heart torn by jealousy she would not admit to herself and by anger at being thus openly insulted.

Next afternoon she met André by arrangement outside of Queen's Royal College. "In the light, as you wanted," she said as they drove off.

"I'm glad. A weight off my spirit."

"Well, have you recovered?"

"Yes, quite recovered. I'm forbidden the house, I take it."

"Yes."

"Then to meet me in the light was wonderful of you."

She drew away the hand he had taken. "Were you driving Cassie about?"

The question shocked him. How much did the police know? "Yes," he said.

"I suppose you've been having an affair with her."

"Nothing like that. She had lost her husband and I was taking her to Fyzabad."

"She wasn't married, André, I know *that*."

"All right, she lost the man she was living with."

"Why did *you* have to take her?"

"She was distraught, I didn't think she would have gone alone."

"Somebody else could have taken her. How far away is Fyzabad?"

"Sixty miles."

"You drove a hundred and twenty miles for her and you don't care about her?"

"I can't tell you all the circumstances."

"That *is* the limit. You and a servant have secrets from me!"

He had parked the car outside the Botanical Gardens. He got out and opened her door. "Let's go for a walk."

She got out without looking at him, her head held high. She did not forget, though, to look in the mirror of her handbag and touch her hair into place. She stepped in a prim, prickly way in her high heels, and the light swing of her behind spoke eloquently to him of her anger. She let him take her hand. They sat on a bench under an enormous spreading fig tree. Both were silent, not because nothing remained to be said, rather because there was too much.

"Have you ever had a black girl, André?"

"Yes."

"After you knew me?"

"Before."

"Was it . . . casual?"

"Casual? I loved her . . . for a little while."

"Was it Cassie?" She smiled wryly, almost ready to strike him.

"No, a girl called Beulah. A servant too."

"You couldn't love her, you're joking."

"No. I wanted love just as she did. And she was . . . utterly generous. I felt she gave me not her body only, she gave me her heart. Who was I to say my heart was better than hers?"

Gwenneth snatched her hand from his and clasped hers together tightly. "I don't think I'll ever understand you, André. Didn't you go to work that day you took Cassie to Fyzabad?"

He thought: "It's just as well to tell everything and be done with this affair." He said: "No. I took the day off. The bakers were on strike. Arnold Walker was going to break the strike, I didn't want any part of that. You understand why?"

"Go on."

"Because everyone wants life to be good, everyone wants happiness, and for that you must be able to eat, to feed the children, to pay rent, buy clothes. . . ."

"But they weren't starving."

"No," he replied in a dull voice. "They weren't starving."

"Oh, I don't care," she said, seeing she had failed him somehow. "You and Cassie, and having secrets from me with her!"

They were both feeling now that they could not bear to give up their love, and that they had wasted themselves on a love that had no future.

"I suppose your father revealed this dread secret."

"Yes. It *had* to come from him."

He stood up. "Shall we go?"

She rose too and looked at him with such reproach, so much wounded pride and so intense a yearning that in a moment she was in his arms and kissing him with abandon. "Can't you tell me everything?" she whispered.

Six weeks before, perhaps, he would have done so, trusting her. But now he couldn't. His world, his uncertainties, his past, his half-seen visions could not be hers. "I felt sorry for her," he said. "I had to help her, that was all."

She wanted to know what he meant by "gave me not her body only" in reference to the servant girl, but the words would not get past her lips. "We'd better go," she said abruptly.

"Not yet, not while you're angry. Sit down. Please, Gwenneth."

They sat with their arms about each other. He was stroking her cheek, her hair, kissing her fingers, but it was as if a long parting stood before them; and so neither spoke, and at last they could stand each other no longer.

When they reached her home she flung her arms around him and kissed his lips though it was still bright day. She promised to meet him that Friday.

That Friday never came for him. As soon as Gwenneth entered the house her mother informed her, bright and gay, that they were sailing to Tobago on Friday.

André never guessed the pain, the doubt, the unaccustomed turmoil of soul that lay behind the cold words of farewell she spoke to him on the phone.

It was all in the social columns what a grand time she was having with Arthur Symmonds. Swimming, sailing, dancing, barbecues—so full were her days and nights she scarcely needed to make the effort not to think of André. The local white planters vied for her attendance at their parties. More than one was in love with her—the breath of life to almost any girl but especially to Gwenneth. But among all these admirers there was not one who could match André. Anger gave way to admiration. She had always admired him but this admiration was for the new and impossible man she had discovered in him, whom she wished she had not discovered.

On her return she phoned him. They met at a Country Club dance. André noticed with joy and terror that her skin was bronzed, that she was slightly plumper and was happier and more self-assured than ever. And why shouldn't she be happier? he asked himself. Arthur was no problem. He saw how Arthur Symmonds ran up to her with a sort of jocular prance, raising his feet high in their glazed pumps, and how Gwenneth laughed and held out both her hands to him. Between them, clearly, were the fondest memories of some Tobago escapades that had drawn them close. André turned to Marie-Louise, who was looking at him with a kind of quiet rapture.

* * * *

Joe had for some time been visiting Elena and taking her out. They went to dances, to the movies and for walks at night. Elena wore a mask of calm indifference to the past and pretended to enjoy Joe's company. Aurelia did not stand in her way: she knew her daughter was unhappy, and Joe she considered an excellent match.

With women Joe was awkward and embarrassed. He did not know how to hold a girl's hand simply, suffered torments before embracing her and then was so clumsy that she felt ashamed and laughed. This was why he made amorous advances under the cloak of a derisive mimicry of tenderness. Elena had become too grave to accept such antics. She felt too deeply, valued truth too much; and their talks were always in serious vein, acid with social and personal discontent that was especially evident when he laughed cruelly at her naive hopes: that laughter covered despair at his own desire for her.

He talked about the labour movement, his plans when he got on the council—building himself up because it chafed him to see that André still occupied all her thoughts. She liked about him best his feeling for the poor, the plain folk, the simple; but with this feeling ran a biting cynicism which jarred upon her because she needed faith in life, and Joe, she fancied, had faith in neither life nor man. All the same, she sensed how much frustration in love and private ambition this concealed. People, he was fond of contending, must be led and must be controlled if we were to live better than we did now—or anarchy. "When I get on that council . . ." or, "If I was mayor . . ." —such phrases were always in his mouth. He felt a constant urge to test himself by challenging life. "I will drink the cup to its dregs," he proclaimed once with a proud sneer on his big handsome face. "It's the only way to live. You have to face fate, you have to face reality, you have to challenge reality to do its worst!"

For consolation he often turned to music. He was playing records one Sunday morning when André came in.

"What! A visit from Mr de Coudray?" he cried with a taunt in his laugh. "Sit down, my boy, I'm listening to one of the finest things in the world."

Because just at that moment he had been thinking of Elena and her enduring love for André and he was playing Beethoven's ninth symphony, which André did not greatly admire.

With a faintly derisive smile intended to conceal his own unhappiness André sat down, thinking: "He's listening as if he really expected that conglomeration of sound to reveal to him the meaning of life."

Joe held up a finger. "Listen to that—listen! No, really, you must admit—"

"False, pompous. Even the Rachmaninoff concerto is superior," André said wildly because it was necessary to talk, argue and convince himself he had not lost the power to make decisions.

"Pure romanticism. He's like a juggler tossing up coloured balls. Can't you see? That certain quality of the mind called character, that power to assess life—that is missing, it resembles a child trying to eat several kinds of sweets at one time. So what do you think life is, just one love song? Come, listen to this. Don't worry about spinning theories, just listen." Joe put on a Beethoven quartet.

In fact the mood of the music suited André's own, but for this very reason it depressed him. "Take it off. It reeks of despair!"

"Not despair, André—resignation, detachment. That is what you need—detachment. You have to learn to accept the inevitable."

"Inevitable? What is inevitable? What are you talking about?"

Joe grinned unkindly. "The acceptance of the inevitable has produced some very beautiful music, and verse too. Look at Mozart's last symphonies. . . . So you think she will marry you?" Joe asked unexpectedly.

"No."

Joe sat up. "Let us talk about it, let us face facts. Look here, do you know what I will tell you? The most demoralising thing in the world is to become a slave to a woman's body. Yes! A slave!" he shouted agitatedly. "Unable to call your soul your own." He began to walk about the room. "Those country club fashion plates? I have never had the doubtful honour of belonging to that set, my friend, but I have seen some of them in action. They can be the ruin of a man's talents—they can ruin the man himself!"

"I am not ruined. No woman will ruin me, especially that woman. I don't want to discuss it."

Joe laughed with a kind of triumphant mockery. This André could not bear. He got up and went out without a word, the laughter blaring behind him. Going through the sitting-room to the front door he came upon Beulah dusting.

"André? Eh-eh, what happen?"

He made an effort to master himself. Tenderness showed in her face. She put her hand timidly on his arm. "You had a quarrel?" she whispered.

"It's all right."

"Sit down. Nobody home but Joe."

He sat. She pretended to dust the arm of the chair in which he was sitting, smiling at him to invite a responding smile, then paused behind him and ran her hand through his hair nervously and tenderly. "And you have such pretty hair," she whispered.

He reached over his head, but she eluded him and went on dusting briskly. He jumped up and took her in his arms.

She tried to push him away. "Suppose Joe see you, man?"

But he pressed her to him and kissed her, and she, pressing her whole body against his, sucked the poison out of his heart. "Tonight," he wanted to say. "Tonight!" But the thought that he was making use of her shamed him and he was silent.

"So long I didn't see you," she whispered with a quiver in her voice that made him shake.

"Tonight, then?"

She smiled. "You'll meet me?"

"At the corner."

She disengaged herself quickly, with a laugh in which he felt only kindness. He went out.

Tonight. In the dark. The more he looked into himself the less he liked what he saw.

Chapter thirty-three

The oil bosses knew Le Maître too well and feared his influence too much to employ him, but Payne and French, less well known, found jobs; both worked for Trinidad Limited in Fyzabad. Not only were these two members of Workers' Welfare, they had joined Boisson's party as well, the Workers' Party. In the Fyzabad branch they monopolised almost every meeting, agitating, criticising, picking out mistakes in administration and policy and pouring scorn on the inactive branch executive. Ceaselessly they called for a militant approach to the workers' problems. Again and again they assured the oil workers that Boisson was not fighting and would not fight his own class. And Boisson's men began going to Diamond Hall to hear what remedies Le Maître held out—this Negro who talked with assurance but who, after all, had less power than the most insignificant of white men on the field. What could he do?

"I can do nothing," he told them. "Boisson can do nothing. It's what you can do!"

They chuckled, some of them. They liked to hear him. What he said made sense, voiced their hearts' yearning. And he spoke with authority. A Negro with authority who was not afraid and who knew the way out. He gave them pride.

One night in October the Workers' Party meeting had hardly begun when Payne was up on a point of order. The chairman, a broad-shouldered, angular, well-dressed young man, a clerk by the look of him, threw himself back in his chair and sighed. "Where's your point of order? Let me hear you," said he with a look of restrained irritation. And he pushed aside some papers on the table as he sometimes saw his white boss do when angry. The gesture seemed to say that in another moment he would give up this thankless job of branch chairman and let these ignoramuses carry on as best they could without him.

"Before the reading of any minutes a roll-call must be taken. I said so last week. I insist on it—a roll-call of members present m-*must* be taken, comrade chairman, as a full, fi-*nan*cial member of this party I insist that this rule taken from the rule book, page three—here it is, here, here!" Payne slapped the booklet, his hands trembled, his breathing could be heard all over the room as if something were burning up inside of him. "This rule *must* be put . . . into . . . *effect.* I want to know why a roll-call is not taken!" he cried. "I want to know why you, as president of this branch, is avoidin' the callin' of a roll. You want to conceal from the comrades that the branch is losing members, you are tryin' to conceal the true f-*facts,* that comrade Le Maître's Welfare Association is drawin' workers away from Workers' Party meetin's. Why, why? I will tell the workers the truth," he said violently to the floor boards, stamping. "The Workers' Party is not a militant body, it has degenerated into a friendly society, and the President General is a scab—"

"On a point of order—" began a tall man.

"He's right. He's damn right, ehn!" another interjected.

"Silence! Comrade Joseph, let me hear you."

Payne sat down, arms tightly folded; he kept wrinkling his nose and blowing through it contemptuously.

"If comrade Payne is on roll-call, let him stick to roll-call, he have no right to call the President General names."

A big, square-chinned man of thirty-five with bright intelligent black eyes and a mischievous smile which never left one corner of his wide mouth now rose and said:

"Mr chair, I support comrade Payne's objection: according to the rules you are supposed to take a roll-call. I move that one be taken now."

He spoke with such quiet good humour that the chairman looked down, thinking: "I wonder what he has up his sleeve?"

"Don' waste people's time, Burnett," shouted a man of middle years with deeply furrowed cheeks.

From others among the old hands came grumblings and sighs. One put his hat on with a gesture of disgust and walked out. Others were looking distrustfully at the chairman. The younger men were smiling, anticipating an amusing evening. It was not uncommon, this scene.

"I will ask the recording secretary to call a roll," said the chairman, adjusting his tie and the papers before him and clearing his throat.

A small man with glasses read out the names.

"How many financial members are present?" Payne asked.

"Twenty."

"Comrade chair, what is the number of financial members in this branch?"

The chairman, conscious that the truth was on Payne's side but unwilling to concede him any victories, nodded solemnly at the recording secretary.

"One hundred and ten," said the latter glumly.

"If the comrades want to see the other ninety members let them go to Diamond Hall, above Yankee shop, where comrade Le Maître is talkin' to them l-like a man, not like a scab, man, not like a *traitor,* not like a deceitful, low—"

"Jesus Christ, all-you lettin' this man come here every meetin' night to spread propaganda for Le Maître?" cried a staunch old Boissonite, springing to his feet. "If members don't attend meetings it's because of this man, Payne!"

"I demand that comrade Payne leave this meeting!" said another. "It's either he leave or I leave. You as branch chairman is responsible for the conduct of these meetings."

"Carry on the meetin', I want to go home," said a third.

"Sh-h!"

"Who you shooin'? I have a right to speak!"

"Comrade Payne have a right to speak too—" French began.

The gavel drowned their voices. Payne was laughing silently, his forehead wrinkled up.

"We will now pass to correspondence," said the chairman. "No correspondence. Any motions? Reports?"

Then someone, a mere lad, got up and complained of the lot of pipe-fitters. The workers listened in silence, some nodding and muttering approvingly. French rose. Someone grunted loudly and contemptuously. "What he goin' to say now?"

"If you are interested to hear," French replied with an air of elaborate politeness, "just keep you' mouth shut and you' ears open—"

"Address the chair, please!" the chairman pounced, using his gavel.

"This young comrade," said French, hitching up his pants, an ominous sign, "hasn't given a full story of the facts. All of us are bachelors. In order to be ready for the truck when it call for us at five-thirty we have to get up at four and cook for ourself. At the present time, as all-you know, we doin' a big job at Erin. No shops near there. You in the bush. It take' us more than an hour to get on the job. We starts at seven. We suppose to stop at eight for food and again at twelve. We leave the job at five. By the time we get back here shop shut. We have to stop on the way comin' back to buy our food for next day. It's not when you gets home tired you want to cook, every man want a little fun then. If we don't cook, what we goin' to eat? Bread an' sausage and bread an' saltfish three times a day? We would be more undernourish than now. And that's not all, comrade chairman and comrades!"

Up to this point French had spoken forcefully yet calmly. But now, conscious of coming to the crux of the injustice done to him and them, he began to rise up and down on his toes and to raise his voice. "When we worked twelve hours a day we were paid eleven cents an hour, but since they agree with Mr Boisson that eight hours is enough for any man they have cut us down to nine cents an hour! Formerly we could make nine dollars and twenty-four cents a week workin' Sundays too. No overtime, comrades! Now to make a little over five dollars a week we has to work Sundays without overtime. Are comrades in this hall content with *that?*" French shouted, and paused, looking about him with wild bloodshot eyes and quivering underjaw. And they knew he saw their wretched state before him in all its complexity, as they could not.

Suddenly his voice dropped to a dramatic whisper. "But further than *that,* comrade chairman," he said, straightening his knees and throwing his body forward, "further than *that* we are carted about like cattle. We are conveyed in an open truck. If rain fall you stop and hide under the truck. You see how a dog does hide? If it rain for hours no hidin'. Many of us have rheumatism from that!" he shouted again, shaking a finger violently at the chairman as if he and he alone was to blame. "Last week we get wet both goin' and comin'. Are we cows, horses—"

"They cover up horses!" cried a middle-aged man. "What wrong wid you? You want dem cover you too? You kean't win no race."

"Comrade chairman! You call you'self a leader? I want to know what you goin' to do," French concluded, controlling his anger with difficulty.

"Have you finished shouting?" the chairman asked, smoothing his cheek with his hand and looking at the ceiling. But some of the men began to roar at him. He banged with his gavel. "Whether it is all fact, as he says, I am not in a position to say. Some of you here are pipe-fitters. If your experiences are different say so." He looked about the hall, and they looked at him and at each other.

"It's true!" one shouted.

"Let us hear *you* now," said Burnett, leaning indolently back on the bench with his head on his hand and smiling derisively at the chairman in the corner of his mouth.

"I cannot tell you what to do. I am not a dictator, I am trying to keep things on an even keel, to be impartial. That is my function."

"Take up you' anchor, cap'n," said the smiling Burnett. "We don' want no even keel, man, we wants to go with the wind."

French turned around, displaying all his upper gum in a silent laugh, and nodding at Burnett.

"My suggestion is a very simple one," said the chairman. "Form a deputation from among the pipe-fitters and interview the construction manager."

"That's right," said a voice from the back of the hall.

Burnett rose and leaned with his hands on the bench before him. "Comrades, do you know what I have myself heard the construction manager say? 'No use paying these niggers too much, they'll go to the rumshop and drink it.' People like him feel black men are cattle—"

"Dat true too!" the voice from the back called. "Some-a all-you only good for one t'ing when night come—grog!"

"You leave out anex' t'ing, Pappy," said the young man who had started the ball rolling.

"If I got no satisfaction from him," said the chairman, banging away, "I would put the matter in Mr Boisson's hands."

Suddenly Payne sprang to life.

"O Gawd!" someone groaned loudly.

"*Mister* chairman, I thought you was a serious man," said Payne, "but I see you's the joker in the pack, you's a *humorist,* you not *se*rious, comrade chairman—no, no, no! Comrade chairman, comrade Payne is on his legs, he has a right to speak, he is a full financial member, that is his *pri*vilege, don't try to shut my mouth or I will get ravin' mad here tonight!" he shouted, breathing heavily, while drops of sweat shone on his pale face. "You know well enough what is goin' to happen when the workers go to present a case: this manager have no authority, that manager say he don't know nothing about it, the general manager says he will consult with the other managers, and the result is nothing from anybody. You kean't expect the general manager to have *pity* on the workers, to talk to him about *pity* is to be talkin' in a s-*strange* tongue, comrade chairman, you ought to *know* that, it's no longer a question of pity, man—" he shook head and shoulders as if flies pestered him—"the function of managers is to exploit the workers, and you are talkin' about *pity—pity?* The workers have to exert *pres*sure! United workers can bring *pres*sure to bear, comrade chairman, but when-a look round now I see all you' pressure gone up in Yankee shop. The workers must lay down the tools and refuse to work. That's *pres*sure, comrade chairman. Hold the employer by his throat, make him beg the *workers* for pity—"

Burnett was laughing silently in the corner of his mouth.

"Hear, hear!" said French with a severe countenance, clapping.

Several others began clapping too.

"Like he talkin' sense in trut' now, *oui?*" a voice said.

A quarrel broke out.

"Why you don't shut you' mout'?" said a scowling young man. "You don't see you old and foolish now?"

"What I forget you never could learn! Old? I have forty years but it wouldn't take me t'ree minutes to t'row you outside. Boisson is the only man who could help us."

". . . get all the pipe-fitters organised," Payne was saying, no longer addressing the chairman but the workers in the hall.

Some rose and walked out. Everyone seemed to be talking at once. The chairman banged with his gavel but no one took notice of him now. "I declare the meeting closed!" he cried, but still no one heeded him. He put on his hat and stalked out of the hall.

"If we get the numbers we can force their hands," Burnett was saying.

"Elect someone to the chair!" French shouted.

It was unnecessary. Payne, standing on a bench, was telling the workers why they should join the Welfare.

For another half hour the meeting continued. Then someone said: "Come go to Diamond Hall."

Several followed him out and the meeting broke up.

Chapter thirty-four

A month later Le Maître addressed one of the biggest meetings ever to be held in Diamond Hall. Some fifty men, most of whom were pipe-fitters, had come to join the Welfare. Many others had crowded in in response to the Welfare's handbill calling upon all workers to attend and hear the reply from the Minimum Wage Committee.

The long heralded Minimum Wage Committee had finally come to life. It had been holding meetings in Port-of-Spain for some six weeks now. As the Committee also proposed to take evidence on the oilfields and sugar estates, Workers' Welfare had applied to the general manager of Trinidad Ltd for permission to give evidence before the committee when it came to Fyzabad. Trinidad Limited refused the request. A letter from the Welfare to the chairman of the Minimum Wage Committee met with the same result.

When the new members were receiving their membership cards and their rule books, going up to the platform one by one, a feeling of enthusiasm, a rough, swaggering spirit pervaded the hall and infected everyone: it was the swagger of a regiment conscious of its numbers and stimulated by this awareness of their power as a mass but as yet untested in battle, as yet unaware of the terrible testing that awaited them. Le Maître stilled the hubbub and the gusty laughter with his gavel. He asked for a postponement of the reading of the minutes and told the recording secretary to read the general manager's reply.

As soon as the recording secretary rose and faced the packed hall he became conscious that the weight of that gathering lay on his shoulders just as it straddled the shoulders of every man present. He frowned, he cleared his throat loudly and leaning on the table with both hands (one of them trembled slightly) he read in a loud accusatory tone:

"*In reply to your letter I have to state that the workers are already represented on the Committee by Mr Boisson, the President of the Workers' Party, a recognised body. As a member of this Committee, I can assure you that evidence is being taken in the most impartial manner from all sections of the community....*"

The gasoline lantern that lighted the hall hissed at the recording secretary as he sat down. For a moment no other sound was heard. Cassie came in quietly, unnoticed.

After a week in her aunt's home she had got a job as maidservant to an English oilfield official. She had come in late, straight from work, because her hours were long and the master demanding. Le Maître alone saw her. To her he was more than a friend: he was the last link between Popito and herself, a link that at this time was stronger than blood because it created a bond of desperate endeavour between herself and all these men. To him she was a woman who, against his will, pervaded his thoughts. But he made no advances. He told himself he wasn't a youth and the job he was doing took all his time, required the utmost in resolution, militancy, a single mind. All the same, he noted now where she sat, close by the door, and wondered if she would hurry out when the meeting ended.

Several people had begun talking at once. French sprang to his feet. Hitching up his pants he looked about him and raised a hand as Le Maître banged the table.

"Comrade President and comrades, this is not the first time nor the second time nor the *last* time that we workers have been insulted and scorned. No! Only two—weeks—ago," said French, pausing between the words for emphasis, "when we went to the manager on behalf of comrade Burnett he chase us out of his office. He said he would have no dealings with us, we were not a trade union registered by law. Now we are told we are not a responsible body. What are workers goin' to think of us—we, the Workers' Welfare!—when they see we can't represent them? We have forgotten what 'welfare' means! If we has to form ourselves into a trade union in order to help the workers, then let us do so at once! They are runnin' from Boisson to us because *he* don' want to help them. But what are we doin' for them?" French looked about him open-mouthed. One could see that in his anger he could not find words to express all that dismayed him. "It's nonsense!" he shouted, paused, then sat down abruptly with an air of determination.

Burnett got to his feet. Smiling as usual in one corner of his wide mouth, looking about him with his intelligent, bright and friendly eyes, he spoke calmly: "Comrade chair, I think not all the comrades here tonight know how I lost my job. I'm goin' to tell them because it is a good lesson."

"What has that to do with the letter we are discussing?" Le Maître growled.

"We are not discussin' the letter simply as a reply to our request to give evidence," replied Burnett. "This letter shows our weakness. That's what I intend to talk about. I left Boisson's party to join the Welfare. Don't try to gag me or I'll walk out of here. There are other comrades who will follow me."

Burnett had not raised his voice, he was even smiling more broadly than before; but something in the smile told Le Maître the man was angry and could not now be opposed.

"Proceed."

"Thank you, comrade. Well, friends, a day three weeks gone the boss on my section call me and say: 'Burnett, are you a Welfare man?' I laughed. 'Yes, chief, I'm a Welfare man; Boisson no good to us.' He nod his head, ask me a question about the work and went his way. That was the beginning of the week. At the end of that week they fire me—the usual excuse, layin' off men. We all know that's not true. The real reason is, they intend to victimise men for belongin' to this body. I could never get a job again on this or any other oil-field in the island. They have me mark down. At Point Fortin, Palo Seco, Pointe-à-Pierre—anywhere, as soon as I give me name they check on me. To get a job I got to change me name. So I must say I have no experience in oilfield work. That means less pay.

"They goin' to pick us off one by one. What are we going to do about that? As comrade French just said, they refuse to hold any discussion of any kind with us. Their intention is clear: they want to draw the workers away from us. And if we sit here makin' a lot-a loud talk—" his smile broadened as he glanced slyly at French—"where that goin' to get us? We want trade unions. Form ourselves into a union at once. That's common sense. If comrade French will move a motion I will second it."

Burnett sat down. Payne, who was close by, swung his emaciated crossed leg, blew through his nose and looked from Le Maître to the floor—clearly biding his time and nursing his wrath.

Le Maître's face was inscrutable. Before he could reply to Burnett a middle-aged man stood up.

"Mr chairman."

"Speak, speak!" Le Maître said impatiently.

The man complained of the lot of cathead men. He, teaching young white lads to drill, earned one-sixty a day while they earned eighty dollars a month. "And besides, when you done reach forty-five the company cuttin' you loose like a kite, they say you mash-up. I have forty-t'ree years now. Just now they goin' to say I old and cold, but I could work harder dan all dem white men . . . !"

He had not finished when Le Maître pushed back his chair and walked to the front of the table. His big head slightly lowered, he looked from under his brows at the cathead man. "And you want the Welfare to help you keep your job—right?" And he slapped the table with his left hand.

"Dat's what I join it for."

"So we form a union. That is simple, the law is there." Le Maître threw out his right hand with a contemptuous gesture. "Then the fun begins. You go to the big boss. 'We are a trade union, we represent the workers.' You beat your chest. He says, 'I don't recognise you. Get out!' So what you will say then? What percentage of the two thousand five hundred workers on this field are organised?"

"We will say to strike!" a young voice rang out.

Le Maître laughed unnaturally, without humour, his face grimacing. "A fine strike! One cathead man, poor Percival on strike. Two chauffeurs—men here and there. That's how you want to strike? When you strike squeeze the boss's balls! Organise the drivers! If we get them we can paralyse this field."

The cathead man was angry. "While you strikin' the table we sufferin', man!"

Smiling in the corner of his mouth Burnett asked: "What is your constructive suggestion, comrade chair?"

"Organisation!" Le Maître shouted, with unnecessary violence it seemed even to himself. "We have all suffered, I as much as any of you. For that very reason I am determined to be strong before I battle with the bosses. Their strength is terrible. Do not underestimate it or you will destroy yourselves—"

"But you is the very man who blame Boisson for not formin' a trade union," the cathead man began.

"If we formed a union," Le Maître interrupted, "where could we strike? The pipe-fitters are the only section where we are beginning to be solid. If the strike was unsuccessful the boss could sue us for damages. He would strip us naked. He would destroy the organisation."

"Defeatist talk, man, defeatist talk!" cried Payne, springing up, waving an arm and shaking his head. "Something *must* be done for sufferin' workers. Face facts! Either we *fight* for these workers or the Welfare become a *friendly* society. Look at the pipe-fitters on the Erin job—they ready to strike now, now, *now!*" He stamped. "It's *fight,* or lose the Welfare."

Le Maître, lips tight-closed, looked intently at his friend. "He fought for their empire," he was thinking, seeing the beads of sweat on the consumptive Payne's pale forehead. "How is it his heart has not yet stopped beating? He is a very sick man but his mind and will are stronger than ever. Is it that I am afraid?"

". . . lose," Payne was saying, "what we have struggled for months and *years* to build, givin' our *health,* every grain of *strength.* Ask the pipe-fitters! They are here. They can fight—lead the fight—!"

"That's right!" French broke in. "Let the pipe-fitters decide."

"It's not I who want to smash the Welfare, it is you!" Le Maître told them. "Study you' head good. If I say do not strike yet, it is because I don't want the Welfare destroyed."

"Let the pipe-fitters decide that!" a new voice insisted. But murmurs rose against him and a man with a very broad nose and a good-natured face and voice said: "Monkey say, 'Cool breeze.' One day we will get the chauffeurs—"

"One day, what, man!" said another angrily, a tall man with an unusually long face. And, unable to find words to express his disgust, he added: "One day, one day, congotay!" All laughed at this use of the well-known child's rhyme, but the man continued without a smile: "It's either to fight or give up the job. What's the use workin' to get sick? I ready to make a stand now. They must provide us wid shelter, give us some overtime. T'ings kean't go on so, man."

"If the Erin boys want to strike, let them strike, yes," Cassie muttered.

"Speak up, girl," a man beside her urged. "Stand up and speak."

The long-faced man, too, pressed her to speak her mind loud. Flustered, Cassie rose and Le Maître, who was speaking, looked at her and broke off, curious.

"What is it, comrade?"

"If the spirit move the Erin boys to fight they should fight!" said she with reckless defiance, as it seemed to Le Maître. "If they have no chance to win, I would agree to wait. But you have a chance and rather than let you' spirit waste—fight! A nex' time might come when the chance is better but you' spirit is low. I see what happen in the bakers' strike in Port-a-Spain. It's true they lose, but the hate that mount up in you' heart through that would make you fight like a tiger nex' time!" Her husky voice rang out at these words and her eyes were hard and dry. Nowadays, reading and joining in their discussions, she saw their trials and hers no longer as the will of fate. White men stood behind them, white men must be defeated if they were to feel the cool wind of happiness on their sweating, despised bodies and their hungry minds. What matter if she never saw the end? In fighting life was given meaning, given dignity, purpose, truth.

Payne leapt to his feet amidst the stamping and "Hear, hear!" from several men. "That's the girl for me!" he screamed, his hand outstretched and quivering with excitement. "Strike while you' blood hot—"

"And starve while it cool!" Le Maître countered.

"Let the pipe-fitters vote!" cried French.

"That would be unfair," replied Le Maître. He thought, looking at them: "A time comes when you can't take any more." He returned to his chair behind the table. "If you want them to vote on the issue you must bring them all here to a meeting. Some are our men, some are Boisson's men. I move that we postpone the vote till Wednesday. Notify the Erin men that it will be a special meeting for them only."

"I second that, man, I second that," said Payne, blowing through his nose, smiling and swinging his crossed leg gaily.

Two nights later the meeting was held.

Among all the Erin pipe-fitters only two voted not to strike after listening to the views expressed by their workmate, French. That the struggle would be hard, as Le Maître warned, did not deter them.

Chapter thirty-five

On Thursday a deputation of Erin workers went to the construction manager's bungalow at six in the morning asking for overtime and tarpaulins to keep off sun and rain.

The construction manager replied that he would "look into the matter"; they would hear from him next week.

French said: "He want time to look about for a nex' gang. He not smarter than me."

"South African bastard!" said another member of the deputation, fearing his power and hating him.

The men refused to climb into the truck. They waited till the office opened. Then the deputation went in to renew its claim for overtime.

The construction manager dismissed them with a few rough words and, jabbing his pipe in a corner of his mouth, returned to some reports that he was checking. The men went out muttering. Outside they cursed him loudly, looking back at the office, wishing he could hear them, wanting to get their hands on him yet held at bay by the authority life had taught them not to defy.

"Well," said one rolling his shirt sleeves higher, "show me the man who say he goin' to Erin today."

They sent the truck away. In half an hour the construction manager drove up. Something about his tone made French sense the unease beneath his anger. He agreed to pay the overtime and promised that tarpaulins would be provided by next morning. The men heard later that he had gone about the barracks calling for volunteers and even tried to get workers from among the unemployed about the streets.

The truck returned and the men climbed in. Stimulated by their success they were in high spirits and joked with one another. French became a hero. In all the gangs of pipe-fitters men told one another how he had gone into the office and addressed the South African. Glad to be acquainted with him, they slapped his shoulder and repeated one of his phrases, turning it into a proverb. At meetings of both the Welfare and the Workers' Party French's action was loudly applauded.

Four days later the construction manager, Blakely, promoted French to the position of pumpman.

"Look, all-you," French warned the rest, "this is a move to get rid of me. As soon as this sick man come back on the job they goin' to lay me off this field."

Every man agreed to stick by him. "If they lay you off they got to lay we off too," they said.

It happened just as he had said. The pumpman having returned Blakely summoned French and dismissed him.

"You took me out of a job to promote me and two weeks later you fire me. What've I done, Mr Blakely?"

"I've got no job for you. Try some other field."

"Very well. I'll know what to do," said French, and left.

When French's comrades heard what had happened they refused to go out to work next morning. They went about among other gangs, urging them to strike for French. One gang composed entirely of Welfare men downed their tools and went in a body to other gangs.

When they heard and saw the bold determination of the strikers and heard that gangs were striking everywhere, workers in other classifications grew restless. The more intelligent among the white bosses sensed this in the way their men laughed, muttered to one another and took orders sulkily.

Almost all the pipe-fitters on the field went on strike. A feeling of excitement and vindictive gratification quickly spread to other workers.

Led by French the strikers assembled on the manager's lawn.

Major the Honourable Ian Bottomley was just finishing his breakfast. He had become a major in the first world war, in which he had served with distinction and been twice wounded. He was Honourable because he had been nominated by the governor to a seat on the legislative council. Not very tall, he had massive shoulders and a beefy face. A square chin jutted out under thin, compressed lips. There was bitterness in his features, but whether from personal misfortune, frustrated ambitions or ill health no one knew. It was not his nature to be communicative. His wife had died some years before. They had had no children. One of his few familiars was the governor, Sir Richard Curry. He came out now in his open-neck shirt and shorts and, seeing how large was the body of men, did not drive them away but called the leaders in and heard their grievances. They stood before him in respectful attitudes, their hats against their chests.

"There's nothing I can do about it," he told them. He had never been known to lose his temper with anyone or even to raise his voice. But no one ever argued the toss with him. "The economic conditions are not of my making. You must try to understand that millions of people are out of work all over the world. Point Fortin laid off two hundred men this week. My company is only laying off fifty. If business picks up I'll take you on again. You don't expect me to make jobs for you, I hope. This isn't a charitable institution, you know. Take your men back to work."

The men went down the steps. A hum of angry talk arose.

"It's a lie, man! They not layin' off men on this field. Any one of all-you hear 'bout dat?"

"Smoke screen."

"Why all-you give in? Talk to him like a man!"

French and the bolder ones again ascended the bungalow's tall flight of steps. The men on the lawn drew closer to the steps and looked up. Again Major Bottomley appeared on the veranda. A dead silence came over the men on the lawn, so that all heard the Major's firm footsteps (he was a heavy man) as he approached the deputation. Bottomley heard the silence. He saw the angry, expectant upturned faces of the workers on his green, well-trimmed lawn with its roses and its neat borders of tea leaves. He listened to the deputation, looking from face to face. Then he addressed the crowd on the lawn and asked for time.

"I am due in Port-of-Spain for a Legislative Council meeting this morning. I can't tell you any more now than I have already said. Get back to work. When I return this afternoon you can come to my office and we'll thrash this matter out. I want you to understand quite clearly that I'm not promising anything."

He scarcely raised his clipped English voice, nor did he increase the tempo of his speech, yet the workers felt in his tone a threat that contrasted with his conciliatory words. French, however, felt he should grasp the proffered hand. He was a man of simple, warm good nature who in calm moments dropped his guard; and now that it seemed a concession might bring them victory why stir up the entire machinery of a state against their small, inexperienced and timid handful?

He nodded. "That's reasonable. Yes, that's reasonable, boys. I agree if you agree."

The others hesitated but Bottomley, seizing on French's acquiescence, said immediately: "Well, get back to work. Just a minute! I'm going to tell you men something which should be of as much interest to you as it is to me. This company is not making any money this year. If you hold up production it won't be the company only that will suffer but all your workmates, your wives and children. You'll force me to lay off other hands. I can't keep unproductive labour. If we're going to get anywhere we must pull together, so get back to work. If you're not going to work you'll have to get off the field." He looked at French. "Come to my office at five o'clock. I don't want any nonsense between now and five o'clock." And with a wave of his hand he turned away, lit a cigarette and went inside.

They put on their hats and went down the steps arguing. The crowd looked at one another. Some feared a trick; others said it was all right, let him go, if he don't decide for Percy French we strike.

French went to Le Maître and reported the result of the interview.

"And you let him go?" Le Maître thundered. He rose from his chair and laughed a biting, humourless laugh. "He has tricked you. What a mistake! Percy! I can tell you now what he will do as if I was next to him." Le Maître ticked off the fingers of his left hand one by one. "He will make sure Boisson is against the strike and get him to pull his men out. Then he will phone Point Fortin and ask for the men they fired there—it is true they fired some. He will phone the police. Then he will come and fire you. The man has gone to prepare himself for battle!"

"But he could have done that this mornin'."

"He was afraid!" replied Le Maître, shaking his open hands before French's face. "He did not know if Boisson was behind the strike. He knew you were not all Welfare men. You should have struck at once. We could have made a solid front with the Workers' Party!" He broke off suddenly. "The men went back to work?"

French nodded.

"*Tonnerre! Foute!*" Le Maître swore softly, slapping his knee. He sat silent awhile. "Go back to them," he said. "You must get the Workers' Party men to form a front with us. Don't try to pull them off the job now. Do what I tell you. A solid front or we are beaten. Go on, don't waste time."

French went about among the Workers' Party pipe-fitters urging them to form a solid front with the Welfare men. He told them that if the strike failed victimisation would follow and men from Point Fortin would be put into their jobs. Some now told him he had been wrong to accept the major's plea for time: as quickly as their militancy had sprung up so now it began to evaporate.

At five o'clock they went to Bottomley's office. He kept the deputation of three men standing before his desk while addressing them briefly and coldly.

"French, I understand that you have been trying to stir up trouble for a long time. I won't tolerate this sort of thing. Go down to Mr Blakely and get your wages. The rest of you will either return to work or get off the field with your belongings by eight o'clock to-morrow morning. I want to make myself quite clear on this point: those who go back to their jobs will only be paid from the hour they started, not as from seven o'clock this morning."

"But you called us here to have a conference with you, Major. We have to put our case," said French, his underjaw quivering with excitement and anger.

"As far as I am concerned," the major replied, "you have no case. Go on, get out!"

" 'Go on, get out'?" repeated the enraged French, his voice rising. "Do you know who you are talkin' to? What you take us for? Because we are black you think you could do as you like wid us? That day is finished!" he shouted. "You English bitches better look out for all-you selves. Uh tell you that!" He darted out the door. "Go on? Get out? What the hell he think, at all!" he cried to the world at large, spreading his arms.

When his comrades outside heard the news they cursed, argued, blamed one another.

"What I tell you?" one said. "All-you too black."

Bottomley descended the four wooden steps of his office and approached his car. He was scanning a document, his mind far from the men he had just dismissed. The uniformed chauffeur opened the door.

"Major! Chief!" Some of the men moved to the car.

The chauffeur shut the door and drove off smartly. A laugh went up.

"This is war, boys!" French said. "Let's go to Diamond Hall. We have to plan our attack or be victimised."

The meeting lasted two hours. Dozens of workers spoke, the majority urging utmost co-operation between the Workers' Party and the Welfare. But some, grumbling, left the meeting and went to make peace with Blakely.

Le Maître addressed the meeting. "It is no use hiding from what faces us now. Bottomley is going to bring in men from Point Fortin or from the streets if he can. The fight is going to be hard. If you are going to fight you must be solid. . . ."

In the midst of his speech word came that Boisson had telephoned instructions to withdraw from the strike. Uproar broke out.

"Son of a bitch!"

"If he don't mean to help we, how we could win?"

"What dem do know 'bout us? He siddown on his fat arse sixty mile away. . . ."

"Me own president . . . traitor!"

"What I tell you long time?"

A fight began. Those close by parted the two men. Shouts, imprecations. More workers left the hall and returned to Blakely.

Le Maître had been scribbling something down. Now he rose. "If we are going to strike," he said, hammering the table, "let us take an oath to stand side by side, solid as a wall, come what may. Over a hundred men entered this hall a while ago. Now we are less than fifty."

The angry and dejected men fell silent.

"This is the oath I propose," said Le Maître.

Slowly and impressively in his deep voice he read: "Though the road be long and hunger give us no peace I swear to stand shoulder to shoulder with my comrades and fight with my last breath this attempt to lower our living standards to make more profits for the rich, to steal food from the mouths of our children, to cast us out of our lodgings to the mercies of the weather, and to turn us into slaves. By Almighty God, I swear!"

He raised his right hand. "All those in favour."

Hands shot up. Some hesitant ones rose slowly.

"Those against!"

The hands fell—and stayed down. Someone said in a stern voice: "Carried!"

"Comrades, I will repeat the oath."

The men listened in silence. Then in their various voices, which blended into one deep, solemn, yet yearning note, they repeated the last line together:

"By Almighty God— I swear!"

Chapter thirty-six

Deprived of their lodgings in twenty-four hours the men sought refuge on the morrow in the homes of relatives and friends. They held meetings in Diamond Hall to give themselves courage. In the village they were martyrs. Within a week they were penniless. Worse, in three days a handful of the unemployed had taken their places.

They began to live on the popularity of Le Maître, who held street-corner meetings and took up collections for them. Heroes the first week they were beggars the second, and in the third Le Maître called for a march of all unemployed to interview the Governor in Port-of-Spain.

The march began and the distance did not dismay them; for in every march of men others are sucked in as water sucks away the land, and so it was this time, they were not alone in their search for justice.

It was not the first time black men had marched, but now the crowds were larger and not only men made up their number but their women too. It made the white men nervous.

Some of the marching women had babies in their arms. The weary mothers shifted the wailing infants from arm to arm, and sometimes a man would take his child; but none gave thought to stopping by the roadside. Instead the women called to onlookers to join them, saying with full faith and fervour: "We goin' to the governor, the only man in this colony who does like po' people. He must fix we up. We have Gawd on our side." For not Le Maître alone had been busy but the Shouters and the Shango priests in their secret places, and their flocks were largely of women.

Earlier that year Sir Richard Curry had been appointed Governor. He had already won popularity by his touring of large areas and his larger promises to the people. And the women went forth with God on their side, giving courage to their menfolk, who went into the shops and begged bread for their comrades and were not denied.

In the afternoon of the second day they came to San Fernando. The crowd now was five hundred and steadily lengthening. The police roped off the road and would not permit them passage through the town. That night was passed beneath the stars. The kinder working folk sheltered the mothers and children, but for the most part the marchers sat and lay in an open savannah while first a woman preached of God and His chosen, and then Le Maître addressed them briefly, reminding them of the oath they had taken. The speakers stood beside a stick on which hung a smoky *flambeau* at head height. Shadows made soft, then stern, their features. But that light, like the light of Hope, caused silent onlookers to line the roadside, and many joined the marchers when in the chilly dawn they rose and went forth to see the man who loved "po' people". They had to make a long detour to avoid the town. At noontide the winding snake of humans rested. As on the day before, sympathetic shopkeepers gave them cheese and the children milk. At nightfall they rose again and marched throughout the night in easy stages; and the next day they rested, and again the following night they trod the hot pitched roads. And the men and women of the villages everywhere were proud to give them food, even clothing, and take them into their huts for shelter from sun and rain. The police stood by, proud of their people, joking and talking with them in low tones while the sergeant was not looking.

Le Maître bullied unwilling shopkeepers for milk and cheese and bread. Raising his big voice, shaming them before their customers, he cried: "How you goin' to live if they can't buy? You want to cut you' own throat? Give them food so they can get strength to go to the Governor and demand work!"

And onlookers and customers took up the cry.

"Give the people food, you stingy coolie!"

"This time he must be have so much-a money hide in 'e mattress he back hurt him when day come. . . ."

"You goin' to see little babies starve? You have no Christian feelings? One Gord above all-a we, man!"

And the grumbling shopkeepers, Indians mostly, would hand out the food amidst encouraging remarks from their women customers.

Le Maître saw with each dawn how the stragglers increased. He was looking at a man who walked in front of him yawning, eyes groundward—tall, flat-chested, stooped, he did not utter a single word, only sighed occasionally and shook his head. Le Maître tried to cheer him, but after a while the man dropped out of the long line and sat, as others had done before him, on the grass by the roadside and rubbed his feet.

The lagging of the marchers, their evident doubts, his own doubts and weariness sent a wave of anger to Le Maître's head. He retraced his steps along the line, shouting:

"No lagging, comrades! Two hours again and we will rest and eat. We have done thirty miles, we are halfway. If any man feels he is too weak for the struggle, let him turn back now. But I want all-you to know I would rather die than go back like a beaten dog."

"Man, keep cool, man," said a rough voice.

"No use gettin' angry, Ben," said a young woman who had waited for Le Maître. "People tired and hungry, man."

It was Cassie. One night in Diamond Hall she had addressed a meeting she had persuaded some servants to attend.

"Some of you 'fraid to join the Workers' Welfare, others feel it have no sense in that, you believe Indian and Negro kean't help one another to make life better. I say, ladies and gentlemen, put that foolish idea out of you' mind. You have children. They will grow up naked, their belly big, their navel swell up. Those who don't go to jail and get the cat will have to make a fight to get eight or nine cents an hour to feed more children to grow up and get the cat. You never try to work out how much servants gettin' but I could tell you. It's three cents an hour. Who that benefitin'? Tell me that. It ain't no benefit to you and those children, the benefit is for who employin' you. Plenty children, cheap labour! If some dead what they care 'bout that? Plenty more comin' out you' belly. We have to make a union. We have to fight for higher wages, shorter hours—yes, less work for more money! Make them pay us! You ever see white people children with swell-up belly and big navel and goin' about naked? Our wages payin' to keep them from that. . . ."

On the morning the march began she waited with others outside Diamond Hall to see the crowd move off. Watching the endless numbers of feet scuffing that already hot asphalt she felt impelled to join them in their trial of strength. They moved in uneven ranks, with good-humoured laughter, as though walking for their pleasure. They were not just men and women, some of whom she knew. They were her kin. Their destiny, whatever it might be, however harsh, unkind, was hers. She must be with them.

She ran to Le Maître. "I comin' too."

"Don't come," he warned. "It will be a tough march. We may not even reach. Stick to your job here, you—"

"Save you' breath, I done make up me mind," she told him, having long put Madam and her needs behind her. Joining some women and a man she knew, she moved along with them.

She was uncomfortable in Le Maître's presence, feeling the harshness in him, yet was drawn to him as she had not been to any man. He was no lover but a demanding tyrant, and yet she felt for some reason that she could give him everything.

He was convinced she was contemptuous of him because he was too old. Well, damn it, what about Popi? He had been older still. Perhaps she thought he couldn't keep her? Sometimes when they met he held her arm a moment, unable to resist touching her. Her eyes mocked him, sparkling. He would think angrily: "You're a fool, Ben, give it away!" But she seemed unattached. He felt deep down that his personality was not unpleasant to her because he had a working mind, just as she had. But lovemaking and all that, damn it. . . . No matter how he cursed himself words evaded him, he was tongue-tied, only glowering with downcast eyes.

"I'll come to see you," he burst out once. "When you'll be home?"

"Any night."

"Right. Tomorrow. Okay?"

He came to her aunt's place and sat there, his big frame filling up the bentwood rocker, talking of bosses and exploitation, of the need to read and cultivate the mind. And in a lowered voice as he was leaving: "So you don't go out with anybody?" As serious as if making an examination of the terrain before an armed assault.

On his second visit, when he was saying goodbye, she, leaning against the door jamb, her head sideways against it, watched him smiling.

"Come for a little walk with me," he murmured.

"Nearly eleven, yes?"

"All the better. Come." He took her by the arm. They had only walked a few steps and his own arm was around her. It had happened in spite of him. She said nothing, didn't smile, didn't reject him. She felt the tension in his arm.

"Better I go back," she said.

"But we hardly walked a hundred yards!"

She stopped. "What have you so tie-up inside?"

"I was married once. You know that?"

"So I hear say."

"A man should never marry a woman who don't love him."

"That is true."

"What about Popi? You loved him?"

She turned her head aside, sighing. "Without Popi what was to happen? Look, it's time for you to go." She leaned towards him and kissed him tenderly, without passion, and would have gone, but he seized her in a vice and pressed his mouth to hers. She broke away and ran. It was like being devoured by a tiger. She admired him, respected him, suffered with him, yet couldn't be sure she loved him. "Now, if he was to make love like Popi I would know what to think."

Between men on the march many days and nights, moving through a world in which open sympathy keeps the nervous master at bay, sleeping side by side beneath the coconut trees, purpose is toughened and the determination to fulfil that purpose. Cassie, sleeping beside Le Maître at noontime, walking beside him in the night, felt not only comradeship but a deepening dependence on his moral strength. Late on the fourth night they went through Reform Estate. The sound of the crowd's footsteps, a laugh, a yawn, bits of animated conversation, snatches of a hymn sung by a group, then silence save for the scrape of uneven footsteps—these sounds departed from Cassie as she sat by the roadside to remove the shoe from her blistered foot. About her she heard only the silence of the night, a silence emphasised by the faint rustle of a coconut palm, the piercing whistle of grasshoppers in the bitter scented bush and the persistent croaking of deep-voiced *crapauds* in a grass-grown ditch. Then Le Maître's voice calling—he had turned back to seek her.

"Ben, ohi!" she called, and startled *crapauds* fell silent.

"What's the matter? You tired?" he asked with concern, emerging from the darkness.

"Me foot blistered so bad!"

He struck a match, examined her foot, then took out a knife, cut away the heel of the shoe and slit the sides. He bandaged the foot with a bit of cloth torn from her slip and tied the shoe to it firmly.

"Try now."

"That's better. Come go," she said.

"You should not have come without stockings, but I hadn't time to think of it," he said, putting his arms around her.

She did not resist him or turn away with a laugh as formerly. Her arms went round his neck. He passionately kissed her lips. She felt his body tremble against her own, and it was pleasant to her. The *crapauds* began to croak again one by one. Suddenly she broke away.

"What's the matter with you? Come go on!" she said.

But he was not to be disposed of so easily. He seized her again. "Look here, Cassie, I'm in love with you!" His voice sounded threatening.

"We kean't talk of that now, Ben," she pleaded in a husky voice that sharpened his desire for her. "They goin' ahead of us. That's where you belong."

"You're afraid of me?"

"Yes."

"Tell me at once—you love me or not? I am not a little boy for you to fool with!"

His impatient hot breath angered her. "No, man, no!"

He pushed her from him violently. "If you goin' to march with us walk up. If you can't keep up the pace we'll find a truck to take you back."

She walked beside him. "You know very well I will walk as well as you," she said with a heavy heart. Tears filled her eyes but she brushed them away with impatient stealth. He was walking with his head thrust forward, bull-like. "If you want to run, go ahead," she told him. "I can't go so fast." He slackened his pace. They walked for a long while in silence.

"You vexed with me?" he asked at length in a softened tone.

"What it is to you?"

He took her hand. "Don't bear hard feelings against me. I am tired like you, the march has me worried and. . . ." He broke off.

Approaching Marabella they stopped to drink from a roadside tap. When they went on he again put his arm about her.

At dawn they caught up with the marchers, who had stopped at Claxton Bay. After resting an hour Le Maître went from shop to shop for food and did not lie down to sleep till midday. At sunset he roused the crowd, noting with anger and despair how increasingly difficult it was to do so every night. Yet he could not let them sleep, for the shopkeepers would not give free biscuits a second time. He went about among his comrades saying:

"We are making for Couva sports ground. It's barely eight miles away. We will take our time and get there by midnight. We can sleep in the stand, under shelter for once. Come, comrade, it's a fine night, not a sign of rain. We'll have a good sleep tonight. Plenty of shops in Couva, we are sure of a good feed tomorrow."

Le Maître headed the column, French took the rear. On either side the staunch and solid hemmed in the womenfolk and the men who limped morally or physically, and halted the column for the stragglers.

"Hold up, Frederick!"

"Frank, ohi! Hold that, boy."

"What happen, flat tyre?"

"No, we stop for passengers."

"Right-o. All-you in front, conductor say hold up."

"Well! B'Christ! This is the longest free ride I ever get. Quite from Fyzabad and I ain't pay a cent."

"Who the hell legs so long in front there?"

Cheerful voices called to one another, halting the column, and then called out still more cheerfully, urging it forward.

"Walk like tourists! Watch the scenery. All-you ever see this part-a you' country yet?"

"In trut', is no difference. Tourists look at scenery t'rough dark glasses, we look at it t'rough dark night."

"All-you start off bold to walk to town as if you expect to take a taxi back home," a thin wag of a fellow said.

In a high, strained voice a woman was singing a hymn. A man's bass took up the tune several thirds lower.

A woman with a child complained that she could go no further.

"Gimme the child," said Le Maître. "Now is not the time to lose courage. We nearly there." He put the sleeping child on his shoulder.

"All-you sleepin', ehn," said the woman reflectively as they came upon the outlying houses of the village, close by the canefields. Dogs barked but in the shacks no one stirred. "Sleep soundly, my dears. You lucky. A-ah, yes. . . ." She nodded and looked up at the stars, so very clean and bright and silent.

The crowd entered the sport ground and filled the spectators' stand. Cassie and Le Maître went up to the topmost tier. Silently Le Maître stretched himself out on a bench.

"Like a herd of cattle," he muttered. "Only they look after cattle."

The despair in his voice brought Cassie beside him. She pulled his head on to her lap, caressing his forehead. About and below them others were yawning, talking, laughing, quarrelling with one another for taking up all the room by lying down.

"No matches! Out with that light!" French was heard shouting.

"Le Maître! Ben Le Maître. Ben, ohi! Anybody see Ben?" a man's voice was calling.

"He gone back home for a rest," someone replied.

Le Maître was stirring. Cassie covered his mouth with her hand. "Rest, man, you tired."

The voice ceased calling. Le Maître breathed evenly. Just when Cassie thought him sleeping he said: "You still love Popi, not so? I looked at you that night when you said the men should strike if the spirit move them. You were thinking of him."

"Don't talk of that, it done pass."

"Cassie, let's get married."

"Eh-eh! Straight so? No courtin'? And you say the other day when a man married he does lose the fight in him?"

"Not all men—look at Clem Payne. Besides, you would be fighting alongside of me. We would give each other courage."

"And what about love?"

"It's for you to say."

She laughed. "Ah, my God! Life funny, yes? Eh-eh! You have a job, nuh? What you goin' to married on?" And again she laughed, this time with tenderness.

"Ha, ha, ha!" he mocked angrily. "Well, go to the devil and leave me in peace!" And he rose from her lap.

"Eh-eh! A body could never make fun with you."

She moved away and lay down. "Ah, Lord!" she whispered, sighing. Popito she had loved, yes, as she might love a child. With Ben she felt safe, sheltered, proud. Well, and you had to live. An instinct told her that he could not but seek to control her whole life if she were his. She didn't want that. She was conscious of her own individuality, her own mind, her strength. Suppose he beat her? Let him try it! Only once, and it was the end! And things were not so bad now, her English mistress gave her ten dollars a month with food. Ben wouldn't know the first thing about money or what to do with it. . . .

Le Maître, too, was not sleeping. He felt a terrible desire to beat her, take her in his arms, bite and kiss her. He knew he was overaweing her, that he must court her gently, but when he saw her walk and heard her voice he could not wait. He was annoyed that she should have so powerful an influence on him without herself desiring it.

"Cassie!"

"What?"

"Come here."

About them in the darkness sounds of snoring mingled with soft talking and a woman's endless complaints.

"You always want to order people about," Cassie grumbled. "I don' want no man orderin' me about, me dear."

"Am I ordering you? I asked you to come and sit by me." She went to him. "I want you tell me straight—you want to marry me or not? You 'fraid to marry me, not so? Why?"

"Give a body time, Ben, but you hurry, hurry. Wait!"

"You are in love with a dead man," he said softly after a pause. "Forget him. Look a live man beside you. Where one can live two can live, you know."

"Tomorrow we have to walk again and I well tired. Leave all-a this talk for when we get back to Fyzabad. Then you could come to *Tante* courtin'." She suddenly laughed merrily. "An' you donno one thing about courtin', man. How is that?" In the darkness she looked into his face and kissed him.

She left him and lay down. And he, too, lay down but it was long before he slept.

In the morning Couva saw near a thousand people in the stand or sitting on the grass in the shade. They had come like locusts in the night. A hum like the sound of swarms of bees filled the air. Dozens of people had joined the marchers, or stood on the roadside talking excitedly, arguing heatedly and with gesticulations. Policemen stationed at intervals along the road kept the people off the road and the traffic moving.

At nine o'clock Boisson stepped out of a police jitney and entered the field. He was smiling and was dressed as usual in spotless white that made him conspicuous among the unshaven workers who had slept five days in their clothes. The well-dressed brown man with the cigar, who was now an alderman and always followed him like a shadow, was shaking hands liberally. Rings glittered on his left hand. Behind him trailed Sub-Inspector Primrose.

The news of their coming visibly agitated the people in the field as a breeze does a heap of fallen leaves. All rose and flocked into the stand for a view of Boisson. On many faces angry looks appeared, but most looked at him with expectation that his coming heralded succour in their plight.

"So they bring police for us, they think they goin' to stop us?" cried French, red-eyed and with a five-day stubble of beard.

". . . Now, my friends," Boisson's voice was heard.

Some began shouting at him.

"That man is a traitor, don't listen to that man!" French cried hoarsely.

"What Boisson sayin'?"

"He want we all go back home."

"After we come so far? What he givin' us?"

"My friends," Boisson was saying, "it is not necessary for all of you to come to Port-of-Spain. Choose two delegates from among you. I will take them at once to the colonial secretary. He is waiting in his office to receive them."

Somebody began to cheer and others took it up.

French and his comrades again shouted: "Traitor!"

"Quiet, man, Percy!" said Le Maître. "Let you' head cool off. You don't see the people tired and hungry? And most of them are strangers to us besides."

French, too, saw that they were glad to seize this way out and rid themselves of their martyrdom, but he looked at them angrily and at Boisson with hate.

At the call for delegates hundreds of throats shouted: "Le Maître! Ben Le Maître!"

He was the only delegate. It was an acknowledgement of the Welfare's leadership, and French was pleased.

"Percy, try to get all the women back home on trucks. Get Cassie to help you," Le Maître told him.

Feeling more like a prisoner than a delegate he got into the front seat of the station wagon, beside the Negro driver, because there was one place for mayors and aldermen and another for oilworkers' delegates. Primrose sat beside Boisson in the rear seat. Besides, it would have set up incalculable social strains if the delegate had sat on the other side of the mayor: the alderman, who was brown, would have been compelled to sit with the driver, who was black.

During the drive Boisson and the alderman discussed the economic situation. Only once did Boisson address the delegate.

"How long have these people been walking?"

Le Maître turned round in the front seat. "Five days. I thought the police would have kept you informed."

Dead silence.

Boisson looked straight ahead and ran his fingers through his hair. The brown alderman looked through the window.

Upstairs in the bleak and dreary corridors of the Red House Le Maître thought he had never seen anyone so comfortable and of such easy mind as the uniformed messenger who smiled, nodded and said "Yessir!" almost joyfully to Boisson when the latter asked to see the colonial secretary. He was shaven, no bits of grass stuck in his hair and he stepped noisily, like a man with a happy awareness of being a fixture about the place, in his polished iron-shod boots. Only when entering the colonial secretary's office did he step on his toes. In a moment he returned and invited Boisson to follow him, speaking in a soft voice and stepping on the balls of his feet in order not to offend "the captain" by seeming too much at ease in the precincts of the Englishman who was Head of State.

"Sit down a moment," Boisson said to Le Maître. "I will let him know you are with me."

Le Maître sat down. Some official in a black alpaca coat passed by with a pile of papers under his arm. He was stooped, middle-aged and dismal-looking and Le Maître had the impression that life-long toil in the building had deformed him physically and mentally. He gave Le Maître a sharp look and his lips made rapid little motions as if he were chewing something or talking to himself. A healthy-looking black youth with a smooth bright-eyed smiling face ran up the stairs. He asked something of the messenger and looked with awe at the colonial secretary's door, which the messenger indicated. The messenger yawned carelessly and leaned his head on his hand. The black youth ran down the stairs and silence reigned, the silence of files and memoranda. Le Maître heard the tap of a discreet typewriter. It made him think of a rodent building a nest of paper.

Having passed twenty minutes in this fashion he rose. "I want to see the colonial secretary," he said in a loud voice.

A look of angry alarm appeared on the messenger's face. "Don't make any noise in here, man!"

"I must see him at once!" Le Maître insisted.

The gnawing of the typewriter ceased. A woman's dark head with ironed hair peeped round a swing door.

"He is there, he is busy and you makin' a set-a noise, man, siddown. You wânt me call police?"

"Jail is just the place for me to get the rest I need," said Le Maître, and without further ado he went to the door through which Boisson had disappeared and knocked so loudly upon it that the messenger gazed open-mouthed at his audacity.

A voice bade Le Maître enter. When, unshaven, with grass in his hair and his clothes soiled with mud, he strode in like an apparition the smile on the face of the colonial secretary was replaced by a look of stern interrogation. Antipathy and embarrassment, especially embarrassment, made Boisson flush and pass his fingers through his hair.

"Who gave you permission—" the governor's deputy began.

"I am the delegate elected by a thousand starving men, women and children who have walked from Fyzabad to see the governor!" said Le Maître in stentorian tones. "This man," he shook a finger at Boisson, "has taken it on himself to keep you unaware of this fact and shut me out in the passage. Mr Symmonds! He knows nothing of the position of these people. And they are only a fraction of the destitute and starving in this colony."

The colonial secretary was pale and tight-lipped. Boisson had informed Symmonds that a delegate appointed by the marchers was waiting in the corridor but Symmonds preferred to talk with Boisson because there did not seem to him to be much point in holding discussions with an irresponsible rabble-rouser whose influence on the people was negligible. But as soon as Le Maître burst in and began to speak Symmonds realised his mistake.

"Please sit down, Mr—er—"

"Le Maître," Boisson prompted.

"Mr Le Maître, please sit down," the colonial secretary continued without rising, first because the man was wanting in respect and second because he himself was rather short and would not cut a good figure beside him. "I was about to ask you in. I'd like to hear what you have to say. In the first place, are all of these people strikers?"

"Only a small percentage. The rest are unemployed workers."

"How long have you had them on the road?"

Le Maître caught the imputation of responsibility but he let it pass. "Five days."

"Shocking!" the colonial secretary muttered. "I can assure you that I am aware of the acute situation. I like it as little as you do, Mr Le Maître. Government's intention is to open up a very large programme of public works to keep these people usefully employed. I am sure it is not necessary to remind you, Mr Le Maître—you are obviously a very intelligent person—of the danger to all concerned of inflaming passions at a time like this."

"To inflame passions would be madness. The people have no arms. But even if we wished to do so it would be unnecessary, the people are already inflamed, they are boiling with rage." Le Maître, spreading his left hand, began to give a precise account of the strike at Fyzabad and its causes.

His eyebrows raised, the colonial secretary doodled on his blotting pad. "Yes, yes," he interrupted, "but as you can readily understand, Government cannot interfere in such matters. If you wish to form a trade union you are entirely within the law, but the question of recognition is one for employer and employee to work out together amicably. To adopt a combative spirit at a time like this is extremely dangerous. You must not forget that you are dealing with an excitable people who have not your discipline or intelligence. I think a wise leader has to bear in mind that the forces he sets in motion might grow beyond his power to control. Mr Boisson has been aware of these pitfalls, he has maintained a very nice balance."

The intimation that he should take a leaf from Boisson's book caused Le Maître to compress his lips contemptuously.

Boisson's flush had not entirely subsided. Smiling and looking only at the colonial secretary he said: "I would just like to point out to my friend in a spirit of comradeship that we can get nowhere by creating dissensions among the workers. Government realises the unemployment situation and is about to take measures to relieve it. To attempt to make political capital for oneself out of the unemployment situation is to show a cynical disregard for the workers. What is needed—"

"Speak clearly," Le Maître interrupted. "You are against the strikers."

"A strike can only lead to a further dislocation of industry."

"Workers are starving, others are struggling to make ends meet and you asking them to show consideration for the profits of industry?" Le Maître laughed without humour.

"They will soon enough care if more men have to be laid off," Boisson warned, smiling at the colonial secretary.

"That is a point you seem to have overlooked, Mr Le Maître," said Symmonds. He dropped the pencil with which he was doodling and drummed with his fingers on the arms of his chair. "Government cannot look on with indifference if through unjust strikes damage is done to one of the mainstays of the island's economy."

"Allow me to ask you: when do you consider a strike just?"

"It is the government view that strikes are entirely unnecessary. Differences between employer and employee should be settled through accepted legal machinery."

"The rule of law," Boisson said in agreement, but also, Le Maître thought, as if meaning: "As every sensible labour leader must recognise."

"Even admitting that is so—understand me, I do not admit that such a procedure is desirable at all—but supposing it to be so, where is your machinery for arbitration?"

"Government is thinking along these lines, Mr Le Maître."

This was not true, the idea had only just occurred to him. He looked significantly now and, as he expected, Boisson rose.

Le Maître remained seated. "You have not told me what message I must take the people from government."

"You can tell them that a programme of public works will in the very near future provide employment for all who want work. They will be advised through the newspapers and the wardens' offices throughout the counties." The colonial secretary rose. "I trust, Mr Le Maître, that at all your subsequent meetings you will keep in mind my conversation with you this morning."

"Good morning," said Le Maître, looking away from him, and preceded Boisson from the room.

Chapter thirty-seven

The Minimum Wage Committee had held several meetings that year in the Red House, on sugar estates and on the oilfields. On 15 December it was holding its last meeting for 1936 in Dollard and Company's boardroom. While the committee discussed golf, drank iced beer and relaxed before engaging in the serious business of the afternoon, the witnesses asked to testify sat on a bench in the corridor outside and whispered among themselves. They were Jacob, the porter, Mrs Elfrida Burnett, a Negro woman who owned a little cook-shop, an old Indian, Ramsammy, who was one of Dollard's customers, and two young Indian men.

Ramsammy had the noble bearded features not infrequently seen among Indians of the older generation. His eyes were large, bright, prominent, full of intelligence, and at this moment they looked about him with some suspicion. What was the aim of this committee, what were they trying to get out of him, an agricultural labourer unable to read or write English or speak it properly? He questioned the young Indians beside him. It did not occur to him to lower his voice when he did so and once, hawking the phlegm up loudly in his throat, he walked with dignity on his bare feet to a large potted palm and spat into it. He wore a turban, an Indian jacket buttoned up to the neck and western trousers.

Mrs Burnett, rather short and very plump, compressed her lips squeamishly and her pink satin dress rustled as she squirmed on the bench. With every movement she gave off an overpowering scent of perfume. She was clearly displeased at finding herself on a common bench—not even a back to it—amidst such company. Yet when she addressed Jacob, who was sitting beside her, it was in a timid undertone without any trace of Ramsammy's bold confidence. Jacob answered her readily in the careless, loud voice of an employee who likes to show himself familiar with all the mysteries associated with the white man's domain.

The witnesses heard laughter in the boardroom.

"They better hurry up, I haven't got all day," Mrs Burnett muttered, raising her eyebrows and sighing.

"Come on, Jacob," said Dollard, opening the door, still smiling gaily at one of his companion's remarks. "Come on, everyone."

"Yes, suh!" said Jacob, springing up at once. "Come, everybody, let's go in, man." And perhaps as a consolation for himself as well as the young Indians who smiled timidly and Ramsammy who was frowning, he added: "They kean't do you nutten, man."

Mrs Burnett rustled in first on a wave of perfume. Dollard put her at her ease and invited her to sit down. "Sit down, sit down," he said to the others, indicating some chairs against the wall.

The Director of Agriculture, Mr Ormsby, was chairman of this sub-committee. He was a portly Englishman in middle life with a pale, round and kindly face. He sat at the centre of a magnificent table that shone like glass. On his right hand was Dollard, on his left Thorn, an English farmer. Boisson occupied one end of the table and the secretary, a young brown Negro, the other. While Dollard rocked himself carelessly back and forth in his chair Ormsby began in his kind and cultured voice:

"I'm very glad to see all of you here this afternoon. As you know, His Excellency the governor has asked us to find out what is the least a man can live on. He doesn't want that man to be paid less than a sum on which he can live. That is why we want you to tell us how you live. I hope all of you understand that for this very important purpose you must give us truthful answers."

He nodded to the secretary and at the same time took out his pipe and began to fill it.

"Jacob Jackson!" said the secretary.

Jacob jumped up.

"Come forward, Jacob," said Dollard.

Jacob rested his hat on his chair and came forward.

"Sit down," Ormsby said.

But Jacob smiled at the half-empty glass of iced beer before the Director of Agriculture. "It's all right, chief, I could stand." He thought it improper to sit before them. Besides, some instinct told him that if he once sat it would be more difficult to speak to them than if he stood. And he wanted to get away from here as quickly as possible. It wasn't the director's official utterance that had troubled him because his mind had automatically closed against it; it was the phrase "you must give us truthful answers", with the stress on the "must". As soon as he heard that he had no doubt that they were going to take something from him. And furthermore, he could not sit down in front of Dollard. Hatred for Dollard lurked deep in him. He had scarcely ever given it recognition, but it was there and it suddenly leapt up in him when he saw him rocking back and forth, smiling "so nice" with these officials.

"You are a porter here, are you not? Come nearer, will you? Are you a porter? I see. And how much do you earn per week?"

"Yes, suh. Yes. Well . . . five dollars a week."

"You live on this sum only? You have no access to other means of revenue?"

"You mean if I does make extra money? Where I goin' to get time, chief?"

Ormsby lit his pipe, puffing several times, and removed it from his lips to ask: "Tell me, Jacob, are you married?" and put it between his lips again.

"Well—you know how it is, suh."

"Extraordinary the number of witnesses who aren't married," Ormsby remarked to Dollard, catching at once what Jacob meant.

"But you have got a keeper?" Thorn said.

He had a small dairy and estates of grapefruit, cocoa and tonca beans. He had accepted an appointment to the Committee because it was vital to him to defend what he had and what he would leave his children. There was always some crop disease or some fall in overseas prices and now they wanted to burden him with a higher wage bill.

But Ormsby, disturbed by his countryman's lack of finesse, came in so quickly that Jacob did not have to reply to Thorn.

"Can you tell us how much you spend on food every day, Jacob?"

Jacob looked up muttering at the ceiling. "About a dollar, yes?"

Thorn pounced. "You earn five dollars a week but you spend seven dollars a week?"

"I has to get credit, chief."

"How many children have you?" Ormsby asked.

"Six, chief."

"How many outside?" Thorn smiled at the director.

Ormsby refused to notice him. "And you have to feed eight people, eh, none of them old enough to work?"

"That is so, suh. Life not easy for people like us."

"What did you eat yesterday, Jacob? Can you remember?" Because he himself could not for the life of him remember what he had eaten the day before.

"Yes, Uh t'ink it was beef and coush-coush, yes?"

"Give us quantities," Thorn said. "How much beef?"

" 'Bout a pound and a half, suh."

"Coush-coush—are you taking notes of all this?" Thorn asked the secretary.

Dollard thought: "If Ormsby isn't careful Thorn will take the meeting out of his hands."

"Pound and a half, suh," Jacob replied after a moment as though meaning: "Take it or leave it."

"A pound and a half of coush-coush! Oh, nonsense, he couldn't eat a pound and a half of coush-coush at one sitting," Thorn said to Ormsby with a look and gesture that appeared to express his conviction that they were unlikely to get very far with such unreliable witnesses. It never crossed his mind that this Negro porter might be trying to make a fool of him. Jacob was looking down humbly.

"Why not?" Boisson asked. "It's probably an unconscious attempt to make up for certain dietary deficiencies. You are considering quantity to the exclusion of quality."

The Indians were arguing among themselves in their tongue.

"Jacob, at your age you have tapeworms? Eh?" Dollard remarked with a laugh to smooth things over, and glanced at his colleagues.

Suddenly hate leaped up in Jacob, it seemed to seize his throat like a hound. He laughed cunningly, a kind of chuckle. It was a reflex action that had become habitual over the years. It silenced the hound. "Man, Mr Dollard," he said, "I have boys eatin' more dan me, yes?"

Now Ormsby: "Well, then, if what you ate yesterday for three meals amounted to fifty cents, what would you say it cost to feed your wife and children yesterday?"

"Well, chief, six children, a wife . . . dat make seven; and if you say it come only to thirty cents a head dat is more dan two dollars again."

"You just said food cost you a dollar a day." This from Thorn.

"That is so. But is not arithmetic you eatin', is food—and you hungry, all day long you pushing dat heavy load." And Jacob laughed his low, throaty chuckle, looking straight into Thorn's face.

"Jacob," said Boisson, "would you agree with me if I said that some days your children don't eat food because you have no money, and they have to live then on mangoes and breadfruit?"

"Hah!" And in Jacob's cry was triumph. "Mr Boisson, you know the business. I don' know what some of us would do when the day come without a breadfruit tree or a mango tree in the yard."

"Man kean't live on dat!" Ramsammy declared magisterially, coming forward with dignity to the table.

"You mustn't come up now, sit down," Ormsby reproved him paternally in his kind voice, waving him away with his pipe.

"Come, Ramsammy, what's the matter? Sit down, sit down, you'll have your turn just now," said Dollard in the gruff good-humoured and slightly contemptuous tone he adopted with customers like Ramsammy.

The old man would not be gainsaid. "Sometimes he buy ripe figs, mangoes," he continued. "What about fruits? Only white people does eat fruits and greens? Suppose him buy tania, dat mo' money. Suppose him buy red beans, dat mo' money again. Plaintain—all dem foods is mo' money dan rice. Suppose buy fresh fish—why no put fresh fish dat list? Dat good for you, dat good for he too, dat mo' money dan beef. . . ."

Ormsby was puffing thoughtfully, eyes on the table. Boisson was laughing.

"It's a very sound objection," he said. "You can put me down as seconding it."

"All right, Ramsammy, this sahib write what you say," said Dollard, tapping Ormsby's shoulder. "You sit down. Just now we call-am and you talk, eh?"

"Tell him write." Ramsammy pointed to Ormsby.

Ormsby, looking up, indicated the secretary with his pipe. "He'll write, don't be afraid."

The old man returned to his seat with proud dignity.

Dollard said: "Do you mean, Jacob, that it's only once a week you and your family have a proper meal?"

"No-o, Mr Dollard, suh. Nutten so, man, Eh-eh!"

"I saw you finishing off a banana yesterday at two o'clock. Did you have a proper meal yesterday?"

"That was just a bite afterwards. Like three o'clock tea," added Jacob, remembering that soon after eating the banana he had had to go upstairs and had seen the office boy taking a tray with tea and biscuits into Dollard's private office. And he chuckled again, so that Thorn thought him a simpleton and turned his eyes away.

"I don't know how it strikes you, Mr chairman," Dollard said, "but it seems to me that we ought not to complicate the question by considering the size of a man's family. After all, that's his own business. Dr Lavalle suggested that twenty-five cents a day could feed a man. He is a doctor, his figures should be worth something."

Thorn had been looking closely at Dollard. "I agree entirely," he joined in. "Some have ten children. Are we subsidising families?"

Ormsby looked through some papers. "Our terms of reference don't exclude the family, you know. I'm inclined to think we ought to consider the average family. From our evidence thus far the average family would seem to be a family of five."

"I certainly would not be a party to any discussion of the worker apart from his family," Boisson declared bluntly.

"Well, take Jacob," Dollard persisted, throwing out a hand as though to indicate that economics was on his side. "He's got a family of eight. Eight times twenty-five is two dollars a day. If he has to spend two dollars a day on food he can't get less than fourteen dollars a week. Business can't afford that. You'll put all the small firms out of business."

And Thorn: "Quite so. What does Mr Boisson suggest we do about the more irresponsible among these people who have two families?"

Boisson, reddening: "No red herrings, please. We are concerned with a family of five."

Argument followed, during which Jacob withdrew somewhat stealthily to his chair against the wall. He tried not to hear what they were saying, it seemed to set the hound baying. "Eh-eh," he remarked with a chuckle to Mrs Burnett, "it's eight of us but they only allowin' for five. What I suppose to do with the other t'ree—drown them?"

"If you worry wid dese *baccra johnny* you go out you' mind, *oui*?" said Mrs Burnett, stretching her lips disdainfully.

Jacob took out a large maroon handkerchief with flowers, leaned over between his knees and blew his nose with two resounding reports.

"When this goin' to finish?" Mrs Burnett wanted to know.

"They not hungry yet. When they start to get peckish they goin' to call for adjournment."

"Even if his food bill is only a dollar a day," Boisson was saying, "what about clothes, what about medicines, what about rent?"

They had Jacob come up again.

"Is your rent in arrears?" Thorn asked him.

They all looked at Jacob, they seemed even to hang on his words.

"You kean't help dat, chief. You bound to get in arrears."

The others dropped their eyes but Thorn continued: "Doesn't your wife take in washing? You must do something to make ends meet. How much does she make?"

But so much at variance were Jacob's requirements with the celebrated Dr Lavalle's estimate of what was necessary to maintain health and good cheer in the working people that Ormsby, knocking out his pipe, suggested laying the question aside for the moment and discussing clothing.

The secretary called Mrs Burnett to the table. Ormsby invited her to sit down and even smiled. Having established her identity and her position in the world he asked: "Can you give us some idea of what the minimum expenditure on clothing for a working woman is likely to be?"

The interrogation to which Jacob had been subjected had put Mrs Burnett on her guard. "Four dollars a month," she replied promptly.

Thorn adjusted his glasses. "Four dollars? Her minimum?"

"Wait a minute," said Dollard. "You say forty-eight dollars a year, Mrs Burnett?"

"No, I say four dollars a month."

"Well, that's forty-eight dollars a year. Suppose we take the question another way. How many dresses will she require per year? How many bloomers, let us say, panties do you think she will require every year?"

The twist that Mrs Burnett gave to her lips indicated that she considered that question coming from a gentleman verged on the indecent. But before she could reply Thorn demanded clarification.

"Are we discussing dresses or panties?"

Dollard threw up his hands. "Well, all right, panties, it doesn't matter to me."

"Panties are a small item, it's probably easier to assess the cost," Ormsby agreed.

"Incidentally, Mr chairman," Dollard added, "I've had a talk to my cook about this, you know. She informs me that some people don't wear pants in the daytime."

Thorn: "Do you mean they wear them at night?"

"Well, I can't see much point in that. I don't know. That was just one woman's point of view, but there you are. . . ."

Ormsby was puffing smoke to the ceiling. "In a climate like this," he remarked, "there are probably other items that aren't considered essential wear. Still I don't think we should allow that to influence us in setting minimum standards." He thought: "Do they all wear brassières?" and recalled various movements.

Boisson, slightly pink, asked politely: "Mrs Burnett, what is the cost of a pair of panties?"

"A cheap one, sixty cents. A good one, a dollar," she replied stiffly.

"How many would she use in a year?" Dollard asked.

"About a dozen."

"You mean she will wear out one pair a month?"

"She has to keep some in reserve."

"No, no!" Thorn said at once. "These are minimum quantities we are discussing. There is no reserve. Could one pair last her three months?"

"Excuse me," said Mrs Burnett, letting her eyes slip over him as if the sight were unpleasant to her, "nobody want to wear the one panties for three months."

"I think there's a misunderstanding here," Dollard said. "We don't at all want to make anyone wear one pair for three months. We're trying to find a minimum. Can you help us find a minimum?"

"Nobody could wear a panty three months," she affirmed pertinaciously. "If she has any self-respect she goin' to change every day."

"I understand Mrs Burnett," Boisson said. "She feels that every woman should have the right to keep herself respectably."

"Mr Boisson, that's right—every woman!" she affirmed.

Ormsby steered them out of that current. "Mrs Burnett, can you tell us something about the cost of dresses?"

They listened in silence now to her replies. There was nothing else to do. It was an extraordinary thing, Thorn thought: as a people they seemed to have no conception of what was meant by living within one's means—none whatever. She went on and on about dresses, hats, even stockings, as if everyone was accustomed to wear shoes and stockings, and as if she expected servants were going to be paid thirty dollars a month instead of the five dollars to which most of them were quite accustomed.

Chapter thirty-eight

Among the new clients who had come to Aurelia that year was Indra Goodman, a girl of Elena's age, partly Negro, partly Indian, who had so fresh and vital a personality and was so different from Elena that the two quickly became great friends. Indra had wonderful eyes, dark and flashing, laughing and caressing all at once. No storms had battered her; she did not leave herself much time to think nor had she any desire to question life, she was too busy tasting it and enjoying its flavours. Through her Elena was invited to parties and dances and stepped out into the world. Aurelia found herself having to face the fact that her daughter must live as other girls did; that it was not possible, and certainly unacceptable to young people, to take the measure of every young man who came calling before allowing Elena out with him. Elena was twenty, yet for Aurelia this was a time of great heart-burning and sleepless nights: in her truncated girlhood no such freedoms had been possible, and now they alarmed her.

Elena began to push André out of her mind. Why think of what was impossible? And when she met Robert La Forest it seemed stupid as well. He was very tall, good-looking, brown-skinned and a devil of a dresser. He possessed no few scholastic attainments. In his year he had just missed the only scholarship that could have taken him abroad to study medicine. His parents having no money to fill the breach he applied for a job in the service. He was blessed with charm as well as talent and, what was more to the point, knew how to employ them to secure his advancement. Already at twenty-eight he commanded an excellent position in the Accountant-General's department.

As soon as Aurelia set eyes on him she knew he was well experienced with women, that he was the type who would boast of his conquests even though they bored him. Resentment and suspicion reared up in her, especially when she saw that Elena seemed flattered by his attentions. Many girls regarded him as a catch, it seemed, and were fascinated by his general air of cynical indifference towards them. This infuriated Aurelia. She lost no time dismembering him morally for her daughter's benefit.

All the same, Elena enjoyed his company and inwardly smiled at her mother's suggestion that he was so dissolute. He was interesting. He danced well, he was well read. Sometimes he showed off and admired his own cleverness. She disliked this in him. But it was pleasant to know she had captivated him, and her thoughts played with the possibility of marriage to this man whose admiration other girls envied her. When her mother, noting that he left his cynicism outside her door and realising from certain remarks that his intentions were serious, began to speak approvingly of him Elena ceased to joke about "getting tied up with Robert" and told Indra, "He's not my type." She felt that her mother and everyone expected something of her and she was not ready. She toyed with the notion in secret, trying it on, as it were, to see how it would fit, now decisively rejecting it, now again coming back to it, now disliking him, conscious how far short he was of the husband she dreamed of, and now admiring him in spite of it because everyone believed she *must be* in love with him, everyone except Indra envied her, and some even expected to hear of her engagement to him soon. Now and then she permitted him an inconsequential familiarity: a kiss on the cheek was as much as he could manage despite all his experience, Aurelia's warnings having had their effect, and Elena did not lack an instinctive knowledge of how to handle the reins. Without really intending to do so she encouraged in him a love he had not yet formed for any woman.

It was one of those bright calm periods in between life's storms. Each storm was the same but no two had the same destructive effect, and sometimes treasures turned up amidst the wreckage.

The firm's financial year had closed in March of '37. In April, Hoo gave the staff a party when the day's work was done. Cakes and pies, sandwiches and soft drinks, cheap wines were spread upon a board on trestles in the office. Hoo had handed out bonus cheques an hour before. The staff approached his bounty timidly. Everyone wanted to eat something, to drink some wine, but they all laughed with one another in a strained manner and tried to seem indifferent to the food, over which flies were buzzing, and the unopened bottles. No one, not even the accountant, wanted to be first to put his hand out for a cake or even an empty glass. Hoo came up and said:

"Come, all-you, eat up, eat up! I see some-a you hangin' back as if you never see so much food, man."

His parchment face cracked and he uttered a dry cackle in acknowledgement of his power and his generosity.

And to everyone now those words were a commandment. It was

necessary to eat at once and drink and appear to enjoy everything, even the cheapest sort of sausage ("horse", a young clerk whispered to Elena with a smile, "the one he lost at the races last month") so as to avert the possibility of incurring Hoo's displeasure. And the word "horse" went round the table in whispers, with snickers, because most of them were conscious of being subjected to an indignity. The accountant, having respectfully filled Hoo's glass first, poured less into every other glass including his own, stood up very straight, called loudly for silence and made a speech in praise of Hoo. He called him "the greatest captain of industry Trinidad has ever seen", and asked the staff to give three cheers for the man to whom they owed "everything in the world". Everyone responded. Hoo, too, applauded, laughing slyly.

The accountant was three-quarters Negro and one quarter Chinese. He considered that he owed his job in no small part to his distant Chinese ancestor and that the delicacy of his position was increased by the fact that his assistant was pure Chinese. Further, he had just received a bonus amounting to a dollar and eighty-five cents a week and was overwhelmed by this sum.

The assistant, not to be outdone, followed the accountant's example. He tried to say in different words what his senior had said. He did not know what the accountant had received but was sure it was not as much as *he,* a pure Chinese liked by the boss, had been given—a bonus amounting to a dollar a week. He was already considering devious ways of discovering how the winds had favoured him, hoping to deduce from this a continuous rise in his future standing with Hoo.

Now all the clerks knew they would have to rise and say something in praise of Hoo—it was done every year. All suffered, some from shame but all from uneasiness lest they find themselves in disfavour by praising Hoo less than the accountant had done. Who could tell? It might mean the difference between a rise of fifty cents a week and no rise at all. Some in the most abject terms, their voices shaking with fright, expressed undying gratitude for the bonus. One said Mr Hoo was one of Christ's true disciples; another demanded outright "prayers for him tonight"; all competed with one another in praise of Hoo, and at every speech Hoo uttered a cackle and applauded before anyone else.

"Miss Henriques' turn now!" he said sharply.

Hoo had given her a bonus of fifteen dollars. She had been overjoyed to receive it. But when one of the girls whispered she had seen the accountant's cheque for ninety-six dollars Elena realised that her own amounted to little more than thirty cents a week. Hoo was paying her four dollars a week for far more work than Miss Marley had done in her place and saving almost half of what he had paid Miss Marley. She had squirmed with contempt and pity for the clerks who had sung Hoo's praises.

With a sedate smile she said that Mr Hoo was undoubtedly a man of great energy and astuteness. No doubt if he had not suffered from the handicap of poor parents he would have outstripped other business-men long ago. She could not but wish him success for it was on his continued success that their own livelihood depended.

The dignity of her few words—which all applauded—came like a blast of cold air into the gathering after what had preceded them. Hoo did not cackle this time.

At home Elena found her mother deep in low-voiced conclave with Miss Richards. It was the latter's first visit since she had borrowed that five dollars almost two years before.

"Eh-eh! Well! Elena, how, my dear?" Miss Richards timidly, conscious that Elena did not like her, yet at the same time expressing by the genuine surprise in her crafty oriental eyes a flattering admiration of the young woman who stood before her. "When I last saw her she was a big girl, Aurelia, but now, my dear—eh-eh! You have a beautiful woman for a daughter, yes, chile? How are you, my dear?" To Elena's irritation she even wiped some moisture from her eyes.

Elena did not yet know that the moisture was induced by the hope of raising another loan, or that the voices were lowered not over gossip but a tale of woe, the bombardment and softening-up before the attack. She went to the kitchen to prepare dinner. Miss Richards did not stay this time. She had seen in Elena's black eyes an unrelenting power of perception unusual in one so young, and a readiness to condemn, which made her feel ashamed and guilty. She went off promising Aurelia in a whisper to return next day.

Aurelia's face lit up when she heard of her daughter's bonus. She praised Hoo's generosity.

She fell silent for a while. It was quite unusual. Then she said in a wheedling tone: "Elena, you couldn't lend Miss Richards ten dollars? Poor thing, man! Her position is terrible. Some days she is without food. Unless she can make up the rent the agent goin' to throw her out. She only didn't stay to dinner because she feels you don't like her."

"Mother, Miss Richards is not getting one cent!" Elena said in a shaking voice because she couldn't bear that unfamiliar wheedling tone, especially as it was so reminiscent of what she had suffered that afternoon. "I'd rather give it all to Leah. Miss Richards knows how sympathetic you are and she takes advantage of it. She is not in the difficulties we are in and she knows I know that, that's why she's afraid to face me. I've run my blood to water for the miserable fifteen dollars—" She broke off, biting her lips to keep from sobbing.

Aurelia was flustered, her face reddened. "It's only Christian, Elena," she said, rising from the table. "It's your own money, do what you like; but I couldn't have it, see friends want and not give—"

"Christianity? What is Christianity?" Elena broke in with passion. "To be made a slave by a man with thousands? To live in degradation because of him, to have to humiliate yourself before him to keep your job? Why must we alone be Christians? It's time for us to be fighting such people."

Aurelia began loudly to defend Miss Richards. But she felt she was defending not Miss Richards so much as herself and her impulsive acts of generosity, and the more she talked the more angry she became, and the more impossible it was to be silent, and the more did she twist Elena's words.

"Who are you to talk? I have sheltered you all your life. What experience you have?" And so on, because she had to defend the only way she knew how to live to preserve faith and truth.

At last Elena went to her room, Aurelia to hers. Elena tried to figure out how to dispose of the money so that her mother would not make it over to Miss Richards . . . cloth for dresses, perhaps, and the shoes they needed.

After lunch next day she complained of feeling ill. Hoo let her go. She went straight to Peter D'Aguiar, who headed the insurance department of a big import-export company with branches throughout the West Indies. It was part of her job to make out Hoo's insurance claims and discuss them with D'Aguiar. He knew her work and respected her for it. He had no job to offer her but: "I have had certain developments in mind. . . ."

"I hope you . . . will be discreet, Mr D'Aguiar?"

He smiled and rose. "You may rely on me."

Stifling her embarrassment and fear she tried another company, long-established and very wealthy, the kind in which, at that time, there would not have been any Portuguese D'Aguiars in authority. Here heads of departments were either British or descendants of old French estate owners.

A well-dressed fair-haired white girl showed her into a private office. "Mr Keening will see you in a moment."

And it all turned out as she expected. Her shorthand was tested, her familiarity with office procedure examined in detail. Then: "No, we need a girl with more experience." As she went out, calm and dignified, she felt the eyes of all the office girls upon her. She alone was coloured.

Almost automatically Elena's steps led her to the cathedral. Its echoing quiet, its hard pews polished by the millions seeking succour, the effigies of the saints looking down upon her in fixed attitudes of piety, the flickering lamps and candles—these and her prayers had often brought her peace. She had come here when she realised that André would not return, when her mother was sued for a debt or the bailiff was pressing his claims; and she had been comforted. Now she felt with despair that she was inextricably bogged down in some kind of foul malodorous mud. Prayers rose from her lips only, not her heart. She thought of Robert, not of God. What ought she to do about Robert? Would they be happy? Was he . . . a bit of safe high ground in that mud?

So quiet was it in the empty church that she heard a sound of whispering. She looked round and saw a thin middle-aged black woman in a floppy torn straw hat standing beside a bas-relief with her hands crossed before her. A washerwoman perhaps. With a surreptitious air she was whispering prayers, gazing with a look of diminishing hope into the eyes of God. How often had she not seen that look on the faces of the poor when they came to beg Christ's mercy? And suddenly she remembered she had seen Mr Keening holding the canopy over the priest in the procession last Corpus Christi. She shut her eyes. "No, no! I mustn't think like that. If I lose my faith what's left?"

She began to repeat rapidly the Our Father, but the sound of whispering drew nearer and she saw the woman in the torn straw hat standing beside a different station. On her face was a look of mingled fear, pleading and a conviction that only by uttering the particular words at each station could she hope to avert the disaster she saw awaiting her. That look so painfully confirmed the doubts in Elena's heart that she quickly crossed herself and left the church.

She took a tram to the Gardens. Memories of André came crowding, memories she wanted both to recall and to forget. She sat and looked at the sanded path, the lush grass, flowers on the vine, and nothing was beautiful, nothing touched a chord; it was all stale, lifeless, without meaning just as life had no meaning—senseless like the days she trod. She felt an aching emptiness. She wept, the tears running unnoticed down her cheeks. She wept because everything was eternally the same, because there was no one to value what was good in her and she was wasted. She wept because tears were soothing. They washed away something that had obscured her vision. The flowers on the vine became young and fresh. Dreams came back in spite of Keening. She heard the rustle of a squirrel in a tree, there seemed a magic in the soft fall of a flower on the path. She listened to the intricate call of a bird. She saw Robert beside her, then she saw André and felt angry and helpless that she had not yet forgotten him. She heard the footsteps but did not look up. She waited for them to pass so she could go on dreaming.

"Elena?"

Her heart leaped, beat wildly, her face grew hot. "How stupid I must look!" she thought staring at him, unable to say anything.

"May I sit here?" André asked.

"Yes." The promptness of her reply angered her. So he was smiling. Smiling! What right had he to smile? How dare he smile! She wanted to get up and rush off, and wanted nothing so much as to stay.

"How have you been?" he asked just to say something, because he wanted to fly away himself with his guilt.

"Very well." She looked him full in the face as if meaning: "Why should I be otherwise?" She watched him slowly flushing. "Have you been all right?" She was in command of herself now.

"Yes, I've been all right. How is your mother?"

"Very well."

"Has she got over. . . ."

"Uncle Popi's death? Yes." She got up. "I must go now."

"Elena . . . may I talk to you?"

"I don't understand." She was pure ice.

"I mean. . . ."

"Why don't you talk to Gwenneth? Aren't you engaged to her?"
"I'm not."
"You're in love with her."
"I don't know how to answer that."
"It didn't work out as you thought it would and now you want me to console you, is that it?" Tears came before she could master herself. She hated herself, she hated him.
He had got up too, and took her hand. "Please!"
She pulled away her hand. "It's all over between us, don't you understand that?"
"I shouldn't have said anything. I'm sorry."
She blew her nose. "I must go home." For an instant he was uncertain if she would prefer him not to accompany her to the gate, but her movements indicated she expected him to do so.
Night lurked beneath the trees. The western sky was burning. People sat outside the Gardens watching the evening parade of cars and the girls on the Pitchwalk. They smiled, chatted, yawned, were slightly bored and thought of dinner. In the Savannah the first fireflies appeared.
Let him suffer, she thought. *Let him suffer! Haven't I suffered? In a moment we'll get to the tram stop and he'll go, and that will be the end, that's how it should be.* "What is she like?" She had wanted to ask this all along.
"Proud—like me. Arrogant. In love with herself."
She laughed. "You proud? And bowing down to her? Anyway I don't want to hear anything."
Night fell. Millions of fireflies were flickering over the Savannah, rising and falling and seeming to sway in waves. The Savannah looked like an enormous jewel sparkling in the darkness.
They were strolling past the Shamrock Club. "Did she enjoy your article?"
"As far as they were concerned I had reached the lowest depths."
"I was glad you wrote it. It spoke the truth. What are we if we can't speak out? You must have known what would happen?"
"I did, but we must own our own *minds.* That above everything. I hate these snivelling fools who say we're too stupid to manage anything. They make me hate the English with a richer hate, a conscious rather than an instinctive hate such as I never felt before."
"Don't talk about hate. You hate them and you love them, you

said so yourself once," she said, her voice fading as if it were torture to utter the words.

He looked fiercely at her in the light of the street lamp. She was not the same Elena who had loved him months before. He was ashamed to be trading on her love for him.

"I didn't mean that," she whispered, looking down. "Tell me, I want to hear."

"All right, Elena. Could I bring Clem Payne home, or Cassie? Life won't let you go beyond a certain point! I have to eat. Besides, would *I* want it? I can't bridge the cultural gap. Yet Payne will do deeds I could never accomplish in a lifetime. I'm talking, he's *acting*. What am I doing to realise myself?"

"It's always like that here. Do you think we could ever find more than a partial solution?"

"I hate partial solutions! For how many more years will we be divided up like this, unable to communicate, speaking incomprehensibly or with enmity to one another? How many hate what I hate? They don't! They mock themselves, they feel only contempt for themselves and one another. You turn from the whites to the coloureds and what is there but this stultifying self-contempt and despair!"

From the wildness with which he expressed himself, she guessed he had not told her the main thing: that he was tormented by the knowledge that he could not break with Gwenneth. She wanted to take him in her arms, to hush him as one might a child because she didn't want the image she had long cherished of him replaced by another, and already he had twisted it all out of shape. Only her fingers playing with a bit of paper she had rolled into a ball gave hint of her inward struggle.

"I know," was all she could say.

She wanted to tell him about Hoo's party and her disgust. "Why should I rake out my soul for him?" she thought and got up. "I must go. I'll take this tram." He got up too. To see the disappointment in his eyes was soothing to her.

Soon after dinner Robert came in. Everything that had been growing in her for him dissolved in a moment. His dress seemed loud, she was offended by the light, careless mockery in his remarks. For the first time she was struck by their self-conscious levity, their superficiality.

"Could I tell *him* about Hoo? How would he understand it? In my place would he have accepted it, would it have bruised anything in him?"

Passionately she resolved: "I'll never talk to André again—never, never, *never!*"

And she began laughing with Robert as if nothing had changed.

Chapter thirty-nine

Gwenneth went out frequently with Arthur Symmonds. With him there was no social problem, he was fun. She wanted André because life would not let her have him. She feared and was fascinated by his singleness of mind and his independence of thought, which would drive her, she felt, into some kind of no-man's land. She felt shame and joy and fear that he could always possess her. She wounded him again and again to revenge herself.

When he heard that she was seen everywhere with Symmonds André felt himself brought to public ridicule. He hated her.

Though he could have gone to the Manzanilla Estate with the family he had chosen to remain at home alone. He was alien among them, he told himself. But he also knew he was hoping that the phone would ring.

He found his dinner awaiting him when he got home after seeing Elena, and the cook anxious to be gone. He sent her off. Almost at the first mouthful the phone rang. He rushed to it, forgetting everything—resolution to be done with her, hatred, hurt pride—everything.

"André?" It was she, in her voice a humble, nervous note he was not accustomed to hear.

"Yes."

"Have you just got in?"

"Yes."

"I rang before. You were out."

"I was."

"Who was the girl you were with?"

So that's it, he thought, and said, "A friend of mine."

"Is she the one you were in love with?"

"Yes, she is the girl I was in love with and for whom I still have much admiration."

"Evidently. I waved, you never even looked!"

"Unfortunate."

"I want to see you."

"I'm alone here. They've gone to Manzanilla for the weekend."

"I'll come about nine o'clock," she whispered nervously.

He threw out his dinner, he couldn't eat with his bowels tangled in desire. He showered, shaved, changed; sat down with a book at the dining table but scarcely understood one sentence in it.

A knock on the kitchen door. He jumped up, suddenly furious. *Hiding, using the back door,* he thought and tugged it open. Cassie faced him. "Come in, Cassie!"

Not knowing who might be in the kitchen she was at once the servant. "Goodnight, Mr André. I only come on a message."

"Come in, come in, there's no one at home. In here. Sit down." He pulled out a chair for her at the dining table.

Cassie looked around her with an open, mischievous smile—the Cassie of old. "So how? You one in this big place? You not afraid?"

"I was, but you're with me now."

She laughed. She was searching for something in her handbag. "I see. Well, I well glad you didn't go too or I would have make a journey in vain. Ben gave me this for you." In her hand was a folded manuscript. "You know, this is the full truth of the strike down south, and the march, and how Boisson cheat us. He want you see Joe Elias and get him print it in the magazine. Tell him he could sell plenty copies down south."

"We need this. The papers published hardly anything. I'll see Joe tomorrow."

She was about to put her handbag on the brightly polished table. "You better not, chile," she muttered with a smile, and slung it over her shoulder. "You safe there, you not scratchin' anyone but the owner."

She laughed, and he was overcome by her charm on which, he saw, she placed no value. He wanted to embrace her and cut that abscess in his breast.

"So how 'bout you? Not married yet, man?"

His face changed. "It can't be with her. You know that, Cassie. And you? What you doing with you'self?"

"Just workin'."

"Are you happy? Tell me the truth—you think life is a pleasant thing?"

She shrugged. "Sometimes. Man, if you livin' you have to live, yes? So things not good?" She was looking at him, smiling, sensing what he felt towards her and wanting to hold his head against her and comfort him. And he began to tell her everything, all that he had been unable to tell anyone else, all the turmoil that he felt distorting his personality and dragging him down.

"I know I despise her, so how can I love her? I feel *sorry* for her. Cassie, could you love someone deeply, you know, give your whole self to someone, and go out and have a good time with someone else the next night?"

"Eh-eh! You sure?"

"Yes!"

"If I love a man I want to stay with that man."

"So in her case it wasn't love, it was only stealing. She stole what was good in me just to amuse herself with it."

She looked at him with a strange smile. "Not you alone could say that, André. What about Elena?"

"Yes, and I'm ashamed. Everything was so confused, different. . . ."

She rubbed her thumb-nail without replying.

"But I don't love Gwenneth, it's a habit, it's vanity—"

"It's she you love," she interrupted, "but she hurt you and you don't *want* to love her."

"I can't love her, she would destroy me!"

"Now you sayin' a different thing. I glad to hear you say that at last, I well glad. She not make for you."

"You know something?" he said, wanting to deface the alluring image stamped on his soul. "She's ashamed of loving, the act of loving—with me!" he cried. "With me!"

"No, man," she reproved him. "She's afraid, André."

"Afraid of what, afraid of what?" He was so worked up now that his lips were pale and trembling.

"It's not a little thing she givin' you, you know. Listen to me good." She took his hand in hers. "She young and not experienced, and she love you. You understand? No need drivin' her, she livin' well. In this Trinidad today they not goin' to let her love you. It's not her fault." All the gaiety had gone out of Cassie's face.

Suddenly she snatched away her hand. He looked up and saw Gwenneth coming through the drawing-room. On her flushed face eagerness conflicted with intense curiosity, suspicion and a readiness to take offence.

"Gwenneth!" He sprang up and approached her.

Though she saw Cassie rising to go she said frigidly: "You needn't bother to get up, I'm unable to stay." She went out the front with her quick step, her frock swinging ominously behind her.

Cassie watched André come back in, his eyes blind with pain. "Don't go," he said.

"You knew she was comin'?"

"Yes," he whispered.

"Why you didn't tell me, man?"

"I needed you, Cassie."

"Love is a hard thing to forget," she said gently, stroking his hair.

He took her hand and pressed it against his forehead. But he could not be still and jumped up, and was hardly up when he sat down again, striking his forehead and again jumping up.

"Stop, man, stop!" she said. "Come with me to Fyzabad."

"Yes. Anything."

"You are with us. Enough difficulties for you in that, don't take on dese white people, they goin' to shit on you, man, excuse me."

"Yes. Yes, all right."

She came and put her arms round him and her cheek against his own. "Don't fret, man, don't fret. O God, I don't like to see people hurt so! So what about these papers?"

"I'll take them to Joe. Now. Come with me. Will you come?"

They went out together.

Chapter forty

In November of the previous year, 1936, Joe had won a seat on the city council. He had joined Boisson's party, but when they declared him unacceptable to them as an election candidate he switched his allegiance overnight to the Workers' Welfare. Standing against the candidate Boisson himself had selected, he won the seat. In all his campaign speeches he had demanded a militant response to the problems in which the great mass of the people foundered about as in a bog. The people had accepted him. No other candidate spoke so well as he; with power, colourfully, boldly, never needing to pause for words; a man of education, this one, clever, not like themselves. They hoped, as they had hoped of others, that when he got into the council things would change. Perhaps rates would fall; but especially they hoped he would champion them because they had no champion.

A heady incense arose from the approving crowds, from the unsmiling readiness of some to follow him, the man of truth, wherever he led. When he was declared the winner there was no lack of hands to touch his coat, to grasp or pat him. To his own surprise he thought: "They are easily fooled."

The craftiness of the politician he learned without difficulty. He made pacts for tactical reasons and broke them to serve his strategies. He would laugh and slap his broad and meaty chest, crying: "You can't put anything over this one!" In the February session he called for increased wages to the scavengers and a general lowering of the franchise. The second was outside the province of the council and he knew this. He intended it as a stick for Boisson's back: the acknowledged leader of the working people had never yet demanded such a measure in the legislative council.

They took the wages motion first. A stout Portuguese businessman was the first to rise in opposition.

"What do you want to do, take money from the poor to pay the poor?"

Joe replied: "If it ever became necessary to raise money from taxation—and I say if—we would find ways and means of taxing business."

The stout merchant reddened, foreseeing that giving to one might well entangle him in an obligation not to refuse the other, his own clerks.

Old Elias, who was sitting among the scavengers on the public benches, was particularly displeased. He had rejoiced at Joe's win. As soon as he met someone he could not refrain from saying: "My son is a councillor now. You saw that? Yes, man, he won by a big margin!" a smile of happy amazement spreading over his face. But now he repeated in a low voice, looking open-mouthed at the faces about him: "The boy is mad, man, the boy is mad!" He kept thinking: "My fault. What right I had to give him twelve hundred dollars to come here and say this?"

While Joe continued to present the scavengers' case for more pay two councillors got up and went into the gallery for a private conference. ("What are they plotting?" went through Joe's mind.) The stout Portuguese, dull-eyed and discontented, summoned the uniformed orderly, who respectfully took a coin from him and went out. Another councillor, a well-dressed, handsome Indian of about thirty, was working out the crossword puzzle in a newspaper. He kept twisting and stretching his neck as if his collar were too tight. A third, a very ugly black man, was intently picking his nose while looking through the windows at the trees in Woodford Square. The orderly returned with a glass of iced grapefruit juice and set it before the stout merchant. This seemed to awaken two other councillors, who summoned the orderly and whispered to him, slipping coins into his palm and pointing to the stout man's glass. The scavengers on the public benches were frowning or smiling in accordance with their temperaments as they listened to their City Fathers debating their future with long and clever words.

"The scavengers' request for elementary health safeguards, such as gloves and high rubber boots, has been ignored." Joe was shouting. *What worms these men are,* he thought, looking at the faces around the table. "I presume Your Worship is not unaware of the fact that more than ninety per cent of them walk barefoot about the streets and underground drains, and are consequently exposed to hookworm. This council has decided to raise the salary of the city engineer. What about these men? Without them the health of the city would be menaced in twenty-four hours."

"Hear, hear!" from the public benches.

The mayor, Boisson, threatened to clear the chamber. Old Elias's expression was like that of a spectator who gazes spellbound at the daring of a gymnast, expects that at any moment he will fall from the wire and be picked up in pieces, realises with amazement that the gymnast is an expert and prepares to burst into applause.

"That's my son, you know? That's my son."

"Powerful speaker," said the scavenger he addressed, because in his heart was hope.

The stout Portuguese had got up. Parting his jacket he put his fat little hands under it behind his back and began in a grave hoarse voice: "I am not sure whether Mr Elias intends his final words to be—"

"What final words? You haven't heard the last of me yet!"

"Order!" from Boisson.

". . . a threat to strike. No one profits by strikes—"

Raucous laughter from Joe. "Why don't you read? All the important gains of the workers have been won by striking."

The Indian interrupted the study of crossword clues to say: "Cool off, Elias. The next election is nine months away."

And again Boisson banging.

"You cannot draw blood from a stone!" the merchant asserted angrily. "Our finances are not unlimited. The report of the Minimum Wage Committee has just been published. What does it say? It says that sixty-nine cents a day is a fair minimum wage. The men who were on that committee are businessmen—"

"Watching their pockets," from Joe.

"—men of experience, not mere youths. And they don't spend their time doing crossword puzzles, they have the welfare of the community at heart—"

"Hear, hear!" ironically from the black man, wiping his finger on his jacket.

"What are we paying the scavengers? Ninety cents a day. We are not robbing anyone. We might like to pay more but we have to live within our means, we cannot allow ourselves—"

"Have you read the report?" nose-picker demanded.

"Yes, I *have* read the report."

"You read the lists of clothing?"

"What is the purpose of this interrogation, Mr Mayor?"

"Don't hide behind the mayor, man. Do you agree that two pairs of panties are sufficient for a woman for one year?"

Laughs around the table. From the public benches a resounding "No!" Bangs from Boisson. "If there are any more comments from the public I will order the chamber cleared!"

"That is the irreducible minimum. Why don't you ask the mayor? He signed the report."

And Boisson, smiling pityingly: "I did not sign the report. I submitted a minority report. I protested and still protest against the conclusion arrived at."

"Face facts!" the black man said to the Portuguese merchant.

"Ah! What's a five-letter word for fact?" the Indian enquired, twisting his neck in its collar.

The brown man with the cigar had an appointment to meet a lady friend secretly at eleven o'clock. "Mr Mayor," he said in a business-like tone, "there is no need for this display. Are we to become another comic strip? I move that a committee be formed. Mr Elias chairman. I'll be willing to serve." He blew cigar smoke to the ceiling.

And in a minute they pushed scavengers' wages out of the way.

But Joe was on his feet again, setting out his reasons for moving a motion asking government to lower the franchise for elections to the council.

At once the Indian began to stretch and twist his neck rapidly and flung down his pen. "On a point of order, Your Worship, this council cannot undertake to ask for a lowering of the franchise. This is a matter outside of our authority—"

"You did not think it outside our authority when you went before the electorate last November," Joe broke in, shaking an accusing finger. "I happen to have been present at one of your election meetings. I heard you say that the franchise served to keep the working masses out and deprive them of a voice."

"Why be dishonest? I made no promise to lower the franchise."

"Dishonest? You couldn't hold a candle to me!" Joe shouted in his small voice.

"I don't take directions from the hooligan element like you. You are openly supporting and encouraging the worst elements in the population. You and they should be behind bars."

Joe had planned this manoeuvre without consulting anyone, only hinting mysteriously: "You will see something." Certain proposals had been put to him by the group of Welfare supporters who had worked to get him elected, but Joe ignored these men and their plans.

The complex inner man was moved by an urge profounder than all their reasonings and their strategies.

The motion was seized upon by the councillors like a shoe by puppies and torn to shreds.

"What do you want to do, bring the barefooted and uneducated into the council?" said the brown man with the cigar, his thin face looking more rapacious than ever. He stole a glance at the clock on the wall.

The merchant: "Make this council the laughing stock of the world. . . ."

The black man—he was a shoemaker who had done not badly—said solemnly and with some irritation: "We are here to give guidance to these people. Why you think they call us the City Fathers in the papers? You really expect these ignorant people to know who to elect to run a city of a hundred thousand people?"

They threw out Joe's motion, much to the relief of old Elias, who had been saying to a coloured drug-store owner behind him: "No, that's a bad thing, man, bad thing. . . ."

Boisson was banging the table and trying to silence Joe, who was speaking again on the same motion.

"Sit down!" the brown man with the cigar shouted spitefully.

"Sit down! Sit down!" came shouts from around the table.

Joe was angered not by their shouts but by his own small voice, which seemed to squeak ineffectually as he strained it.

". . . and there is not one of you—not one—" with a wave of his arm he expressed scorn of everyone, but the gesture was so grand he also succeeded in expressing disapproval of himself—"who realises the condition of the masses in this country. The depression is supposed to have passed yet there are more people hungry and walking the streets in search of work than ever before. Unless we make them vocal a very serious situation is going to develop, there's going to be an explosion—"

"There'll be an explosion right here if you don't shut up and sit down, Mr Mayor . . .!"

". . . you are afraid of losing your seats, you are fully aware that on the present franchise you don't represent the people—despite the fact that a man has to pay only five dollars a month rent to qualify as a voter. I warn this council that it cannot dam forever the human being's sense of injustice—"

"Sit down!" Boisson shouted, red-faced.

"I defy you, it is my right to speak for the people! Sooner or later their anger will burst its banks. I tell you solemnly, we will all be in danger of being swept away—"

"Escort Councillor Elias from the chamber!" Boisson cried to the policeman on duty.

"Throw him out! He got no right in here with this talk about revolution," the shoemaker agreed.

Joe laughed raucously, and with satisfaction. "Throw me out? Try it, try it!" His face was red and perspiring. He was overcome by an ecstatic lust to pit the strength of his mind, his moral purpose and even his muscles against them all; he was imbued with a joyful, reckless fury. "I will not sit down, I will not walk out. I defy you!"

And he lay down flat and stiff on the floor.

Everybody got up to look and some began to laugh.

"Take him out," Boisson ordered.

The constable could not refrain from smiling. "Come, Mr Elias," he said respectfully.

"You'll have to find some way to do it, me boy, I'm not helping you."

The shoemaker felt personally insulted by this unheard-of display of contempt for the city council's public image. He called to the orderlies for assistance. They came and helped the policeman to lift Joe up and carry him out.

"Goodbye, gentlemen!" Joe cried with a sneering laugh. "Until tomorrow."

The scavengers were quietly chuckling, but old Elias felt so ashamed he did not know where to look. With a flushed face he got down from the platform and left the council chamber, stepping softly on the balls of his feet so as not to attract attention.

Chapter forty-one

Towards the end of March old Elias suffered a stroke while at the home of one of his women. In a few hours he was dead. Joe was sent for. He found the Negro woman, who was by no means old, weeping in a stifled manner, as much upset by this dramatic public exposure of her secret life as she was frightened by the death that sat with her. In her reddened eyes was grief. The emotional prop that gave life meaning had snapped beneath her.

Looking at his father's remains Joe felt aversion and pity and horror, and a secret satisfaction that he himself was in splendid health, as vital as usual. Both to him and the woman it was a relief to know he could call someone in to do what was necessary and they need not look on death any longer—at least he was sure she felt as he did. He rang the undertaker.

When he broke the news to his mother, sisters and ten-year-old brother a hushed atmosphere of shock, dreaded expectation of seeing the dead body and a morbid curiosity settled on everyone. As soon as the body was brought in the wailing began. The servants came to look. Afterwards they whispered: "You saw him? Death really change him up!" And one smiled. The boy saw this. He was frightened not by death but by a sudden feeling of insecurity, by a vague, incomprehensible, terrifying development in life. He climbed a guava tree in the yard and stoned the hens. Why should a foolish creature like a hen live and pick at the grass while of his father nothing remained but that cold body? Such was his unexpressed, scarcely comprehended reflection.

Joe had never before set eyes on death. That very morning he had spoken to his father, who had seemed well enough. Now here was this body which in a week would be full of worms. And whether it took a week or another forty or fifty years he, too, would make a meal for the worms. It was a very ancient thought, but suddenly he had understood it so intensely and so personally that he was sure he could never be the same, could never again feel that naive confidence, born of unawareness, that he had felt in the council chamber this afternoon. What made it worse was coming upon his mother late that night, when the others were in bed, kneeling beside the coffin, weeping. He felt she was weeping for her own life which soon must end. Then a kind of rage overcame him as well as terror, and he wanted to run out of the house, away from death. He thought how he would die, how his closest friends would stand at the graveside and wipe their eyes and then, going home, would crack jokes and laugh just as before. He found this hard to accept. What was the use of all this bickering in the council and lying down on the floor? Why this striving to embarrass Boisson? Why the determination to win more money for the scavengers? We all were worms! You could not escape that essential fact—the uselessness of all one's efforts. And everyone was deserving of pity: the scavengers, Boisson, that fool of a shoemaker—all! But at the very next committee meeting he attacked the brown man with the cigar and hotly supported the scavengers. "Why am I doing this?" he thought, suddenly depressed. He had to make a great effort not to lose interest in the point he was making.

Waking in the mornings he thought: "I'm alive! How good that is! How do I feel? What are the indications of incipient heart trouble? Cancer? But where's the sense in being glad to be alive if living is so useless?" And again depression would come down upon him like a huge, wet, dark cloud. To want to live, yet to feel that all life was futile, his especially—this drove him to fits of melancholy in which everything seemed dark as night.

He could not communicate with anyone. Death had never come near André, he never gave it a thought. Once he confessed he had thought of killing himself; but to Joe that only indicated his complete unawareness of the shattering destruction that was death. "Death?" Joe said. "You don't mean death, you mean unconsciousness." And he tried to explain what death meant to all who knew it the first time. But to André it was all words, he saw, just words. Manny Camacho laughed and shrugged at his friend's repeated references to death—"as though he's exempt", Joe thought with irritation, feeling old and tired.

In April, Le Maître came on a brief visit to Port-of-Spain. He sought Joe out and expressed a desire to discuss the magazine with him. "And Coudray and Camacho too!" he said in his forceful way. "Let's all have a talk."

Joe invited them to meet at his home. He now occupied his father's study. It had quite a different appearance, it seemed more spacious and full of light because Mrs Elias had hung new curtains for her son and had disposed of the old roll-top desk, the safe and the ancient rattan chairs. She had ordered shelves put up and he had lined one wall with his books. "She's afraid I might leave home," he thought, sighing.

There was truth in this, but she had made the changes mainly because his melancholy distressed her. She felt relieved when she heard his voice raised in argument in the study. Then, she felt, life was stirring in him as it ought to do in a man his age.

The magazine's continued existence had for some time been in doubt. Le Maître valued the magazine less because workers would read it—few could afford it—than because it could win allies among the middle class, who were unaware of or simply indifferent to what simmered at their back door.

Before he entered the study where they were gathered, as soon, indeed, as they heard his fearless voice at the front door they felt his presence. Joe went out to welcome him. André looked at the door with a smile that indicated his personal liking for Le Maître, whom he was beginning to know.

"Hello, André, how?" Le Maître said as soon as he entered. He was glad to see André; he expected much of him.

Joe brought in a jug of sorrel; also a bottle of rum and some wine. Le Maître chose sorrel.

"How many copies of the last issue you sold?" he asked, wasting no time on the usual preliminaries such as health, the weather or bits of gossip.

"Two hundred or so."

"Many in the south?"

"Yes, this time. Your article on the strike and the march. . . ."

"It pays?"

"We have to raise money among ourselves to pay the printer," said André.

Manny came in with a chuckle. "I can generally raise a few dollars from my old man."

"He approves?"

"He doesn't disapprove," said Manny, adding with youthful confidence and superciliousness: "For a man of his narrow shop-keeping mentality he might even be described as a liberal."

"We have to make use of them. All the same, we can't run a magazine in this way."

Joe, lying back in his comfortable new chair with his feet up, said:

"That's not news. What's your suggestion?"

They all expected Le Maître to offer a solution to the problem of raising money. He pressed the top of his thumb reflectively against his front teeth. "The magazine should draw readers' attention to the workers. We should write about the workers. In the last issue you have a poem about death. The workers don't want to read about death."

Joe abruptly sat upright. "Oh, they don't? Let me tell you, death is the greatest of all realities," he said pontifically. What did this man know about poetry anyway? "I'm surprised you don't realise that. Wages, conditions—and suddenly you come face to face with death. Doesn't that compel you to question your values?"

Le Maître was about to say: "A fine thing! They're struggling to live and you're preaching to them about death." But instead he asked gently: "You were very attached to your father?"

"He was a worm. But he was also a man. How can you get away from that?"

"I am not afraid of death," said Le Maître, as one might say, "I am not afraid of bees." Joe almost laughed but refrained when he remembered Le Maître had fought in the 1914-18 war. "When I die I want to die serving the workers. If every man was to sit down and think how he was goin' to die tomorrow what would happen? The capitalists would tighten the ropes."

"Anyway," said André in the silence that followed, "the poem was too personal an expression of an experience to mean anything to ordinary people."

"What you want—that I should bring the magazine down to the level of the uneducated?"

"Why not, Elias?" (Le Maître never called him Joe. He was conscious of an arrogance in Joe, an intellectual and class arrogance that Joe was not aware of in himself. Already he had fixed notions about Joe and his role in society.) "To free ourselves of colonialism we have to emancipate them, and to do that you must educate them."

"Oh, educate them!" Joe said exactly in the tone his father had used when asked for money. "What—lessons in history? Rubbish. That's not my function. Let me ask you this. Have you considered the middle class?"

"They're a very important class but they haven't got the economy in their hands. In my view we should use the magazine to win them as allies while at the same time helping the workers to realise their strength."

"Of course." Manny rose. "Quite correct, my boy, quite correct." He put his hands on his hips, smiled benignly and moved about the study. He peered short-sightedly through his spectacles at some books on Joe's shelves. "Those opinions don't coincide with Joe's, I'm afraid, Ben."

Joe waved a hand disdainfully. "A magazine to cater to some sort of momentary political exigencies? A Workers' Welfare magazine? Nonsense, piffle! What we need is an outlet for philosophical discussion, for works of art. Political discussion too, but to confine it to Workers' Welfare politics would be a huge mistake." And he sat forward on the edge of his chair. "Look, you must have vision—"

"What sort of philosophy are you promoting?" Le Maître interrupted. "A philosophy of death, of resignation to death? Is that going to help anybody?"

"Le Maître, listen to me. A man's soul needs time to breathe. Intelligent people need spiritual oxygen. You want to supply them with one set of ideas. Do you realise what you are leading up to? Dictatorship. Imprisonment of the human mind! Look at what Hitler and his Nazi rallies are doing. Is that what you want? Look at Stalin!"

Le Maître pouted. "I asked you what sort of philosophy you are promoting," said he in a hectoring tone. "The answer to that is everything. We need a philosophy to make our people conscious of their strength. Do you agree with that?"

"Yes, yes. So what?"

"Once they are conscious of their strength they will stand up to the boss, they will fight colonialism. It is the only way!"

Once more Joe was astonished by what seemed to him the narrowness of Le Maître's vision. Yet he envied him that narrowness and at this moment wished that life's colours did not flash before him in such rich variety. "What a lot of heads the boss will lop off, Le Maître," he sneered. "Just one cruiser—and where are you?"

"In jail or six feet under. But that is not the point. We cannot sit here forever and preach collaboration, damn it!"

And André, his heart beating fast and the words tumbling out: "You're right, you're absolutely right, we can't! But where's the point in risking destruction? Why destroy the very morale we need to build, Ben? The people are not all like you and a few others."

Joe laughed at Le Maître. "A revolution?"

"Who's talking about a revolution? Don't be a fool, Elias. I am talking about a revolution in the mind! Look at the vile short stories the newspapers print. They're written to make people laugh at themselves, to make us believe we are savages. Why don't you get people to write stories for the magazine to show the oppression we are subjected to?"

"I am for that as much as you. Listen. There is room for both of us, Ben. I believe—you know what I believe, my friend?—*Forward* should be open to all kinds of discussions. It should air many different philosophical concepts. Political concepts. At the same time I have a job to do on the council, and you have a job to do at grass roots level."

Le Maître finished off his glass of sorrel. "It's very good sorrel," he said. He was thinking that he knew just what would happen: there would be discussions on art no one would understand, and abstract discussions about Nazism in Germany; some professor would declare that the shape of the Negro's skull proved he could never be the white man's equal in intelligence, and some Negro schoolteacher would put an opposing view; and nothing would be achieved, people who were jobless and hungry would know nothing of those who were suffering on the oilfields, the sugar estates, nothing would be done to bring them together—it would all end in armchair chatter.

Joe was pouring him another glass. "What is your opinion?"

"What are you achieving by lying down on the floor in the council?" Le Maître could not resist asking.

"A buffoon, that's what they call you," André remarked with a laugh.

"The middle class. The workers understand the position much better, my boy." Joe brushed him aside with a smile to cover his discomfiture.

"If you are trying to make yourself a rallying point for resistance to Boisson that is not the way to go about it," Le Maître told him. "Workers are realists. We are back again at this same problem of educating the workers. It is vital! You *can't* win anything for them by shouting and lying on the floor. They will soon discover that. A thing like that should be made clear in *Forward*."

"And the police?"

"I am not asking for a call to strike, but the tactics you use should be discussed. If I write an article attacking you will you print it?"

"Of course I'll publish it. I tell you straight, you'll never change people as easily as you think, Ben." Joe laughed indulgently. "So you want to challenge the British Empire? You want to make yourself a hero?"

"I want to stand up, I want everyone to stand up! Not lie down like you." Joe, encased in mocking laughter, seemed invulnerable, and this annoyed Le Maître. "You are incapable of understanding this in a fundamental way, Elias. If you had been born a Negro or a coloured man it would have been different. What you say, André?"

André nodded. "When you're inside, in the fire, it's different. You understand too much."

"The System weighs on everybody, everybody without exception," Manny said, sipping his rum as if it were wine. He did not enjoy it, he drank it rather to deny his youth.

They fell silent. They were in agreement yet not in agreement, and each one, except Manny Camacho, felt unhappy in his own way at their inability to harmonise their differing viewpoints and form a solid phalanx against the enemy in their midst.

If only there was some one vital truth that they could all grasp and work for because it showed the way, André thought. Surely there was some such truth that was more important than all others.

* * *

Old Elias's estate amounted to half a million dollars. Joe received thirty thousand in cash and four properties that together brought in five hundred a month. As manager of the stores he drew a thousand a month and shared the profits with his mother, brother and sisters.

His mother had always given him spiritual support, they were close to each other. He immediately saw to it that she had numerous comforts she had never enjoyed. She assured him they were unnecessary, she had done without them all her life; the children's needs were the only necessities she permitted herself to recognise. Joe ignored her scruples, bought her a car and hired a chauffeur. He encouraged her to go down the islands for a month with the children. In her absence he had the house repainted. He hung new curtains, added new furniture. On her return she looked about her with delight and a guilty conscience.

"Oh, my, Joe! What a lot this must have cost!" she said in a whisper.

"Mamma, forget the past. This is what you should have been enjoying long ago. You are not poor, you know," Joe added in a lower voice so the servants should not hear, and in a significant tone.

Mrs Elias felt she could not afford to grow old. Four children still remained to be educated and married. Erica, who now had a baby, came frequently to spend days with her and unwittingly caused her to relive the days when she had tended her own. But this was all joy, pure joy, undiluted by responsibilities. Under the care of a doctor whom friends had recommended (he charged the highest fees), her health improved and she shouted orders in a louder voice still. It seemed to Joe as if, with his father's passing, a malignant growth had been removed from her heart.

On his election to the city council Joe had become a hero to his clerks. When he championed the cause of the scavengers and flayed his opponents the clerks congratulated him even in the presence of his surly father. When old Elias died they all felt that now at last the son would be able to demonstrate his goodwill towards the masses in a practical way. One after another they approached him in secret, each trying to be the first to tap the source of gold, knowing that with every demand the output would fall. Joe's resentful surprise astonished them all.

"You must wait till the end of the financial year. I hardly know whether the business is making money or not."

His father had never loaned money to the staff, but now they came to Joe, one to borrow the wherewithal to bury his mother, another for an operation on his child, a third to keep off the bailiff. Joe could not refuse, he loaned what they asked of him. But he sighed, they thought, just like his father.

"O Lord, O Lord! This will have to stop," he muttered as he counted the slips in the till. He was sure he would be ruined. "One talks and talks but one has to face reality. Some adjustment will have to be made in their wages but not before the end of the financial year. And I'm not going to keep any loafers! What is one to do? It's a tough world. Manna doesn't fall from heaven any more."

When he spent over a hundred dollars on new gramophone records it seemed almost a sin, he took precautions to hide the purchase from his clerks, not to speak of it on the phone. In two months, however, he had quite forgotten about sin; without a second thought he would ring up the music shops and have them charge up what he wanted.

He found that business intrigues, which he wished to avoid, sought him out. His money gave him power and he was expected to use it. His money also implanted fear in him. To protect himself and extend his field of operations he joined the Chamber of Commerce and helped form a bloc against the big businessmen who were attempting to monopolise certain trade. Being young, eligible, a councillor with a growing reputation as an intellectual, a prospect for legislative council honours, he was invited to the home of well-to-do Syrians and introduced to their daughters. He became a member of the Syrian Club. They wanted to make him a committee member, but he declined. Business people more white than black thought: "Better a Syrian for a son-in-law than a nigger," and invited him to their dances and parties. He could not always refuse, it would have been unbusinesslike. So engaged, he had less time for the magazine. It became a bimonthly but with its appearance greatly improved as it was no longer set up by an old handpress in a Belmont backyard but by a printer well-equipped for the task. Joe continued to write poems on the incongruity of man's end despite all his striving.

The scavengers patiently awaited the outcome of the committee's deliberations.

It was Joe who moved that government be approached for a loan.

"And suppose you don't get it, what will the scavengers think?" André asked when he heard this.

Joe was about to say, "You can't draw blood from a stone," but checked himself in time: these were the words of the fat councillor so ready to warn against "excesses". "That is such a naïve approach you're taking," he replied. A laugh, the laugh of a disillusioned man, was cut off short in his throat. "Life, and especially political life, is a matter of compromise. There are no absolutes, my boy. To achieve an objective very devious characters and aspirations must be made to cohere, and that can only be done by compromise."

André wanted to say: "Will the scavengers understand that?" But he was silent. He felt that Joe was in an unenviable position. How pleasant was power, he thought; with what luxury it grew, climbing, ever climbing, like an enormous tropical vine choking the trees that supported it.

"Let's play some music," he said.

"Yes, let's have some Beethoven. The last quartets." Joe sighed. "He never compromised. He never needed to."

He shouted loudly for some sorrel to be brought him and lay back in his easy chair.

Chapter forty-two

Not being a pipe-fitter Clem Payne had taken no part in the strike. They had fired him just the same—he was a torch they could not put out. Only by assuming false names did he and French and many another manage to find employment on other oilfields. It proved to be of brief duration. Early in '37 they again were jobless. Managers learned their names were false or saw the dreaded fire in them. The fields, they said, were cutting production—and this, too, was true.

For six weeks Payne paid no rent. The landlady needed the money to keep her own head above water, and sympathy went out the door with Payne. He took his family to a disused bush shanty. Once it had belonged to a peasant who had grown crops of vegetables on rented land. A single drought had sufficed to drive him off his land. The shack fell into disrepair. The roof leaked, the wooden windows sagged on their hinges, the steps rotted away, covered in slime. Payne repaired them with a whisky box. Unable to climb on to the roof he put his two cots out of reach of the dripping water.

They lived on what Rosie could make by washing and ironing; not much, for the unborn child got in her way at the washtub and weariness tied her limbs. Three of the four children helped their mother. They went to the white people for dirty clothes, which they brought home in enormous bundles balanced on their heads; they fetched water in buckets, walking to the nearest standpipe half a mile distant.

Friends brought Payne oil drums stolen from a field. Into them, with an arrangement of slit bamboo, they fed water from the roof.

When Le Maître heard what had happened—and this was not for some days—he roused Yankee from his cot that very night and ordered a parcel of food made up. "For Clem? Sick velly bad?" said Yankee, and offered one of the two fowls he had in a coop.

Cassie gladly took the sleepy, squawking bird. "So you only chargin' for the fowl, ain't that so?" she said encouragingly but with an expression that showed she would not be pleased if he refused.

He laughed. "Aw light, aw light. That guy's a good guy."

"Good! Add a tin of salmon," Le Maître said at once.

Yankee made up two big parcels and, loaded up, happy, they set off for Payne's. It had been raining, but now the stars came out.

It was long after ten. Lights in the village were going out. Le Maître had felt depressed and discouraged all night, and now he felt irritated by the darkness and the backwardness of village life. "An oilfield village besides," he thought. "That last light going out . . . like a man's life." And immediately another thought followed: "Leaving only darkness behind." Just as swiftly he rejected it. While he did so with his mind, tonight his heart could not relinquish the thought: "I will never live to see a change. Darkness, only darkness. . . . That fool Elias!" he reflected in sudden anger and disdain. "Poems about death . . . 'the greatest of realities'. The fool! Death will never conquer Payne."

Cassie was humming gaily and the further they went into the darkness the merrier she felt. That they were doing this for Payne fanned the flame of her feeling for Ben.

"No moon tonight?"

He made no answer. In him was no poetic response to nature.

"Why you so silent, Ben? What you thinkin' about?"

"It is a terrible fight," he answered slowly and in a low voice as if not wishing to be heard by a third person. "A merciless battle. We will die and not see the end of it. You realise that?"

"None of us think it easy, but what we goin' to do?"

"Cassie, I wouldn't confess this to anyone but you, but sometimes I wonder if we are benefiting in any way at all from this struggle. When I see how frightened so many of us are, how our spirits are crushed, I wonder what is the good. That is the most terrible thing, that our spirits are crushed!"

"What you sayin', man—hush! Our people not so. I never see them with so much fight as now. This ain't no time to old-talk so. If we don't live to see a change our children will see it."

"Yours and mine?" he asked softly.

"Eh-eh! I didn't say so, nuh?" She laughed. "Well I never! Look the moon," she added, breaking off, a note of joy in her voice.

An old moon, misshapen, was rising over the trees. Leaves that were covered with raindrops shone in the moonlight. Long shadows lay across the road, which was still wet. From the bush on either side came the sleepy, high-pitched buzzing of grasshoppers, the croak of frogs.

"Moonlight. . . . Ah, Lord!" she sighed, touched by the poetry of the night's mystery and loneliness, its tempting eeriness. She had no words with which to express the thoughts of heart and mind.

He heard only the huskiness of her voice, which was music enough to him. He heard it when alone, he heard it in his dreams. It disturbed his thinking and his sleep. She maddened him at times. Once he had angrily upbraided her before the men in the hall for failing to bring more servants to the meetings.

"My whole life is dedicated to one purpose!" he cried in a melodramatic voice while his lips grew pale and trembled. "Whoever tries to stand in my way will do so at his peril. We have no time for dances and frivolities, we have a terribly serious task before us!"

She saw he was frustrated and mad with jealousy, and this pleased her even while she was infuriated by the bully in him. She jumped up, lashing him with scornful laughter. "Who you think you are? Jesus Christ? We make you a leader and we could unmake you. Don't come tramplin' on me—"

"I asked you whether you would undertake the job of organising them. You promised me faithfully—"

"I told you when I have a day off . . . !"

Many in the audience were murmuring against Le Maître. Observing this he fell silent. Percy French, laughing silently, hid his gum behind his hand. He knew that what angered Le Maître was Cassie's unyielding resistance to his advances. She flung a last shot at Le Maître—"we lookin' to get rid of bosses, don't come bossin' me!"—and left the meeting. All the way home she wept silently, dabbing her eyes quickly: that he could make her cry angered her. Next day Le Maître asked her forgiveness when he found her alone. "I hate to see you try to make you'self a big man by laughing at people," she told him, her anger still not expended. "If you can't respect me as a woman as well as a comrade, keep away from me."

He knew she was right. He knew also that this fault in him was aggravated by his hatred of their degradation and his impatience with their slavish reliance on him alone, while at the same time that reliance instilled in him a beguiling and dangerous consciousness of his power. But he said nothing of this because he did not like looking into himself before others.

"Moonlight," he said now with a curl of his lips, "is so deceptive. Before beautiful moonlight can please me I must know that under that roof there is a worker who lives in comfort with a full belly."

He jerked his chin at Payne's shack which they were approaching. It was dark within, but the roof was shining, a wild lily scented cloyingly the air, muddy pools ensnared a gliding moon, and raindrops gleamed as they ticked away the seconds in their plopping from the bamboo guttering. Destitution was covered over with a shining film of poetry.

They crossed the deep earth drain by the two coconut tree trunks with which Payne had bridged it. At that instant Cassie heard the sound of drums in the distance. The night lost its charm. She was seized with vague horror; saw the *hounbonnor* with his fixed, fanatical gaze; heard again the terrible blows Duke struck Popito. The cock, sensing she had stopped walking, squawked in apprehension and vainly fluttered in her grasp. Her fingers tensed about the warm, sinewy base of its wings. Standing close behind Le Maître she gripped his arm.

The door opened a few inches to his prolonged knocking. A woman's tied head appeared, outlined by the candlelight behind her. "Not in!" she said harshly.

"I want to see you. It's me—Ben."

She admitted them. Evidently she had a headache: to either temple adhered a square of brown paper over a smear of soft candle. The two eldest girls were sleeping together on a mattress on boards raised off the floor by boxes. In one of the beds a boy of two slept with his mouth open beside his five-year-old sister. On a dilapidated sideboard a bit of candle burned in the cover of a cigarette tin. There was a stale smell in the closed-up room. Through a tear in the jute bag that covered one window a shaft of moonlight streamed, but Rosie, thinking the night air baneful, had pushed the sideboard to bar its entry.

She was thin and narrow, her face and arms were long and thin, her breasts, though inclined to fullness now, were long, and she had shiny shin bones and slippered feet. To Cassie, who had long not seen her, it seemed that she was stretching like elastic. She was one of those honest people who speak their minds without remembering the feelings of others. At this moment her highly expressive face said everything. It bore a look of mournful desperation. When Le Maître said: "I brought some things for you—milk and so," it lit up with relief and shame.

"Thanks," she said in her deep voice, taking the parcels and putting them on the sideboard as if they were of no consequence. "Cassie, how, chile?" She went into the next room and brought out two bentwood chairs.

"I good, yes, Rosie? Like you have headache?"

"Bad enough, girl."

"Look, I bring a fowl for you."

"In truth, I didn't notice," Rosie lied, smiling like one unaccustomed to smiling. "I see it, in truth, yes? But I was 'fraid it wasn't for me so I didn't watch it. It not goin' to bawl long in here, I tell you that!"

"Where you goin' to put it, chile? I say if I tie it under the house snake might take it."

"Snake have no chance with me."

With alacrity she untied one of the parcels and with the string tied the squawking bird to a table leg in the other room.

"Where Clem?" Le Maître asked.

"Since mornin' he gone down Point Fortin. He not back."

"He has any chance of a job down there?"

"Which job, Ben? You know he kean't get no job again. He gone to talk, talk an' make people lose they job as he lose his," she replied sharply.

"He has gone to try and make them courageous fighters like himself," Le Maître said softly.

"Ehn-hehn? And what his courage do for me and his children? Tchps!"

Their voices woke the sleeping boy. He sat up crying. In the daytime he ran about naked but at night he wore one of his father's shirts. His arms were lost in the sleeves, which hung down below his knees. Rosie took him up automatically and rocked him on her knees while talking.

"The last boss he had tell him he got consumption, he must go to hospital."

"Clem would never stay in hospital, Rosie, you know that," said Le Maître, "even if there were hospitals for his sickness. Inactivity is death to Clem."

"Because of you! It's you drag him down to this, it's you have him half out his mind. All-you mad, you not goin' to drive me mad too, you hear? Hush-hush!" she ordered the boy, rocking him violently. But he kept crying in a sleepy voice.

Cassie said: "Look bread in this parcel."

Rosie took the loaf that Cassie gave her and broke a piece off for her son. At once he sat upright, swallowed his sobs and with babyish awkwardness tried to stuff it all into his mouth at once. Rosie took it from him despite his protests and broke it smaller yet. He ceased to regard the visitors and fixed his eyes on the bread in his mother's hand while he chewed. The tears on his cheeks ran into his mouth but he did not notice them.

As if she had smelled the bread in her sleep one of the two girls on the plank bed sat up and said timidly: "Ma?" She had enormous eyes and eight short plaits sticking out like horns about her head.

Rosie gave her a piece of the loaf. "Don't wake you' sister," she said in a threatening tone.

The little girl tugged at the bread with her teeth and chewed rapidly, her big eyes fixed on the parcels on the sideboard. Her gaze wandered to Le Maître. Almost ceasing to chew she looked at him long and curiously. There was something strange about him which only her eyes could see.

"Gracie, how are you?" he asked.

"Well, thanks," she said slowly in a deep voice like her mother's. She looked shyly at the bread in her hand, returning her eyes to his face as soon as he looked away.

They heard a truck stop outside then drive off at high speed. Payne entered.

How pale he looked, Cassie thought.

"Eh-eh! You find *zandolie* hole, then," Payne said with a frowning smile that sought to ridicule his situation. "Cassie, how you keepin', girl?" His voice was hoarse. He flung his hat down and sat carelessly on the bed with his old dash—Le Maître remembered it well—leaning back on his elbows and laughing at them.

"You're a hell of a man! Why you didn't tell me what the position was?" Le Maître asked.

Payne blew through his nose contemptuously. "Clem could stomach a lot, boy, but not that."

Rosie was re-wrapping the food parcels. She handed her husband a three-cents loaf with ham between the halves.

"Where that come from?" It was hard to tell whether the resentment in his tone was genuine.

"Just fall down from heaven," she answered dryly.

"That's the first good deed I see heaven do," said he, tearing at the loaf with his teeth.

"Turkey tomorrow," Cassie said, eyes twinkling.

He laughed. Rosie put the boy back on the bed. "No more tonight," she told him.

"Mamma," said Gracie, "piece more for me?"

"You ain't hear what I just say?" Rosie's tone was harsh.

Payne crooked a finger and Gracie ran to him. He broke a bit from his loaf and gave it to her. "Go to sleep—fast!"

"Thanks, Pappa." She ran back and at once ducked down in the mattress, curling up, clutching the bread. The visitors could not help smiling. Nor could Clem, but suddenly something quivered in his face and he burst out:

"I went down Point today. The position ripe. When I speak to them, boy, it's like a match to gasoline. The bosses there 'fraid me for so! They have me name and description circulatin' all about, all about. I will never get a job again. But so I mean for them! If I have to go into every *house* and talk I goin' to get them, I, Clem Payne: chauffeurs, pipe-fitters, boilermen—you never see trouble so in you' life yet."

He loved his own courage. He liked to display it publicly, for then he forgot himself, then he rose above everything and nothing inspired fear. At nights, alone with Rosie, he felt annihilated. Then he had to summon a different courage, a quiet patient courage, and ignore the cold hands of death that were reaching out for his.

"And when they take and lock you up?" said Rosie.

"A truck could kill me tomorrow."

"Don't tell me that! When you dead you kean't help it, but so long as you livin' you have a responsibility to you' children."

"It's true," said Cassie.

"It's you to look after the children, I kean't live long enough for that. What little breath I have leave back in me is for workers, man."

Rosie broke down then. "But what I one could do for the children?" she pleaded with Le Maître, her voice shaking with tears. "They not kittens I could drown in the bucket. You fightin', you fightin', but you have no strength against dese white people, man. You don't see dat?"

Le Maître, his lips closed firmly, looked from Rosie to Clem. He agreed with Clem yet sympathised with Rosie and felt the impossibility of resolving the contradiction between them. It was Cassie, with her capacity for quick decisions, who did so.

"Rosie, give me Gracie. I will look after her."

"That is it!" Le Maître agreed at once. "Let somebody else take the two other girls and you keep the boy."

Even though, perhaps, it was the best plan at this time Rosie could not bring herself to say, "Yes, take them." She blew her nose in the hem of her dress and glanced at Gracie, who peeped big-eyed from Cassie to her.

"Cassie, I know I could trust you to look after them, but who else I could trust, man? Who it have I could trust?"

"Burnett's wife will take one," said Le Maître. "Keep cool, Rosie, we will find comrades who will take them. Clem, why the hell you don't stop makin' children, man?"

"Too powerful."

"Mamma, a spider!" Gracie sat up nervously.

A big tarantula, furry, with red-tipped legs, was crawling down the wall. Rosie took the broom and crushed it with a well-aimed thrust. "And sometimes in the night scorpions on the floor, yes?" she said with gloomy restraint.

"It's the bush," Le Maître said, "the bush. You too close to the bush, you must get out of here."

"Rosie, I goin' to talk to *nen-nen* 'bout Gracie. As soon as you ready I will take her. Don't fret you'self. Ben, let us go."

Rosie brought the stump of candle to the doorway. "Mind the step as you go down, do."

"Right-o, Clem, I gone," Le Maître called back.

"See you tomorrow, Ben."

They crossed the bridge of coconut trees. It was dark and depressing. "Mm! Moon gone," Cassie muttered. A light wind had sprung up. In the dark rustle of the trees she fancied something evil. Rain was coming, she could smell it. But suddenly moonlight drenched the earth, bringing with it rich odours, sounds and colours. At the same instant she felt an irresistible surge of the heart towards happiness and love and calm contented days. She pushed Clem and Rosie out of her mind. "Let's take a walk," she said.

Le Maître had automatically headed homewards, his mind busy with schemes to help his comrade. Somehow they must get Payne a job. Not heavy work. He could drive a truck. On some field where he wasn't known. Comrades would have to *order* him to halt his reckless, inflammatory assaults on all the injustices that needled men, divided them and walled them in. Clem must *live!* He must be made to value life, not thrash about in it like a mad dog, needlessly sacrificing himself and his children. "He must eat proper food, damn him!" he reflected. "Why should we lose such a man? He must be made to see that."

At that moment Cassie said, "Let's take a walk," stopped and turned her back on the village.

"A walk?" he said in surprise. At once a lightness, an eagerness filled his heart. Without being aware of it he jettisoned Clem and his kids and Rosie. "All right," he said. And his arm was around her, holding her close as they walked.

She saw the moon racing through the clouds, hiding, rising, emerging, seeming to tear the clouds in its rush. She felt something wonderfully majestic about it; an impenetrably mysterious poetry such as she had never observed or tasted till this moment. She gazed upon it till she felt giddy, till she was assailed by a vague sadness, she knew not why. The wind was rising. A warm and scented darkness enveloped them, swept over them and was gone, and again the moonlight flooded their hearts not so much with happiness as with the desire for happiness and the expectation of it. It was there for the taking, it must be taken; or like the moonlight it would pass them by and only dark clouds would remain. What is yesterday compared with now? What is tomorrow? Let moments of happiness be enjoyed as we find them. So we say in our Carnival. So we have said in our history, for slaves seek to enjoy life even as the free enjoy it.

Darkness again, and now the rain treading the tree-tops as it advanced towards them. They ran into the bush and climbed a steep bank towards a saman tree. Against the scaly bole, briefly sheltered by the enormous spreading limbs, they stood close and breathless. Lightning split the darkness and seemed to bind them closer, her arms round his neck, her lips on his. She heard the roar of the pelting water yet did not hear it. She felt the heavy drops on her shoulders, but perhaps they were the shoulders of someone else. She was one with the water that ran into her shoes, she was one with the scent of earth and leaves. She was utterly one with him in her giving and receiving. . . .

"Getting wet? This is dangerous, you know."

"No, man!"

"Lightning could strike the tree and we would be killed."

"It's so? What I care." She laughed.

"But I care," he said. "You are so precious to me now. You know that? You believe me?"

"I bound to believe you now."

"It's such a strong feeling . . . bad as well as good."

"Bad as well as good? Eh-eh!" She was resentful.

"It's so it is. Bad and good always mixed up in everything."

"You talkin' stupidness, man."

"You right. To hell with it! Come home with me tonight."

"What! You mad?" She laughed. "And what people will say tomorrow?"

"Tomorrow we will go straight to the courthouse and get married."

"Much you know about it." She was greatly amused. "You have to put up banns. Three weeks."

"What sort of stupid law is that? Come go. We must make up our minds to get soaked. I don't like you under this tree."

"Where you like me?" There was laughter in her voice.

"Everywhere. All over. Come, watch you' step, everything slippery."

"If people watch us now they'll say we mad."

"Madness is a great thing. Not all sorts, though. You know something? Life is an extraordinary thing, a terrible thing, a wonderful thing! You ever felt that, Cassie?"

"What I want to talk about that for, boy? You just stay close by me with you' arm like this, and the devil could do his worst, I don't care."

"By Christ, you're a wonderful girl!" he cried out suddenly, stopping in the rain to embrace her.

She closed her eyes. Glorious, she felt then, was their madness.

And now a shift in the wind brought to her the distant sound of drums and frenzied singing, but as they hurried towards the village it died away as the past dies, leaving behind but a lifeless memory.

Chapter forty-three

They married three weeks later. Cassie's aunt—"nen-nen"—took Gracie and Cassie worked to keep them both.

"That's a *good* thing you did, Cassie, a wonderful thing," Le Maître said more than once. "If only I lived a different life, a more secure life . . ." he added regretfully, and for a moment was silent. "But that's not possible," he added abruptly.

New feelings, thoughts and aspirations arose in him continually, to his surprise. Such unexpected flexibility of heart and mind was both strange and wonderful. Tenderness, an emotion with which he was not much acquainted, seemed almost a weakness, a thing he indulged with a guilty pleasure for Gracie and Rosie and others less fortunate than he thought himself. Vague hopes of a different future would not quit his mind. He tried to put them out of sight, afraid lest improper indulgences weaken his will, corrupt his purpose. He who had but rarely noticed the beautiful things in life, and to whom beauty had seemed a snare when he beheld it, could not tire of looking at Cassie's eyes and smile, her limbs, her breasts.

"Don't move, don't move! Stay just as you are." And he would gaze at her body with a kind of rapture.

"But what happen to the man!" Cassie would say in her husky voice, both pleased and embarrassed.

He wanted to say then: "You are the most beautiful creature in the world." But at once he reproved himself. How the hell could she be the most beautiful creature in the world? That was stupid, dangerous! He said: "You are beautiful. Not I alone see that. I'm sure I'm not the only one to see that." After all, it would be stupid to be carried away by middle-aged ardours.

"And you handsome, darling," she teased, laughing.

He laughed with her and at himself, feeling with relief that his accustomed sense of emotional balance had returned to him.

But as soon as she spoke with another man, especially one younger than he, he was assailed by jealousy, fear and anger. He would pretend not to notice her, but his voice as he spoke to others boomed louder, and he laughed loudly and cynically as if he had never seen such fools as those who spoke with him.

The promises of government had been like so many promises, light as the cotton that flies from the silk-cotton tree in March, but seedless, fruitless. In the south the idle thickened, spread like a pestilence, infecting the land with demands and questions no one heeded. The official world was so convinced we were a happy people, needing little, and paid no great attention when men went hat in hand, in vain, from boss to boss. They did not seem to notice when men gave up hope. Whey-whey gambling, the illegal manufacture and sale of rum, petty thefts of every kind, highway robbery—these must be stamped out. A menace to the law-abiding!

On the sugar estates the white overseers—and how well they knew the Indians, riding among them all day long, not shy of enjoying the comforts some black-eyed daughters could provide—yes, they knew, they were convinced the peasants were content with a half-day's work. Three days' work a week for eight months of the year, it was all the sugar trade would carry. Doctors often found the bodies full of hookworm. Independent doctors claimed the hookworm was due to ill-nourishment and filth; company doctors claimed the ill-nourishment was due to the hookworm. Perhaps both were right, but it was beyond question that the family cow with uncovered ribs was healthier than they. For carting canes a man earned fifty-five cents a day, the highest wage. And six cents a day for the children, the weeders. And still ingratitude. One could not please them. Grumbling and threats when, by Jove, if you'd given them a whole week's work they'd have gone off in the afternoons to sleep or fish, or tend their vegetable gardens.

The best that Boisson's dozens of hangers-on could do was to point with pride to his picture in court dress when in May he attended the coronation of George the Sixth. But Workers' Welfare was growing apace. Payne got a job as a truck driver on one of the smaller fields. He formed branches of the party in the Point Fortin area, to the south-west of Fyzabad, and in Point-à-Pierre, the big refinery twenty miles north. The drivers flocked to meetings. Their quarrel was chiefly with overtime. Instead of getting it from the ninth hour they got it only from the tenth, and even then not time and a half but time and a quarter. Further, they claimed that if they must sleep "on call" in the companies' barracks instead of at home they were entitled to pay from the time of entering the barracks. They were demanding, in addition, extra pay for Sunday work.

At street corner meetings Le Maître mocked: "Look at Boisson—Little Lord Fauntleroy! Knee breeches, stockings and sword. Kissing the king's backside but what is he doing for you? He and the king and the whole damn lot of them—what do they care about starving workers. They are spending millions of pounds on the coronation, entertaining the fascists, the very beasts who are slaughtering the Abyssinians, our people. And Boisson is sharing in that, taking a pride in it. If he had the workers' needs at heart he would spend his time in England getting some help from the English workers, explaining our position to them. He is hiding under the cloak of working-class speeches. The time has come when we must reject such leaders!"

Shouts, approving laughter and angry murmurs arose from the crowd. In Port-of-Spain they had marched in protest to the Italian Consul. Thousands expressed their sympathy for their African brothers by holding meetings and cabling protests to Mussolini.

There was more than restlessness among the workers. There was a mystical, wild spirit, anarchistic, whipped on by accumulated hates and piled frustrations. They hungered for a spiritual homeland that would give them pride and strength and assurance to face the white man boldly. Some few asserted that white men and black had been equals in the distant, groping past. Before sugar came. Could that be believed? Was it true that once, in a time long gone, African cities and scholars had flourished where now only the jackal howled? "Yes, man, it's true!" those few insisted, enraged by the wanton rapine of Abyssinia, a sovereign state; clinging to the Lion of Judah because in Trinidad they were nothing, not beast, not man. Of their African heritage hardly anything remained, neither language, nor religion, nor their several arts; they had died, forbidden, spurned, exterminated. And the cold wind of the white man's contempt blew about their spirits, which were clothed in tattered memories as their bodies were in rags. They were reduced to accepting Britain's image of themselves, submitting to it and laughing at their nakedness. To laugh was to live, and one must live, not die. But what sort of man was he who accepted the thought that he was nothing? Under the laughter, in the ashes of the past, the sparks were smouldering. Behind every Chinese, every Indian, lay timeless accretions of wisdom and culture their hands could fondle and the spirit relish; but behind every Negro lay the barren windswept earth and the ghosts of a time too long vanished, too long forgotten to nourish the soul. Britannia ruled. Ruled with the chains that didn't clank, the slave mind fashioned to make men hate their own and turn from themselves in terrible disquiet and cry out: "Save me from myself, kind master!" What of that?

Towards the end of May, Workers' Welfare men were calling for a general strike on the Fyzabad fields. Resolutions in favour of strike action were carried without a single dissentient vote. Payne pleaded with them to hold back. Surprise struck them dumb, then some began to attack him. Trembling with excitement, stamping his foot, emphasising every other word, Payne showed them that simultaneous strikes on other oilfields would powerfully aid their cause; they would shorten the duration of the strike, they would "stun" the oilfield bosses—he used the word with appetite more than once—and help to force a quick decision in the workers' favour. A voice laughed out loud with joy. When he called for volunteers to address Point Fortin workers on weekends several hands shot up.

With the loss of the November struggle in mind they disputed with those who advocated a walk-off and urged a sit-down strike throughout the fields. Some disagreed: they would be chased off anyway. "Let them chase us off, let them lock us out," French argued. "The workers will have the initiative, they will shut down the field. If only we have unity we will succeed."

"Ah, unity! If only we could have unity."

"Ah tell you, show me the man who would dare to break the strike!" cried a man in a wild hoarse voice, shaking a massive clenched fist.

Strike committees were formed. Le Maître drew up demands. He sought interviews with manager after manager. They refused to receive him or any deputation from Workers' Welfare. They could neither see nor believe in the gathering storm. They could not conceive that the sun which warmed them might go out.

Le Maître wrote to the governor.

". . . the workers feel it is unnecessary to go into detail with you about their poverty. They consider that you have travelled so extensively throughout the island and showed such interest in the lot of all working people that you cannot have failed to see their desperate position. However, they wish to bring to your notice that the oilfield officials have refused to grant them even an interview. Unless Your Excellency can persuade these officials to see reason, the workers will be on strike from the 18th June. It is impossible for any of us to fortell the consequences. . . ."

The governor, Sir Richard Curry, did not receive this letter. At public gatherings he had expressed the wish that employers as well as workers should not be unmindful of their obligations to one another and to the social order. And the men who held the reins, sensitive to his dignity as the King's representative and their own prestige, fearing lest he appear to accede to threats, had Le Maître's letter intercepted at Government House. The sentence, "It is impossible to foretell the consequences . . ." caused the manager of the Fyzabad field, Major Bottomley, particular concern. He informed Colonel Cambridge, the English commissioner of police, that a strike was imminent. They were in complete agreement on the need to arrest Le Maître. Deprived of his influence, the workers would quickly surrender and return to the fields. Uninterrupted production was essential for Trinidad's economy.

Le Maître's consciousness of the workers' growing militancy and the strength of the Welfare sometimes made him forget to choose his words when addressing public meetings. On Sunday night, 13 June, a member of Boisson's party wrote down some of Le Maître's inflammatory statements in the presence of a detective. As soon as the typescript reached the commissioner of police he ordered Le Maître's arrest on a charge of sedition.

Strange, and yet not strange: the very constable ordered to arrest Le Maître sent a messenger to warn him. Le Maître went into hiding. To his surprise it was Betsy Solomon's conservative father who sheltered him.

Chapter forty-four

Suddenly, after twenty years, they had fired Tom Solomon. "We're cutting production," they told him. But Tom knew the real reason: he was forty-eight; and he was embittered because for twenty years he had worked faithfully, without complaint, accepting his lot and always taking their side, and now he was trash thrown out the door.

Living on credit like everyone else he was soon enmeshed in a web of debts, buzzing vainly in them like a fly. Betsy, however, was a girl of resource. She arranged to hold a dance at home, got friends who were musicians to play at a reduced fee, and sent out printed tickets which began: "A Dance At The Home Of Miss B. Solomon", and ended in large letters: FOR THE POOR.

Tom had borne long hours in the fire of the day. His wife had washed and ironed for whites so that Betsy could go to college, acquire learning, become a teacher and so earn a respect the world had never accorded her parents. There was no profit, economic or social, in being a shop clerk. She always carried an umbrella over her, sun or rain and, with unhurried step, looked to left and right, delighting in feeling herself on stage. She was not popular among young women, her aggressiveness made them prickle, but her men friends were numerous. André found her scintillating. He liked her boldness, the assertion of her right to independent thought. He was fascinated by her figure, so perfectly moulded, and her skin like a dark silk from Africa. And she did not hesitate to show she enjoyed his company and his admiration.

He came to the dance.

Every room but the one in which Le Maître was hidden was stripped of its furniture. Beds, chairs, presses were all piled up in the yard and covered with a tarpaulin. The musicians in their shirt sleeves played in the tiny front veranda. Dancing couples, obliged to be content with vertical motion, rubbed against one another in the warm night scented with sweat and perfume. When the music stopped the men pushed their way down the back steps to the yard and clamoured for drinks at the kitchen window. From the yard, in which the smell of the cesspit mingled with that of rum, there came a sound of vomiting. As usual, the music drew a crowd of onlookers before the house.

Betsy moved about among her guests with a conscious dignity, her head cocked to one side and slightly back, smiling triumphantly. She seemed to spread her feathers as men came up and paid her compliments with their eyes. Her laughter was loud, and she talked with many gestures.

The sweating musicians had a bottle to themselves. At intervals they passed it around. Each tilted the bottle higher than his companion as he drank.

At half-past midnight the violinist, attracted by a bright glow in the sky, leaned over the banister as he fiddled. "Fire, all-you! A well on fire," he said excitedly to the band.

"Strike—big strike!" said the double-bass player with a determined look, plucking the strings vigorously and nodding his head as if to urge the music to a speedy end.

The tempo quickened. The young saxophonist, his face puffed up with blowing, was unable to utter a word and his eyes moved pleadingly from face to face, questioning this mad gallop that made him play more false notes than usual. He abandoned the instrument and leaned over the banister. "Burnin' like hell, man!" he announced.

They brought the music to an abrupt conclusion, running out of the house, crying joyfully: "Well on fire!" Guests, repeating the words, magnifying their import for others by their looks of alarm and intense curiosity, pushed others aside and followed the musicians. Voices cried out that the house next door was on fire. In a moment only the drunks in the yard remained, everyone else had mingled with the villagers, who were streaming towards the flames that roared at heaven. All about them as they ran bicycle bells were ringing and people were shouting or laughing with vindictive gratification or expressing with customary coarseness and intemperance their opinions of the oilfield bosses. But Betsy, mindful of her dignity as a schoolteacher, and her dress which had cost her more than she could afford, stood by the roadside and chatted in a loud, animated voice with those about her.

The fire was the signal agreed on between the Fyzabad and Point Fortin workers to indicate the commencement of the strike.

Two jitneys sped by crowded with policemen. The continuous and hysterical blare of their horns excited everyone still more. Those who had cycled ahead could now hear the roar of the mutinous flames. Immense waves of smoke tumbled upwards over one another, shutting out the stars. The crowd thickened and solidified the nearer one got to the fire. Firefighters could be seen silhouetted like black dolls, running about and dragging something.

Some of Betsy's guests returned to the house.

"They can't control it, it's going to spread," André said to Betsy, the whites of his eyes showing as he faced the flames.

"Damn good for them," was her comment.

"I gone to pack up me belongings, chile!" cried a woman who was running in slippers and dressing-gown back from the fire.

"To strike is one thing," Betsy heard a man say gravely, "but they shouldn't try to destroy the field."

A young oilfield worker turned to him angrily. "Who tell you they tryin' to destroy the field? Use you' head, man. People so foolish as to destroy they means of livelihood?"

"You right, John," Betsy agreed. "Pay the people a decent wage and none of this would happen."

The musicians returned. Betsy and her remaining guests crowded about them to hear the news they brought.

"Let's go in and dance!" she cried, and seized André's hand.

The rest followed them in.

"A hot calypso!" she ordered.

And hot it was, wild, bacchanalian. Some formed a ring, swung the tops of their bodies forward and back, flung upraised arms to one side and hips to the other; moved to one another with forward thrusts of the hips, then back; then with arms about waists, side by side, executed a prancing, bowing, half-bongo step that expressed complete abandonment of customary restraints, a surrender to elemental joy. In this Betsy was foremost. André stood against the wall, of it yet not with it, agitated, excited but not knowing how to take part, unable to throw off all that had bred him and let go. Hilarious guffaws rose above the rhythmic prancing. All clapped their hands on the off beat. The whole house trembled sensuously.

A truck stopped outside with a squeal of brakes that rose above the music, but no one cared to notice it.

Suddenly the music broke off abruptly.

"What's the matter with those fellows?" a man's breathless voice asked amidst cries of disappointment.

Everyone was stricken silent as two young men came into the room supporting a third between them. The third man was French. Blood was streaming down his face. Some of the guests had seen him at street meetings. They remembered a man who, with wild bloodshot eyes, shouted and shook his hands at them as if they were his enemies, rose up and down on his knees and hitched his pants up angrily. They did not at first recognise French in this half insensible man whose shirt was soaked in blood.

"Miss Betsy, help us—help us to stop the bleedin'. Give us a bed to put him on," said one of the men supporting him.

"Police beatin' all workers off the field," his companion said to the guests who questioned him. He spoke unwillingly, as if cherishing a store of wrath he intended to expend physically on the police once French was attended to.

Betsy lost her head, screamed, ran to the door of the room in which Le Maître was hiding and banged on it with her fists. André followed her and seized her hands.

"What's the matter with you? Get some bandages!"

Le Maître opened the door without showing himself.

"French! The police beat him . . . all over in blood. . . . Don't let him come in here!" she cried as he shut it.

Le Maître gave her a violent shake. "What's the matter with you?" he whispered. "Control yourself! Go and bring him in here."

"How you want me do that? I have a government job. The police will come here for him—"

But French's companions had already brought him to the door and were turning the handle. "Miss Betsy!"

"Let him in!" Le Maître ordered.

Weeping, Betsy did as he bid her, slipping out and shutting the door.

"This is not a hospital," she said to some who tried to console her. "Let them take the man to a hospital. Enough trouble in this house. I have a job to think of—"

Suddenly the closed door opened. Regardless of the fact that he was betraying his whereabouts Le Maître appeared in the doorway and shouted angrily: "Stop snivelling and bring some bandages! You want the man to bleed to death?"

Talking in low tones the guests began to leave the house. Everyone understood not only that dancing was now impossible but that the strike was a terribly stern and difficult struggle for all the workers and was far from being a cause for wild rejoicing.

Only two drunks remained. They were singing loudly in the yard.

Chapter forty-five

André remained in Le Maître's room with French, the men who had brought him in and Betsy.

French smiled weakly at André while they bandaged him. "You're the last man I expec' to see here, André. What you doin' this part-a the world?" He felt an affection for him, he trusted André's heart.

Before André could reply Le Maître said to him: "You have your car?"

"Yes."

"Percy needs a place to rest. Will you take him?"

"Of course."

They went out with French, leaving Le Maître in the bedroom. Le Maître called André back. "Are you returning to Port-of-Spain?"

André sensed that Le Maître needed him. "Not if I can be of use here."

Le Maître turned to Betsy. "Will you let him stay?"

"It's okay. Let the boys help us bring in the furniture." She was subdued now, ashamed of her panic.

They brought the furniture in—it was little enough and quickly done—and André drove French to a worker's home as the men directed. He returned to Betsy's. She had made him a bed in Le Maître's room.

Le Maître was agitated and seemed to need an audience. Speaking in a forceful whisper he discussed with André the events leading up to the strike. ". . . The biggest luxury for them—" he was referring to the oilfields' managers—"is a heart. They cannot afford it. Each man is afraid for his job. They are cogs in a vast machine. The mainspring is in London. What are we to do? There is nothing else for us to do! Perhaps we'll lose out. So what? A bank account, comforts—" he gestured—"that's not the most important thing. I tell you, spiritually and morally we are in a superior position. The workers will never forget this struggle, it is a lesson for all of us. It is the beginning of our spiritual manhood, André!" He spoke boldly yet thought of his wife, their love, happiness and peace. "Peace is impossible now," he whispered, half to himself, sadly.

"What about the guests?" André asked. "Can you trust them all?"

"They won't give me away," Le Maître said. But then he shrugged. "Who knows?" he seemed to add.

He closed his eyes. In a short while he was snoring.

André slept little. His surroundings were strange and Le Maître's snores disturbing. Also, from the moment they had brought in Percy covered in blood his heart had taken a decision. When Betsy had wept and beaten on the door with her fists he had felt ashamed and pitied her. Percy had not weakened. Nor, he thought, must he, André, morally.

In the morning Le Maître asked him if he would take a message to Cassie.

"Of course."

Le Maître gave him the message. Looking at him searchingly he added: "What about going to the meeting in Diamond Hall? You could sense the feeling of the workers better than me. I am too close to them, and I can't leave here."

"And you mean that I am not close," André thought at once, meeting his attentive look. "Yes, I'll go," he said, looking away and rising.

A strange fellow, Le Maître thought, wondering what he could have said that offended him. You could never tell with these people, they lived in a different world.

André found Cassie at home. He gave her the message then began to tell her about French, but she had already heard it all. He understood then how closely the villagers stood together. After breakfasting with Cassie he unwillingly surrendered the role of envoy and his new sense of mission to do some business for Ganz Products. Among his more successful customers he found almost universal condemnation of the strikers' action in firing the wells. Afterwards he went to Diamond Hall.

At half-past ten in the morning it was packed. Workers were even standing along the walls. The speaker had a thrusting jaw and chin that belied his calm, pleasant expression and the frequent smile in one corner of his wide mouth. It was Burnett. He spoke with forceful logic. The packed hall listened in silence as he told of the previous night's police attacks on the unarmed strikers. He called on everyone to continue the strike "come what may, till victory is ours".

"Who you is? You know you have no right in here?" a young

worker said truculently to André with a look that indicated readiness to hustle him out.

Three others turned to André. "You's a member of Workers' Welfare?"

"No, but—"

"You have no right in here!"

Some called from the middle of the hall for order. Some in the back said, "Leave him." Others insisted: "He have no right in here, put 'e out! Police spy. . . ."

André went out. The account of the bashings and the workers' mood of angry determination to repay blow with blow convinced him that this was no ordinary strike but an impending war of which only the preliminary skirmishings had taken place.

As soon as he returned to Betsy's Le Maître asked if he had attended the meeting and questioned him about his impressions. He fell silent after André had spoken. "I wonder how Percy is?" he said reflectively.

"I could find out."

"No, no, you mustn't go there. Don't expose you'self. What will Ganz Products say? And the customers?"

"Who would know?"

"It is always safe to assume you are being watched. With the police yon never know. Sometimes they do the most stupid things—look at last night. But not always."

Later he said confidentially: "They're going to hold a meeting in the yard across the street from Diamond Hall, this evening at six. I must be there."

"They'll nab you, Ben!"

"Maybe, but I don't think they would be so foolish. Not with three or four hundred people around me. What you think?"

André thought of those strikers he had seen in the hall. "You could be right. How will you get there? I'll drive you."

"There must be another way. I don't want to ask you to do this, if I'm arrested in your car don't have any illusions, you'll be without a job tomorrow."

"Sure, it's Sunday."

Le Maître did not appreciate the jest. "We must think of some way," he said, pressing his thumb against his teeth. "Who has a truck?"

"Why are you so determined to go?"

"I am afraid of violence. They would massacre us. I must try to calm the workers."

In the end they filled the car with some of Le Maître's close comrades. Seated among them he was not as readily noticed. They got out at the gate and, surrounding Le Maître like a bodyguard, entered the yard. André drove away, left the car in a side street and returned to the yard.

People were streaming in, some of them running: the news had already got around that Le Maître was speaking. André could barely see the top of his head. He joined those who were crowding onto a stack of timber against one wall. There was a movement in the crowd about Le Maître. Someone had brought a chair. He stood on it and continued speaking.

Close by stood Cassie, arms folded under her bosom, frowning. She had heard Duke was in Fyzabad. Suppose they sent him to arrest her husband? The crowd was with him, surrounding her and him, he could still be taken away, hidden. . . . A woman interjected something. Quick as a snake Cassie turned and spat some words at her.

"You right, girl!" others cried, supporting Cassie.

Women in the crowd began to speak loudly and threateningly about what should be done to "them white sons-a-bitches who only good for set police on all-you."

"All-you, hush!" a man's voice called out authoritatively.

Le Maître was saying: "You must be prepared for every kind of police provocation. The reason is simple. If we win this strike workers' wages will go up through the oilfields. What will be the result? The sugar estates will be compelled to raise their wages too. We, the oilfield workers, will give the lead to all the workers in Trinidad. The bosses realise this. They are determined to fight us. If you let them provoke you to violence they will crush us. Stand firm. We will force them to pay. . . ."

André's attention was distracted by the arrival of a car pulling up in the gateway, blocking it. Two white police inspectors, a black constable and the detective Duke jumped out of the car hastily and with determined steps approached the crowd. André's heart beat faster as he recognised Primrose, whose features now were stern, cold and colourless.

The senior inspector, Campbell, strode impetuously into the crowd.

He was a plump, short, broad-faced man with hardly any neck, a snub nose and a pugnacious expression. Holstered revolvers slapped the hips of both inspectors. A dozen men and women ran away, laughing but frightened, to the safety of the gate, but many more were pouring in at sight of the armed police. The crowd—and by now at least four hundred people had packed into the yard—stirred agitatedly, seemed to fall back, opened up, then closed in like a fist around the police.

Perhaps it was that first falling back that deceived Inspector Primrose, that confirmed him in his opinion that they were cowards. Suddenly he realised he was hemmed in. It crossed his mind that Campbell's action had perhaps been injudicious.

"What do them?" voices were asking. "What they think they goin' do now . . . ?"

"People behavin' peaceful and quiet, is they want to make trouble. . . ."

"Provocation! Hold them and bus' they arse! I's only four-a dem. . . ."

". . . b'Christ! They never take Ben down tonight—not so long as I here!"

Those standing on the woodstack jumped down and pressed nearer to the police, standing on tiptoe.

The snub-nosed Campbell pushed his way to Le Maître and said something to him.

"Which warrant? Take it and put it up you' arse!" cried a voice.

"But look he, nuh! White bastard. . . ."

"Silence!" Le Maître shouted. "What is the charge? Read the warrant."

There was a momentary lull in the shouting. André stood on tiptoe, supporting himself with his hand on the shoulder of a man in a sweat-soaked blue shirt. He saw the agitated but forbidding expression on Le Maître's face—he was still standing on the chair—but could not hear what was being read.

"Read louder, man!" cried the man on whose shoulder André was pressing, and others took up the cry.

The constable was mumbling over the warrant because he was intimidated by the hostility of his own people.

A woman with a basket of mangoes was standing near André. "Some cook-up charge they bring for us," she said.

"We kean't hear dat warrant!" others said.

". . . kean't accept dat warrant!"

". . . what you t'ink we is—children?"

André heard Cassie's voice rise above everyone's. "They want to take our leader down but they will never take him. To take him they will have to take every one of us!"

A new high voice began rapidly to re-read the warrant.

That high English-sounding voice following upon Cassie's challenge was more than the man in the sweat-soaked shirt could stand. He grabbed a mango from the basket of the woman in front of him and threw it at the tall Primrose. It struck him on the shoulder and burst. As if this were a signal a big man with a beard like Haile Selassie's snatched the warrant from Inspector Campbell's hand and hit him with a thick piece of wood. With relentless and furious looks others began striking the police with their fists. The callalloo that had long been cooking had come to the boil.

The woman with the basket tried to back away but found it impossible in the press of people. "O Gawd!" she cried, vainly trying to protect with her hands the source of her livelihood. "Stop it—thief! All-you is mad people, man. T'ief—police—!" And in her desperation she took a mango herself and flung it in the face of the man who was using them as ammunition.

Suddenly shots were heard. The fist opened. André fell back with the crowd. He heard several more shots. The retreating police officers were firing into the air and the ground. André had an impression of frightened and angry people running in all directions. He became conscious that he too was running, and he tried to stop but was pushed on. He saw the huge broad-shouldered Duke, head down, in full flight through the gate with the infuriated crowd in pursuit. The police car had sped off. Le Maître's bodyguard was hustling him away. André ran up to them.

"The car is around the corner. Wait here for me," he said.

They had him take them not to Betsy Solomon's but to another worker's home. Le Maître sat silent and grim-faced.

"Things are bad, André," he said abruptly. "Don't stay in Fyzabad. Thank you, you've done a terrific job for us. Listen." He lowered his voice. "Try and see Cassie before you go. Tell her where I am—but she mustn't come. Right? Goodbye."

When the inspectors drew their revolvers and began shooting, Duke boldly ran up to Le Maître and seized him; but he, too, saw only the surface phenomena with which he had long been accustomed to deal, saw only the same people against whom he was accustomed to wreak his spite. Cassie and several other men and women immediately set upon him. He fled across the road into Yankee's shop, jumped over the counter and hid in the back room behind bags of flour. The toe of his boot gave him away. Men threw aside the bags of flour as if they were pillows. Great as was Duke's strength it was no match for the rain of blows that descended upon him. He fled into the next room. The only exit was the window. He jumped, realising too late that the drop was eighteen feet. He lay on the ground in agony, one leg twisted under him, unable to move.

When the crowd rushed into the shop Yankee pulled out the cash drawer, quickly buried it in a bin of rice and sat on the lid, a chopper in his hand. The scale fell from the counter with a crash and flour whitened the floor as people rushed into the back room. Foremost among the crowd which was now fighting its way out was Cassie.

"Pitch oil—gimme some pitch oil!" she shouted at Yankee.

He scarcely recognised Cassie in this young woman with the wild look of invincible resolution.

"You take, take and go," he said. "I don't gi'e you. Get out the shop. He come here, play big shot, take cigalettes, beer, food, don't give any dough, say he's Duke. Okay, let him Duke now."

Cassie ran out with a gallon tin of kerosene. She was not fully conscious of what she was going to do. She was a part of that boiling lava of mob hate that demanded action and forced the suspension of all restrictions, moral and mental.

A grey-haired man tried to take the can from her. "Where you goin' wid dat, chile?"

She struck him in the face and ran on, feeling herself the instrument of all those behind her.

Duke's eyes were leaping from face to face as he pleaded for mercy, the sweat pouring from him. The crowd was triumphant, thirsting for revenge, laughing, yet aghast at the possibility that lay before it, waiting upon some movement on his part or on theirs that would decide all their fates.

"T'row it, t'row it!" a woman urged Cassie. Blood oozed from a gash on her forehead and the dress had been ripped from her left shoulder.

At sight of that hulk wriggling helpless on its back Cassie could not bring herself to throw the kerosene upon it. Pity seized her—something she had thought not possible—and, as well, despair, despair at being robbed of her prey, and a sense of loss at being cut off from this baying crowd, which she could no longer influence because she was as a stranger in its midst.

"Gimme de t'ing!" The woman tried to snatch the can from Cassie. A man's hand struck her. The can was torn from Cassie's grasp and its contents flung on the pleading Duke.

"O God, no!" Cassie moaned, pushing her way through the crowd to escape it, to escape the madness that horrified her, threatening to suck her in. As she ran she heard Duke scream amid shouts of rage, and the hushed cries of those who now began to run away from their collective guilt.

At home Cassie found herself alone and was not ungrateful. The house echoed with Duke's screaming. She sat down, waiting for the sense of guilt, of horror, of failure to pass, but it grew worse. Her personal hate had withered. Her head was full of jumbled fragments of thoughts. Gradually one came clear. "We are all of us like that. Are white people better? Why? We should be walkin' this earth like lions but we only barkin' like stray dogs. Such hate in our faces, man, such cruelty! Why, why?" She was oppressed by a new awareness of her ignorance and her blind groping for comprehension of a world beyond her, groping for a truth by which to steady her soul, give it direction.

After a while, automatically she began to do what she did every night at this hour, preparing the evening meal.

Someone knocked. Her heart pounded but she went to the door almost with relief and flung it open boldly. On the step stood André.

"Come in."

He noticed at once her state of shock. He gave her Ben's address, adding: "He said not to come. He'll get in touch with you."

She nodded.

"What's the matter, Cassie?"

"Nothing. You heard anything?"

"No. What should—"

"All right. So nothing happen. You goin' back to Port-a-Spain?"

"Yes."

"Go then. A lot-a things bound to happen now." She sighed heavily.

She wasn't looking at him nor was she really looking away from him either.

Knowing nothing of what had happened he imagined she had raised a class barrier between them, that in her eyes he had become suspect. He took her hand, but it lay in his cold, limp and unresponsive. "Goodbye, Cassie."

"Okay, man, good."

He went out with an uneasy, unhappy feeling that he ought not to leave her.

Chapter forty-six

Inspector Campbell had been taken in haste to the company's hospital: his foolhardiness had earned him a broken jaw, and a scalp wound drenched him in blood. Though in great pain he was all for returning to battle as soon as the wound was stitched and his jaw wired. Small both in mind and body he had long been frustrated by the knowledge that, though white, he could never rise higher than his present position, there would always be an Englishman above him. The black rank-and-file policemen thought it was well this should be so: with Campbell at the top their lot could be even worse than it was now.

Primrose, the Englishman, had none of that dislike of blacks that Campbell, bred in Trinidad, bore within him like an ulcer. During the first carnival he had witnessed he had been surprised by the immense diversity of the Trinidadian face and the endless variety of its beauty and its ugliness. While looking down imperturbably upon the reckless merrymaking from the back of his horse he had secretly wished he could join in the jump-up with the women himself. But it was very secret, this wish, for he had those safe and narrow views which made men of his upbringing suitable candidates for police work in colonial outposts. His reserve, and his conceptions, which were like a harness, were reinforced by the attitudes of the white colonial society in which he moved.

When he saw and felt the unrestrained anger of the mob; when he saw Cassie, who had been so meekly submissive in the judge's service, calling on the mob to resist; and when he and Inspector Campbell had to flee for their lives, he prepared to take measures to impose the rule of law and instil in these brutes a proper respect for authority.

When the company doctor ordered Campbell to bed the conduct of the affair fell into the hands of Primrose. He telephoned San Fernando for reinforcements and prepared to make another assault on the village to suppress the rioters and arrest Le Maître. An hour later he learned of the burning alive of Corporal Duke. The crime outraged him. He felt that it thrust upon him a new, solemn, inescapable responsibility. He tried to get San Fernando on the phone again but by that time the strikers had cut the lines.

The villagers, now horrified at what they had done, felt themselves pressed against the wall and committed to violence. They were convinced the police would show no mercy now.

Around seven-thirty that night the police raided the village in force. The villagers met them with stones, bottles, revolvers, hunting rifles, chamber pots—whatever came to hand. Primrose would countenance no retreat. He gave his orders calmly and rushed forward at the head of his men straight into the mêlée. And someone, hating him perhaps for that very courage that was born of pride of race, fired from a garret window, and Primrose fell. The police fired haphazardly despite their orders not to shoot, and again they fled, taking Primrose with them, but not before firing three shots at a man who resembled Le Maître. Before midnight David Primrose died.

The governor radioed Bermuda for the despatch of a cruiser.

Learning of this next morning some of the workers chuckled sardonically: "Nothing for Duke, but a cruiser for the limey."

Only in the bright light of that morning, with the cooling of tempers, was a detachment of armed policemen, followed by a detachment of Light Horse composed of white men, able to enter the village and begin a house to house search for weapons and the body of Duke. The villagers watched sullenly as mattresses were torn to ribbons and crockery broken. Suddenly the search was called off. The Honourable Member for St Patrick had come to address his constituents.

Events had driven the governor to come down to Fyzabad to confer with Major Bottomley and other members of the executive council. In the midst of this conference the Honourable Member for St Patrick requested permission to speak to the people. "I am appealing for moderation, Your Excellency. It is not too late for me to ask them to disperse quietly."

Major Bottomley, his broad and beefy face flushed, got to his feet with deliberation. His steely eyes seemed riveted to Saturday night's horrors, his expression suggesting that he was so appalled by the request of the Honourable Member for St Patrick that he could not bring himself to look at the faces about him.

"I protest, Your Excellency, against any such suggestion. The time for speech-making has passed! In view of the events of last night I consider Your Excellency has no alternative but to carry out an immediate search. Le Maître and his accomplices must be arrested!"

He spoke so firmly and precisely that everyone felt his words were intended as a rebuke not only to the Honourable Member but to the governor as well. And evidently the governor regarded it as such for his flat, grim, thin-lipped face grew still grimmer.

"This is not the first time I have found myself at the head of a government in similar circumstances," he replied. "While I am grateful for your advice, Major Bottomley, I am of the opinion that everything should be done which can possibly be done to calm these already over-excited people. I wish the Honourable Member for St Patrick to receive every protection from the police during his mission." He looked at the commissioner of police.

Colonel Cambridge was tall, lean and heavy featured. A faint smile lowered one corner of his wide lips. He rose, put his eyeglass in his eye and glared through it at the Honourable Member for St Patrick. It was not intentional, it was only the distortion caused by the glass. Nevertheless the honourable representative coughed apologetically as if to say it was not his fault if the governor sided with a coloured man, and he regretted having witnessed a rebuff administered to so important a person as Major Bottomley. He went out with the colonel.

The house to house search was halted. From atop his car the Honourable Member appealed to the people to disperse and return to work. The governor, he assured them, was now, at this very moment, giving consideration to their demands.

They met him first with silence then with violent abuse. French, raising both fists above his bandaged head, screamed:

". . . *agent provocateur* . . . want to trap us! Pay no attention to this man sent by Government to lull us into a false sense of security.

Not one single assurance has been given of an increase in wages. I say we will not go back to work for the same starvation wages. They must negotiate with us now or we will break them. Not all you' police can frighten us!"

The Honourable Member, quite losing his temper, waved his fat brown hand and shouted above French's voice something about "ungrateful . . . led by fools . . . the law!" A roar of shouts silenced him. He got into his car and a nervous police posse shepherded him back to the executive council meeting.

There were no further searches that day. Colonel Cambridge feared a repetition of the previous night. He withdrew his police from the village and retired to wait on the cruiser.

Le Maître consulted with those about him. Further police provocation, they felt, was on the cards. There was no doubt, however, that the workers would accept the challenge and give battle: like heated iron their composition had changed. They had neither intended nor wished for violence; but having tasted blood, their first horror at it passed, they would hasten to expend their long pent-up wrath before it cooled. The numbers on strike were growing hourly. Even company officials' domestic servants had quit their jobs.

Now that he was temporarily free to move about the village Le Maître went home. He found Cassie stern and gloomy. He assured her he was safe for a while at least.

"Safe? Who safe today?" she answered him. "You know as well as me they only bidin' they time till the cruiser come. What you hear 'bout Duke?"

"They burned the man alive. It was a terrible thing! But who you goin' to blame—the people?"

"Police to blame. And we to blame too because we only like stray dogs barkin', man! Nobody 'fraid stray dogs. You pick up a stone and they run . . . I was there."

"You?" he asked softly, looking at her intently.

"I had the tin-a pitch oil in me hand, yes? But I couldn't t'row it. After all, he's a human bein'."

"Yes. A bad human being but still not a stray dog." Taking her hand he made her sit at the table beside him. "This one terrible thing will make some white people believe we are not human, so they can shoot us down. Who threw it on him?"

"Who to see? Man or woman, it don' matter."

"Arrests will follow. You were there—"

"Let them hang me!" she cried out. "To dead now or later, is all the same. To hide you—that I been contemplatin' whole night."

"Who goin' to hang? Don't talk so! The people not givin' anybody away. I'm only sayin' because you were seen there—"

"Leave it, man, leave it! I ain't make for war, not this sort-a killin', but people forcin' it on us."

"We can't do anything about it. Not now. Our hope is to get the workers at Point Fortin and Pointe-à-Pierre out on strike; get the stevedores in Port-of-Spain to walk off the job, the railways workers —paralyse industry! That's the only hope to make Government see reason."

"That is so, but you have to hide. I settle it in me mind this mornin' when the police come—"

"They were here?"

"Look in the bedroom if you doubt me."

He went in. The mattress was slashed in several places and its fibre scattered about. The sheet lay on the floor amid books and clothing and broken glass.

"You see why you have to leave Fyzabad? Only one way: as a woman."

"We will talk of that later," he muttered, pressing his thumb against his teeth. "And you? You will stay?"

"I will stay."

Boisson, on his way back from the coronation, was sending telegrams expressing regret that the workers had permitted themselves to be led into violence by certain hooligan elements.

Chapter forty-seven

Oilfield officials all over the south of the island were thoroughly alarmed by the events that followed one on the heels of the other from Friday night to Sunday morning. Refineries Limited of Point

Fortin locked out the workers and manned the gates with policemen and Light Horsemen. The managers felt themselves, and not without justification, to be guardians of a lonely outpost; that on their shoulders had fallen the burden of upholding British prestige and safeguarding British capital. They sang praises to Primrose: "Very courageous chap . . . hadn't even drawn his gun . . . an honour to have known him. . . ."

Cloudless was Monday morning, bright and dewy, as if neither blood nor tears had fallen, and no man would die. Keskidees screamed joyfully or angrily at one another and dived from tree to tree, there to sing defiance or call a mate. A light breeze lazily searched the leaves.

Ten men were behind the gates. Seven were white. Of these one wore the uniform of a major in the Volunteers—Bullen, the South African. The others belonged to the Light Horse. The remaining three were black policemen. They stayed to one side, by themselves.

One of the Light Horsemen was Jack Lorrimer. At this moment a tall raw-boned auburn-haired young man with freckles and projecting teeth was telling a joke. Jack Lorrimer, squatting on the butt of his rifle, which he straddled like a horse, laughed loudly. "Hi!" he said, jumping up to give one of his own so as not to be outdone. He broke off abruptly when he noticed a young Negro in a blue shirt outside the fence. Through the ten-foot-high wire fence the Negro was looking at them with a nervous, puzzled expression. Perhaps he found it difficult to understand why, if the gates were locked, its guards were armed. Lorrimer strode to the fence. His slightly bowed, strong and healthy legs, which were accustomed to scoring winning goals, were encased in shining leggings and heavy boots. He liked to hear them creaking. They lent him, he knew, an air of irresistible authority.

"Beat it!"

Out of respect for his major, Bullen, Lorrimer did not swear at the Negro.

"Beat it? You feel you is somebody now you have a gun?"

Lorrimer pointed his rifle, feeling with pleasure that Major Bullen, who was also his boss in the plant, was watching.

The young Negro didn't move. He looked Lorrimer straight in the eyes, only something in his face quivered. Nothing like this had ever happened before and Lorrimer was furious. He put the rifle to his shoulder. "Get away from the gate!"

And suddenly everyone was a little tense and nervous.

Major Bullen, his thin face stern, put a restraining hand on Lorrimer's shoulder. "The plant is closed," he said to the youth outside the gate. "There'll be no work today. Go on. Don't stand in front of the gate."

The Negro turned quickly as if he had made up his mind about something and walked away. Once he looked back angrily.

"I'd like to pick him off," said Lorrimer. "A bastard like that shot Inspector Primrose, I bet!"

"They say he was a damn fine chap," said the auburn-haired joker.

"Who fired the bloody shot-gun?" asked another who had come up.

"Take a dozen out and flog the shit out of them," said Lorrimer. "Someone would talk then, I bet!"

"Quite wrong," said the newcomer with a smile. "You can't punish the innocent for the guilty."

"What? After that Duke business . . . !"

"Horrible!" said the joker. "How can people do that sort of thing?"

"Niggers."

They fell silent. Lorrimer felt that silence expressed their devotion to justice without regard for personal danger. He felt that though he was not yet a hero he might soon become one. He had felt this since Saturday night when he had heard of the murders; he had felt it with special force when, on Sunday, it had been decided to call out the Light Horse and he had put on his uniform and his leggings. Early this morning Bullen had exchanged a few words with him about the events of the weekend—that Bullen who kept aloof from all locals, black or white. Just before dawn, it was, when they were waiting to relieve the overnight guard. They had been alone for a moment.

"They tell me you're a good shot."

"Not bad, sir."

"You'll take your orders from me."

"Sure, sir."

Bullen had nothing more to say to him. Lorrimer prodded:

"Hanging's too good for those niggers who murdered Inspector Primrose and Corporal Duke."

Looking somewhere into the distance Bullen replied: "I've seen this sort of thing in South Africa. You've got to deal with them very firmly."

"Pretty bad there," Lorrimer agreed. "So few white people!"

"We're a handful. But we hold our own."

Lorrimer thought he detected a note of pride. "Yes, that's right! Terrible in the States too."

"They're savages, of course," Bullen said without malice. "A lot of people are only now beginning to realise that fact. You see," he added after a pause, "you may educate a lot of them, but they revert. What traditions have they got behind them?"

"That's right!" Lorrimer agreed.

Just then the others joined them and they were driven to the gate.

Bullen's aloofness had always inspired respect in Lorrimer, not to say fear. But after this conversation Bullen was no longer the exacting boss of whom one had to be wary, they were comrades in arms, they might even be killed together. In the early dawn he stood by the gate, looking, waiting, not knowing what to expect, yet hoping for some desperate encounter in which he would perhaps save Bullen's life or, better, take command of the unit when the other whites were killed and beat off the attackers. In the back of his mind arose an image of a white girl he knew, a girl of excellent family, in the arms of her father's black chauffeur. He had heard more than one story of this kind. Now, suddenly he saw himself dashing into the village houses, tripping some, kicking others, cowing them with his gun. The occupants would themselves have brought him the murderer of Primrose. And at the same instant he thought of a black girl he had seen in a shop in San Fernando last weekend. She had a figure and a half, that baby! He could have her, he felt sure. Niggers had very little moral sense anyway.

His reverie was interrupted by the arrival of a group of some thirty workers. In a loud voice one of them was emphasising something in a way that made his companions laugh out loud with typical naive, carefree West Indian humour, a humour that held nothing sacred. Lorrimer's hackles rose. He glanced round at Bullen. The latter had been walking up and down with an English Light Horse officer who had come to join them. He did not cease walking nor did he even glance at the workers outside the gate. Lorrimer was conscious of an extraordinary calmness, rectitude and strength in Bullen. Though Bullen passed within two feet of him he could hear nothing he said: he knew how to project his voice so that it reached only that person with whom he desired to communicate.

"Look, all-you, the gates locked, man!"

"So, what happen now?"

"Eh-eh! They get out the guns, boy!"

As they came up to the gates the workers fell silent. A middle-aged man who had worked in the plant for years came forward.

Bullen approached the gates. "Go back home, the plant is closed down."

"Let us in, chief, we ain't on strike," the middle-aged man, who wore glasses, said to him with a smile.

"I said, go back home, the plant is closed down."

Other workers could be seen arriving in a steady stream.

Lorrimer had been standing with his rifle butt resting on the ground. Now he threw up the rifle and caught it in both hands—at the ready—he knew not why. The auburn-haired joker did likewise, thinking perhaps he had been slow in perceiving the danger that faced them. The others, handling their weapons clumsily because they were not accustomed to use them, positioned themselves along the fence.

Lorrimer felt just a little twinge of disappointment mixed with relief that none of the workers appeared inclined to force the gates. Instead of dispersing they sat on the grass by the roadside discussing the meaning of the lock-out.

"They 'fraid us."

"They mean to fire us all. They make so much-a money they could afford to siddown idle for a month and watch us starve."

"You see this move, all-you? They means to take it out of us for what happen in Fyzabad."

"They should-a kill some more Saturday night!" the young man in the blue shirt shouted directly at the white officers behind the gates.

A truck arrived full of workers. All jumped down except a very thin man wearing a collarless shirt and a jacket patched in several places. This was Clem Payne. Standing on the truck he began to attack the employers. He urged the workers to turn the lock-out into a strike; thousands of their comrades were already on strike at the Pointe-à-Pierre refinery thirty miles away. "If you want to get you' *just* demands, if you want to end all this trouble *quickly*, let us shut down *all* the fields *and* the refineries. We can do it! They kean't *work* anything without us, they kean't *move* anything without us. . . ."

The workers, some five hundred now, were gathered round the truck. Some were listening intently, eyes downward now, and now on the white men behind the gates; others shouted approvingly or applauded with gusto. As soon as Payne had finished another man got into the truck and began speaking—"whipping them up", thought Lorrimer. He heard the sincerity of their voices, he saw it in their faces, and yet he heard and saw nothing. Momentary doubts, like shadows, flickered across his mind and were gone.

The crowd made way for a semi-trailer laden with pipes. Bullen and Lorrimer unlocked and opened the gates. The semi-trailer went in. A truck came out of the gates and another semi-trailer, also laden with pipes, was allowed to pass in. Close to a thousand they numbered at this stage. Payne made another speech, this time with an enthusiasm that seemed to weld the crowd into a massed and eager and solid opposition to those who were depriving them of their right to work.

So mercurial are our Trinidadian folk that in a moment they can turn drama into farce, or make a drama out of nothing. No one had thought of returning home, this was an entertainment not to be missed. But after Payne's second speech they knew that they were masters of the situation, the joke was on the boss. They laughingly taunted the armed whites. They yelled merry abuse at the truck drivers and some black workers moving about the oil storage tanks and buildings behind the fence. When other trucks came up they refused to let the boom gate be raised.

"Strike on, boy. Go back home," voices said merrily.

"T'row the blasted pipes in the drain."

"Chum, you' holidays come. You not glad?"

"Go take a rest on Manzanilla beach. Come back wid you' pipes in two weeks."

Bullen called for an axe. When one was eventually brought to him he handed his rifle to a subordinate and stepped out escorted by Lorrimer and the auburn-haired joker. The latter was pale, his freckles standing out prominently on his rounded cheeks.

The crowd jeered as Bullen cut the boom with the axe.

"Let him cut. What he thinks this is?"

"White people bad, in truth."

"The red-hair one shittin' 'e pants a'ready."

The boom fell and Bullen turned back to the gates. The trucks made no attempt to move forward, the drivers had joined the workers. Some in the crowd were eating watermelon and bananas. Laughing, they flung the skins at Bullen and his guards. The nervous Lorrimer involuntarily ducked as a banana skin struck his arm. Bullen felt a piece of wet watermelon skin strike the back of his neck. He was white with rage when the gates closed behind him.

"Fire a volley!" those up front in the crowd heard him say.

Weeks later, at the enquiry, he declared he had intended them to fire in the air.

Lorrimer fired at the young man in the blue shirt. He heard him cry out and saw him call as he turned to run. The policemen further along the fence, not making out Bullen's order but startled by the shots, also joined in the firing. The crowd scattered and ran. Lorrimer, his mind empty of thought, worked his rifle bolt rapidly and fired at the moving targets. One boy of about fourteen who was eating a banana fell forward abruptly on his face. His outstretched arms fluttered on the asphalt like broken wings while his blood oozed over it. A man fell with a newspaper he had been reading clutched in his hand. An Indian boy of twelve who had come to deliver milk fell from his bicycle with a crash. The bottles of milk rolled over and over or burst open on the road.

"Cease fire!"

For some reason Lorrimer kept his rifle trained on a wounded man who was bawling as he crawled away on hands and knees by the ditch.

Overhead keskidees cried out with joyful sounds. The sunlight glittered on the milk bottles scattered over the road. The breeze, which had died down, again arose with a light rustling, but now from another quarter, so that it carried the cries of the wounded and dying to their executioners behind the gates. The auburn-haired joker was staring open-mouthed at the dead milk boy, not understanding how or why he had killed him.

Some of the strikers approached the wounded. Lorrimer, now very pale, saw a thin brown Negro with an angry face—one of those who had made speeches—run to the boy and turn him over among the milk bottles. The gun seemed to go off of itself. When Lorrimer saw the man fall he was even for a moment not sure who had fired.

"Cease fire, I said!"

"Sorry, sir," Lorrimer mumbled, frightened at having disobeyed his boss's orders.

Those who had been approaching the wounded dived behind the trucks or ran for the ditch or huddled clumsily against the unyielding earth.

The last man to be killed was Clem Payne.

Chapter forty-eight

Perhaps no man could say: "Clem taught us this or that," or: "Clem led us in such a struggle." Many resented his cruel tongue; disliking him, some repeated rumours to his discredit. But he was a fighter, had given form and substance to their half-formulated dreams, and no man had he feared. For this they had listened when he spoke. Had any ignorant white youth shot him dead five days before no hearts would have burned as from a personal blow, no tongues would have called the lightning down. The spirits of the slain stood among all men like their own dumb ghosts, but in death Payne's voice rang everywhere, calling to battle. Tirelessly, thanklessly had he watered the seeds of their pride and human worth. They grasped his fire and blew their breath upon it that Monday morning. Six thousand walked off the job at Pointe-à-Pierre.

Oil refining ceased. At the Usine Sainte Madeleine, the sugar refinery two miles outside of San Fernando, the workers, hearing of the new murders and the thousands out on strike, cast off in an instant their age-old submission. The mildest-looking Indians and Negroes cursed and beat white bosses and damaged machinery. The cane workers went out not only on strike but seeking militant leadership and committing senseless acts of violence when they could find no organised outlet for their desire for vengeance. In Rio Claro bare-footed, ragged agricultural labourers went in a body to the warden's office to demand more pay. In their hands were the tools with which they earned their bread—hoes, cutlasses, agricultural forks. Yet as the Warden stood on the steps addressing the workers police rifles cracked from behind the hedge and more were slain by a spirit of fear and hatred that stalked the land.

Who could now ignore the smell of blood? None could do so, and every man took a side.

When at nine o'clock that morning workers from Point Fortin and Pointe-à-Pierre came to Fyzabad and told of the shootings and the thousands everywhere on strike Le Maître and his close comrades decided to do all possible to bring the waterfront and railway workers into the battle.

"Let the slogan be 'wages, not war'," Le Maître said, clutching in despair at his head, which was tied with a white cloth like a woman's.

" 'Wages, not war'?" French repeated with a scornful laugh. "You losin' you' nerve, Ben. Look at the people—look! They want both—wages *and* war. Not even you could hold them back. And they are right! Let us have war."

"You fool!" Le Maître shouted, springing up. "War with what? At any moment English sailors will come here with machine guns. Our duty is to hold the people in check, to bring them out on strike for wages and trade unions, but to hold them back from violence. Like the blows you get Friday night have you stupid!"

French swung away with an impatient gesture but at once turned back to Le Maître, his underjaw trembling with excitement and anger.

"Look," said he. "I am going to Port-of-Spain now. I know I can get the stevedores and wharf labourers to follow me. What you want me do if the police shoot at us—run away? Kneel and pray? The people themselves will take matters out of my hands. Clem is dead. More of us will die, we know that, we not afraid."

"You can't avoid the violence, Ben," Cassie broke in firmly, recalling the mob lust that had possessed her on Saturday night. "It's too late for that now."

"All right, damn it! But we don't have to encourage it."

"Come what may," Burnett said quickly with his crooked smile, "we must encourage the people to withhold their labour. It's not we who is responsible for the deaths, it's the police."

"It's a waste of time arguin' who is responsible," Le Maître told him impatiently. "Every government is based on violence. But where's the sense leading workers to be slaughtered if you have no arms? What will become of our organisation?"

"Percy, use discretion," said Cassie. "You hear? Do the best you can. How you act is how you see the situation at the time. Only God could guide you then."

"Don't waste time, go!" Le Maître added. "Damn it! I shouldn't be bottled up here like this. That's the right word: I only makin' noise like a fly in a bottle."

Burnett laughed happily, like a boy mocking a companion who has been hoist with his own petard. "That's your job now—to be quiet, unseen, unheard."

"Dress up like *jou' ouvert*," Ben growled.

French hitched up his pants and tightened his belt. "I'll say goodbye."

He shook hands all round in solemn haste and went out.

Cassie sighed, seeing her husband writhe in his frustration. "You have to face the facts. You see what happen Saturday. If you in a crowd and they try to arrest you it will cause more violence, the very thing you want to prevent."

"They not so foolish to try that a second time."

Cassie and Burnett held a meeting in the street. A great crowd had gathered, strikers from Point Fortin, Fyzabad and Pointe-à-Pierre. They detailed their own police to stop all traffic while the meeting lasted. First they detained, and then commandeered, passing trucks and buses. The cars they let pass, turning back only those in which oilfield officials were travelling. Since Sunday morning the military had not dared enter the village. The workers were masters of Fyzabad, conscious of their power both as individuals and as a mass. It was a power they had never tasted. It inflamed them with a jubilant, mad and fearless arrogance, inspired a needless, reckless cruelty: for such freedom would not last, that they knew, no one entertained illusions that he was unmarked. But in some few was a solemn sense of responsibility to many more. These would sell their lives dearly, for they were caught up in something far larger than any one man or group of men—the fate of a class, even, they felt, the fate of a nation, hung on their words and deeds, and no one could tell what this surging torrent of life would ask of him.

All Cassie's actions became positive. When she mounted a truck and saw all the people before her she felt more herself than ever, yet one with them as never before. Their voice, that clamoured for justice, came from her throat. And they saw truth in all her words and, longing for leadership, they gave themselves to her will with the relief that action brings.

"Comrades!" she cried in a strained voice, her hands on her hips, but not knowing how she stood, nor caring. "We must blockade San Fernando. Stop all goods comin' by sea or by rail. Percy French now gone to Port-of-Spain to bring out all the railway workers and the stevedores on strike. We have trucks and buses here now to take us to San Fernando to do the very said thing. Stop the merchants' profits! Stop the oil. Stop the guns and the soldiers comin' in from Port-a-Spain. This is the only way we could force them to stop the shootin' and pay us so we could live like free people and not slaves. Let us show them now that slavery done!"

"Take the guns for weself!" cried the thin voice of an Indian. His thin, bare brown arm brandished a glinting cutlass in the scorching sunlight no one noticed.

"Yes!" Cassie made a violent sweeping gesture with her arm. "If you could get them take them—yes. If you don't take them they will give them to the white people to shoot us down. They come quite from England to take what is ours and treat us like dogs—"

"Kill the lot-a them and done!" a voice interrupted.

"No. The governor done send for a cruiser. They bringin' trained fighters to kill us. They could drop big shells on us— women, children, old people—what they care? If you get the guns t'row dem in the sea. It's money you want or war?"

"Money, man!" some said.

"War! War!" cried others. "They declare war on us!"

Cassie raised her hands. "Nobody could feel more than me to kill some-a them. But I tell you truly it ain't no use. It got plenty more white people to come in ships and shoot us all down. Stop their profits, comrades! It's not their life they value so much as their profits! Look twenty trucks and buses here. Don't waste time. Take them. Let us go at once to San Fernando and bring out the workers. By tomorrow the cruiser will be here. Come go *now* while they still frighten'-a we." She looked about her. "Who comin' on this truck with me?"

Several men, including the Indian with the cutlass, leaped on to the truck. The crowd splintered. Their police shepherded them to the waiting vehicles. Cassie climbed down into the cab beside the driver. He revved the engine. The roar of revved-up engines joined and even stimulated the enthusiastic shouted comments, the farewells, the angry taunts, the jokes simple and coarse. The wound-up spring began to uncoil. Cassie's truck moved quickly through the crowd, leading the way.

When, fifty minutes later, they reached San Fernando they came upon hundreds hanging about the streets in groups. Some were strikers; many were the jobless who for months had hung about breeding discontent in stagnant pools. All were now conscious that the law's oppressive hands were fully occupied elsewhere. Cassie stopped her truck. The police ran down the line.

"All out! We goin' to march . . . demonstrate . . . !"

When they saw the column of strikers, a few of whom had bandaged heads or arms, and heard they were from Fyzabad and Point Fortin the idle workers stepped in among them gladly.

"Where all-you goin'?"

"To pull out the railways boys and the stevedores. Where all-you from?"

"Pointe-à-Pierre."

"All out?"

"Every man."

Sometimes the men drew in their women. The word flashed back and forth across the streets.

"Who they is?"

". . . goin' to stop the trains. The white people bringin' guns. . . ."

"Everybody stoppin' work. . . ."

"No police, all gone south!"

And laughing, cursing, servants left madame's shopping and joined the men. Where this would lead God alone knew. Who cared? It was an entertainment, a freeness, a madness. O God, how grand a madness to see the madames run, fleeing to Port-of-Spain! "Who to stop us now? The town is ours!"

Cassie was striding swiftly, leading the crowd, Burnett beside her. When they reached High Street steel doors were hastily rolled down in face of the menacing power of that uncoiling spring. Shoppers hid in the stores or ran to their cars and drove away. A young white man, very neat and clean, ran to his car, glancing behind him with a frightened face. That pale and frightened face shook yet another fetter from the workers. With a roar the foremost flung at the car whatever they could find. One scooped up fresh horse dung in his hands and flung it through the window. A man with a length of iron pipe in his huge fist dealt the windshield a smashing blow. A young white woman in the car screamed in terror and covered her weeping child with her body. A woman seized a stone from a man and flung it with all her might at a white woman running to hide in a side street. The stone hit her on the buttock. A mocking yell went up.

The crowd had become a wild, shouting mob. They smashed cars, overturned others. In vain did a few plead with them to hold back. Hate rose out of them like vomit. When the slim young Indian with the freshly sharpened cutlass that glittered in the sunlight cried: "Le' we take the telephone exchange!" the cry was at once taken up: "The telephone exchange! All for the telephone exchange!" The crowd fragmented, momentarily losing its impetus. Burnett ran back, trying to hold them.

"It's the waterfront workers we want," he pleaded. "The railway men. Stop the trains, boys!"

"We goin' there too, man," they insisted. "First we must cut this town off from communication with the police further down south."

"We must go with them," Cassie told him. "Some of you go to the railway station. We goin' to the exchange." She saw this was the only way to keep some sort of rein upon them.

They passed on. One young Negro, holding a broomstick in both hands over his head, began to shake and jump up in Carnival style. Cassie wrenched it out of his hands.

"What you think this is? Where you' brains? Workers dependin' on us for bread and jobs and you tryin' to mislead people? Get to hell out! This ain't no merrymakin' business."

"This ain't carnival, this is war!" the Indian with the cutlass asserted threateningly.

A pale, irate grey-haired Englishman was insisting on driving his car against the oncoming flood of people, his finger on the horn button. The crowd flowed around it. A dozen arms quickly, without fuss, overturned the car. The crowd moved on with accelerated step.

A lieutenant and four coloured Volunteers—light brown office clerks—were guarding the entrance to the telephone exchange. The lieutenant was a white Trinidadian of Scottish ancestry, puny and hump-backed. Though his deformity had caused him much secret grief it had never stood in his way. Securely pedestalled in society, and with the assurance bred into him from birth that he was master, he had hardly ever deemed it possible that as a lieutenant in uniform, a leader, he might look absurd. And in fact he did not: all his movements were imbued with an energetic authority that commanded respect. Gun in hand he was defending a civilised way of life, decency, womanhood. He would have spurned himself had he feared the mob bearing down upon him. He saw a young woman in a white dress in the very front rank. As they came nearer he recognised in her movements and her eyes fixed on his little force that same dogged resolve he felt within himself. Beside her was an Indian with a cutlass. Lieutenant McDougall fired his revolver in the air. The flood roared onward. He spoke an order sharply. The Volunteers raised their rifles and fired over the heads of the crowd. It halted. It banked up. Some screamed imprecations at the soldiers, others sounded the retreat.

"Go forward! What the hell do all-you . . . ?"

"Go back! You want to get killed?"

"Comrades, rush them and take the guns!"

In the front ranks and at the sides men and women were retreating hesitantly. Lieutenant McDougall snapped an order—he might have been on parade, so nerveless did he seem. He himself aimed at the woman in the white dress.

Cassie felt the impossibility of resisting the tide about her. "Some go round at the sides!" she ordered.

"You expect to fight dem wid stones?"

"That's why we need the guns. . . ."

Some ran off to attack the building from the rear.

Manny Camacho, excited by all that André had told him, had come to San Fernando by bus, intending to go farther south if possible. When the driver refused to go beyond San Fernando Manny got out and wandered about the town, disappointed to find himself, as he phrased it, "far from the thick of the fighting". Hearing of the demonstration he rushed to meet it. He arrived in time to see the Volunteers taking aim. He gazed about him open-mouthed, bewildered by the laughter, the rage, the reasoned arguments and the reckless urgings that bubbled up in the crowd.

"All-you sons-a bitches!" cried a woman with a distraught expression, pushing to the front of the crowd. With her hair in stiff short plaits, and her bloodshot eyes, she looked to the Volunteers like some *diablesse* from the spirit world. "They kill me man in Point this mornin'!" she shrieked and flung a stone at the kneeling Volunteers.

One rushed and several followed. Burnett grabbed Cassie and flung her to one side. She fell headlong and this saved her. The lieutenant's bullet brought Burnett down. Cassie heard the shots, the screams of "Murder! O Gord, they shootin' . . . !" saw the fallen bodies, the running feet. The most desperate, determined to seize those rifles with bare hands, had stormed the steps and were driven back, falling and crying. The Indian had reached a nearby telephone pole. He was ascending it swiftly, the blade of his cutlass between his teeth. Lieutenant McDougall fired. The Indian threw up one hand, the cutlass fell from his teeth and he after it.

Camacho, who, a year before, had stood up at a meeting of

journeymen bakers and cried, "Sooner or later we will have to man the barricades. We will not run when the police bring their rifles," now fled in terror from the screams and the bullets. One had nicked his ear and blood was flowing down his neck. Cassie had got up, but seeing Burnett lying still upon the ground she went to him. She had not seen much of death, but that hole in the head meant one thing only. Holding him in her arms she yelled wildly at the lieutenant:

"Bastards! You deserve to burn in hell forever!"

She did not hear the clicking of the rifle bolts. She laid him down and got up and walked away. "O Lord, O Lord!" she cried aloud, weeping with rage and despair.

All of an hour passed before she could muster a body together to march to the railway station.

That day the governor radioed for a second cruiser.

Chapter forty-nine

When André told Joe that he had witnessed the attempt to arrest Le Maître in Fyzabad Joe questioned him closely about the events of that day and the preceding night and, in particular, the living conditions of the oilfield workers.

"Stupid and arrogant Englishmen! What folly! They will never understand us.'

"The folly is that they are here," André replied. "Only the folly is not on their part but on ours."

"What would be left? If they were to walk out now what would they leave behind them?'

"Is that our fault? Have we made ourselves what we are?"

"All right, all right. But you have to admit, the murdering of Duke and Inspector Primrose were terrible crimes—stupid! Ignorant workers goaded by poverty and led by ignorant, half-baked revolutionaries? My boy, there is no worse combination. I am convinced of it."

André looked at him in angry astonishment. "What other combination do you propose?"

"What's that? What combination? Look here, look here! Do you think it is so simple—"

"Would you have led them?"

"They need a rein on them! Where is the sense flying in the face of the British Empire?"

"Sense? What is in here makes sense to me?" André struck his chest harshly.

"You supporting revolution? In this country? Now? Useless turmoil. Face facts. The British are ruthless. We are only a tiny island. Trade unions—that's what we need, I've said so all along."

André reddened. Joe was right, and yet he was wrong because he had not seen Percy or Duke or that crowd in the woodyard. "How can you blame the people?" he protested, pale, and now uncertain. "How can you? Duke was a brutal beast. In that situation. . . . And there are things you don't know."

He broke off, feeling with dismay that Joe and he were miles apart. Joe, the influential man of business, was not Joe the clerk. Some new, very personal and closely secret vision held his eye. For its realisation old friends were useless.

André experienced once more, and now with desolation, his severance from the world in which he had been born and bred and had a place. His father had sternly condemned "the rioters". Despite André's passionate account of the preludes to Saturday's killings—"What on earth were you doing among such people?" with a look of disgusted incredulity—Mr de Coudray had declared, his face going red: "Your friends need expect no mercy, I can tell you!" and stalked off to his favourite chair. The rest of the family had maintained a frozen silence, as they might have done in the presence of some unspeakable, impolite odour. His mother cleared her throat occasionally as her fingers fluttered over the crochet work for which she was famous among those who understood such things.

In the office on Monday morning Arnold Walker declared flatly that: "Those murderers will swing, mark my words!" André, wiser now, said nothing.

When in the company of Le Maître, Betsy and French he had been certain that truth was on their side; now the openly expressed hostility of relatives and friends and, in some cases, their ill-concealed desire that the rebellion be suppressed by the harshest means, made him recoil in distress and anger. He learned once more that the loneliness suffered in being solitary is not to be compared with the spiritual isolation one might suffer from being too different. He was not now with Joe, but to what degree was he with Cassie, Ben and Percy French? And they with him? How tenuous, indeed, were the threads that bound man to man. "If I disagreed with Ben what use would he have for me? Only an idea links us, just as ideas separate Joe and me, my parents and me. Man himself, the essential personality, is coloured by an idea for which he is spat on, kicked aside, or worshipped." He felt that he had much to give. To whom, to what, then, should he give it? Was it wanted? You made a superficial contact that left the good and the bad, the true and the false, in yourself and them untapped and unrevealed. You wandered as in a shell, intact, a sterile seed. Neither thorns nor fruit came forth if you were not committed, not entrapped by life's harsh kisses and its wild embraces. Yet, after all, could a man's soul bear too close a linking with any other, too close a scrutiny? *One* of them would stifle. To draw too close was to compel separation; yet separation was necessary for that drawing close that was like a fruitful rain on heart and mind.

By midday on Monday all Port-of-Spain was discussing the fresh shootings in the south. The military, composed mostly of young men of Lorrimer's age, guarded the telegraph office, the telephone exchange and other places of strategic importance. André felt still more irritated and angry when he saw Volunteers outside the fire brigade stations and heard the comments of businessmen: " . . . ignorant people . . . riots . . . going to burn down the town. . . ." That afternoon the stevedores heeded French and walked off the job. Many railway workers followed them.

Tuesday morning's press issued communiqués of war spiced with tales of horror. The besieged whites were heroes. More of the strikers had been killed but no white man, thank God, had fallen after Saturday night.

The strikers attempted to seize the arms being loaded on to the train for San Fernando. They failed through hesitancy and lack of resolution when faced by mounted police with guns. Some charged the police barehanded, but the white Inspector shot one man and the rest withdrew amidst roars of rage and flying stones and bottles.

French worked mightily to hold them together in a body, to make of them a fist. They marched through the principal streets of the city, no songs on their lips but with hearts hot like the sticky asphalt beneath their feet, shouting desperate challenges to the world about them yet inwardly shackled with a sense of their own weakness.

Where were the sheepish smiles the merchants recalled seeing in the hunger marches two years before? Those were different men. Their ugly mood, the million rumours, the footsteps falling like the endless rains of June made the merchants quake. They rolled their steel doors down. They stayed down all day.

Joe was no exception. He was especially sensitive to the mutterings of his many clerks, whose eyes seemed to slide from his in accusation. "People want bread and you givin' them bullets. Shootin' them down like dogs. What they did? So black people always have to suffer, my dear. . . ." Joe, too, closed up. He went to the city council meeting that had been called in haste. The scavengers would take no more of the councillors' political war cries and denunciation of government for holding up the loan. They had waited endless months. Their chance had come at last, it was time to take it.

Approaching the Town Hall Joe saw that Woodford Square was packed with people. They were listening to a speaker in the bandstand. With immense conviction he was shouting God knew what and waving his arms; now and then he hitched up his pants and strutted from side to side like a puppet animated by strings. Joe recognised Percy French and, sniffing with feelings of curiosity, resentment and a strange ridiculous jealousy, he approached the crowd. Many of the scavengers were on its outskirts. As soon as they saw Joe they surrounded him.

"Mr Elias, suh, the men want money. They say the council have to pay them forty-two cents more a day. The old demand for ten cents no good any more. They determined to strike if they don't get it tomorrow."

Their spokesman was a plump, round-faced, barefooted Indian in a khaki shirt and pants. Some of the men with him were young and wiry, others grey-haired with grey moustaches. All looked at Joe grimly, searching his face. Hadn't he always supported them?

Removing his cigar from between his teeth Joe said sternly: "What's that? Forty-two cents? Boy, you have no idea what you're saying. Do you realise that is almost a fifty per cent increase? If that's your attitude I'll wash my hands of the whole thing. As far as I'm concerned you won't get anywhere by threatening to strike."

He put his cigar between his teeth and crossed the lawn to the Town Hall. Some followed him, crying their hardship, reminding him of his promises.

"To hell wid he!" one shouted. "Tomorrow we strike!"

They stopped, swearing softly and bitterly in their disappointment, and turned back to join the workers listening to the spell that French was weaving.

Joe's tone concealed shame of the situation in which he found himself and resentment that he should be embarrassed. His heart was with them still. But to countenance strike action now could put him, in the eyes of frightened businessmen, on a par with the rioters. His own clerks, then, would hopefully press him harder. And a voice kept whispering: "I could be mayor of this city but I must play my cards right."

The idea had insinuated itself into his mind during discussions with certain business friends who were sufficiently tinged with patriotism to want to extend the powers of Port-of-Spain's city council. It was the only body that was close to ordinary folk, and was elected by them. Members of the legislative council were hand-picked by the governor or elected on a very narrow franchise. They felt that the antics of the shoemakers, shopkeepers and other dubious types on the city council were bringing the capital into disrepute. They wished its powers curtailed. Joe's new friends dreamed of controlling it, of placing it in the hands of "responsible" citizens who would oblige the government to concede an extension of its powers. The worm of Joe's ambition had begun to gnaw him.

At the council meeting he spoke of the "necessity to face the facts of the situation" and the "economics imposed upon us by a heedless government". He would "not surrender to lawlessness". All looked at him in surprise, his friends turning into enemies and his enemies, friends. The former began to cry out and shake their fists. Joe waved them aside.

"No one is going to dictate to me how to act! Neither you nor any body of misled workers. We are responsible to a city of a hundred thousand people. Do you realise that?"

And he consoled himself, thinking: "No responsible politician can think in a small and narrow way. If I were mayor and the right people sat around this table we could bring pressure to bear on Government such as Boisson does not dream of!"

On the following day the press gave prominence to a long letter over Joe's signature. The need for trade unions, he asserted, could not be disputed. Government's short sight in this matter must be deplored. Britain's trade-union centre should have been asked to provide assistance in training responsible leaders. And much more.

Some of the workers thought Joe was on their side. This made Le Maître laugh bitterly. "Do you think he would regard any of us as responsible?" he asked them.

Some businessmen reluctantly accepted Joe's propositions; most declared our workers "too ignorant" to be entrusted with the control of such organisations, which could only play a useful role in society by pursuing the principle of negotiation.

Boisson, on his return, praised Joe's foresight. It was from this period that they began to see eye to eye on many matters.

Chapter fifty

On Monday Le Maître had written to the governor. This time he took the precaution of sending the letter by special messenger. He asked Sir Richard to select an equal number of strikers and oilfield managers to explore the question of increasing wages. The governor's reply was stern and emphatic: no negotiations while the strike continued.

"He is in the hands of these oilfield swine!" Le Maître said, crushing the letter in his hand. "Stop the strike? They can't see anything except their own point of view. They might as well try to stop the tide rising."

The Volunteers, fully mobilised, were patrolling the south in trucks. Here and there they were greeted with showers of stones. The machine guns mounted on the trucks spat bullets and more of the jobless fell.

At dawn on Wednesday Trinidad police and English sailors from the *Ajax* swept like a wind through the homes of Fyzabad workers, seizing knives, cutlasses and one or two shotguns, leaving a trail of destruction behind them and a searing, bitter frustration. They arrested

Percy French and several well-known militants. Le Maître had slipped through their hands. The night before, still disguised as a woman, he had fled with Cassie to Winchester's home in Port-of-Spain. French had arranged with the old man to hide him. Government was offering a reward of five hundred dollars for information that would lead to his arrest.

"Bring him, man, bring him," Winchester had said, not fearing now to speak patronisingly to French of the man he envied and disliked.

Gwenneth Osborne went shopping on Wednesday. Phyllis Lorrimer had intended to accompany her, but having seen Tuesday's "rioting niggers" she stayed home and advised Gwenneth to do the same. "God knows what they wouldn't do to you!" she said.

"Nonsense! We've got to stand up to them," said Gwenneth, repeating her father's words.

She felt it was required of all the English, and particularly of herself as a close friend of David Primrose, to be unafraid. She walked down Frederick Street with head erect, as if all Port-of-Spain were her estate, and the times could not change, nor black men throw their rags behind them.

Today the stores were open and all was quiet. Here and there groups of strikers or unemployed workers were reading newspaper accounts of the latest events in the south. In the stores it was difficult to get served. Few of the clerks now concealed the animosity they felt at this young Englishwoman's clipped tone and distant, foreign manner; they showed it in the display of indifference with which they laid dress materials before her while talking with one another animatedly as if she were not present.

Eleven o'clock found her drinking tea in Stephens' Tea Room. Someone cried from the veranda: "The sailors! The sailors from the *Exeter*!" Everyone got up and rushed onto the veranda. Down Frederick Street marched a column of British sailors, rifled, cool, every arm swinging in unison. Their disciplined and measured tramping menaced all disorder. People ran out of the stores and gathered on the sidewalks. Several little black boys swaggered alongside the column and behind it, mocking the sailors' stride and the stern bearings of their officers as all little boys will. The *Exeter*'s plane roared overhead very low, adding to the excitement. Leaflets warning solemnly of retribution spiralled to earth, there to be picked up, read with varying response or simply ignored.

Gwenneth's heart swelled with pride and her eyes shone as she looked down on her young countrymen.

"Aren't they wonderful?" she remarked to someone beside her, a woman she did not know. At any other time she would not have dreamed of addressing a stranger.

One of the sailors winked. Gwenneth responded with a wave of her handkerchief. All along the street the verandas, which overhung the sidewalks in the old Spanish style, were full of fluttering handkerchiefs, waving hands, excited, welcoming faces. The white woman beside Gwenneth was even weeping. Very reassuring was the sound of those tramping boots. What power there was here, what majesty in their bearing! Thank God for law, for justice!

"Our troubles are over, I guess," said a blue-eyed young American. His arm embraced a very slim girl in a bright floral frock.

One of the managerial staff, Gwenneth concluded, of an American oil company. The girl was clearly one of those who had fled from San Fernando. Gwenneth smiled at them, conscious of being linked in this victorious moment with innocent victims of a wicked and senseless riot.

As her eyes turned away they caught André below on the opposite sidewalk. Her heart bounded. He did not look up and had not seen her—or had he seen her and purposely did not look up? Not since the night she had gone to his home and found him with Cassie had she seen him. Ever since then he had been avoiding her, he had never once phoned though she had left message after message. At this moment she knew she loved him, a coloured man; that she was tied to him by a bond that existed between her and no one else. How dare he avoid her! She had heard he had been seen out with Marie Louise. In spite of all logic, all reason, she had to find out if he still loved her.

All day the vision of him standing there was with her. Beside him all men seemed nonentities. Why hadn't she realised this when he had asked her to go away with him?

"No, I don't want to see him! There was—there must be!—something between him and Cassie. They look down on me, laugh at me. What sort of woman am I? I'd give anything to have him back. I want him, I don't care!"

* * *

The telephone rang.

His mother said: "It's for you, André."

It was Phyllis Lorrimer wanting to know if he could come over at once. "There's something I want to talk to you about. Urgently."

Phyllis Lorrimer. And urgently, almost in a whisper: "Is Gwenneth there?"

"Gwenneth?"

"Yes. I see she is. You aren't very good at dissembling." He sighed. "I'm no longer interested, Phyl. Just tell her that." He put down the phone.

He went to his room. He lay on his bed a long time, not thinking, just trying to give his ruined love, that tormenting ache, time to settle into that limbo of the soul where one hides the worn-out, the unwanted and the failures.

Chapter fifty-one

"So you have turned woman, friend," Winchester cackled in his thin voice, surveying Le Maître's dress when the latter arrived at night with Cassie.

"French told me you have a room for us," Le Maître replied abruptly.

"Of course, man. Poor as I am, I don't forget my comrades. Sit down. You'll take a drink?"

"No, thank you."

"What about you, Cassie?"

"No, thank you, Mr Winchester."

"No use being sad, man," said Winchester, again glancing with amusement at Le Maître's dress. "Julia, come and meet the ladies," he called to his wife.

His derisively patronising manner drove the blood to Le Maître's face.

Winchester's wife called out that she was preparing the room. Cassie rose and went in to help her.

"Well, boy, you put you'self in a proper mess, yes?" Winchester said to Le Maître. "When you have madmen—"

"When you speak of a mess, remember your journeymen bakers' strike," Le Maître interrupted curtly.

"Oh, I failed too, I failed too. But I used what is the better part of valour," Winchester said, smiling. "You see, man, from the moment you said on Saturday to the people you were addressing in the yard : 'Don't let them take me down!' your case was—"

"The papers lie!" Le Maître broke in angrily. "I never said so."

The old man, frowning, put his finger to his lips and peeped out the window. "That voice—you must be more careful. You know what madmen like French give, man," he continued in a lower tone, motioning scornfully with his bony hands, the skin of which resembled cracked leather. "No discretion . . . no . . . no forethought." He fished out this word with satisfaction.

But Le Maitre said: "Speak of what you know and you will be silent."

This angered Winchester. He laughed. "Oh, speak of what I know, ehn? You want to know what I know? I know you are no longer a leader. You have dishonoured your position. Men, women and children killed, but you run away."

The vain old man took pleasure in Le Maître's dependence on him and no longer feared him as formerly.

Le Maître made an effort to control himself. Patiently he explained how the violence had started, the indiscretions of the police and the deliberate provocations of the people by white men determined to teach the blacks a lesson. But he felt uneasy and wished he had not come to this house.

It was a very small wooden house, as old as Winchester, and black with years. In the living-room were six highly polished straight-backed chairs of which Winchester was very proud and a bentwood rocker, all with antimacassars. In the centre, close together, stood two round tables overburdened with gaudy glass knick-knacks; against one wall was an old china cabinet with a brightly coloured tea set. Behind it stood a photograph of Winchester as a young man, dapper, even handsome. Opposite was a large coloured magazine portrait of Lord Kitchener. The antimacassars, the knick-knacks, the pictures suggested to Le Maître that basically Winchester, despite all his fluent talk, valued the approval of his masters more than the approval of the workers, who were not yet strong.

"We have come to the wrong place to hide," he said to Cassie when they were going to bed.

Silently she put her arms about him, pressing her cheek to his. "Better you hide one place and I somewhere else. I never like Winchester," she said, recalling how he had sneered at Popito.

"You know of any place else?"

"Not for you."

She began to undress. Lying in bed he watched her every movement as if seeing her for the first time. "It is an amazing thing how beautiful you are in spite of everything," he said in a hushed voice in which she heard a note of sorrow. "Take it off," he said when she came to lie down beside him. She removed the slip in which she slept. He took both her beautiful breasts in his hands as she leaned over him. "I never thought it was possible to love a woman so much . . . or permissible. . . . But I would understand if you didn't wait for me."

"Wait for you?"

"If they catch me it's two or three years jail at least."

She covered his mouth with her hand. "How you could ask that question? Who else I goin' to wait for? And what about me, when they catch up with me?"

"Don't be afraid of that. They have to have witnesses."

"The police know me."

"And you know the men who lighted the matches and. . . ."

She pulled him down upon her. "Don't talk about it. . . ."

For a while they loved in silence rent by half-stifled cries and joyous moans. . . . He lay relaxed, staring up at the ceiling. She smoothed his brow, trying to drive his thoughts away.

"Some people not meant for happiness," he said. "It's only a suffering or a fighting. With me so, now—how you can be happy?"

"You talkin' stupidness, Ben."

"It is impossible for you to wait for me," he said brutally. "To live you must have a man, surrender your body to him for cash! It is better to shoot you and myself than be tormented by this thought while I am in jail."

She looked at him in anger and astonishment. "After all we gone through together I goin' to leave you for a next man? You losin' you' nerve or what?"

"How you goin' to live? Tell me that!"

"Get a job. So this is the first time I have to live without a man to help me? What you take me for? How you could even ask such a question?!"

He was silent for a while.

"It was stupid, forget it. It's not your problem, it's my problem. You have come to mean more to me than my life, my safety, more than the workers. When you first came to Fyzabad I was afraid that would happen. I want to stay out of jail now not for the workers but for you. It is a terrible thing: as soon as I am beginning to enjoy life it is taken from me."

"As Percy would say, that is defeatist talk. They ain't catch you yet. You could go to Barbados, Grenada."

"Too small. You can't hide me, I am too big. No. The thing is to wait till the workers get tired. Once they have no more use for me I could go to jail."

"I hope they never get tired," she said, sighing fervently, thinking that the struggle then would have been in vain.

Next day messengers from the south came to discuss with Le Maître the progress of the strike. Winchester was alarmed. "What you want to do, man, attract the attention of the police?" he whispered loudly, his long moustaches quivering.

"Who will go to jail, me or you?" asked Le Maître with cold anger.

That night he attended a secret meeting on the outskirts of Fyzabad. Hundreds of police and Volunteers were patrolling the south, menacing and breaking up even the smallest groups of people whose only purpose in meeting was to pass the time of day. The strike leaders met in a peasant's hut in the forest. The Workers' Welfare had formed a strike committee, but to collect adequate finance proved impossible. Many who might have contributed had turned against the workers after the events of the past four days. Now worker must collect from worker. It was a poor pittance that could feed nobody. Le Maître suggested it be spent on propaganda.

Thousands of leaflets were secretly printed. Despite terrorism workers distributed them in Fyzabad, Point Fortin, San Fernando and Pointe-à-Pierre. Five were arrested.

Every day members of the strike committee came to Winchester's house to see Le Maître. Le Maître did not remember it was not his house. He would sit with them in the living-room, forget to pick up the antimacassars that fell off as he moved chairs, and thoughtlessly pushed out of his way the round tables with their knick-knacks. Cassie would come and whisper in his ear. "That damn old fool again?" he would say. "Let us go in my room where we can talk in peace." Everything about Le Maître jarred on the jealous Winchester. He came to hate him. His size and strength, his big dynamic voice, his positive approach to all problems, his readiness to defend every point with argument that punctured fond beliefs, his manner of speaking as if laying down the law for everyone—all this filled Winchester with jealous rage. He felt he was no longer master in his own house. He was afraid of these strangers who destroyed his accustomed peace and endangered his security by making a nest of conspiracy of the home he had worked so hard to build.

On Friday some of Point-à-Pierre's six thousand strikers returned to work. It was a trickle at first, but the numbers rapidly swelled. Some of the leaders were angry and discouraged. They brought the news to Le Maître. Though he spoke to them in his room, his voice carried all over the house.

"You must look at it this way," he said, and held down the first finger of his left hand. "There was no preparation for the strike in Pointe-à-Pierre. No strike committee, no preparation of the men's minds for struggle. It was a spontaneous thing. We cannot expect more from them. They have stayed out almost a week. That is wonderful! They have never been on strike before. They are not going back to work because they don't believe in the strike; their empty bellies are driving them back. And we have to be prepared for the same thing in Fyzabad and Point Fortin. The workers of Fyzabad have been prepared, but none of us expected these murders. They have disrupted our plans. Comrades, we must assess the situation this way: when all the Point-à-Pierre workers are back in a few days' time the workers in Point Fortin will follow. Our people will stay out longest, but they won't be far behind. It will be impossible for them to stay out more than three weeks. Food, food! Where are they to get it?" He paused and looked at the gloomy faces before him. "To know when you are defeated is as important as the determination to struggle. We must be prepared to tell our men to return to work—not now, we still have a chance. But they will want to go when Point Fortin men give in." Again he paused, but no one spoke. "We have lost important comrades," he continued. "It would seem as if we have lost everything. Don't be defeatists. The workers have gained valuable experience in open battle. Next time they will use the strike weapon more effectively.

We have suffered like hell to make this small advance, but we have made it! I tell you *nothing* can hold back the colonial workers!"

His audience, two men only, were looking at him yearningly. Their eyes flashed. One, a tall man with a very long face—he who had amused the workers by saying with exasperation in Diamond Hall: "One day, one day congotay"—slapped Le Maître's shoulder. "Right, Ben. We despised West Indians one day goin' to make these islands our own. Either the white people treat us as equals, man to man, or we pack them back home."

"That day won't come of itself," Le Maître told him. "We have to learn from every battle; but don't fool you' head, they learnin' too. It's we have to make the sacrifices, not them—their guns against our history."

All this time Winchester was walking from the kitchen to the living-room and back again, sitting in his bentwood rocking-chair with its soiled antimacassar, and in a low voice contemptuously repeating phrases Le Maître uttered. "Tell them to return to work—it is well for you that you realise that much. You should have done that long ago. Leader! You are a leader? You will fool these stupid people, but not me. Who committed the murders? 'To despair is to surrender to the enemy'—so you want to fight again? 'Successful end to the workers' struggle'," Winchester cackled loudly and angrily. "Mad!" he muttered.

When the strike leaders left he could contain himself no longer. He entered Le Maître's room. "So you want war. 'Successful end to the workers' struggle!' You are a menace to the workers! I am twenty-five years older than you, I have experience of life and workers in this place that you could never hope to have, I tell you you are a lunatic, man! War with the British Government? Who freed us but them? You goin' to throw them off, little you? Then who will swallow us up? Hitler and Mussolini? You don't think! You call you'self a leader? All you want is confusion. Innocent people killed and you run away!" His voice rose on a high note. Le Maître pressed his thumb against his front teeth and said nothing, seeing a crisis was at hand. But his look, contemptuous without knowing it, stung the old man to fury. "You want to conspire against the government in my house. None of that! Find a next place to stay."

Hearing his raised, excited voice the women had come in. His wife tried to pacify him.

"Where you expect us to go?" Cassie asked angrily, her breath coming rapidly. She turned away without waiting for an answer, trying to control herself.

Winchester, waving his arms, was screaming at his wife not to interfere in what was none of her business.

"Leave him, leave him," Le Maître said to Cassie, and lay back on the bed.

"Yes, I am an old fool, that is what you think—!"

"Did I tell you so?" Le Maître demanded.

But conscious of being in the wrong, of making a fool of himself, but unable to control his tongue, Winchester replied in a threatening voice: "You will find you have made a mistake!" and quickly left the room.

So unreasoning was his jealousy of Le Maître that even the latter's silent presence, the sound of his breathing, the shape and motions of his lips, their characteristic pout—all were offensive to him. Winchester left the house and, without giving himself time for reflection, went straight to the police station.

Le Maître, left alone, expected the worst. Cassie came to bed and they talked over the situation. Le Maître made up his mind to return to Fyzabad. The police would not look for him there now.

"I'll take *Sweet Violet* first thing in the morning," he said, and at once went to tell Winchester he might be easy, both he and Cassie were leaving. He found that Winchester had gone out.

The old man came in at midnight. When his wife told him Le Maître was leaving, he became thoughtful but made no reply.

Dawn was just breaking when he got out of bed and, without a word to his wife, slipped out of the house.

At half-past five detectives and police silently entered the yard and with guns drawn barred all avenues of escape. A white inspector hammered on the back door and uttered the fateful words.

"They have come," said Le Maître, who was putting on his woman's dress. He dropped it. "The bastard!"

Cassie flung her arms about him. Her breath came in gasps, the tears ran down her cheeks. "O God, O God!" she whispered.

"Don't let them see you like that," he told her sternly. "Wipe you' eyes—quick! The workers are behind us."

He went out and admitted the police.

Winchester's old wife had grown fond of Cassie. She wept for her, and wept no less for shame of her man's black deed.

The police handcuffed Le Maître and Cassie, put them in a waiting car and drove off at high speed. There were few people about the streets at this hour, but the inspector stood with a drawn gun on the running board. The sight attracted every eye. Their way lay past the Eastern Market, where thousands of workers and servants were buying the day's food while their madames, white and coloured, soundly slept. Some glimpsed Le Maître's big head and pouting lips. The words passed from mouth to mouth: "Le Maître!" And suddenly gusts of laughter swept the people on the sidewalks. "He playin' cowboy!" they said of the inspector. "Hop-along Cassidy!" they shouted derisively as the police car slowed to cross a drain. "Fall off and bus' you' arse, you son of a bitch!" they cried, pelting the inspector, as it were, with their laughter. Le Maître, leaning forward slightly, was able to greet the crowd with a smile before the detective beside him pushed him back.

Chapter fifty-two

At a meeting of the Legislative Council on the following Monday the governor reviewed the strike in a speech that ended his career. Big Business regarded the general tenor of that speech as totally unacceptable. Such sentiments as "if we are to stamp out the cause of the recent disturbances and prevent their recurrence employers of labour must realise more fully than they do their responsibilities to the people . . ." and "my sympathy goes out to those who . . . were seeking ways and means of calling the attention of their employers to their plight . . ." created much resentment.

William Dollard and Major Bottomley agreed that evening that this was not the kind of governor the island needed. Two days later Dollard was on his way to the Colonial Office in London, in his briefcase a copy of the governor's speech and letters of introduction to very important people.

Le Maître went before a jury two weeks later. Long discussions with a well-known Indian lawyer had convinced him that his conviction was so strong a possibility that legal arguments would serve little purpose. He decided to conduct his own defence on humanitarian and social grounds. The jury, nevertheless, found him guilty. Justice Osborne, who presided, handed down the maximum sentence of three years with hard labour.

*   *   *   *

Year after year Mr de Coudray's estates went through their peaceful cycle, and lightning did not blast the trees, nor storms uproot them, nor did the pests blight many when they came. The fruit was picked and taken to market, sent to the factory for juicing, boxed and shipped across the seas. No one complained. Except at times, perhaps, the master. Until the upheaval came. It was impossible to escape its tremors, far though he was from the centre of that mighty storm. Overnight, wantonly, all his kindness to them notwithstanding, his labourers destroyed fruit trees and came to him demanding higher wages. Demanding! His wife enjoined him to "send them packing". Mr de Coudray compromised with small increases. His labourers returned to work. The interrupted fertile cycle was resumed. And the daily domestic cycle, slightly soured, continued on its inevitable round.

Now, six weeks later, see him lying in his Berbice chair, his feet on its extended leg rests, in that corner of the veranda hallowed by years of after-dinner rest and reading. He shakes the London *Times*. Much talk of Hitler. The Czechs seem truculent. You can't keep Germany down forever, England's right. On his left his wife, pale wrists jerking as she skilfully works the crochet hook. On his right Clotilde, rocking her rocking chair, her eyes fixed on the honeysuckle vine that makes so cosily private this broad veranda with its handsome balustrade like a row of soldiers. She sees not leaves and yellow flowers, she sees the past, when life was good, and comprehensible, and she had her place in it. She has no place in it now.

Into this joyless atmosphere André steps, why he knows not. If told it was because he needed the family's warmth he would deny it. He is too young to see his father's heart behind his stern, proud eyes, or sense its helplessness behind all that grand demeanour; or that his mother, with an attitude fixed and frozen, conceals a bewilderment that she has failed this son despite the best she did, and fears for him now that he has grown so strange. He is too close to see these things, and much too hurt. He has come, it seems to him, to crow of a victory they can hardly stomach.

"Hear about the trial?" he says to his Aunt Clotilde.

"Trial?" she says, smiling because she is fond of him. She hears less and less these days. "Tell me," she adds, half turning to his father, "what about those people who burned the poor policeman to death, have they tried them yet?"

"The trial finished today—finished today!" Mr de Coudray shouts, leaning towards her.

"Ah!" she cries, raising in grateful approval her thin white hands with their swollen blue veins. "Guilty, of course. Going to hang them all, I hope? They deserve it, you know."

Her brother gives his head an abrupt shake of disapproval. "They got off."

"What? Got off! The jury let them off? What fools! We will be murdered in our beds next and they will do nothing. What a disgraceful state of affairs!" Clotilde's face flushes, she wriggles in her chair, sits more erect, her posture emphasising her utter dissociation of herself from this miscarriage of justice.

"Why did they get off?" Mrs de Coudray asks.

"The evidence was too conflicting," André says. "By the way, Cassandra Le Maître, the principal one of the twenty-four accused, was once a servant of the trial judge."

The Times is lowered. The swiftly moving wrists are still.

"I know her," he continues. "She's the last person you would expect to kill anyone. One said she had a can of kerosene in her hand. Another said she was nowhere near the spot. A third was sure she was in the yard but nowhere near Duke." He laughs.

Aunt Clotilde gazes at him open-mouthed. "You know this creature, this—Charlotte Corday?"

The Times is raised and the wrists are moving now.

"Yes, I know her. She isn't what you'd think. Quite a person. Soft and kind, yet bold and fearless."

Her lean white fingers tightly gripping and clawing at the arms of her chair Aunt Clotilde leans forward, straining to hear. Abruptly she shrugs. "But where does he get these ideas, my dear?" she appeals to her brother. "They don't run in our family."

"The governor is going back home," Mr de Coudray says.

"Ill health?" his wife asks.

"Not well? Drinks too much?" Aunt Clotilde is sensing scandal.

"I understand he's being recalled because of his handling of the riots," her brother answers.

"His eyes? Troubling him?"

"The riots! The riots!" her brother shouts with sudden, furious and unexpected annoyance. "He handled the affair badly from the start."

She looks at him open-mouthed, then shrugs. "There's no need to shout, *mon cher*, I'm not deaf."

Inside, the telephone rings. Yvette jumps up, she is smiling.

André, too, leaves them. "Shall I go to her?" Already, however, his steps take him to the car and he is heading for Elena. He has heard talk of "some Robert or other". "I guess her mother'll hate the sight of me. But I must find out. And Elena herself, perhaps she, too, can't stand me. Why am I going?" But he cannot turn the wheel and go to Joe, to Marie-Louise, to others . . . what others? He now feels quite alone. . . .

Elena had come home bursting with the news of Cassie's victory, and Aurelia's heart was light. It was especially light because of the ring of happiness in Elena's voice. The days of books and brooding were behind her. She still read a great deal, but frequently now the reading was interrupted by a horn, a hurried conversation through the window with the carful of young people in the street, a rush inside—"Mother, we're going to Macqueripe Bay!"—the door banging, the revving of the engine—and silence, the empty silences to which Aurelia listened, hardly knowing any longer what was right or wrong, whether to be strict as formerly or. . . . She prayed for guidance.

* * * *

Miss Richards called out to Aurelia from the sidewalk. "You there, Aurelia?"

"Yes! Come, come. I'm alone."

Reassured, Miss Richards went in. "You still at it, my dear? Poor you."

"Still at it, man. What to do?"

"I heard from Cyril, my nephew. In New York now two years, my dear. Jumped the boat, you know. They didn't find him. He doin' well these days, much better than if he was here. . . ."

Aurelia only half listened. She kept thinking of André, who was again visiting Elena, and of how difficult it was to judge character. She imagined with mounting rage that which she most feared coming to pass—that he would hurt Elena a second time.

"But why is she such a fool!" she cried out.

"Who?" Miss Richards asked in bewilderment, breaking off.

"Nothing, man. Something just cross me mind, that's all."

"You worry too much, Aurelia. Everything in this world is for the best. Look, I nearly forget to pay my debts."

Cyril, it appeared, had sent her fifty dollars. She had come to repay the money Aurelia had loaned her long ago and lost hope of ever seeing again.

"Eh! Thank God. Just in time, chile," Aurelia said, and began to feel that things were not so bad. While listening to her friend's chatter she recalled how André had smiled at her. She listened again to the tones of his voice as he talked with Elena, to his inflections, to his laugh, the ideas he expressed, the words he used, striving to understand the soul of the man, weighing him in the light of her accumulation of harsh experience, and preparing to bare her teeth to tear him apart if he should hurt Elena.

"No," she thought now. "How could he be a bad man. You have to have faith in people. . . ." She put everything aside and turned to her friend. "My dear, I always said if I could have reach New York I would do well. You know how many times this was in my mind? But Elena prevented me. After all it's still not too late. If I could sell everything and raise a couple hundred and get just *one more* sou-sou hand—my God, life would change for me, I feel sure! God looks after us but we have to help Him, my dear."

"They say a war comin' just now. Hitler really got all their heads hot."

"War? Which war? There's always some war or other. If you worry with that you will never succeed."

"If war come some will be dyin' for king and country, but we here will be eatin' and gettin' fat."

Neither of them had any suspicion of the enormous events that were unfolding in Europe and would soon overturn and refashion the life to which they and all Trinidad had so long been accustomed.

Picador

☐	**The Beckett Trilogy**	Samuel Beckett	£2.50p
☐	**Williard and His Bowling Trophies**	Richard Brautigan	£1.25p
☐	**Bury My Heart at Wounded Knee**	Dee Brown	£2.75p
☐	**Our Ancestors**	Italo Calvino	£2.95p
☐	**Auto Da Fé**	Elias Canetti	£1.75p
☐	**Hidden Faces**	Salvador Dali	£1.95p
☐	**Nothing, Doting, Blindness**	Henry Green	£2.95p
☐	**Household Tales**	Brothers Grimm	£1.50p
☐	**Meetings with Remarkable Men**	Gurdjieff	£1.50p
☐	**Bound for Glory**	Woody Guthrie	75p
☐	**Roots**	Alex Haley	£2.50p
☐	**Growth of the Soil**	Knut Hamsun	£2.95p
☐	**Meanwhile**	Max Handley	£1.50p
☐	**When the Tree Sings**	Stratis Haviaras	£1.95p
☐	**Dispatches**	Michael Herr	£1.75p
☐	**The Greenpeace Chronicle**	Robert Hunter	£2.50p
☐	**Three Trapped Tigers**	G. Cabrera Infante	£2.95p
☐	**Man and His Symbols**	Carl Jung	£2.50p
☐	**China Men**	Maxine Hong Kingston	£1.50p
☐	**The Woman Warrior**	Maxine Hong Kingston	£1.50p
☐	**The Other Persuasion**	edited by Seymour Kleinberg	£1.75p
☐	**The Case of the Midwife Toad**	Arthur Koestler	£1.25p
☐	**The Ghost in the Machine**	Arthur Koestler	£1.75p
☐	**Janus**	Arthur Koestler	£2.25p
☐	**The Roots of Coincidence**	Arthur Koestler	£1.00p
☐	**The Thirteenth Tribe**	Arthur Koestler	£1.50p
☐	**The Memoirs of a Survivor**	Doris Lessing	£1.50p
☐	**Albert Camus**	Herbert Lottman	£3.95p
☐	**The Road to Xanadu**	John Livingston Lowes	£1.95p
☐	**Short Lives**	Katinka Matson	£2.50p
☐	**The Snow Leopard**	Peter Matthiessen	£1.95p
☐	**The Man Without Qualities, Vol. 1**	Robert Musil	£1.95p
☐	**The Man Without Qualities, Vol. 2**	Robert Musil	£1.75p
☐	**The Man Without Qualities, Vol. 3**	Robert Musil	£1.75p